Hot Splices
THE AUTHOR'S CUT

Mike Watt

Encyclopocalypse Publications
encyclopocalypse.com

Splice. *Noun.*

A term used to designate any joining of one piece of film to another when editing. One method uses tape. Another permanently cements the two pieces together. This method is known as a "hot splice."

This book is for every film addict out there.

It is especially for Andy.

And always, and always, and always
To Amy.
Especially because we survived all of this.

TABLE OF CONTENTS

NEWSREEL
THE FINAL SCREENING OF HANOVER COBB'S MAGNUM OPUS

"To be an artist is to give yourself to your art one hundred percent. It demands nothing more than your entirety."

> — "Who is Hanover Cobb and Why
> Does He Scare Hollywood So?",
> *Movie Outlaw*, Dec, 2003.

The event was widely advertised. Cobb was respected, though not well-known, but the screening was open to the public. Turnout was practically guaranteed.

Held open-air in a vacant lot in the Welles, the curious filed in, greeted by ushers nearly ghoulish in their glee. They'd gotten an advance preview. The corners of their eyes twitched. Flecks of foam gathered in the corners of their smiles.

Cobb was expected to be present, and indeed he was. The sun sank behind the jagged teeth of the city skyline. The film would begin, but first, the ritual:

First, the screen was set up. He'd shaved first, before the flaying. The flesh of his chest and back were stretched between chrome bracings. At the corners were his tattoos: unblinking eyes staring back at the viewer.

Second, the projector was prepared. His cornea and

retina were smoothed across the machine's lens, an eye for an eye. Belts to drive the reels were fashioned from his intestine, the smaller of the two. The noise it made sounded like distant weeping, far away and in the dark.

His lips and tongue formed the speaker, and flapped in crystal synch with the soundtrack, as designed. The clatter of the shutter was like chattering teeth.

Then the film began.

Those who could bear to watch beyond the opening credits felt the chilling sensation that they too were being watched, from something far behind them, and far below.

As it played on, the film beckoned the audience to join it, to fuse with it, to allow their atoms and essence to join in the cinematic fun. From them, it wrung their tears, it laid their hopes bare, it shattered their illusions, and it took from them all it needed to. The *entirety*.

When it was complete, as the film faded out to the inevitable black, the end flapping on the final reel, there was no one left to applaud. The ushers swept up the dust. Something out in the darkness smiled and, thumbless, gave its approval nonetheless.

MAIN FEATURE
THE CINEPHAGES

PRE-CREDITS SEQUENCE
INTERIOR: UPSTATE NEW YORK, 1978 - DAY

Her director smiled as he used the hand-crank to wind the camera spring. In just a few seconds they'd be ready to shoot again. She trembled, listening to the blood running from her leg, where her foot used to be. Spilling over the side of the table, softly pattering on the floor. They'd be ready to shoot again in just a few seconds.

Several takes ago, her throat ruptured from screaming, filling her mouth with blood. Now the only noise she could make was hitching, rasping moans.

Fortunately, the scene didn't require her to deliver any lines.

The Director sighed, very happy with her performance. The crank stopped. He had a full wind again. Placing the camera to his eye, he framed the shot, filling the square aperture with her beautiful, naked form—white peeking through the streaks of wet red.

He captured her agony on razor-thin strips of plastic. Later, he'd process the footage himself, cut it into his larger work-in-progress. Then his critics would finally feel what he wanted them to feel: her pain and the pain of so many others.

His finger twitched on the chrome trigger. The girl began to fight again, weak as she was, her arms straining against the rubber tubing holding her tight to the metal table beneath her. Without taking his eye from the camera, he reached out, and his slender fingers found the scalpel, the metal tacky from the drying blood. He smiled at her. "Just one more shot," he told her and, smiling at his little joke, "and then we'll cut."

CHAPTER ONE
THE ADDICTS

"I believe that the only end of all human activity—whether it be politics, art, science, etc.—is to find enlightenment, to reach the state of enlightenment. I ask of film what most North Americans ask of psychedelic drugs. The difference being that when one creates a psychedelic film, he need not create a film that shows the visions of a person who has taken a pill; rather, he needs to manufacture the pill."

—Alexandro Jodorowsky, "El Topo:
The Book of the Film," p. 97

SCENE ONE:
BOONE AND THE AGENT MEET CUTE

As he left the lobby of the Arc Theater, trading the cool air for the wet slap of humid, dying summer, the fluorescent glow of the interior from the flashing lights of the marquee above, Boone and Shel, the Agent, met for the first time.

Boone hadn't been screening anything that night, down in the Welles, at the Arc, but still the man sought him out through the dwindling crowd. The Fedora was back in style, wrestled from the hands and heads of the hipsters, and the man wore his at a jaunty angle, the brim shadow across his eyes, a sharp slash of negative space down the line of his square all-American jaw.

"I saw your movie," he said, "*Comedown*. A bar was playing a bunch of shorts on their big screen. I liked it the best."

Tom Boone nodded, said thanks. The usual etiquette. *Comedown*. He shot that years ago, back when he was a student at Griffith. Used that experimental brand of Super-8 before it got caught up in the military ban. The stock gave the movie its texture; a creaminess you didn't get out of Ektachrome. Not as orange as the remaining back-alley Kodachromes. With the death of commercial film stock, the black market was the last resort for those directors with the coin to spare. Those directors were a dying breed too. The digital 1s and 0s had all but replaced the photochemical.

"That movie really stuck with me, Tom. Can I call you Tom or do you prefer Boone?"

Either.

"Stuck with me for days. Wormed its way into my dreams. What was it, four minutes?"

Six.

"Zoomed by like four," said the man, and he held out two long fingers, between them a biz card the same shade as a new projection screen. "I'm Shel," he said. "An Agent. I wanna talk. Seriously."

No need for an agent. No plans to go Out West. Out There. No thanks.

"I know," said Shel. The Agent. "I'm not that kind of an Agent.

You'd be wasted at the Studios."

That's kind.

"You've seen all the classics, I'm betting. I don't bet loose, you know?"

Sure.

"But I got access to some stuff that'll really sharpen your eye."

Again, two fingers, this time, a single frame of film. Four perforations high, 1 3/8" inches wide. 35mm. Boone took it, held it up to the light of the Arc's marquee, bulbs on the border firing in psychotic sequence. Maybe a second went by. Boone sent an eyebrow up, holding the little window, like a square of stained glass, very close to his eye he looked at Shel through one of the sprocket holes, the tiny rectangle perfectly framing the Agent.

Composite from three-strip Technicolor, Boone thought. *"The African Queen."* Not a question. "1951. John Huston."

The Agent smiled, showing straight white teeth. Nodded. Quizzing. "No Bogart in that frame. No Hepburn. Just a shot of the river."

Boone shrugged, pleased with himself all the same, but taught to be aloof years ago by his one-time professors at Griffith Academy.

"How'd you know?" asked Shel. "C'mon, you gotta tell me."

Couldn't be anything else.

Shel nodded. "Taste it."

Again, an upward eyebrow, but no question.

"No worries," said Shel. The Agent. "It's not laced. You flix, right?"

Sure.

Boone did as was suggested, placing the frame on the center of his tongue. The frame tasted *green*. The *correct* green. Not over-processed. This was no dupe print. As the emulsion dissolved the warmth of the shot spread directly from his tongue, up through the soft palate, tingling the sinuses, as the heat of the jungle coursed through his bloodstream. He looked at Shel, "This from the original negative?"

"Interneg," said Shel.

Of course. Stupid. Release print. Reissue. 1955. '56 maybe.

Shel smiled. All teeth. Like tiny drive-in screens. "From Russia," he said.

Boone almost swallowed but resisted. "With love," he

said, a Pavlovian response.

More smiling, more nodding. First taste is free. "Sat in a Vault until 1988. Screened twice. After *Perestroika.*"

Eyes feeling heated. The light around him bloomed. Bogart's voice, speaking as his character, Charlie Allnut, turned the inside of his head into Dolby speakers: "A man takes a drop too much once in a while, it's only human nature."

To Shel, Boone said, "Thanks."

"No sweat," the Agent said. "You know what you need to see? One of the Borgia films. Ever seen one?"

"Of course," he said. *The Pioneer.* The second one of the series of experimental art films. The first and last could be had for a small fortune, but he had seen parts of the third, *Rape of the Archangel,* in the documentary about Luther Borgia's trial. That's all that was left, of course, since the footage had been destroyed, as far as he knew. At least the original negs.

"That's the fairy tale," said Shel. "I got three and five, access to one and two. Four's in the Carcosa lab's vault. The Archives. Right here in Bethlehem."

Can't be. *Osculum Infame* had been destroyed.

"Ever see yourself as a Cleaner?"

Shel was better than his word. Before the end of the year, Boone was a Cleaner. A few weeks later, he was inside the Vault. As promised. Three down and two to go before the Borgia Quintet, the pretentiously named "Divine Heresy", was ready for screening.

The Addicts were clawing at his door, begging him to hurry along. Everyone needed to see between the frames.

SCENE TWO:
EXPOSITORY FLASHBACK

The Addicts found each other immediately. They recognized each other by the gate chatter of the bloodstream; heartbeats that echoed like a shutter clicking open and closed. They'd all come to the Griffith Film Academy like pilgrims, bypassing Fulsail, USC, and NYU. At the big schools you learned how to make movies. At Griffith, you learned "how to become one with cinema." At freshman age, that slogan didn't seem pretentious at all. It sounded like a clarion trumpet calling them home.

Boone remembered all the advice in the past. "You wanna land a career in movies, you go to UCLA. Make the connections. Do your time as a production assistant on the big jobs. Shoot two music videos and you'll get feature offers dropped in your lap." All that well-meaning is what sent him to Griffith, the ghetto of film academies, the Miskatonic University for the frame addicts, the flicker freaks.

"Don't go Out There," said Doc Bailey, having gathered them all into his classroom the day before the Graduation Screening. "The Studios are Auschwitz for visionaries. They take new minds and shovel them into their ovens. Bake at 600 degrees and spit out formula on the other end." Bailey smoked cigarettes compulsively, even when he taught, even when handling nitrate film—so flammable it even burned underwater. He was leaning on his desk, speaking in his halting monotone. They all leaned in to hear him. "Go to Yage," he advised. More advice. "Go to Cor, go to Carthage, go to Meridian—go to all the spokes. Backpack through South America. Visit, learn, capture, photograph. Then come back to the Hub. Come back to Bethlehem. We'll raise an army. Burn the studios down. Until only sprocket holes are left."

Like Boone, few of them were interested in storming the Kingdom. The location wasn't the message. The message came from the flashing shadows, spit out through the Elmo projector, captured through the Arris and the Eclairs. Hollywood was irrelevant. The Studios were irrelevant. The real movies were produced underground. Same as it ever was. And on and on and on. Let The Studios decay. Art was for their eyes, their cameras, their editing bays.

Digital was the new weaponry, but Boone and the other Addicts had a thing for film. The edges were sharp, for one thing. ("Sharp enough to cut your tongue." A line from one of their student films. Almost didn't matter whose.) It existed. It was tangible. It wasn't just binary on a hard drive. It was photoelectric. Alchemy. It didn't stream. You didn't download it. You blew it to life with kilowatts of light and created god on the screen before you.

Sure, downloading was the easiest delivery. Movies captured instantly on phones were the New and Living Art. But digital lacked frames. And it lacked the spaces between the frames. It lacked flicker. It lacked biochemical connection.

They all knew this instinctively. It was whispered in the corners of Griffith, the sort of transgression verboten at the Tisch School of the Arts, spit upon at Fulsail.

But that wasn't what sent Tom Boone to the Lab or the Vault. No it was again, advice, but different advice. Nothing well-meaning and certainly miles beyond his best interest. And that was what he liked about that advice. That's why he followed it. To find the spaces between the frames.

After graduation, most of the Addicts went their separate ways. Bill Z. returned home to Ohio. Kearns disappeared first into New York, and then committed the mortal sin: he moved Out There, worked Out There. Darryl was killed in Yage, during the riot that followed the premiere of *Cunt Killer*.

Boone traveled the spokes, as Bailey suggested. He backpacked, like countless vagabonds before him, following the festivals. A day of glimpsed sunshine meant that a screening, somewhere, was missed and that was the worst of tragedies. Following in the footsteps of Sayles and Waters, cameras were always at the ready. The move to digital was inevitable and, sometimes, sickening. But he had to evolve with the media. For Addicts a roll of film could mean the difference between the "feel" of a photograph or shot, or admission to a fest. A cheap handheld handicam and USB cable afforded the opportunity to both capture and uphold the mission. To see. To view. Darkness on three sides and bright magic in front.

The Studios' "discovery" of Yage and Eastern Bethlehem for cheap location production value was part of the reunion. Despite the Bailey's urgings to amass an army, sometimes you just had to go where the work was. And if you were intent on avoiding the West Coast, you still wound back in the center of the Hub. And finally, back at The Squat, formerly "The Cathedral", formerly "Orson Hall", their old dorm building. Sitting in the dead center of The Welles, one of the least-worst sections of Bethlehem.

Because it was an arts district, The Welles was always flooded with mundanes and hipsters, clutching their wallets through their pockets, eyes darting for danger as they dashed into the "hip" theater of the week. Meanwhile, the citizens, addicts, and voyeurs of every strain, peered out at them from the shadows, acting out whatever movie played in their heads. The Welles had resisted gentrification throughout the years for this very reason. Never more than a seedy Harlem, a ten-square block 42nd Street, The Welles grew movie theaters like teeth, new ones sprouting up out of the grime and decay of the one before it. A little city of phoenixes, playing the movies until the movies swallowed them up yet again. It was a place to watch movies, while the movies watched back.

A decade later, the reunions at the Squat felt less like fate and more like contrivance. Were their lives a movie ("were"— the idea would be laughable in their later years), the Addicts finding each other again, after so many years, would have felt like a forced twist, a MacGuffin to move the story along. Something hackneyed out of every mercenary film, out of *The*

Muppet Movie. "Getting the band back together." One of the Wretched Clichés. One by one, the survivors of Griffin returned to roost.

Alyce—"Lys"—wound up crewing on some of the Big Pictures in Yage. When she returned to Bethlehem, she had the means to buy the Squat. By then abandoned by Griffith, students relocated to better digs in Hightown, the Squat was crumbling from within. Their Chelsea Hotel had decayed and become Gormenghast, the painted murals of all the greats slowly chipped away by time. On the Northwest corner, Clark Gable's ear was missing, brick showing through, while time and age dissolved Olivia DeHaviland, in his arms for eternity, until eternity was done with them.

The usual sexism was implied: Lys blew the right people, bypassing the Production Assistant (P.A.) level and going straight to Second Assistant Director (A.D.) on her first show. A Big One that came complete with panic and near endless budget. The job led to other shows. As hollow as cheap chocolate Easter Bunnies and just as mass-produced, but the cash did flow. Money solved problems, not gaffer's tape. And Lys's talent lay in problem solving. Money saved went directly into her fund to purchase the Squat.

By this time, Boone was surviving as a critic, not as an artist. Fest admission came free with the prestige but he felt his mercury plummeting. When film negative is exposed to light, the emulsion turns black. When processed, that portion is washed away, leaving its image behind. That image, in positive, is the photograph. As a critic, Boone felt that more and more of his emulsion was getting washed away. Soon he'd be a blank frame. Returning to Bethlehem, meeting Shel, brought him back to his proper exposure.

After a dozen years, the Squat needed a classier nickname, but no effort was made. Lys's remodeling had brightened the dead motel atmosphere, but it still retained the corruptive presence of the Welles. Where there had been bare futons were now couches and real beds. The TVs were bigger. The speakers installed instead of patched.

Within weeks of the Addicts' return, those new-bright walls were once again hidden by posters, though framed now. DVDs in cases and sleeves still littered every horizontal surface—that did not change with "maturity"—but filthy plates and rotting food were no longer found during excavations. Tastes had matured. Obsessions had not.

When it had been Orson Hall, when it housed the students who would become known as "The Addicts", the building had all the charm of the Bradbury Building, made famous by Ridley Scott's *Blade Runner*. The first four floors had been modernized to house new humanity, but everything above five was wrought-iron bannisters, hardwood floors, its own shuddering elevator complete with a manual gate. Less of a dormitory, more of a towering warehouse for human storage. Naturally, floors above five were off-limits to students living in the housing, sectioned off for offices that never were rented out.

Also of course, few of the students obeyed these rules. Orson Hall starred in more than ninety-percent of student films, a ready-made vertical landscape of skeletal girders and German expressionism. The higher you went, the crazier the architecture, as if the builders had succumbed to some Lovecraftian madness of geometry halfway through construction. Orson Hall, The Cathedral, The Squat, towered over The Welles, standing nearly as tall as the Nazareth Building which marked the center of Bethlehem, The Hub, with the circular highway nicknamed "The Strangeways Path" wrapping around it like the arms of a lover. No better place in the world to shoot, in their opinion. The kind of place Burroughs or Cronenberg wouldn't have left in a hurry. Their chosen land.

The film boom that descended upon Yage and Bethlehem earned Griffith quite a cap-feather. With the Studios and the Suits fighting each other for the best locations and the cheapest labor, the school's students were endless grist for the movie mill. The curriculum intensified, degrees were fast-tracked. You could earn a BFA in less than three years, get spit onto a set right after graduation. That is, if you weren't already employed as a runner, a P.A., or any number of euphemisms for slave status. Three days on a set qualified you for full credit in Independent Study—practically a major for the students graduating just after Boone and the Addicts.

Griffith Film Academy finally got what it always wanted and was lifted from ghetto status in the eyes of the world. Consequently, improvements were made all around. Crippled, skeletal Orson Hall was abandoned in favor of shinier new buildings north of The Hub, furnished more like apartments than the opium den cells The Addicts had been used to. Griffith's main building was rechristened Zanuck, a not-so-subtle prayer to Old Hollywood's demi-gods, and received upgrades to every classroom. Every piece of post-war era equipment got upgraded. The old CPs and Frezzolinis, once standard for television "Film at Eleven," with their Mickey Mouse-ear magazines and barrel-heavy balance, found their way to Ebay or the lobby display cases. Museum pieces, these awkward, heavy dinosaurs of the Jurassic era, replaced by Reds and Scarlets and 4K "capturing" devices, tethered to hard drives and heavy cooling units. "Film" was dead. Long Live the New HD video Flesh.

Lys had gotten lucky. The Squat went up for auction, as did the remaining primordial machinery. With the money she'd gotten for her work on Coppola's *Codename: Dragonfly*, and the surprise hit *Raging Beauty*, price wasn't much of a concern. Aside from a Chicago-based theater conglomerate wishing to purchase the building and raze it to parking space, she had been the only interested party. She became the proud owner of the medieval ruins after a little anemic bidding. Griffith, of course, had basically washed its hands of the place. Orson Hall was a glowering reminder of the school's former status of poverty row in the eyes of tuition-paying parents across the world.

Remodeling was done under radar. No time for human

interest neighborhood rejuvenation stories when Tom Cruise was shooting on the roof of Nazareth. North of The Hub was booming, growing, surging. The Welles dwelled in the South of The Hub, the Squat, and the Arc Theatre sharing the same block of Abaddon Street. Old neighborhood. Skid Row. As if someone had tipped the city and all the garbage rolled to lower ground, to the bottom, to The Welles.

Only *Movie Outlaw* had been interested, particularly in the Arc, due to the publication's fetish for decaying theaters wherein Paul Morrissey may have shot up. *Movie Outlaw* was the last of the underground film rags, having survived *Film Threat, Hollywood is Burning*, even *Entertainment Weekly*. It may as well have been born in The Welles. Editor Joe Sisto had on staff only one writer familiar with the area, and that was, of course, Tom Boone. Boone, living on old Broadway Dave's couch in Yage, about to be evicted as no one, especially not the landlord, had heard from Dave in almost a year. His documentary on Carthage swallowed him whole and he never returned. The apartment's heat was off. So was the water. The old lady landlord was forcing Boone out, starving him of utilities. With nothing left to lose and nothing left to stay for, Boone accepted the assignment and caught a long bus ride back to Bethlehem.

Boone returned to The Welles more or less as a free man. He owned no cell phone, smart or otherwise; everything he had was crammed into the army surplus duffel bag, nearly as tall as he was. The sky above was pissing slush, but across from the bus station was the Fulton Theater and it didn't matter what was playing. Inside was warm and dry and dark. Surely, one of the Wretched Clichés would rescue him. He'd meet cute with an old friend, a chance co-incidence to twist his current plot. It was the way of the world for The Addicts: put your faith in the film the Elder Gods were making. Cinemagog, dark father of the deiwos of film, would provide the next scene.

Sure enough, after trading currency for a ticket, the moment Boone's foot touched the now-colorless red carpet of the Fulton, his scene changed:

INT. THE FULTON LOBBY - NIGHT

Boone sees Lys for the first time in ten years.
And she takes him home.

SCENE THREE:
ORSON HALL

"Can you believe it?" Lys asked him, her dark eyes glinting, whole face beaming with pride. "It's all ours again. Bought it right from Griffith for near nothing."

Actually, he could believe it. He'd always admired Lys's tenacity. Even in school, she'd pulled off miracles before others had even conceived of an attempt. Half of them would be only starting on video projects and she'd already be in edit. Name your cliché: "she took the ball and ran", "she jumped the gun", sports phrases for the driven artiste.

For half of a decade, the Orson building had been their home. Never a dorm-like atmosphere, always more of a flophouse hotel for struggling film students. The slum where creativity thrived. Standing back inside the narrow foyer, faced with a decision of twin staircases leading to opposite wings, the area cast with a urine-colored glow from the ancient light fixtures above, it was like the open arms of a welcoming family, of inbreds and psychopaths, exalting his return. Lys chose Staircase Two, leading to the East side of the tower. Boone followed.

"The first and second floors I rent out to the kids who can't afford to stay in the Zanuck dorms in Hightown," she said, taking the steps two at a time, like a giddy sprinter. "The rest of the building I saved for us."

"'Us' who?"

"All of us. The Addicts are back, babe." For Lys, this was a happy triumph. Boone took that news as a sad stab to the heart. Had any of them made it out?

"Kearns came back first," Lys said, then dropped her voice to a stage whisper, lest the words echo and bounce around. "It was right after his last job with The Studios. He was shattered. Wait 'til you see the scars on his wrists from where they kept him chained up." Stopping hard, she leaned in close.

"Rewrites," she whispered. "Almost killed him."

Copper, she told him, never really left. He'd leased out the attic right after graduation and set up his studio there, commuting back and forth from his mother's house until she finally succumbed to the sad life she'd led. Gradually, he turned the studio into his residence, cutting away at his Big Feature. His semi-girlfriend, Mya—who Lys had never actually met—had apparently resigned herself to his constant absence. Only Rusty Pennick—an entering freshman, Boone recalled, showing up at the doorstep as the rest were hurling their grad caps into the air—his production assistant and company. Well, Rusty and the deities that Copper honored.

While they ascended, Boone trailed his fingers along the age-smoothed wooden balcony railing, across the cool tile of the walls. He could feel the history humming within. All too familiar. This return was melancholy. To him, seeing the dim halls, knowing that behind each door, an Addict, new or known, was flixing away to a personal film festival. Preferring the dancing shadows to the life outside of The Welles.

"The rent's whatever," Lys said. "And you pay for your electricity. That's the main rule. Everything else is like it used to be."

Communal, Boone thought. A vertical barter town. Eat, sleep, watch movies, and flix to whatever you brought with you. The Addict definition of Heaven. Except that this was the *Twilight Zone* twist to that idea. In many ways, reaching this nirvana felt so very much like failure. Lys was gathering up the Addicts and, like the recommendation on every film can, storing them in a cool, dry place.

Finally, they'd reached their destination, and Lys handed him an old fashioned metal key, to go along with the ossified door. "411," she said. "I saved your old room for you."

SCENE FOUR:
DYING HARD FOR OLD HABITS

Like most of the Addicts, Boone turned on to flixing in high school. During his Junior Year he served as an apprentice projectionist at the Parkway Theater in Samedi, west of The Hub. He learned all about flixing from "Broadway Dave" Desmond, the wizened chief projectionist, a Merlin who talked about the practice in the same way Burroughs waxed ecstatic about heroin.

"As long as there've been movies, there've been flicker freaks, man," Dave said, breaking down the print of *Terminator 3* on the ancient rewind table. The Parkway operated a three-platter projection system; a burnished aluminum plate for feeding, a second for take-up and a third for reserve during the rare times the theater had a second feature booked. A feature film consisted of six-to-eight thousand-foot reels of 35mm film. Spliced together end-to-end, you had a precarious four-foot circular slab of loosely coiled celluloid. During a break down, the projectionist took the tail of the giant slab, fed it back onto one of the original 1000' reels and reversed the process of making a movie. You had to make sure you put the right head and tail countdown lengths on the right reel or else you'd make hell for the next poor box-jockey who had to rebuild the print in second run.

"Even the guys who only see this as a job, you know? Not really movie guys, just collecting the paycheck? They'll suck on a frame during a showing. Passes the time mostly." Broadway Dave rode the take-up motor as the film returned to its reel. He spoke around a cigarette, a permanent part of his creased face, white burning tube shoved into the middle of his unruly gray goatee. "And I don't care who you are, union guy or fanatic, you keep frames off of every print you build. It's an obsession. Gets snarled in your brain. Snag something from the head or tail of each reel. Real butchers will find a scene in the middle and steal a frame from that. That's why the prints jump around in the second-run houses. Some sadistic pricks'll steal the frames with the 'cigarette burns', which used to be a real fucking pain when you were running two projectors. Never knew when to do the change-over."

Broadway Dave had his own stash of frames inside a yellowing envelope tacked to the corkboard hanging over the manual rewind table. Before too long, Boone had amassed a small collection of his own, trimming frames from every print he built or broke down, regardless of what it was. He swore to himself that if he decided to try flixing, he'd do it at home, in a safe environment. That promise was broken less than a week later, during a showing of *Breathless* (*À bout de soufflé*, 1960, directed by Jean-Luc Godard). He'd chosen a single frame of *Pink Flamingoes* (1972, John Waters). In hindsight, the faded print going pale magenta, riddled with scratches and tears, was probably a poor choice. Midway through the French gangster film, the overwhelming stench of b.o. and dogshit invaded his nose from the inside, and his vision swam with washes of pink and green. On-screen Jean-Paul Belmondo morphed into the image of Divine painted large across his eyeballs, and Boone didn't find it amusing. Which was worse? The sour taste in his stomach, or the unwanted, throbbing erection? By the time the credits finally rolled, he swore he'd never flix again.

That weekend, he and Trish Medvitz each did a frame of *Sirens* (1994, John Duigan) and fucked until the sun came up. Still tripping on the mental images of Elle MacPherson and Portia DeRossi, he hid in Trish's closet until her parents left for work. Trish, still in the midst of orgasm, claimed stomach cramps and together they skipped their morning classes.

After that, he flixed in class. He flixed at work, while driving, whenever he could. When his own frame stash ran out, he began swiping from Dave's collection, tasting the frames from older movies, better prints. Boone's waking life was a kaleidoscope of Technicolor imagery.

Returning to the Squat, after all those years trying to

"make it", put him in the mood for rock bottom. Staring up at the ceiling from the provided couch that served as his bed, it hit him that he really had nowhere to go. No real job outside of the meager *Movie Outlaw* earnings. He hadn't made a movie in years. No girlfriend, no family, no ties on Earth save Lys and The Squat. Anxiety began to eat its way out of him.

His last bottle of Jack Daniels had worked its way to the bottom of his duffel and it took some digging to unearth it. The former occupant of his apartment had left behind a chipped Daffy Duck coffee mug and into it he poured a respectable shot. Two hours later he wouldn't remember what had happened the hour before. But the liquor would need some assistance.

Fingers drumming along the rim of his mug. Again. Each time it took Tom longer to notice. Before him, the apartment's flatscreen was alight with Miike's *Gozu* (2003), noisy, colorful, surreal to the point of incoherence, a film version of panic.

Drumming. Drumming. Nails clinking on the porcelain. Fine. No use fighting it. What was the point?

Without pausing *Gozu*, he returned to his bag, attention split, one eye on the screen, the other on the hunt for the familiar age-crumpled and yellowed envelope that had accompanied him on every journey for the past decade. Envelope found, he shook some of its contents into his hand. No two from the same movie, 35mm rectangles mixed with the smaller gauge 16mm, and the even smaller Super-8mm. Never been able to score a frame of "regular" 8mm. Not that the flavor would be any more condensed than the Super-8mm—which actually had a larger frame of exposure due to only one side of sprocket holes—but because it was harder to come by, the rarity made the delicacy automatic. Select a frame, hold it up against the flashing shadows. Squinting. *Bullitt* (1968, Peter Yates), chase sequence through Fisherman's Wharf. McQueen's 1968 390 V8 Ford Mustang GT fastback suspended in midair, leaping a hill. Boone shook his head in time to the word 'no' in his brain. Going on midnight, the speed would clobber his nervous system and he had to look for work in the morning.

Discard. Select. Squint. *From Hell* (2001, the Hughes Brothers). Jack the Ripper's knife glinting in a dark alley. Abstract. Possibly dangerous.

Back into the envelope. Select. *From Here to Eternity* (1953, Fred Zinnemann). Another re-release print. Crisp black and white. Surf washing over Debra Kerr's long bare legs. *Gozu* is framed inside a sprocket hole. Applying pressure with thumb and forefinger, the frame bowed, edges held between fingerprint ridges.

Back into the envelope. Twitchy now, anxious, he fished around and grabbed one at random, rested it on his tongue. Old Hollywood slid down his throat, up through his saliva glands. It had a molasses taste, which could only mean Capra. Too smooth for Preston Sturges; not enough bite for Ford. *Destry Rides Again* (1939, George Marshall). Fine.

Normally, he didn't care for mixing genres. When you're watching, say, *Two Mules for Sister Sarah* (1970, Don Siegel), you don't want to pop a frame of *Chicago* (2002, Rob Marshall) or even *Paint Your Wagon* (1969, Joshua Logan). No, you maybe grab a *Guns of the Magnificent Seven* (also 1969, Paul Wendkos), maybe a shot from *Bandolero* (1968, Andrew V. McLaglen) if you're lucky enough to score a length. You want the same grit and sand inside as you're watching outside. Never understood guys who'd pop *The Shining* (1980, Stanley Kubrick) while watching *Last Tango in Paris* (1972, Bernardo Bertolucci). Or the reverse: *Day for Night* (*La Nuit américaine*, 1973, François Truffaut) while watching some hideousness like *The Frozen Dead* (1966, Herbert J. Leder). It made his brain nauseous. But this was one of those proverbial "desperate times".

The contrast between matinee western and psychotic Japanese gore was almost too much. His body bucked once, violently, then again with less force. Color and monochrome swirled together. Subversion dancing with formula. His teeth chattered with the rhythm of a shutter.

By morning he hadn't slept. *Gozu* ran through twice and he replaced it with *The American Astronaut* (2001, Cory McAbee). After the first flix, he continued to grab frames at random. He vaguely remembered taking three at a time, the bits of film stuck together with old splicing tape residue. One had definitely been the crummy Van Damme movie, *Double Impact* (1991, Sheldon Lettich). Another was definitely *The Doctor* (also '91, Randa Haines) with William Hurt. Those two melding together overwhelmed the third—or was it the unidentified third that sent his minds' eye spasming?

True hardcore flixers would go without eating, drinking, or even excreting during a marathon. You got hungry, you just found the appropriate eating scene, suck on a frame or two. The cinematic food tricks the body into feeling full and nourished. Couple of guys upstairs in the midst of finals tried to commit suicide by swallowing entire reels of *Le Grande Bouffe* (1973, directed by Marco Ferreri), thinking they were clever because the premise of the film was about four men, including Marcello Mastroianni, eating themselves to death. Maybe they could have, but all they'd been able to run down was a beaten-up release print from the basement of The Arc. Most of the flavor of the film, the color, had been washed away by too many screenings, poor storage. Reel four had started to weep vinegar with rot, and that doesn't work as a salad dressing during a flix binge.

As the sun streamed through the room's single filthy window, a glint of wet told him that he was bleeding. One of the side effects of over-flixing. It had happened to him several times before, the first following a freshman year binge. Flixing for four straight days, sucking the emulsion off one frame after another while he popped DVDs in succession—starting with Sergei Eisenstein's *Battleship Potemkin* (1925) for some reason—it wasn't until around the 76-hour mark that Boone had noticed all the crimson.

Just like the first time, his arms were crisscrossed with parallel train tracks of tiny weeping wounds, all of them perfectly identical, rounded-off squares, as if his skin'd been run over again and again with a patterned tool, a sprocket wheel. It may have taken him longer to notice if a blood tear hadn't dripped down his nose. Hanging there for an instant, long enough to tear his attention away from the Russian fantasy *Mechanosets* (2006, Filipp Yankovsky), he watched it fall onto the envelope of film frames in his lap.

That triggered a response, evoked movement from his body, one of barely a dozen over twelve or so hours. Jumping up, immediately half-sober, he held the bowl up to the TV light, to find which frames had been contaminated by his blood. He found only four, and immediately cleaned them off on the surprisingly stiff sleeve of his black *Nightbreed* hoodie. Defying the laws of probability, the spattered frames had all been base-side up. Any scratching from the sleeve cloth would be minimal. The emulsion would be fine. The flavor of the movie intact.

Gingerly, he placed the wiped-down frames—Christ, he wished he had some acetone—back into the envelope with the others. Feeling another drop gathering on the point of his chin, he bolted into his bathroom. Thanks to Lys, the fifth floor rooms didn't share communal showers at either end of the hall. From four up, there were separate facilities, one for guys, one for dolls. What were they if not the pretext of civilized?

Fluorescent stuttered and buzzed to life as he entered, gradually coating the room in sickly green. If he were to shoot film in there, he'd have to use a filter to keep the color balanced. He didn't take the time to try and remember which filter; he wasn't a director of photography, after all.

The mirror image was an ugly sight. Splashing away the freshest blood, water revealed tracks across his face, neck, scalp, neck, shoulders. Crusted tracks on the backs of his hands, dried blood where it'd seeped the longest. Hoodie sleeves had soaked up the oldest tracks. Probably broke out during *No hoi wai lung* 1995, Bun Yuen. English title *Tough Beauty and the Sloppy Slop*— that'd be appropriate. He'd expected more from vintage Hong

Kong action but it was a pedantic and predictable cops-n-robbers thing, completely wasting the talents of Yuen Biao and Cynthia Khan. Best thing about it was the goofy English-translated title.

From the waist-up—and that was as far as he wanted to explore at the moment—he was thoroughly sprocketed. Each set of tracks was exactly (precisely) 34.98 mm apart (give or take 0.03 mm). The wounds looked to be Kodak Standard, rounded rectangles 2.794mm at the widest part by 1.981mm high (or .0780" by .1100" inches wide. .020 inches diagonally). His skin could be run through a standard projector at a rate of 24 frames per second. Each set of four perforations equaled one standard-sized film frame, sixteen frames per foot. Even if he could see his back clearly, he wasn't up for doing the math.

There was almost no pain, just a stinging itchiness and a lot of subdural blood. Back at Griffith, it wasn't unusual seeing his classmates bearing the faint scar tracks of similar movie marathons. Of course, he thought, you never think it could happen to you.

Stripping down, he jumped into the shower, hosed himself off for a couple of minutes. Just as he'd suspected, the wounds went all the way down, even to the bottoms of his feet. Red water circled the drain, reminding him of—what else?—*Psycho*. The fluorescents kinda made the blood look black. Without a towel and without really caring, he dried off with the sweatshirt and wrapped it around his waist. No sense in even getting dressed.

After the shower, his eyes were still watering, checking the mirror he saw why. There were tracks across the white of his eyes, same gauge but seeming huge in perspective. Tears were pinkish, running down his face.

Jesus. But what was he gonna do? Hit a hospital? Doctor would just tell him to take a fast from movies. Wasn't like he'd ever do that.

Sleep, he thought. Sleep would heal him up.

Maybe Andy Warhol's *Sleep*…

He'll be careful from here on out. Perfing that first night back—that'd be his wake-up call.

CHAPTER TWO
BORGIA

"What else is there to talk about?" he asked Shoard. "All religion is about death and art's about life. Religion is there to say: hey, you don't have to worry — there's an afterlife. Culture represents the opposite of that — sex. A very stupid Freudian way of looking at it, but one is positive and one is negative. [...] I don't know much about you,' says Peter Greenaway, [...] 'but I do know two things. You were conceived, two people did fuck, and I'm very sorry but you're going to die. Everything else about you is negotiable.'"

—Peter Greenaway. Shoard,
Catherine. 2010. "Peter
Greenaway's pact with death." The
Guardian. March 18.

SCENE ONE:

SETTING THE BLOODY SCENE

("The Archetype Murderer: The Serial Killer as Artist" by Chris Balun. *Movie Outlaw*, Vol. 3, No. 1. 1999. Continued from page 24.)

...Convicted of the murders of Etta Tarquinio and

Heather Grenedy, Luther Borgia was executed by lethal injection in his home state of New Jersey on December 13, 1982, just four months after the death penalty was reinstated in that state. He was the third person in the country to die by that method.

Born October 7, 1940, the son of Anthony and Loretta Borgia, Luther Borgia was a top student at New York University, studying Philosophy and Social Sciences.

In 1966, he first began to experiment with 16mm films. His early works are largely unremarkable, studies in motion and superimposition.

In 1968, he joined a camera club and began to experiment more freely with the art form.

In October of that year, three days before his 28th birthday, Luther Borgia discovered the remains of the works of his grandfather, Rupert Borgia (1855-1902). Rupert was a successful machinist and friend to inventor Thomas Edison. Intrigued by Edison's development of the "Kinetoscope" movie camera in 1889, Rupert Borgia followed the inventor's achievements with the device and often assisted in tests, including the first-ever public test in 1891. Acquiring one of the later prototypes, Rupert experimented with his own short films. After the birth of his only son, Anthony, in 1900, Rupert's films were discovered by San Francisco authorities. Depicting the deaths of three young women–later identified as Amelia and Elizabeth Street and Mildred Ocznakowski–Rupert Borgia was convicted of first degree murder–the first time in history that films have been used as evidence in a murder trial–and was hanged for the offense in March, 1902.

Restoring and incorporating this ancient footage into his works, Luther began to craft what he would later call "The Divine Heresy": a series he referred to, tongue-in-cheek, as "a five-part trilogy" (predating author Douglas Adams own description of his famous *Hitchhiker's Guide to the Galaxy* novels). "The Divine Heresy" was heralded by the early underground movements of punk and avant-garde artistry as a brilliant exercise in violence and blasphemy.

Largely experimental, "The Divine Heresy" consists of the five short films:

The Magus (1977)
The Pioneer (1977)
Rape of the Archangel (1978)
Osculum Infame (1978)
From Gomorra to Golgotha (1979)

Borgia's techniques improved during the course of the "trilogy", but even his most rudimentary talents are on display in *The Magus* (in which the last supper is depicted as a cabaret show held by a cheesy stage magician, in top-hat and tails. Host wafers are produced from behind ears, a wine chalice is filled by the slit throat of a young girl volunteer, and, in the end, the magician is literally carved up and eaten by the audience). In between the rather linear story, Rupert Borgia's rough and admittedly horrific turn-of-the-century images are interspersed, along with very violent depictions of sexuality.

Borgia would continue these themes of violence, sex and offenses against religion—particularly Catholicism (though the artist himself was raised Methodist)–throughout the rest of the trilogy, culminating in the final part *From Gomorra to Golgotha*. This final installment was actually banned at several artistic exhibitions for one image in particular: Christ, crucified naked, between two rotting corpses (the thieves from scripture), is approached by (assumedly) Mary Magdalene, who then proceeds to fellate the dying Messiah.

While the horrific murder and rape that pervades his films were at first assumed to be special effects (echoing the realistic special effects that were all the rage in mainstream cinema at the time), it was later determined that, like his grandfather, Luther Borgia had murdered at least two young women, runaways from Brooklyn. When it was proven that two girls in particular, Etta Tarquinio (18) and Heather Grenedy (16), from his home state of New Jersey, were definite victims, Luther Borgia was arrested and, in 1988, finally convicted of their murders. Both girls murders could be seen, it was argued, in the next-to-last film, *Rape of the Archangel*, though Borgia insists that they were alive when filming was completed. He failed to elaborate whether that meant that he had actually staged their deaths and was innocent of the crimes, or if his torture of the girls was real and that they died only after he had finished filming. Borgia was not allowed to testify on his own behalf, as his council had built an insanity defense around the case. The press depicted the charming, smiling artist to be not only sane, but a cold-blooded killer and the jury thought likewise. It was suspected, but never proven, that many other of his celluloid victims, male and female, were more than actors cast in gruesome fiction. Tarquinio and Grenedy remain his only confirmed kills, despite cinematic evidence.

"The Divine Heresy" has never been exhibited publicly in its entirety. Even during his freedom, Borgia would show one or two, at the most, three, of the series. After his conviction, the confiscated films were sealed as evidence by the New Jersey District Attorney's Office.

In 1998, VHS transfers of *The Magus*, *The Pioneer* and *Rape of the Archangel* surfaced on the Internet among "bootleggers" and collectors. *Osculum Infame* and *From Golgotha to Gomorra*, admittedly rarer, are rumored to exist on VHS among collectors from the underground '80s scene, though proof of their existence has yet to surface.

Borgia is known to have influenced and have been admired by such experimental artists as Stan Brakhage, who appreciated his style and sense of humor, and, not surprisingly, practitioners of the "Cinema of Transgression", headed by filmmaker Nick Zedd and photographer Richard Kern. The films of these two men are also notorious for their sexual and violent imagery, especially in such films as *Fingered* and *Hardcore*, (continued on page 28)

*****

It is a popular misconception that Luther Borgia had never screened the entire "Divine Heresy" publicly. To the contrary, there were at least two known exhibitions, both in New York. Andy Warhol, Borgia's most famous admirer, screened all five films at The Factory in 1980. Among those in attendance were Paul Morrissey, John Cale, Jean-Michel Basquiat, Martin Scorsese, and Kenneth Anger. While Borgia supplied the prints, he was not present at this last screening. Warhol had made the decision, rather than show the films back-to-back, that he would play them in random order, much as he had done with the individual reels of *Chelsea Girls*. Following the initial screening, the films were continuously projected side-by-side for the remainder of the evening. For nearly eleven hours, the segments of Borgia's "trilogy" unspooled while the artistic elite partied, drank, and proclaimed themselves important.

Warhol's diary entry for this event is spare. The films are not mentioned by title, nor Borgia by name. Andy seemed more concerned by the nosebleed he awoke with which continued to plague him throughout the day. He also wrote that he was plagued with a headache, "not quite a migraine," that made him want to avoid light and company.

The second and final exhibition was organized by Borgia himself. He rented The Rialto on 42nd Street, a 200-seat blackbox that alternated between arthouse films and hardcore pornography. Of the fifty recipients of private invitations, only twenty-two attended. The screening was open to the public but only a handful of walk-ins bought tickets. Official reports vary on the total attendance, but most agree that it remained at less than fifty. By the end of the night, only six people remained in the audience.

Later that evening, two of the remaining six took their own lives. Two others were arrested for assault and attempted murder of strangers. The fifth succeeded in butchering a transient sleeping on a subway train, stabbing him repeatedly with the shattered neck of a wine bottle until little remained of the victim's face. Attempts to arrest the perpetrator resulted in injury of two transit officers and three uniformed policemen who subdued their attacker with borderline-deadly force. The assailant was Daniel Silver, a freelance food and entertainment journalist for *The Village Voice*. After two days spent in a holding cell, alternately raving and near comatose, his body was discovered during a watch-change. Silver had swallowed his own tongue.

The sixth and last audience member was a young man named Arnold Lipiniski. He was Etta Tarquinio's cousin, had recognized her during *From Gomorra to Golgotha*, during a violent scene where she is shown being disemboweled by St. Peter, played by Borgia himself. It had been over three years since Etta Tarquinio had disappeared from her Jersey City apartment. Lipiniski's testimony proved key to Borgia's later conviction, despite the fact that Etta Tarquinio's body was never found.

It wasn't until later, a year before Luther Borgia attempted to hang himself in his cell of New York's infamous prison known as "The Tombs," that Borgia finally led police to Etta's remains, sealed inside a metal drum and partially buried in an unfinished garage in Hoboken. Dental records, at first, were deemed inconclusive. In 2009, DNA testing revealed that the remains were, in fact, those of Etta Tarquinio. Luther Borgia had been dead for more than a decade.

SCENE TWO:
ART VS. COMMERCE

None of the other Addicts had a copy of *From Gomorra to Golgotha*. Lys had held on to a VHS copy of *The Pioneer*, but of all the Borgia movies that was the easiest to come by. It could be viewed in its entirety on YouTube. Snippets from all of the films, save the last, were archived all over the Internet, particularly among those who considered Borgia a cult figure like Manson or Gacy. The serial killer sub-culture. Everybody had their thing.

"The dude killed people in his movies," Josh said around a mouthful of pizza. "It's not a *Faces of Death* thing or news photos. These are pretty much snuff films."

Boone shrugged, took a swig of Guinness. He was responsible for the night's feast, courtesy of his surprise signing bonus from the Carcosa FilmLab, unusual in and of itself considering the owner, Josef "King" Ghast, was known far and wide as an evil bastard who wasn't above embezzling his own employee's pensions. With the recent IRS woes that came down upon Ghast, he guessed his new boss was trying to put up a good front. That, or an attempt to finally attract good employees. The lab's revolving door spun like a gyroscope with hirings and firings and walkouts. Either that or Shel the Agent had pulled some strings. Either way…

"I'm not one of those 'endurance test' guys," Josh continued.

"I'll stick with the Video Nasties if I need a good stomach-churn."

"C'mon," Lys said. "You edit autopsy videos for a living."

"And the stars of those are already dead," he said. "I've seen the Bud Dwyer news footage, why would I want to see a couple of girls actually die for some asshole's pretentious show?"

Actually disappointed, Boone spelled out the obvious, "Because they're rare. Barely anyone has seen any of them. It's history."

"So was the Black Plague. I wouldn't want to watch that shit either." Josh tossed his crust back into the box. It was another annoying habit of his. Lys rescued the leavings, picked away anything that may have touched the man's teeth, chomped it like a bread stick.

"His grandfather murdered people too," she said around the mouthful. "Worked for Edison. Shot them dying with one of the first cameras ever made. *That's* history. That's like Jack the Ripper caught on surveillance video."

Guttural disgust from Josh. "You're acting like that's nothing."

"No," Lys dug a pepperoni from the cooling cheese, flipped it into her mouth. "I'm just saying I'm intrigued."

"I don't support murderers. Sorry, I have standards."

"Yet, you love Polanski," Lys said.

Josh's face flushed with indignation. "That is completely different."

"How?"

"*Chinatown,*" Boone said.

Lys said to him, "So Polanski gets a pass for rape and pederasty because he made a good movie?"

"I didn't say I gave him a pass," Boone said. "And he's made nothing *but* good movies."

"It's the art versus the artist," said Josh.

"Then why are you against the Borgia films? Because he's not talented enough for you?"

"You know, you're the one who loves Woody Allen. He fucked his own daughter."

"And you know that's not true, either."

"Sorry, but I can't have any respect for him."

"Who? Woody or Polanski? How about Victor Salva, Josh? He get a pass too?"

"No, his movies are shit."

Lys looked to Boone for assistance. He simply smiled.

"I'm not justifying anybody here. Borgia's a serial killer, Salva's a pedophile, Polanski's a degenerate. They've all played their parts in film history."

"Not Salva," Josh muttered. "Fuck *Jeepers Creepers*."

Boone finished his bottle, grimaced against the dregs. "Plus, nobody's seen these Borgia movies in thirty years. We'd be the first."

Then a new voice said, "Wrong." Everybody jumped. They'd forgotten Kearns was back there, on the floor behind the couch, watching the original *Zatoichi* on his tablet, seemingly lost in a flixing haze.

Lys kneeled up and peered at him over the back of the couch. "1980. At The Garden in SoHo," she said, partly reminding him and partly schooling everyone else. "Five people died after that screening and two were arrested for murder. It was the screening that led to the investigation."

"Yeah," Kearns conceded. He placed the tablet on his stomach but didn't look up at her, keeping his eye fixed on a spot on the ceiling. "But that wasn't the last screening."

"Okay, even I know that's bullshit," Josh said. "All the prints were destroyed."

Kearns said, simply and again, "Incorrect." Even in conversation, Kearns' voice had a hostile edge, far removed from the gentle tone Boone remembered from school-chum Kearns.

"How do you know?"

"*The Magus, The Pioneer* and *Golgotha* were shot on color negative. Borgia made three or four prints of each. *Rape of the Archangel* and *Osculum Infame* were shot on 16mm reversal, so he had to have a negative struck from both. That's why those two are the hardest to find, but they exist. Warhol had a complete set. So did Richard Kern. So did Michael Snow. So does Joe Coleman. In fact, Joe was the guy who lent *Archangel* to Chris Balun to do his documentary on Borgia."

Boone opened another Guinness. "Coleman's the guy who does those really intricate paintings, right?"

"Yeah. The microscopic pictures in the margins. The blows-himself-up guy." Kearns still refused to look at them. Or, rather, he wouldn't deign to do so. "And Balun put on his own screening of all five in 2008. In the order Borgia intended them to be seen."

Josh tossed away another crust, missing the box. The bread skittered under the TV stand. "And I guess everyone went nuts there and killed each other too? That's why we all heard about it on, oh, nowhere?"

Kearns just shrugged. "Google 'Gas Leak in Ohio Multiplex, 2008'. Fifty-some people burned to death."

"Because of the films?"

"Because fucking Chris locked everyone in and blew the place up."

"Uh, Kearns," Boone said. "No disrespect, but you know I knew Chris, right? I wrote for *Movie Outlaw*? Mag he co-founded?"

"Did he tell you when he was dying of lung cancer?"

"Well, no he did not."

"Then why would he tell you that he nuked a bunch of film ravers after they lost their shit?"

"Okay," said Lys. "Who told you?"

"What do you think I was doing Out There for six fucking years? I was working on a script based on all that. I wrote eleven drafts of that stupid shit. My first day on the job I got locked inside a room with the FBI while they *let* me read all these redacted files. Couldn't take notes. Had to remember everything. They treated it like some Roswell thing. Still read like the stupidest slasher movie ever. Fucking Lee Benway was supposed to direct it." Which was how Kearns always referred to the infamous director. "Fucking Lee Benway"—as if that was his full formal name.

Since he'd been back, this was the most Boone had heard Kearns talk about his time spent Out There. Of course, the man's complete change in personality from graduation spoke volumes. As did the scars on his wrists and ankles from his studio manacles. Once upon a time he was happy, charming "Bobby K." He dreamed of being a pro-screenwriter. He was the only one of them who'd made it. Now they were all back where they started, Kearns eyes looked out of his haunted face with a thousand-yard stare. ("Only things missing are camp numbers on his arm," Josh once remarked.) He'd worked for auteur and super producer Fucking Lee Benway almost exclusively, and nothing he'd ever written was produced.

"It was supposed to be Fucking Lee's big horror masterpiece," Kearns said, returning the tablet to its upright position on his chest. "He wound up making that Tallulah Bankhead biopic instead."

"Which one?" Josh asked, before Lys could stop him.

"The one I didn't write," Kearns said.

It wouldn't cut the tension, but Boone asked anyway, "You still have any of those drafts?"

"First couple," said Kerns. "Along with Fucking Lee's People's Choice Award."

"Mind if I read them?"

"Wipe your ass with them." He did not add, though it was implied: "Fucking Benway did."

It was obvious that Kearns had again recused himself from the conversation. The others returned to their pizza, arguing over which movie to put on so they could all flix.

The next morning, Boone found a thick envelope wedged under his apartment door. Inside was the multi-colored "Fourth Draft" of Kearns' script.

Lee Benway would like to invite you to a screening of the last movie you will ever see…

24 F.P.S.:
24 FRAMES PER SLAUGHTER

Screenplay By
Robert J. Kearns

FADE IN:

INT. GILES THEATER - NIGHT

THE CAMERA drifts along the empty corridors. The old multiplex seems deserted and quiet.

Suddenly, an EAR-PIERCING SCREAM rips through the silence. A terrified YOUNG WOMAN rounds the corner and runs down the hallway towards the camera. Her escape ramps down to SLOW MOTION as we see what's chasing her: an armed and ANGRY MOB of people from all walks of life—punks, suits, people in casual clothing, folks in bondage gear—all tear down the hall after her, brandishing various weapons.

The young woman is barely ahead of them and makes for the lobby. She hurls herself against the exit doors.

THE DOORS

don't budge. They're held fast with a loop of chain.

THE MOB

is on her now. She sinks to the ground in despair as they close in around her.

CREDITS

As the credits roll, we have a montage of computer screens receiving the same email, which we can read in chunks as the sequence continues:

> "Come to THE underground screening of the year! "The Unearthed Films of Luther Borgia" will be screened for the first time ever! The convicted serial killer descended from one of the most vicious murderers of the nineteenth century was rumored to not only have filled his home movies with footage of his victims but for splicing in footage of those killed by his grandfather, Rupert Borgia, who used a camera designed by Thomas Edison himself! These movies have never before been screened and were once thought to be an urban legend! This is a rare opportunity – but keep it to yourself! Be at the Giles Theatre at 7pm Saturday night! Tell no one!!"

Interspersed with the email are shots from various websites dealing with both lost films and urban legends. The faces of both RUPERT and LUTHER BORGIA stare out at the audience from the websites. Little looped frame-grabs from the movies are all that seems to be available of these "Lost Films".

                    THE CREDITS SEQUENCE DISSOLVES TO:

EXT. ROOF - DAY

DIANA FRIEDMAN, dressed in a conservative suit belying her carny ways, stands with her eyes closed. She exhales hard and opens her eyes.

Fluffy clouds drift lazily above. Several golf balls lie at her feet. She kicks one away as she walks towards the edge of the roof.

THE GOLF BALL

Rolls off the edge. We follow it as it hits the ground and bounces.

PARKING LOT

The ball bounces again, over the heads of a LINE OF PEOPLE waiting outside the building. The golf ball continues to bounce past the rows and rows of cars that fill the lot.

DIANA

Peers over the edge of the roof, staring down at the enormous crowd that has gathered outside her building.

                        DIANA
          Showtime.

As she turns, she nudges another golf ball off the roof.

We FOLLOW the ball to the ground as it falls.

EXT. THE LEWTON THEATRE PARKING LOT – DAY

The ball hits the ground, and bounces past a set of feet. The feet belong to CHRIS BALUN, who is shooting the crowd with a mini hand-held digital camera.

The theater itself is a big steel box, a disused multiplex waiting for life to thrive inside it again.

It's late in the day, nearly dusk. And the cracked lot is filled with cars.

FILM FANS are lining up around the building to get inside.

As we further follow the line, we pass groups of our primaries, picking up LITTLE SNATCHES OF CONVERSATION as we pass.

In the center, DAN and RALPH (20s), two scruffy little film geeks, gape around at the crowd.

> DAN
> I thought this was supposed
> to be some kind of underground
> screening?

> RALPH
> It was.

> DAN
> What's with the eight-mile
> poseur line?

Further down the line stand a pair of reasonably well-dressed men in off-the-rack suits. They both

look moderately dis-gruntled, however. They are
writer KURT CARRINGTON and his agent, THOM WADE.

Carrington looks at the crowd with a sour look.

Wade is scanning the faces, looking, it seems,
for a way to make a buck.

                    KURT
          I can't believe you couldn't
          just get passes to this thing.

                    THOM
          No passes. General seating.

                    KURT
          I am standing in line like
          a friggin' nobody! I wrote
          "Aurora Borealis" for Christ
          sakes!

Further down the line is a quartet of people
that couldn't be more polar opposite. PIKE
and KRUSTY are a pair of pierced and tattooed
punks, somewhere between raver and goth, in wild
clothes and unkempt, multi-colored hair. Behind
them are DAVE and SARAH, dressed much more
conservatively. Dave is grinning wide, while
Sarah looks uncomfortable.

                    SARAH
          So what is this thing about?

                    DAVE
          They're experimental movies.
          They don't have plots. They

        were made by a crazy guy who
        ended up killing two girls.

                    SARAH
        I love your idea of a romantic
        evening.

A BRIGHT PINK CAR pulls up near the back, swerving
to barely miss a group crossing the lot, and we
follow it to the rear of the lot.

INT. PINK CAR

is clouded with smoke. Inside is PHOEBE WELSH
(late 20s), smoking a joint.

The front seat is a mess of magazines, business
cards and other detritus.

She pulls into a space, parks on a diagonal
that will prevent anyone on either side of her
from accessing their own cars and starts shoving
things into a too-small purse.

She pulls some business cards out of her glove
compartment.

INSERT: BUSINESS CARD

        Phoebe Welsh
        Fucking Awesome Magazine
        BACK TO SCENE

She finishes her joint, stabs it out in the
ashtray and checks her makeup in her rear-view

mirror.

> PHOEBE
> You're one smoking-hot bitch
> tonight! Hell, yeah.

She takes a quick nip from a hip flask, stuffs that into the purse.

She looks back into the mirror, her eyes harder than they were just a moment ago.

> PHOEBE
> Just keep it together. They're
> not smarter than you. They
> can't hurt you.

Her eyes focus on the crowd outside the building.

She swings herself out of the car, pulling on the hem of her skirt.

She sees SEVERAL GUYS in the line staring at her.

She hesitates, her face almost sick, then, with a smile and a wink, she lets the skirt ride back up.

She starts working the line.

> PHOEBE
> (to GUY)
> Phoebe Welsh, "Fucking Awe-
> some". We have to talk after
> the movie, doll.
> (to GIRL)

Hey, pretty. Phoebe Welsh. We
have to talk. I totally love
your shoes.

Behind her, guys snicker and high-five each other
over lewd comments.

Phoebe freezes almost imperceptibly, makes a
quick fist, relaxes and goes back into her act.

SHE PASSES BY SARAH AND DAVE and the camera
lingers on them.

Pike and Krusty are talking amongst themselves.

              SARAH
    So this is like an art exhibit?

              DAVE
    Yeah, sort of. There's gonna
    be a band and a buffet table.

              SARAH
    But, ultimately, we're going
    to be sitting in a big room
    watching a weird movie.

              PIKE
    Standing.

              SARAH
    Excuse me?

              PIKE
    Sorry. Didn't mean to butt in.

              DAVE

No problem.

                    PIKE
Yeah, there are no seats.
It's standing room only. This
place hasn't been a working
theater in years.

                    DAVE
Oh yeah?

                    PIKE
It's gonna be like a movie-
rave.

                    SARAH
Did you hear that, Dave? A
movie-rave.

                    KRUSTY
              (to Sarah)
You know about these movies,
right? How the guy who made
them either killed the people
on screen or probably killed
them later?

                    SARAH
              (glaring at Dave)
No. I hadn't heard that.

                    KRUSTY
It's gonna be wild. That's
the reason these movies have
never been seen before.

                    SARAH
        Wow. How utterly romantic.
        Our one day off together and
        you took me to see a snuff film.

                    DAVE
        Sarah,   seriously,   you're
        gonna be glad you came.

                    SARAH
        Yeah. Because now I totally
        want to make one.

Pike and Krusty snicker at this.

Dave tries to keep grinning but fails.

Sarah looks annoyed.

Chris rounds the corner and films the crowd.

We FOLLOW him

SCENE DELETED

EXT. PARKING LOT - NIGHT

Ralph pulls a nasty, wrinkled piece of paper out
of his knapsack.

Dan unfolds it, reads it over.

                    DAN
        There: "Tell no one!" This
        was supposed to be a private
        invitation.

The camera spins around and DASHES to the door where, flanked by the NEWS CREWS, is Diana, the promoter responsible.

                    DIANA
          This   is   a   one-of-a-kind
          opportunity,   not   just   for
          horror   fans,   but   for   film
          scholars   across   the   world.
          The   films   of   Luther   Borgia
          have   never   been   screened   for
          the   public   in   their   entirety.
          They   were   thought   to   have   been
          lost   for   years   after   they   were
          used   as   evidence   for   his   1982
          murder   trial.

This   sends   the   reporters   into   a   frenzy.   She calls upon #1.

                    NEWSCASTER #1
          Ms.   Friedman,   don't   you   think
          it's   socially   irresponsible
          to   screen   these   films?

                    DIANA
          I   think   it   irresponsible
          not   to.   This   is   history,
          as   valuable   as   the   music
          of   Charles   Manson   or   the
          paintings   of   John   Wayne   Gacy.
          Samples   of   which,   by   the   way,
          have   sold   in   auctions   for
          thousands   of   dollars.

                    NEWSCASTER #2

How do you guarantee that the
films are genuine?

DIANA
I've had world-famous film
historian Harry Murdoch,
author of "Hitch, Truffaut
and Me", verify the films'
authenticity. He gave his
personal voucher to Variety.
I assure you that a screening
like this will not come around
again.

NEWSCASTER #3
And how did you manage to
obtain these films, Ms.
Friedman?

DIANA
Through a very convoluted
series of coincidental events.

Another hand shoots up in the back, and Diana
seems reluctant to acknowledge the owner.

NEWSCASTER #4
And what can those present
tonight expect from the
screening?

DIANA
Well, such unique movies
deserve a unique event. We
have the band Blackheart Mary
playing before the movies

                begin.   Refreshments   will
                be available throughout the
                evening and once the doors
                close, they will be locked.
                No one will be permitted to
                leave until the films have
                completed. This is for legal
                purposes, of course.
                We can't have details of
                the films leaked to the web
                before they're even finished
                premiering. Oh, and to that
                end, all cell phones and
                cameras will be confiscated.

                     NEWSCASTER #5
                Isn't that dangerous?

                       DIANA
                I can assure you that every
                precaution has been taken to
                ensure everyone's physical
                safety.

                       CHRIS
                What about their mental
                safety?

Diana freezes and looks to the back of the crowd.

Chris Balun has his camera up as he pushes his way past the crews.

Diana looks annoyed, but remains cool and confident during the following:

DIANA
Ladies and gentlemen, noted
internet writer and fanboy,
Chris Balun.

CHRIS
What about their emotional
safety? Did you take that
into consideration?

DIANA
These are the personal and
experimental films completed
by a pair of serial killers,
Mr. Balun. Be that as it
may, they are arguably very
intense.

CHRIS
There is every reason to
believe that the victims in
those movies were actually
murdered in real life.

DIANA
Neither Luther nor Rupert
Borgia were convicted of
their crimes by using the films
as evidence. In both cases,
the movies were dismissed as
works of fiction.

CHRIS
Those are the details of the
case, yes.

> **DIANA**
> Those are the findings of the legal system, Mr. Balun.

> **CHRIS**
> And what about the documented cases of people going mad after having watched the movies?

> **DIANA**
> What about people who vomited during "The Exorcist"? I can't control degrees of delicate nature, nor, as an exhibitor, should I be expected to.

> **CHRIS**
> Twenty-three people, Ms. Friedman. Twenty-three people have gone mad after just seeing segments of the movies! Of those twenty-three people, sixteen assaulted family members and friends.

> **DIANA**
> Circumstantial, Mr. Balun.

> **CHRIS**
> Documented fact!

> **DIANA**
> (talking over him)
> And I think it's safe to assume that today's audiences

are much more sophisticated in the ways of film magic.

CHRIS
It is the opinion of the film community that the films of Luther Borgia are cursed and should not be publicly exhibited.

DIANA
Yes, Mr. Balun, and everyone knows how popular censorship is in this country. Why, the founding fathers were all for the suppression of information.

CHRIS
This isn't about the First Amendment! This is about projecting… live deaths for a paying audience!

DIANA
And there you have it, friends. "Live deaths" for the mere price of $20.

CHRIS
There is every reason to believe that some of his onscreen victims were actually murdered during filming. These are snuff films, Ms. Friedman!

> DIANA
> So they do exist? Here I
> thought that was something
> made up by "E! True Hollywood
> Stories."

The crowd laughs.

Diana looks pleased.

> DIANA
> Now, if you will all excuse
> me, it's time to open up.

The newscasters erupt into a renewed frenzy, but
she waves them off.

The CROWD has grown larger. Ralph and Dan are
still grumbling, but have taken their places in
line.

> DAN
> This is bullshit, dude. We
> should jet.

> RALPH
> Nah, we came all the way down
> here. Besides, where are
> you gonna see these movies
> otherwise?

> DAN
> Ten minutes after the screening
> ends, guaranteed you'll be
> able to download them.

```
          RALPH
I'm staying.  It's the theater
experience.


                         CUT TO:
```

...Flipping through the script, Boone could read Kearns' frustration right off the page. Characters drifted in and out of this first act set-up, their sole purpose to skewer the clichés of filmmaking and fandom. He recognized the archetypes: the shallow, preening bloggers, the fanboys strutting their vast knowledge of obscure film history, the exploitative show-woman trying to make her mark with an outrageous event, the faux outrage. All of these characters painted with a tarbrush of traits and ticks. They were the cannon fodder. Numbers for the body count. Any semblance of deeper humanity were obviously washed away by the notes from the producers, as indicated by the rainbow pages, a cascade of changes. Whatever statement Kearns was trying to make was drowned by whatever committee the writer had to answer to.

Whatever historical value the "Divine Heresy" provided was also lost in this over-boiled stew. The movies were discussed by the characters in line, setting up the mythology, but no great meaning was assigned to them. The films, in this script, were merely the MacGuffin—the insignificant thing to get the plot moving towards the bloodshed and chaos. Interestingly, when the movies begin to play, Kearns never specifically slugs a shot directed at the screen. Only the audience faces reacting to seeing the Borgia films as the madness seeps in. To visualize the supposed mind-altering power of what amounted to five pretentious "art-horror" shorts, Kearns had those most affected by the madness weeping tears of blood. A shortcut to let the audience know who to root for and who to fear.

So powerful were these movies, implied the script, so great the evil within Luther Borgia, that the images themselves razored through rational thought, infecting the minds with cancerous insanity. In the script, those most-affected sprouted physical pulsing tumors of rage, Cronenbergian body horror. The audience in the story succumbs to barehanded violence, gang rape, cannibalism, surrounded by a trough of horror tropes and in-jokes.

For example, twin redheaded nurses, dressed in hospital togs of white fetish vinyl, unspeaking and unspeakable, as the story unfolded. It was a nice touch, Boone thought, taking the creepy twins from Kubrick's *The Shining*, aging them to something more lust-appropriate, giving them the mantle of William Castle's nurse-garb "assistants" who would make moviegoers sign release forms before the screenings of *Homicidal* or *The Tingler*. "…specially-trained medical experts will be on hand to assist those who succumb to the fright and terror…No refunds will be given if you leave via the 'Coward's Walk'."

But these little touches were shoved aside for the gore and the shock. The whole script reeked of "pushing the envelope" with "balls-out horror". The too-many cooks at the top inflicting their will. And yet, beneath all of the misunderstood dross, there was still little more than a base and banal story. "Forbidden movies turn crowds into killers." *Grand mal* hysteria, rioting, lynching. Boone wondered about Kearns' underlying message: horror movies *really do* create psychopaths? "Tipper Gore was right and so was Frederick Wertham! They'd just focused on the wrong medium of entertainment."

This was a script designed with shock, shriek, and howl. This was a Halloween haunted attraction of a story. The theater opens, the audience enters, nobody comes out. What was the point? He wanted to storm Kearns' apartment and demand answers. Where was the poetry of his earlier work, the scripts he wrote when they were all students? Did those Out There beat it out of him, or did the cynicism eat the romantic from within without help from the studio suits?

The further Boone read, the more determined he was

to see Shel's project through. He had to see for himself the five movies, in order, that were whispered to literally warp viewers' minds. Was the quintet a puzzlebox out of which would spring Borgia and a cadre of cinematic cenobites? When they reached the end of *Golgotha*, would Luther Borgia stand before them, resurrected by the films' power? What would they do if it happened? How disappointing would it be if it didn't?

The answers lie in Carcosa's vaults, where the missing films from the "Divine Heresy" were nestled amongst thousands of cans containing thousands of films. Boone still had no real plan of how to go about liberating them from what he assumed was an intricate series of safeguards against theft. Shel hadn't yet come forth with those details.

While he read, Boone thought about the coming days, descending into the former slaughterhouse turned industrial factory, where he now worked—thanks to Shel's connections and Copper's car to get him there—as a "Cleaner".

He spent his days winding reels of film by hand, holding an acetate-soaked cotton rag to the base and emulsion between thumb and forefingers, removing years' worth of dust, debris, grease pencil marks, and general age, prepping the reels for whatever their next lifeform would be. Handling the original camera negatives that the filmmakers themselves had handled. Using the old methods, the dying ways of preserving celluloid.

The subterranean film lab had a poorly lit dungeon feel, the rooms connected by dark passageways and tunnels, Morlock technicians shuffling in and out of the swallowing shadows. Working with arcane machinery gave Boone the feeling that he'd aligned with some secret cabal working tirelessly to preserve history itself against the ravages of time and the onslaught of new technology. Cleaning film felt like washing a corpse, preparing it for burial within the very cinderblock tomb that housed it, where the sun never reached and the air hung heavy with chemical fog.

All around him, behind heavy doors and through

blackened chasms, machines hummed and screamed and spooled film between reels and buffers and rollers. The only thing separating his new reality from that of Lang's sweltering *Metropolis* was the absence of the steam clouds that billowed from the German auteur's nightmarish industry. In Carcosa, the clouds were invisible.

Boone kept to himself, doing his best to avoid contact with the fishbelly-pale technicians who worked in the cacophony of the droning developing machines, breathing in the poisonous air without masks or filters of any kind, their bodies adapting to the photofluid so completely that—like the people of Lovecraft's Innsmouth—they'd need gills to breathe clean air ever again, should they crawl and slither their way out of Carcosa's pits for more than the precious hours between workdays.

While he reeled and cleaned and spooled, Boone stared straight ahead through the lab's double glass doors, leading to another dim hallway that unfurled like a tongue from the vault at the heart of the labyrinth. All day, his mind consumed with the riches sealed away within that vault—vestiges of *The Other Side of the Wind* or *The Day the Clown Cried*; the original negatives to *Gone with the Wind*, Corman's *Poe* series, *Night of the Living Dead*, still wrapped with packaging bearing the original title, *Night of the Anubis*. Somewhere, lost amidst the rows upon rows of canisters and reels, were the lost Borgia films, the missing pieces of The Divine Heresy. When the time was right, they'd find their way into his eager hands.

CHAPTER THREE
SHADOWY FORCES

"Film as dream, film as music. No form of art goes beyond ordinary consciousness as film does, straight to our emotions, deep into the twilight room of the soul. A little twitch in our optic nerve, a shock effect: twenty-four illuminated frames a second, darkness in between, the optic nerve incapable of registering darkness."

—Ingmar Bergman

SCENE ONE:
SETH AND THE SOUP CANS

Seth returned to the Squat with a bullet hole in his side and a steel film can in either hand. The latter caused the former, but for the time being he felt reasonably sure he'd lost his pursuers. Stumbling through the heavy wooden doors, he kicked them closed behind him and dropped the cans on the ceramic floor, shattering new crack webs to the filthy ancient tiles, the echoing sound of a truck ramming a dumpster. He eased himself down on the wood foyer steps. No shadows passed by the door window, greyed to smoked glass by years of dust and dirt. Nothing had followed him in.

Beneath the black *Evil Dead* hooded sweatshirt, his chest was bare. His also-black t-shirt was torn in two and tied around his waist as an emergency bandage. Heavy sigh, deep intake of breath, he unzipped the sweatshirt and carefully peeled the ersatz dressing away, tried to inspect the wound in the dim light of the sputtering fluorescents above. Clean shot, through-and-through, blood still wept from the button-sized hole. Blood had soaked through, the spreading stain invisible on the black cloth save for the wet that sheened when it caught the light. Already clotting, turning brown and black around the small angry tunnel through his love handle. It didn't look like Harrison Ford's wound, in the exact same place, in *Witness*. Not even Christian Slater's in *Kuffs*. Just an unblinking demon's eye made by a .22 caliber derringer stuffed up a coat sleeve, on a wrist-spring like Travis Bickel's. In the streetcar parking lot, a sneak attack he should have seen coming. Classic ambush cliché.

Pain was starting to fade and ice crept through his body. Going into shock. Had to act fast but he'd never make it up those stairs. Not with the soup cans. Not with the film on the heavy steel reels. Help.

Vision was starting to fog but he forced his way through and scanned the mailboxes for a name, anything familiar. "Roth, C., 6A". Couldn't possibly be Cris, could it? He hadn't stepped inside the Squat since graduation, way back when it was still owned by the school. Fifteen years ago? Couldn't remember the last time he'd seen her. Not outside of the news coverage of her great on-set accident. It didn't make sense that she'd be back here. After being Out There? Even after the accident, two dead stuntmen and one very big Name, also dead, her star hadn't plummeted. So why come back to Bethlehem? To the Welles? To the Squat?

It took him three pain-shot tries to reach the buzzer button below her name. Had to maneuver himself up onto one of the soup cans so he could answer the tinny speaker voice that said, "Who is it?"

"Seth," he choked out. Freezing, but sweat poured down his face. She demanded he repeat his name. When he did, he'd had to think hard, remember what his last name had been back in school. "S-Seth…Salem." That's right, his real name.

Long pause. Angry: "This a fucking joke?"

"I'm hurt, Cris…help."

There was no response, but footstep echos fell like lead snowflakes, drifting down from the upper floors.

Seth wasn't afraid of dying. His image had been preserved in a handful of movies and videos. He'd live forever as an electric shadow. It was what was in those cans that needed him alive. To keep it safe. The rarest spools of celluloid on the planet. Something, to all of film's history and historians, considered long lost, a grail, Holiest of Holies. The soul of Tod Browning himself and Seth wasn't about to let it slip into the hands of any corporation.

Even as the footsteps grew louder, Seth fought for consciousness and soldiered on. To battle shock and stay awake, he pushed raised one film can, then the other, bringing each one down hard on a marble step, the impact of metal on stone exploding through the building like a rusty gong. Pain shot through his body, his legs spasmed—he felt the wound in his side gasp with him, sucking and racing the lungs for every breath of air.

Again—*Clang! Clang!*—then he heaved himself upwards another step, using the cans as leverage, leaving a pool of blood behind as he moved. *Clang! Clang!* Another drag forwards, forcing a choked groan from his chest. As his vision wavered, his body slipping under the dark frozen waters of shock and unconsciousness, his saviour's face swam into his view. Exactly as she'd been more than a decade ago. Dark hair falling into her eyes, chalk-white skin reflecting the feeble, stuttering green sodium light from above. Cris Roth. His one-time partner. One-time lover. With an unsurprising strength she took a can from his left and hoisted him to his feet.

SCENE TWO:

INT. CRIS'S ROOM

"Who's after you?" she asked him, up in her room and safely away from street level. Nervous chit-chat borne from curiosity.

"Everybody," he said.

It was the next thing he knew. Dim memories of a ride skyward in a claustrophobic elevator, Cris's arms wrapped around his chest, keeping him upright. Audio hallucinations: blood pattering on the elevator's tiled floor, the pain singing through his muscles and veins with every breath or movement, an electrical storm of agony. He remembered the chill coming over him, sapping pigment from his face, forming frost across his lips and teeth. He remembered the soft darkness that came next.

She'd cleaned his wound with alcohol and dosed him with Vicodin, which was doing its warm and fuzzy job quite well. No sewing needle could be found, so the lack of thread was moot. The super glue she used burned like hell but the narcotics kept him from caring.

"I'll bet." Pressing a freezing hand against both sides of the wound, she kept her eyes on her work and continued. "Who plugged you? Yakuza or Feds?"

"Actually," he said, "I'm fairly certain he was MPAA."

"You're kidding."

"Not even if I could." Some pain found its way through the narcotic haze but he talked his way through it. "Either them or someone from the Jack Warner hit squad."

Cris shook her head. "MGM movie," she said. "So it'd be a Goldwyn death squad."

"Or a Mayer."

"Did the guy look like Thalberg? That'd be ironic."

"Getting killed by the namesake of the Lifetime Achievement award? That would be funny. No. Didn't see his face, but I can't be sure it wasn't Timothy Agoglia Carey," he said the name carefully, drawing out each syllable. Thank you, Vicodin. "That's the minimum bar height for scary."

"Carey's dead," she said.

"Why should that stop him?"

Testing the weld on the wound, her top hand stuck to his skin. He hissed, made bulging eye contact. Making a face in way of apology, she tore her hand away quickly and he bucked under the shock. She forced him back onto the sprung couch.

"I think you'll live," she said. "You're a film critic. Why do you keep getting shot?"

He tried to laugh but the pain choked it down. That was a reference to a film festival where an angry feminist blogger pumped a slug into his shoulder because he took a stand against her attempted censorship. Of what was predictably a dire atrocity of a film. *Cunt Killer*—not a porno, just misogynistic dreck. Her opinion was correct, no argument. But every movie deserves to be seen. *Ars Gratia Artis*. "Art for art's sake". The MGM coat of arms. No argument as to what constituted *artis*. Weakly, he pointed a thumb at the bloody film cans.

"What's in them?" Cris asked.

"Holy grail," he muttered in response. As she reached for one, he caught her wrist. "Don't open it!" It was a command hissed through clenched teeth, keeping a scream at bay from the too-quick movement.

"What's it going to do—melt my face off? Fuck is it?"

"Old," he whispered. "Don't expose it to the dirty air."

"Where'd it come from?" she said, demanding. "How do you have it?"

He wanted to tell her about the images swirling through his drug-addled consciousness, but nothing held still long enough for identification. He remembered the old man with the grey goatee, the endless rows of film cans lining the walls of his cavern; the cherry-redwood library towering over them. There was the deal, but what were the terms again? Why was it too late to say more? Who was the girl who'd led him there, lying unconscious on the couch, eyelids fluttering? Who were the men crashing through the windows? How did the man know he was part of the f.p.s. Underground? How did he get out and where was he running to?

Then the roar of the gun—a blinding flash from the darkness of the alley—and the lead searing through his side, removing part of him as it exited through the back. Then there was the running, with the burning, bloody hole in his side and his shoulders screaming from the weight of the soup cans. Traffic noises. Headlights. Panic. Then instinct.

"Doesn't matter," he said. "Don't open them," he said again, and let the darkness consume him.

SCENE THREE:
BACCHANALIA

The bright crack of a whip and a sharp feminine cry brought Seth out of his deep sleep. As slight as she was, Cris had managed to somehow hoist him into her bed, bandages gone pink now, the bloodflow stopped. Still, there was a towel beneath his side to protect her sheets from any leakage. She'd stripped him naked, wrapped him in a thick comforter emblazoned with the face of Maya Deren. His clothes were nowhere to be found in the smallish room. Across from him, Alain Delon gazed down at him with his patented icy stare—Cris' framed *Le Samourai* poster keeping watch over the dying man. It hurt, but he managed to arch his head back, see who stood guard above him: just two silhouettes against a barren landscape: *Badlands*.

Another whipcrack and accompanying squeal made him sit up too fast. Another scream banged against his teeth and he swallowed it back, gingerly fingering his bandage, trying to ascertain whether he'd reopened his wound. No new blossom of blood. That was good.

Much more gently, he eased his legs over the side of the bed, tested his balance as he got to his feet. Thrown carelessly over the foot of the bed was a dark red kimono. Whether or not it was meant for him didn't matter. After the third whipcrack/ yelp, he shrugged into the faux-silk robe and opened the door. Padding down the barewood hallway, feeling ridiculous, he heard voices grow louder. The hallway opened into a dungeon.

A young blonde girl was tied naked and ass-out on a St. Andrew's standing cross. Her assailant stood behind her, dressed in a remarkable replica of Tawney Kitaen's bondage outfit from *The Perils of Gwendolyn*—just a crisscrossing of black straps hiding the bare minimum of flesh. She held a cat-o' nine tails in one hand: the source of the whipcrack. The girl on the cross, with a red blush covering her body from nape to kneecaps, was the source of the squeals.

And at the other end of the room, Cris stood, cigarette in one hand, Hi-Def camera in the other, taking all in. His swimmy mind brought forth a fact about Cris and he used it as his opening line: "So, your Golden Globe," he said. "Did they just have an extra one lying around?"

As the dominatrix was in mid-swing, Cris called "Cut!" Then, to him, pleasantly, "And fuck you very much."

From somewhere else in the room, another girl appeared, fully dressed in jeans and a turtleneck, clipboard in hand. She jotted down a note then helped the dom unshackle the little blonde sub, draped a white robe across her pinked shoulders. Cris toed a power strip at her feet and turned off the bright studio lights. "Go back to bed, Seth," she said, still amused by his bemusement.

"Seriously, is this what you do now?" he asked, lowering himself into a chair. "Christ, you were cleared of all charges. They blacklist you Out There?"

"Yes, it's exactly that simple. And before you judge, look at this." Thrusting the camera under his nose, she pressed play. The digital viewfinder sprang to life. The scene he just watched came into being before his eyes: light streaming between the uprights of the cross, giving the young sub a beautiful halo, sparkling her sea-blue eyes. The camera tracked out to reveal more of the scene, introducing the dom, the whole shot slightly over exposed to give the image a dreamy haze. The technical aspects washed away the word "porn" and revealed "erotica".

"I take it back," he said. "Pure *Story of O*." Also directed by Just Jaekin. That explained the *Gwendolyn* outfit.

"And yet you first snorted in derision."

"Caught me off-guard. You were doing action movies the last time I read about you."

"One in Majorca," she nodded, fiddling with the camera. "Didn't go anywhere. What I'm making on movies like this, and the fetish webcams, is paying for my Doctorate." She waved her arm around the room. "Welcome to Ravenous Pictures."

The blonde girl inserted herself between them, whispered something to Cris that he didn't hear. "Oh, sure, honey. Everyone take five," she called out. The girl in the turtleneck returned to her notes. The dom sat down hard on a divan and lit a joint. Cris cleared her throat at the woman in black straps. "Kitchen, Wanda! For Christ sake."

The dom, Wanda, apparently, stood up on her spike-heeled boots and wobbled out of the room. "Models, man," Cris said to him. "Gotta walk them through breathing sometimes." She winked at something behind his head. Before he could turn, a pillow sailed out of the hallway, missing both of them. The little sub had lousy aim. "I'm kidding, honey! Love you!" Cris turned back to Seth. "One-hundred and ten grand just last year. Know what *Murderworld* got me? $14K and a 'not guilty' charge on manslaughter."

Seth nodded, forced a smile. The *Murderworld* trial was a sensation half-a-decade back. Two stunt guys, one biggish actor making a desperate returning bid, killed in an explosion. Pyro guys claimed that 'the woman director' called for the gag too early. In the face of tragedy, the mens' club tossed the female under the bus as it crashed through the glass ceiling. A bucket of clichés raining down upon her. She'd had no business telling men what to do anyway. Who hires women directors? Blame the producers too. "I'm 'Leni' here, by the way. No one else in Orson knows my real name."

"It's on your fucking mailbox."

"So's your name," she said. "Alyce Reynolds bought the Squat but didn't do much else."

"Who?" he asked.

She ignored his question. "It's just a coincidence I wound up in the same room."

"I thought sure they'd torn this place down."

"They really should have," Cris said. "Before it falls down on its own. Burns down, falls over, *then* sinks into the swamp," they said together. *Monty Python* jokes. No trauma too great to dampen a good reference.

Panic seized him by the scalp. "Where are the cans?"

"Safe," she said. "Relax."

"Safe *where*, Cris?"

"Oh, for fuck's sake, they're under the goddamned bed. *Handcuffed* to the legs, by the way. And also: you're welcome. And also, you owe me for everything you leaked blood on."

"Use the bloody pillows in your next scene," he snapped. He could smell Wanda's marijuana wafting from the kitchen. His whole body turned into longing. "I could use a hit of that."

Cris ignored him. "You think whoever shot you will come after you?"

Seth shrugged. He legitimately didn't know.

Cris nodded. "Well," she said, "welcome back. The place has hardly changed."

"I just need to hole up here until I can get word to *f.p.s.*"

"It's fine. You can stay here or I can talk to Alyce and see if there are any other rooms available. Not like the place is crowded."

"Thanks."

"You sure came at an interesting time," Cris said. "Actually, you showing up with your mystery film only comes in second on the weird meter."

"How's that?"

"A bunch of Addicts living here decided they're going to put on a private screening of the Borgia films. Last I heard, they'd dug up prints of the first three or so."

"Seriously?"

"Apparently. You ever seen them?"

Seth nodded as the memories flooded back. "Once," he said. Screams echoed in his mind.

He saw the Rialto, the theater in flames. Heard the desperate pounding on the doors, the begging to be let out, as the flames consumed. Outside, he and Chris Balun padlocked the last of the exits. He couldn't decide which was louder—the crashing of the chains holding against the bulging doors, the howling of the damned from inside, or the laughing clatter-chitter of the projector, reaching out to listeners through the cracks in the concrete, as the images it showed devoured them all.

*****

CUT TO:

EXT. PARKING LOT - NIGHT (CONT'D)

The camera sweeps towards the doors where Diana and Phoebe are exchanging phony "hello" kisses.

                    DIANA
          Sweetie! You look amazing.
          Your skin is glowing.

                    PHOEBE
          That's just the vodka blush,
          pretty. Any chance I can
          sneak in early? I still have a
          bladder the size of a fanboy's
          penis.

                    DIANA
          Oh my god, say no more. Go
          right in. Make sure you mark
          your territory - it's going
          to be an eventful night!

As Phoebe heads in, Chris Balun rounds the corner.

                    CHRIS

               Phoebe!

                    PHOEBE
          Chris Balun, holy shit!

                    CHRIS
          Seriously, Phoebes, you don't
          want to stay for this.

                    DIANA
          Oh, Christ, Chris. Fuck off
          already.

Diana turns her attention to the English actors,
while Chris slips into the theater after Phoebe.

INT. LOBBY

Phoebe and Chris exchange a quick hug.

She offers him a hit off her flask.

He accepts.

                    PHOEBE
          How'd she score these anyway?

                    CHRIS
          No idea. As far as I knew,
          there were only the masters
          and those were supposed to be
          sealed with the court records.

                    PHOEBE
          Wow. Art finds a way, huh?

                    CHRIS
          Sure.

                    PHOEBE
          How sick are these things
          anyway?

                    CHRIS
          The truth?

                    PHOEBE
          Of course.

                    CHRIS
          Pretty fucking sick.

                    PHOEBE
          Can't wait. Rest room?

Chris points down the hall as he passes back her
flask. As she exits, Diana and the Press burst
through the door. Chris launches back into his
spiel.

                    CHRIS
          I really have to warn you
          folks, it's a bad idea.

                    DIANA
          Keith, get him out of here.

                    CHRIS
          The movies are cursed! It's a
          documented fact!

Diana stomps over to him as KEITH, a burly

bodyguard, ushers the confused-looking reporters around the corner.

Diana looks like she's about to hit Chris.

Then she can't hold it in anymore and starts laughing.

                    CHRIS
          Worth the two grand or what?

                    DIANA
          You're laying this on so
          friggin' thick.

                    CHRIS
          You wanted controversy! You
          wanted a brand new urban
          legend. You're the William
          Castle of the new millennium.
          How's it feel?

                    DIANA
          Did you see that crowd?
          There's a thousand people out
          there.

                    CHRIS
          At twenty dollars a head…

                    DIANA
          It feels pretty fucking
          amazing.

                    CHRIS
          You're welcome.

                    DIANA
Any truth to that bullshit
you're slinging?

                    CHRIS
You gonna tell me how you
scored the tapes?

                    DIANA
Allow a girl some mystery.

                    CHRIS
Then allow a film geek the
same.

                    DIANA
Nobody died?

                    CHRIS
Not from watching them.
Making them, obviously, is a
different story.

                    DIANA
Their loss was not for nothing.

                    CHRIS
              (with admiration)
Christ, that's cold!

                    DIANA
So now let's get things
started.

EXT. GILES THEATRE

Diana throws open the doors. The crowd cheers.

There is a bit of pushing as people crowd the doors. An CASHIER just inside the door takes their money. An USHER beyond takes the tickets.

A table with a pair of SEXY NURSES has Pike and Krusty sign waivers.

                    NURSE #1
          Sign here please.

                      PIKE
          What's this?

                    NURSE #2
                 (mechanically)
          By signing this form, you
          are   absolving   the   Giles
          Theatre,   its   signatories
          and   its   employees   from
          any   responsibility   should
          you   suffer a   heart   attack,
          an   aneurysm   or   a   nervous
          breakdown while watching the
          film.

                    KRUSTY
          Fucking-A! This night's gonna
          rock!

Diana looks inordinately pleased as the crowd files in.

THE CAMERA FOLLOWS Pike and Krusty through the lobby, past the usher and into the main hallway.

There are two theaters set up – one marked "Screening Room", the other marked "Party Room".

After a moment of decision, Pike and Krusty head into the Screening Room.

SCENE DELETED

INT. LOBBY

Diana picks up a small walkie-talkie from the desk and speaks into it.

> DIANA
> (continuing)
> Norm, what's the status? The
> walkie crackles to life.

> NORM'S VOICE
> We're all set, Diana.

> DIANA
> Sound check good? Projector
> up and running?

> NORM'S VOICE
> You're right next door. You
> don't trust me, get your anal
> ass over and check it out for
> yourself.

> DIANA
> On my way.

> CHRIS

"Anal ass"? Whatever you're paying him isn't nearly enough.

                    DIANA
          Laugh clown.

They exit. The CAMERA FOLLOWS THEM to

INT. THE SECOND PROJECTION ROOM

This one is at the rear of the Screening Room. The band's MUSIC streams in through the cutout windows. NORM, a greasy-looking career projectionist sits in a chair smoking a cigarette.

                    DIANA
          Put that out, Norm.

                    NORM
          Woman, please. I worked a
          theater that had open cans
          of kerosene sitting next to
          carbon stick projectors.

                    DIANA
          Two words: "Cinema Paradiso."

                    NORM
          Go frighten people with your
          stolen snuff films.

                    DIANA
          I don't need technical
          difficulties at this stage of

the game. I have two thousand
angry,   violent   people
downstairs.

NORM
You this bossy in bed?

DIANA
You'll never know, will you?

NORM
I'd be afraid your pussy has
teeth.

DIANA
Lovely. When this is all over,
remind me to punch the shit
out of you.

NORM
I'm sure you'll remember.

She leaves. Norm lights another cigarette off the
remains of his previous one.

CUT TO:

CHAPTER FOUR
THE SQUAT

"Our battle, our struggle, is to create art. Our weapon is the moving picture. Because we have the moving picture, our paintings will grow and recede; our poetry will be shadows that lengthen and conceal; our light will play across living faces that laugh and agonize; and our music will linger and finally overwhelm, because it will have a context as certain as the grave. We are scientists engaged in the creation of memory... but our memory will neither blur nor fade."

—F.W. Murnau (as played by John Malkovich) in Shadow of the Vampire (2000), written by Steven Katz, directed by E. Elias Merhige.

SCENE ONE:
LURE OF THE TABOO

When word of a *Divine Heresy* screening got around Addicts started emerging from the shadows. Before too long, the rumors had reached the lower floors where Griffith housed the students who couldn't afford to stay in the upscale dorms. The Borgia name transcended his art; Boone doubted if half of the Film I or II students had seen more than the muddy screen capture of *Rape of the Archangel* that appeared in their *History of American Film* text book. In the *History*, both Borgias merited less than a paragraph, their art and crimes summarized in forty-nine words.

It was the taboo that lured them. Forbidden documentation of insanity and murder in super-saturated color. "Underground" in the purest sense of the word—these were movies not meant to be seen. Censored. Condemned. Redacted. Hidden. Choose your own adjective. Collectively, *The Divine Heresy* was the Holy Grail of Outsider Cinema.

Beyond the lure of witnessing real death was the mythology of the films' quality. So seldom seen, Luther Borgia's movies had been elevated to the greatest rumored heights of art. Pure, raw talent pouring from the imagery, or so it was told and retold. It wasn't the content that drove the audience mad: it was the beauty.

"Like anyone really believes that bullshit," Josh grumbled, barely loud enough to be heard over the booming roar of *The Guns of Navarone*. Boone had already managed to find *The Magus* and *The Pioneer* in Carcosa's labyrinthine vaults. Even as they sat, watching the fruits of Gregory Peck's sabotage, the colossal cannons tumbling into the sea at the film's end, Boone knew that the machines in the Lab were scanning those films, carefully, lovingly, one frame at a time, to digital files. No one—not his managers, nor the heads of the departments—had questioned Boone's work orders. At Carcosa, any semblance of caring had been long since leached away. It didn't matter that he was just a Cleaner. He was a Cleaner with the proper paperwork.

"Like they're the *Necronomicon* or something?" Josh continued. "It's a fucking cliché anyway. Carpenter did it with *Cigarette Burns*, and that was a cheesy *Masters of Horror* episode."

"*The King in Yellow*," Boone said. "Forbidden text—"

"Bull. Shit."

Finally, words fell on receptive ears. Lys's head lolled on

her shoulders, rolling back to look at Boone sitting behind her, seeing him upside-down. "What are you babbling about?"

"Movies that can make you go crazy and kill people," he said.

Lys nodded. "Still?" She was floating on a cocktail of cheap weed and a cracked frame of *Defending Your Life*. Josh was merely stoned. Not that they were ever on the same wavelength. Still, she managed a snort of a laugh. "Of course it's bullshit," she said. On the flatscreen, the credits rolled. Already the group was exchanging telepathic messages debating what to put on next. "But so what?"

Josh echoed, "So what?"

From far away, lost in his own haze of beer and *The Big Lebowski*, Boone answered. "You sound like you'll be disappointed if they don't fuck with your head."

"I just don't think we should get our hopes up."

"So you do *want* us to end up killing each other?"

"I mean with all the hype they're probably not going to be all that. And we shouldn't expect them to." He added, "Be. All that."

"We'll hide all the sharp objects just in case," Lys said. A full second later she laughed at the thought. Sometimes a good flix came with a delay.

Credits over, the DVD returned to its static menu. Boone shifted forward, stared at a Jenga stack of movies on the floor, scanning the titles through blurry eyes. In his bloodstream, the Dude abided. (*Abade? Abode?*) "Hey, Rusty?" he said. "What was the thing Copper always tries to get us to watch?"

At the back of the room, Rusty looked up from his laptop, away from the little video project he'd been editing. Pushing his perfectly round glasses up the bridge of his nose, he stared at the impaired group for a moment, as if studying other life forms. "*Salo?*" he said by way of a question.

"No, the other one."

That snapped the younger man out of his distraction,

evoked a laugh. "Oh, 'the other one'." Once upon a time, Copper had been the biggest Addict of them all; there wasn't a movie made during his lifetime he hadn't seen. Of course, he was gone now and had been for some time. "Gone," as in, upstairs and uninterested in anything but his work. Still, Rusty ventured another guess. "I don't know. *In a Glass Cage?*"

Boone snapped his fingers and pointed at him with a smile. "That's the one."

"Dude, that's in Spanish," Josh said.

"So?"

"So, I'm high as balls. I can't deal with subtitles tonight."

"Philistine," Boone said.

Rusty, the only sober one in the room, returned to his laptop and his project. He liked to get things done. It felt like, in some small way, that it would make Copper proud of him. Copper was the first person to see Rusty as he was. He didn't deadname him or shame him. Copper didn't care who Rusty had been before arriving at Orson, or what his mother had named him, or that "tomboy" had been a slur that followed his every step. To Copper, Rusty was Rusty, and that bought eternal loyalty.

Tonight, The Mentor and the Master was tucked away in his attic penthouse that night, like most other nights, working on his own opus. Smiling, Rusty finished another page of his rewrite. He couldn't wait to show Copper the new pages when—*if*—he finally emerged.

With the thought, Rusty felt a stab of guilt. No... *shame.* An old shame, different from what had been a constant adolescent companion, but still fresh. When they'd first met, Rusty'd quickly fallen in fawning awe of the older filmmaker. Copper had worked on *real* features—worked his ass off, as a production assistant (P.A.), a grip, a grip-electric, schlepping cable and hauling crates of equipment, pushing heavy dollies laden with camera and crew, always smooth, never halting. He did this to facilitate his own film. Every dollar he made with The

Union went into *Spires*, his masterpiece.

Maybe it was a need for a father-figure, or an older brother, but Rusty gravitated to Copper almost from the second he'd stepped into Orson, fresh-faced film student eager to get started on his own great works. Already something of magic in his mind, Rusty, like the others, worshipped the great Film Art. But when Copper told him of the Deiwos, the Gods of Film, wonder became reverence. Copper revealed the Names of the Gods, their function and origins: Vastane the Adversary, Goddess of Assistant Directors, created from the tools of Yapim, God of Producers; Cinemagog, the Father of All Film.

But so early in their relationship, Rusty failed to realize that Copper was Abraham and not Uncle Remus. For Copper, the stories were Law. To Rusty, naïve and so eager to please his new mentor, they were inspirational fables and nothing more. He was so proud when, for a Creative Writing class, he'd written a story incorporating Copper's deities.

INTERLUDE

RUSTY GETS AN "A", BUT NOT THE ONE
HE WANTED FILM GÖTTERDÄMMERUNG
By Rudolph "Rusty" Pennick

Cinemagog, father of the Film Gods, chief among the Panoptheon, supreme ruler of all modern artistic endeavors, puffed on a cigar the approximate length and width of a table leg and gazed down at all in his dominion. The Kingdom of Hollywood, the usual focus of his benevolence and wrath—his Athens, if you like—was chugging away nicely, as usual, churning out both crap and quality in almost equal amounts. The sprockets, as he liked to say, were driving the celluloid.

Outside Hollywood, the other Meccas were doing just as well. Bollywood, Pinewood—all the 'woods, present and accounted for. The newer bastions, New Zealand, for instance, and Vancouver, had no problems to report. Art and shit in steady supply, coming from all over the world. With his dominions slouching ever onward, he turned his attention to the smaller tribes that toiled under him.

In short, out of a sense of mischievous boredom, he decided to mess with some "Indies".

At any given moment, there are literally thousands of young—and not so young—independent filmmakers (and "filmmakers") hard at work making movies, thanks to the boom of affordable digital video equipment. Once upon a time, only the truly committed could make a movie (overzealous fathers with Super-8 cameras not-withstanding). Cinemagog thought about those days and felt both nostalgic and nauseous. You would think that with so many people running around with cameras, paying homage to the Film Gods whether they realized it or not, that the Panoptheon would be more powerful than ever.

You *would* think that, wouldn't you?

A hacking cough over his left shoulder—Dollirostrum, God of the Grips, announced his presence. He wasn't well. The cough came as much from his two-pack a day cigarette habit as from the weakening of his followers. "Anyone schleps a cable calls himself a grip," Dollirostrum grumbled often. "None'a them knows a Beefy Baby from a Mighty Mole."

Cinemagog felt his pain. The True Equipment Names, the names of power, were falling by the wayside. It wasn't just light stands that went nameless; the proper names for gels, for lights, even lenses were being dropped from the vernacular of the Indies. Latham-ascdop, God of Cinematography, lamented with the rest of the *deiwos* over this fact. Usually at sundown. His "special time".

"Golden Hour," Latham-ascdop would correct.

"The home computer has killed me!" This from Kem-Daly, God of Editing. "Just store me in a cool, dark place. I'm ready to go."

So many of them weakened: Yapim, God of Producers; Vastane the Adversary, Goddess of Assistant Directors; Galvanivolta, Goddess of Gaffers;

Poesner, God of Hair, Make-Up and Waredrobe... Only Meizahn, God-Goddess of Directors and (by virtue of so many of the young filmmakers being male) the Special Effects God, Geissler, seemed upbeat and healthy these days.

For those who worshipped at the altar of digital video, without knowing they even did so, paid tribute to a relatively young god, Digitalis. And those in the Panoptheon didn't care much for Digitalis.

"He's a dick!" This from Ifirs, God of Executive Producers. And then he'd mark down the insult in his ledger, just to keep track.

Cinemagog couldn't help but agree. Digitalis made them all feel old. Very, very old. Older than the hundred years-plus that they actually were. For the fact was, compared to the Muses—as Calliope and her sister, Terpsichore, delighted in pointing out—the Panoptheon consisted of infant deities.

This fact pissed them off too.

"Who's up?" asked Dollirostrum, rasping with excitement. "Who do we destroy today? Let's make it rain on their only exterior day. Ooh, no, we'll make half their actors not show up!"

"Praxinothespis would never allow that," Cinemagog said. Indeed, the Goddess of Screen Actors was very protective of her followers. Her "family", she called them. "We're just one big troupe and have to support each other," she'd say, whether anyone was listening or not.

"Even those who deliver dialogue like they're taking an oath of office?" asked Vastane. "With a mouthful of frogs?"

"*Especially* those," Praxinothespis would respond. With a pride that would make the rest of them vow to spit in her egg white omlet.

"Okay, fine," said Dollirostrum. "Let's go with the rain, then."

Cinemagog looked down thoughtfully at one set in particular. "I think I could whip up a sudden rain day," he said. "Or a freak snowstorm. That'd be one for their blogs."

Dollirostrum winced. *Blog*, he hated that word too. It ranked right up there with *CGI* and *Zebravision*. Terms made of crap. Digitalis's new terminology.

"Alright then." Cinemagog sat up suddenly. Then, distractedly, he realized his cigar had gone out. Even fire was avoiding him today. If he called Dollirostrum's attention to it, though, he'd just blame that on Digitalis as well. "Snowstorm, noisy neighbor with a leaf-blower and a fucked up circuit breaker. That'll show 'em."

"And locust, too," said Dollirostrum. "Whip up some of those."

"I'm doing sabotage here, not plagues."

"Fine."

Cinemagog fired up his cigar once more, casually as possible so as to avoid more bitching from Dollirostrum, and set to work.

It started small. An unauthorized butterfly flapped its wings in New Zealand, buzzing a third assistant director on the set of *The Hobbit*. Moments later, just outside of Akron, Ohio, no-budget filmmaker Danny Goodwin was just about to call "action" on his latest lesbian vampire opus as the first fluffy white snowflakes began to fall. His jaw dropped. "You're kidding me! It's almost May!"

His actors looked at him, wondering what to do. Confused, frustration growing, Danny ducked down, hid behind the viewfinder of his camera, and tried to decide his next move. They had at least a dozen shots to go before they could move inside. Half of his six-person cast was clad in flimsy nightgowns. He hadn't even noticed the temperature dropping— he'd just been happy when Mr. Douglas next door decided to *finally* put away his friggin' leaf blower. The seconds ticked by. Danny wallowed in indecision as Mr. Douglas' fired up his weed whacker.

In Denver, Rudy Tolliver, head of Puttin' on the Shiznit Productions, watched in horror as each of his three halogen garage lamps exploded in order of expensiveness, dousing his stepfather's basement, and his set, in darkness. His lead actress, Suzie Tolliver, threw up her hands, announced that she couldn't work like this, then stormed off face-first into a wall.

Phoenix: Director of Photography Norm Reyfield was shocked to discover lens flares invading both sides of his frame, despite the three-man reflector team doing their jobs. Despite, in fact, the sun being behind him.

Hoboken: "Can you play back that last take?" director Joy Burton asked LeVar Gedrick, sound engineer. Handing her the headphones to his digital recorder, he did as she asked. There was no mistake. The dialogue of her urban thriller had recorded in Swedish.

All across the world, fuses blew and batteries died. Microphones turned into feedback machines. In Wheeling, WV, the ceiling sprinklers burst to life in SonicWow Studios, nearly drowning everyone on the $250 per hour green screen set. The actors playing the aliens saw their prosthetic noses wash away.

Molly Heder, winner of the cherished Jim Feldman Award for Most Improved Actress, reached the crucial point in her monologue where her character admits she has cancer. Sense memory working overtime, images of dead pets swirling in her mind, and totally *in the moment*, Molly's first tear fell from the corner of her right eye. At that very moment in time, two produce trucks collided outside her studio apartment with a sound like a junkyard hurled down the stairs. Horns blared. Molly's line became, "I'm trying to tell you, mom, I have—*holyfuckingJesusshit*— *What the fuck was that?*"

"Be honest," said Cinemagog to Praxinothespis, who was doing her best not to laugh in spite of herself, "that was Molly's best take of the day."

In Great Falls, during a tense "Killer's P.O.V." shot, Sam Maritz, Minnesota's most accomplished Steadicam operator, was suddenly overcome with St. Vitus Dance. Yapim and Ifirs, the Producer Gods, refused to hide their giggling.

Urged on by their enthusiasm and guffaws of the most schadenfreudean, Cinemagog just couldn't help himself. The chaos spared no production; no budget was safe. Kansas City, Kansas, on the set of *Subsidy Dreams*, during the crucial corn-shucking scene, Cinemagog gave in and let loose the locust. Both Sally Field and Martin Sheen were forced to take refuge in Zack Braff's trailer. Worse for Zack: they wouldn't let him in.

High above, all of the deiwos, the principals of the Panoptheon, the Gods of Film and Filmmaking, were holding their sides in hysteria, wheezing phlegmy guffaws. "Do another!" begged Galvanivolta. "Blow up a circuit breaker!"

"No, wait, better!" said Poesner, clutching her combs and her suit tickets in delight. "I say, let there be nothing but fluffing in pornoland!"

Through the cackles and chortles Cinemagog

struggled to maintain focus. He *was* the King of All Film Gods, after all. Dignity was expected. As he was just about to snarl up traffic and ruin a modestly-budgeted car chase in El Segundo, when from way in the back, a pair of throats cleared.

Wiping tears from their eyes, the deiwos turned to see who desired attention. Coming up out of the fog, in the most heroic of hero shots, came the most-satisfied of the Film Gods: Meizahn, God-Goddess of Directors and the Special Effects God, Geissler (who'd provided the fog). "Hot set!" announced Vastane the Adversary. "Director on the boards!" But that just got everyone going again.

Cinemagog held out his hand, a conciliatory gesture, hoping to diffuse any hostility that may come from the only two gods who were still respected by the artform they watched over. "Just blowing off steam," he said to Meizahn.

"Well," said the God-Goddess of Directors, pausing for emphasis (which secretly delighted Praxinothespis, who so-loved a dramatic beat or two), "*We* say, 'go big or go home'."

With that Geissler nodded towards Vancouver, his jeweler's loup never budging from the eye that held it. The rest of the gods turned, followed his gaze. In the center of the dazzling Canadian city, working so very hard to look like downtown Manhattan, was Steven Spielberg and his crew of thousands.

The auteur was perched on a camera crane, right next to Vilmos Zsigmond, acclaimed cinematographer. Before them: Sir Anthony Hopkins, repetant Nazi commandant, was about to confess his conscience to Mother Theresa, played by Dame Judi Densch, wearing a nun's habit originally designed by Edith Head. Waiting just out of frame was the entirety of Industrial Light and Magic, ready to cue the alien invasion. It was *the* signature shot:

The crane would start high and lower, perfectly framing Sir Anthony and Dame Judi against the setting sun, then *dolly in* to an exquisite two-shot, wherein Sir Anthony, as "Ubergrubenfuhrer Klaus Klass", would unburdon his soul. At the critical moment, just as Mother Theresa was to lay her hand upon his forehead and absolve him of all Holocaust-related crimes—*KA. Fucking. BOOM!*—the charges would go, the Chrystler Building would topple and the Martians would rise in insurrection. Most of the latter would be added in post, of course.

That was what drew Geissler's wrath. "CGI implosion? Digital aliens?" Geissler's mouth twisted into a sneer of a smile. "Kiss my ass, Digitalis."

"And screw you, Spielberg," said Meizahn.

With cheers and thunderous applause, the Film Gods joined hands and fixed their attention on the Dreamworks production.

And Hell rained down upon it.

During the Academy Awards the following year, extra time was dedicated to those who lost their lives and careers on that fateful day. Despite all weather forecasts, meteorologists and climate scientists world-wide were at a loss to explain the devastation that met *Steven Spielberg Presents: The Day.* No one could have predicted six tornadoes. Or that they would somehow catch on fire.

And McG took home the statuette for Best Director.

BACK TO SCENE

Rusty couldn't wait for Copper to read the story, to see

how the stories had touched him, how he'd taken them to heart. Instead, Copper had retreated alone to his attic and stayed there for almost a week, which was not unusual. He had not permitted anyone to visit. Again, not unusual. Except that now, "anyone" also included Rusty.

It didn't take long for fear to creep in. Copper hated the story, but didn't want to tell him. Copper hated the story and now hated Rusty. Copper liked the story and was jealous…that seemed too impossible. The older man was an Artist, a Visionary. Rusty was a neophyte. Not even an acolyte.

Finally, Friday afternoon, Copper emerged from his sweatbox at the top of the Squat. Possibly cajoled by Lys, possibly of his own accord, Copper descended the narrow stairs and returned the sheaf of paper to his surrogate little brother. He wore a sad smile, sadder than his normal, and nodded. Rusty relaxed, but only a little, and even that amount of relief vanished when Copper said, simply, "They're not benevolent. It's not a game for them." Then added, "They don't love us."

After that, Rusty didn't ask about Copper's deities. He didn't want to hear the darker tales of destruction, or the sacrifices they demanded of the filmmakers that lived beneath their heels. He didn't want to hear about the artists who the Deiwos had tortured to death, taking their own lives to escape the suffering of the business created by man in Their image. He remembered one of the first tales Copper had spun, about Donald Cammell, director of *Performance*, who went only a little mad during the making of that film, but took his own life after many defeats, countless failed projects. From Copper's point of view, Cinemagog had cast Cammell into some pit of molten plastic, doomed to watch his failures for eternity. All for the amusement of the dark Gods of Film.

Rusty continued to love Copper. Copper loved him back. They worked on *Spires* together and kept to themselves. But in the corner of every movie he watched from that moment on, Rusty could see the shadow of dark wings rustling in the corners of perfectly-framed shots, and red glowing eyes beneath the bed of inevitable love scenes. From then on, he saw that the scratches that marred old films had been made by talons.

*****

                                                    CUT TO:

HALLWAY

A CAMERA CREW is waiting.

                    DIANA
                 (to Keith)
          Is everybody in?

                    KEITH
          Seems like it.

                    DIANA
          Screw the latecomers, then.
             (turns to camera crew)
          Here we go, then. Ready to
          roll?

                    CAMERMAN
          Just a sec…all right, we're
          recording.

                    DIANA
          Okay, it looks like everyone
          is inside and eager to view the
          "Borgia movies". As promised…

She starts down the hallway. The camera crew hurries after her.

There is a chain around the doors. Diana picks up a heavy padlock and holds it up in front of the camera.

> DIANA
> From here on, until the movies are done, nobody gets in.
> (she clicks the lock closed)
> Or out.

She smiles, satisfied. The cameraman shoots a close up of the lock.

> CAMERAMAN
> And if there's a fire?

> DIANA
> (smiling maniacally)
> Then we all die.

The crew looks uneasy.

> DIANA
> Guys, I'm kidding. Cut tape.

The cameraman puts down his camera.

> DIANA
> (continuing)
> Seriously, this is all for show. Every precaution has been made, the fire depart-ment has been alerted. The building is completely safe. That lock isn't even real. You could rip through that

> door in a heartbeat, okay?

That seems to satisfy everyone. Chris wanders up behind her.

> DIANA
> Now I think the band is wrapping up. Go shoot some stuff with the crowd. Some of them are pretty wild!

They head up the ramp. Chris cocks an eyebrow at Diana. They talk as they walk up the ramp.

> CHRIS
> That lock is real.

> DIANA
> Yes it is.

> CHRIS
> You never called the fire department.

> DIANA
> Didn't have to. Two 'g's to the fire marshal took care of that.

> CHRIS
> So if there is a fire?

> DIANA
> Then we all die.

The camera moves past them into the screening

room. The crowd is rocking out to the band, which finishes its set with a loud cacophony and a series of outstretched middle fingers. The audience loves that. Diana takes the stage.

SCENE DELETED

INT. SCREENING ROOM - NIGHT (CONT'D)

The Crowd is chanting:

> CROWD
> Movie! Movie!

> DIANA
> (into walkie-talkie)
> Roll it, norm. Before they
> set the place on fire!

Norm doesn't respond. The lights dim as the projector roars to life.

White light washes over the screen, followed quickly by the academy countdown leader.

TITLE: WHITE ON BLACK "THE MAGUS"

The crowd cheers loudly. People start "shushing" each other.

Images accompanied by discordant music. The imagery is violent from the start.

Sarah winces immediately. She shrinks into Dave's arms. Dave is clearly enjoying what he's seeing.

Pike and Krusty are cheering along with the rest

of the crowd. They pause to exchange a long, wet kiss.

Kurt looks bored; Thom plays with his smuggled in cell phone.

Diana and Chris slip out.

SCENE DELETED

THEATER

The images are still coming hard and fast and gruesome.

Keith gives the crowd the once-over.

Near the screen, a mosh pit has broken out. People are shoving each other, cheering the movie on.

Keith sighs and stomps down the aisle.

In the mosh pit, a punk kid, Dirk, stops for a moment, staring up at the screen. His eyes roll, his head lolls on his shoulders. With a smile, he pulls a knife and, eyes still rolling, lifts it into the air.

CUT TO:

SCENE TWO:
CARCOSA

Shel the Agent had cleared a path. Every week, Boone found himself in another department. No longer "just" a cleaner, he now prepped reels for editing, worked the poison-spewing Photoguard machine, cut trailer snipes for projection. As he traveled the cavernous former slaughterhouse, he avoided the work-release employees who labored in the packaging department and hugged the walls as they passed. He possessed a badge that they did not, and somehow that was all the protection he needed. He'd heard of interns being stabbed in the dark corridors of Carcosa, by the crazed prisoners who rotated in and out of jail cells. He'd also heard of the disappearances, and of the machines that were heard roaming the halls during the Midnight shift.

During his first week there, an editor—someone he only knew of as "T"—had vanished from his workstation without putting away his project. By the end of the week, no one else in editing—or in the rest of Carcosa, for that matter—could even remember the now-missing man. His disappearance had removed him from their memories. He'd been completely edited out. And that's how people were treated in Carcosa. Despite the technical demands, management held that everyone was replaceable. Anyone could wind up on the cutting room floor.

The closest thing he'd made to a friend was a chance meeting with Nick, one of the night shift guys. Nick worked in the ass-end of the building, in the Optical Printing department, fighting ancient machinery to replace damaged sections of film negatives, using a technical system called "Wet Gate" that Boone didn't completely understand, but didn't really need to. It was Nick's job, not his.

Nick was about Boone's age, but looked at least a decade older. Working in the building's subterranean section, breathing in clouds of chemical fumes and bathing in the sick green fluorescents, his complexion lacked color, shiny and watery like the separated liquid floating at the top of cottage cheese. Even his eyes, so pale a blue they too were practically colorless, and sunken deep in the sockets, surrounded by swollen lids, accentuated by the sharp cheekbones barely covered by flesh. His hair was patchy and receding.

"I feel worse in the winter," he told Boone one day, when they were both desperate enough to sample the sewer-water urine the ancient break room machine boasted as "coffee." "I get here after sundown and it's still dark when I leave. Have to sleep during the day so I never see the sun."

"They make these UV bulbs," Boone said, trying to find common ground with helpful sympathy. "At least you'll get the Vitamin D."

The sallow man laughed, a cross between a cough and a bark. "Yeah, I had one of those back in the Optical room. Stopped working."

"The bulb?"

"The vitamins."

Not knowing what else to say, Boone took a swallow of coffee and immediately regretted it. He grimaced and forced it down. Nick gave him a thin smile and drained his cup. "Gotta get back," he said.

A fear shot through Boone that he didn't quite understand. Just that he didn't want to be alone again so soon. Quickly: "What are you working on?"

Nick, who should have been taller than Boone but could not seem to bring himself to stand fully upright, slouched in the doorway. "I have to repair a section of *Some Like It Hot*," he replied, his voice without inflection. "Then it's back to that 'Jesus film'."

'That Jesus film.' That's what the whole lab called the project. The dream of an evangelical missionary to spread the word of Christ around the world via a very expensive, very bad-looking film. Shot in Jerusalem, using locals as extras but still starring a blond, handsome Christ, "That Jesus film" was meant to change the world. God via celluloid. Competing with the Copper's gods who knew the truth so much better. Still, the loneliness had crept up on Boone and wouldn't go away. "Enh, take a break. There's no one around. Who'll care?"

"The Oxberry," Nick said, referring to his ancient printer lurking in its lair way the hell down past the developing room. "It doesn't like me to be gone too long."

Trying for more light sympathy, Boone let out what he'd hoped was a knowing chuckle. "Yeah," he said, "the film cleaner calls me at home asking if I'm seeing another machine."

Nick smiled back, but without humor. As if he'd forgotten what humor actually was. "The Oxberry doesn't know where I live. Thank fucking God."

Then he left and Boone was alone again. He could hear the silence echoing through the walls. Once upon a time, he reminded himself, near the turn of the century, this windowless building of wet concrete and slimy ceramic served as a slaughterhouse. The violence of the past practically hummed within the walls.

Finally, more than a month into his employment, Boone received word to report to the vault. A new shipment of negatives was coming in, to be stored until the rightful owners could be found, the result of another middling studio going bankrupt. Their films were being abandoned to political asylum. Boone would be needed to receive and sort. Overtime was not available. Nor, apparently, was supervision. As soon as he received his instructions and a key card to pass through the vault's security, he was utterly on his own.

Though there was no hurry, he leapt at the opportunity. Carcosa's vault stretched seemingly for miles in all directions, racks upon rows upon shelves of film cans. Most were marked. Some were not. Picking an aisle at random, Boone let his finger trail across the titles scrawled on yellowing cloth tape that sealed the cans. *The Pit and the Pendulum* from 1964. Orson

Welles' *Othello*. If there was any order to their placement, the arcane system was lost on him.

Carcosa didn't believe in computers. The King thought the expense was unnecessary. Every film in the vault was logged by hand into giant, cracking ledgers. The ledgers held neither rhyme nor reason either. Films were grouped by lots, it seemed, in order of arrival. Nothing was cross-referenced. Nothing was indexed. If the Borgia films were indeed within these temperature-controlled walls, only luck would guide his hand.

For hours he wandered the stacks, trying to take note of every title. Three-strip Technicolor negatives were squeezed in between student films and educational loops. 16mm abutted 35mm and Super-8—the miscegenation was practically appalling. But the chaos hummed to him. Rounding a corner, a folded and very aged slip of paper met him at eye level, jutting from between two broad cans holding prints of *Gone with the Wind*.

Using his finger to hold its place, he unfolded the slip. It bore his name and an instruction:

"Boone," it said. "Start here."

The slip was decrepit, the ink almost unreadable. As if this note had been written centuries before, waiting for him to find it. No matter. He worked diligently. For hours he crawled across the floor, scanning the titles at the very bottom shelves. Nothing of interest. Nothing of importance. Nothing to indicate he was on the right track, yet nothing to say he was on the wrong path either. He made his way down one side and back, raising his line of sight one row at a time. Time vanished beneath him. Inside the windowless cavern, it was impossible to tell day from night. Neither of which really mattered.

Finally, four rows up on the left and six shelves down towards center, his finger found the word "Golgotha". It was scrawled across both the side and top of a small 16mm film can. Aside from the ancient Kodak label, the can displayed no other legends. Excited, he tore open the can with his fingernails. A tomb's gasp escaped as he pried away the lid. Inside was a small metal reel, film wrapped eternally around its core. Aged white tape had flaked away and the film wound loose, threatening to escape if held the wrong way.

Scrawled across one of the spokes of the reel, in grease pencil so faint with age it could barely be read, was one word: "Borgia".

Over the next several hours, Boone climbed the shelves searching for the film's intended companions. Finally, he had to admit defeat. Aside from *Golgotha*, he'd come up empty. The films he'd been employed to sort still lay untouched in their boxes at the top of the loading dock. Still, his mission was more important and tomorrow would be another day.

The resealed can in his hand seemed to pulse with a greedy life. Idly, Boone wondered if he held the can out in front of him, would it lead him to its brethren like a celluloid divining rod? He tried. It didn't. Still, he'd succeeded where so many others had failed.

It didn't matter who'd left the note. Clearly, it couldn't have been Shel the Agent, but who else could it have come from? Shel had obviously ventured deep into Carcosa's past, penned the note and placed it there for a long future until Boone was ready to find it.

As it turned out, there was no set procedure for signing the films out. No record seemingly kept for order amongst the chaos. Without bothering to question, Boone left the vault at the end of his shift and walked unhurried out the door. Outside was a long corridor of hurricane fence topped with razor wire, giving the lab's exterior the air of a prison camp. He traversed the corridor to the parking lot, passing the empty guard shack, skirting the ancient, battered, and (secretly) non-working metal detector, and made his way to Copper's car.

Leaving the lab behind him, silhouetted against the dawn sky, it seemed to him that the sun was actually rising *in front* of Carcosa, as if the lab sat on some distant planetary island between the earth and the sky. The illusion wreaked havoc on his empty churning stomach. With *Golgotha* sitting safely in the passenger seat, Boone left the lab behind as fast as he could, watching the sun in the rearview mirror as it eclipsed the rotting building.

SCENE THREE:
ALYCE SWEET ALYCE

Down the hall, Boone slept in the room she'd provided for him. Which was fine. Lys—Alyce—was most productive during late night and early morning hours. Nocturnal, much like the rest of the Addicts. Unfortunately, she had company, and it was hardly the company she wanted.

Kerns had twisted himself on the bed, chest-down and heels down. A gimbal in his spine? "See, your problem is that you never had any conflict in your life," he said, hissing each word's end. "Not real conflict."

Sitting at her desk, Alyce tried to ignore him, continued to tap out letters on her laptop. She didn't care what order the words were in. All that mattered was that she typed to spite him.

"You want to write about life, yeah? Real life. Problem: you've had no real life." Untwisting, he let his head hang upside down off the foot of the bed. "You and Boone, you were nurtured as kids. No abuse. Only support. What's the worst argument you ever had with your mother? Skirt length?"

Nerve hit. She stabbed "Return."

He'd come into her room without knocking, stripping off his shirt and writhing on her bed, watching her write, finally deciding to destroy her train of thought. His mouth was the dynamite plunger. Her train derailed, rending limbs from ideas and vital organs from dialogue. He shattered her scene as effortlessly as taking a breath.

"You were never a junkie," he whispered through his rotting teeth. She glanced at his reflection in the mirror above her desk. His eyes were turned toward the ceiling, his thousand-yard-death-stare boring through the crumbling plaster. "Never prostituted yourself. No sexual abuse. I can tell that much. Experience any death at a young age? Aside from some distant aunt or uncle?"

Ignore the question in favor of typing.

"Even stood up on a date?" She flinched. "Ah. Okay. At least you had some tragedy."

Mocking her. What was he flixing on? *Les Liaisons Dangereuse? Who's Afraid of Virginia Woolf?*

"Poor Alyce. All alone in the rain on prom night in her taffeta dress." Kearns pulled at his clothes, tugging his shirt up over his emaciation-hard abs. "Not, 'poor Alyce, dumped post-rape into a gutter after her third gangbang.' That's the kind of thing you can hang a screenplay on."

Taptaptaptaptaptap…

"But now…There you go, there's your real tragedy! Ha! Poor Fictional Alyce's had four abortions from unwanted and violent pregnancies. Poor Fictional Alyce is cracked-out in a bus station toilet. Poor Fictional Alyce cooks up junk cut with Draino for her pimp lover. She cleans up, puts all the sorrow down on paper and what happens? Studio tries to figure out how to purify it all. How would it look for Cameron Diaz shooting up? It's not Oscar season. Maybe it could be a comedy? Does she have to have the abortions? Can't she turn Christian at the end? Does Alyce have to be a woman? Male leads draw more box office."

She squeezed her eyes shut against the tirade hitting the back of her skull. Fingers just convulsed on the home keys, generating page upon page of gibberish. This was Kearns' regular screed.

"So you do it yourself. Direct and star. Do it as an Indie. Trouble is, where does the money come from? No angels out there ready to finance some Sundance entry. What do you do? Does Poor Real Alyce go the way of Poor Fictional Alyce? Does she whore out? Figuratively—as a ghost or doctoring on some Sandler schlock? Or does she *really* whore out? Are we gonna see Poor Real Alyce in the gutter any time soon?"

She spun around—his long, thin face, unshaven and flaking psoriasis, upside down and just inches from hers. His left eye winked, though it may have been a twitch. There was a frame stuck between top front teeth. Tongue worked against a corner, clicking. Her rebuke dried up unspoken in her own mouth as he went on. "What does she do with her life? Why, she returns to her old school, tail between her legs, buys the old dorm and shines a beacon to alert her old comrades that home is home again. And a parade of the dregs arrives at the door, but not the one person she'd hoped. Not the one person she'd rebuilt this Tower of Babel for. Until, finally and *finally*, her knight strides out of the storm, his battles won and lost and forgotten, to declare his love for her." Kearns' dark eyes focused suddenly, with a laser precision, and bored into her own. "But he doesn't declare, does he? He just walks right in and makes himself at home. As if to say, 'Of course. Of course, she would do all of this for me.'"

Smiling to himself, Kearns let his gaze rise back to the ceiling, to some random point in the tile pattern, his tongue clicking against the film frame between his front teeth. Quickly, Alyce snatched it out, slicing his gum and happy about it. He didn't even notice. He would later. Holding it up, the light helped her identify it. Richard Dreyfus at a piano. Of course. *Inserts*. Failed screenwriter turns to porn in the '30s. It was one of his favorites. It fed his self-loathing.

Slamming the laptop closed, she stood, flipped the frame back in his direction. It landed on point, stabbing his eye. He didn't even blink. Both hands were jammed down the front of his filthy jeans.

"Don't come on my sheets," she said, slamming the door for punctuation.

The same boring tirade. Kearns, Josh, all the Transgressives too afraid to literally burn Hollywood down. So they whined it to death. Or would if the town were listening. All their words did was add to pollution in the air, the negativity that blanketed Bethlehem like funeral ash. She stopped at the thought. "More fucking pretention," she said out loud. The words filtered down through the iron railings, littering the tile many floors below. Disgusted. Kearns had infected her. Had she written that down, the "funeral ash" line, she would have burned herself with a cigarette as punishment.

Angrily, she bent the frame between her fingertips then let it spring into the air over the rail. It flittered to the ground to join the rot and the mold and the broken promises below. She'd let him drive her from her own room. Room? The whole goddamned building was hers! He was there by her good graces alone! She should tell him that. Remind him of her generosity. Remind him of what a broken, twisted wreck he'd been when he'd finally escaped his chains. Eldritch-pale, skinny, the wild eyes of a Borneo geek. He stumbled through the doors of Orson looking for all the world like Jodorowsky at the end of *El Topo,* just prior to the character's self-immolation. The sweet-faced young man she'd known in class, practically her second-love after Boone, but much closer to an older brother, filled with kindness and support—that was all gone. "Fucking Lee Benway" had squeezed it out of Kearns like a toddler with a tube of toothpaste. His humanity had been wrung out and his soulless shell left to dry on a line.

When Kearns had his "bad days," he reeked. Of unwashed loathing and crazy. It was a smell that bubbled up through his skin, leaching through his pores like a wetbrain's alcohol sweat. The rough scars on his wrists and ankles seemed to pulse with a demented heat of their own, reminding the bearer that they would always be there. They were the sole surviving witnesses to his destruction and resurrection. Only, instead of any phoenix-like rise, Kearns had emerged from the ashes an exhausted, pure-white shuffling corpse. He breathed decay. Nothing inside him was healthy. All day long, he drank rum, watched movies, and flixed on whatever was on hand.

Alyce turned and put her back to the railing, glared a hole through her own door. Behind it, Kearns was writhing in some unspeakable fashion to the film in his bloodstream, rubbing his filthy body over every surface she held sacred. Or worse, he was reading what she'd written, fueling his disdain of her, his disgust for her. He'd escaped from Out There, but only barely. She'd been able to leave it all behind. That's what killed him the most, she told herself. She hadn't let Out There's acid dissolve her away to nothing. Out There hadn't beaten her. It didn't matter that she'd been his savior—or the savior of everyone else now living inside Orson—she'd survived where he'd failed. It was unforgivable.

When Kearns'd first come back from Out There, Alyce had been overjoyed to see him. He didn't look like the sweet, scruffy kid he'd been when he left, but that was to be expected. Five years working for the Studios, change was inevitable. But the talent he'd had—even their most jaded professors praised his writing, his sense of story and character. They couldn't wait to see what he'd do Out There. He'd be a feather in the Griffith cap for certain.

But Kearns returned like he'd clawed out of the grave. He was a shade, a ghoul, his skin giving off a kind of sickness that you didn't want to expose yourself to, risk catching the infection. Hardly a teetotaler in school, he spent hours in the Common Room draining bottles of rum and binging on Buñuel. "We'll never escape," he told her one night, eyes rheumy with alcohol joining the poison already within. "There's an exterminating angel standing right outside the door."

The Kearns who'd left had been their harlequin. He defused the tensions, particularly around finals when the Addicts abandoned sleep and nourishment to finish their final projects. When Boone joked that he would hurl himself from the top of Orson Hall, Kearns belted out a sea shanty, a bellowing non sequitur that had the rest of them howling. He dragged them from the editing bays and projected *The Man with Two Brains* right on the front of Doc Baily's pristine white office door. More than once, he prevented the apocalyptic ending of *If…* No one took up arms against the school. They graduated with honors, with honor, with passion.

After he'd been back a month, swilling booze in the

Common Room, rotting away inside his old dorm apartment, Lys had had enough and dragged him out into the daylight. His clothes and skin gave off a stench, not so much unwashed but stale. Like something abandoned then rediscovered, stuffed in long-undisturbed corner.

She wanted to take him somewhere, out of the Squat, out of his own head. But like the other Addicts, Lys still only thought in terms of movies. The Arc was a nighttime theater now, so she dragged him uptown, to the Regent, where *Shaun of the Dead* was playing.

At the start of the film some of the old Kearns began to emerge. Certainly, he identified with the slackers played by Simon Pegg and Nick Frost, the slovenly job-jockeys who lived for video games, beer, and fart jokes, but he seemed to delight in the set up. When the zombies arrived, he actually perked up, guffawing at the sight gags and bloody humor. Lys found his laugh disturbing, though. It lacked the youthful music she'd been so accustomed to before he'd gone. Now it was scratchy, a sputtering engine dying underwater. But it was a laugh.

Midway through the film, just as the mayhem was ramping up, the couple in front of them pulled out their cell phones, bathing the rows behind them with too bright, intrusive light. Kearns laughter faded and then shriveled in his mouth. The guffaw became a low growl of warning. Diplomatically, Lys leaned forward. "Excuse me, could you—"

"Bitch! You don't pay my phone bill! I'm talking to my daughter!"

Then the male member of the couple joined in. "Dude, control your bitch!" he said to Kearns.

Lys tried again. "Can we please be adults about—"

"Fuck you both! We paid the same as you."

Violation. A breaking of the unspoken Treaty of Movie Theater Patrons. To hell with the request to "silence your phones" preceding the feature, following the instructions to obtain popcorn and Coca Cola. A peacepipe had been ground beneath an uncaring heel. The phone's importance superseding courtesy, decency, cohabitation.

Around them, the other patrons sank into their seats, offering no help for either party, willing both sets of antagonists to disappear.

Lys never saw Kearns move. First he was in his seat, slouched low and growling. Next, he dragged the man by the hair out of his chair and into the aisle. There was a gun in Kearns' hand, the barrel was in the man's mouth. His face was a blank mask, eyes burning hatred into the woman's skull.

"Turn off the phone, cunt!"

"You can't do that! Let him go! I'm calling the cops!"

"Call the cops, and he's dead." It was a statement of fact, not a threat. Still, no one in the theater moved. Not even to call for help.

Kearns forced the man to his knees. Tears spilled from terrified eyes. The offending light vanished. The woman had dropped her phone while crying, softly, "Oh, please. Oh, please. Don't. We have babies…"

"Fuck your babies," Kearns whispered. "They should have been destroyed." It was the calm in his voice that Lys found terrifying. His eyes flashed in the darkness. On screen, Shaun beat back zombies with his cricket bat.

Kearns stared down at his victim. "What's your favorite movie?"

The man tried to talk around the gun, but as Edward Norton said in *Fight Club*, all that came out were vowels. Viciously, Kearns pulled the gun from the man's mouth, the barrel sight splitting a front tooth. The man howled and spit blood, phlegm, snot.

"What is your favorite movie?" Kearns said, demanding an answer.

The man stuttered, still sputtering and tasting metal. "Fu—"

Kearns pressed the gun barrel to the man's eye. "Answer

me."

Finally, the weeping man, formerly such a tough guy, formerly so imposing in his own mind, went back to his childhood. "*Star Wars.*"

Kearns nodded. The answer was acceptable. Still, he held the gun steady. To the woman, he said, "You bring a phone to another movie and I'll fucking find you. I will burn down your life and torture your babies in front of you. I will leave you destroyed."

The woman moaned, "You won't... you—"

The man with the gun in his eye screamed: "Shut up, bitch!"

Kearns hit him, hard, the barrel of the gun smashing two more front teeth. "Be nicer." He said. The man dropped to all fours, blood pouring from his mouth.

As in school, Kearns still wore steel-toed combat boots. They'd been *de riguer* for all of the Addicts. The toe of his boot met the man's forehead and his whole body arced backwards, almost in slow motion, blood blossoming in the air like perfume from an atomizer. His woman screamed, then whimpered as Kearns eased down the aisle towards her.

Still, no one in the audience moved. The Regent was a multiplex, staffed only by kids not much older than Alyce or Kearns had been when they were in school. Minimum wage slaves. The era of the usher was over. There was no authority in the auditorium. While *Shaun* played on, Kearns was authority.

Sobbing uncontrollably now, rocking in her seat, the woman made a mewling noise as Kearns stopped beside her. Keeping the gun trained on her face, he reached down, fumbled on the floor until he found her phone. A raucous song played over the speakers. Shaun and Ed were beating a zombie with pool cues, their violence matching the beat and rhythm of the song. Lys stayed where she was, frozen in her crouch.

Kearns held the phone in front of the woman's face. With a deft swipe of thumb, he found the phone's flashlight and shot the beam into her eyes. She tried to move away, shield herself from the piercing, screaming white light. Without another word, he switched off the light then flung the phone away, into the dark of the theater. Somewhere in front, it clattered against bare concrete floor. Everyone could hear it shatter.

And then…

Like the rest of the audience, Lys remained still. Not just immobile, but solidified. She couldn't inhale. Even the blood in her veins had stopped its flow, waiting for the next terrible thing to occur.

And then…

Kearns ducked down and exited the aisle. Ducking down—so as to not block anyone else's view of the film as it reached its climax. Remaining in that Groucho Marx position, that Hawkeye Pierce avoiding the whirring blades of the helicopter, Kearns returned to his seat. After a moment, Lys did the same. Kearns' laugh had vanished. Died. As the credits rolled, the woman in front of them whimpered prayers to Jesus. The man in the aisle moaned softly but didn't get back up.

When the house lights went up, Kearns and Lys left through the emergency exit. There was no urgency in his step, just the wish to avoid the rest of the audience. It wasn't until the heavy door slammed behind them that Lys finally heard shouting. Screaming from inside the theater.

After that, she never went with Kearns to the movies again. After that, she did her best to avoid him entirely. It wasn't always easy. They'd shared a moment. A sin met with a sin. In that moment, she'd been complicit. To Kearns mind, they'd completed a bond, sealed a covenant. But she knew that, in her inaction, he'd judged her and found her wanting. She'd never seen him with that gun again, but he no longer needed it. Being Out There had turned him into something she couldn't identify. He'd become one, she decided, with one of Copper's dark gods. And this thing wearing Kearns' body was now living comfortably beneath her roof.

In buying the Squat and welcoming him in, she'd somehow opened that puzzle box from *Hellraiser*, and the demon that emerged looked just like Kearns. Since then, she'd do anything to leave his presence.

So, turning her back on her own safe space, even as Kearns defiled it, Lys walked down the hall towards Boone's chamber, the sanctum she'd bestowed upon him, the asylum she'd provided. Seeing the dangers of Out There firsthand was her motivation for saving, for purchasing The Squat even as Griffith was content to let it rot. They were all there by her grace, by her mercy. But she didn't need their accolades or glory. It was enough that she knew: she was their salvation.

Boone's door had no lock—she'd made sure of that long before he'd even returned—so she slipped inside quietly. Once her eyes adjusted to a different level of gloom, she was able to orient herself. None of the Addicts were particularly fond of light. All of the windows could be boarded over and barely a soul would protest. From outside, the building appeared looming, crumbling, forgotten, abandoned. But instead of boards, every window held a movie poster shielding the dweller's from intruding sunshine. One-sheets were the new drapes. Quads were the new tapestries.

Over his windows, Boone had hung *Miller's Crossing* and *Hard-Boiled*. A *Fright Night* poster, signed by Chris Sarandon, turned the kitchenette into a cave. The only interior light came from the TV, beaming its almost friendly blue from the dead A/V channel. Boone was sprawled naked on his couch, bathed in the azure video glow. Dried blood had crusted on his chest, seeping from the crisscross perf tracks on his skin. He must have been flixing all night again. One of the series of wounds had tracked across the bridge of his nose, traversing both cheeks, just below his eyes.

Without waking him, she walked softly, on the balls of her bare feet, into the bathroom and found a clean cloth to wet. Bringing it back, she washed the blood away from his cheeks, caressing him softly as he slept. Or, rather, pretended to sleep. Looking up from her task, she found his eyes, glinting in the darkness, waiting for her gaze.

Neither said a word. Slipping out of her oversized and faded *Critters* t-shirt, the cloth sighed as it met the floor, and she climbed on top of him. Beneath the shirt, she'd been naked too. The Addicts had always been unselfconscious around each other. It didn't matter to her if Kearns caught glimpses of what she had beneath her clothes. It did matter that Boone see her in whole.

They were both pale, white as some species of subterranean reptile, their skin glowing in the dim, reflecting the video blue back into the room. He trailed his fingertips from the hollow of her throat down her chest and over her breasts, just barely touching her, but sending an electric charge through her. Flesh from both of them responded. And soon they were devouring each other. He was Jack Nicholson having Jessica Lange on the kitchen table, in the remake of *The Postman Always Rings Twice*. She was Kathleen Turner and he was William Hurt, the movie was *Body Heat*, and he was driving her face into the sofa cushions, tugging at her hair like a horse's reins, and she cried out in delight. He went down on her, Michael Douglas and Sharon Stone in the deleted scenes from *Basic Instinct*.

Mouths opened wide, met, and sealed together. Her tongue explored and found, hidden between his teeth and jaw, a film frame. Greedily, her tongue seized it, wrestled it from his mouth and took it into her own. She didn't recognize it at first; the imagery flooding her senses was colorful and blooming, but also dangerous. Something dark. The snarling, gnashing, *fucking* flowers copulating during "Empty Spaces," animated in *Pink Floyd's The Wall*. A wailing guitar lick steamrolled through them and over them, a wave of pulsing pleasure as their bodies met again.

While they flixed, their bodies became one unit, merging, morphing, changing. Her sex bloomed, open and greedy against his *shaftjohnshaft*. Her breasts collapsed into her chest and regrew on his. She found herself biting his lips as they became hers. She knew her face had adopted his features. Sweat-sheened skin slid over skin, fusing together at a molecular level.

What shall we use...

to fill...

the empty...

spaces...?

Inside her, he laughed, and the sound delighted her nerves. Enveloping him, she shuddered with pleasure, echoing his. Sensation from scalp to sole, a tingling, electric, chattering tremor of more and more and more. At climax, their heads snapped back, ears almost touching backs, and through their open mouths, flickering light splashed the ceiling. The images projected from the depths of themselves superimposed and vibrated—all the clichés of trains and tunnels and mushroom clouds, of bubbling champagne, of the waves rushing in to caress Burt Lancaster and Debra Kerr on their beach of *Eternity*.

Exhausted, she collapsed on top of him, shivering, the sweat alternately steaming from their bodies and frosting over. He laughed with her. Then his hand dropped below her vision, grasping for something under the couch. *An icepick?* She thought. That would make *him* Sharon Stone, then.

Instead, it came back up clutching a small metal can. She didn't need to read it to know what it was. '*Golgotha*,' he whispered. *I found it for us.*

CUT TO:

LOBBY

Diana heads towards the stairs. Movement down the hall catches her eye.

She looks over.

A MAN is walking down what had just been an empty corridor. She frowns.

The Man seems to be flickering.

                    DIANA
          Excuse me? You can't go down
          there.

The Man doesn't stop. He rounds the corner.

Diana hurries after him.

                    DIANA
          Hey, asshole! You deaf or - ?

Reaching the corner, she finds only an empty, dead-end hallway.

                    DIANA
          What?

She turns around. Surrounded by empty corridor. There is nowhere for the man to have gone.

She rubs her temples.

With a frustrated little snarl, she returns to the lobby.

THEATER

A PUNK COUPLE are groping each other in the back. Sarah is trying not to watch them, but that would mean she'd have to watch the movie.

The Punk Girl sees her.

She licks her lips lasciviously and flashes her. Sarah turns away.

Dave is transfixed by the images on the screen.

Red light splashes across his face.

                    SARAH
          How long is this movie?

                    DAVE
          This is just the first one.

                    SARAH
          Jesus, Dave, I can't watch
          another one of these. Can we
          go when this is over?

                    DAVE
      No.

                    SARAH
      What?

                    DAVE
      I said, no.

She stares at him. He looks down at her, seeing her for the first time. He shakes his head, clearing it.

                    DAVE
          I mean, they locked the doors,
          remember? We can't leave.

                    SARAH

Well, can we go into one of
the other rooms, then?

                    DAVE
Sarah, you're really missing
out. This stuff is amazing.

                    SARAH
I don't like these kinds of
movies. You know that.

                    DAVE
Then why the fuck did you
come?

                    SARAH
To… to be with you.

Dave stares at her, then breaks into a smile and
puts his arm around her.

                    DAVE
Anything you say.

He turns back to the movie. She stares at him,
then turns away. She catches the Punk Couple in
the back still going at it. The Punk Girl is
beckoning her over to join them and laughing.

Sarah stares down at her feet.

The doors open and Diana slips back in.

She sidles up behind Chris who looks pissed.

                    DIANA
How's it going in here?

> CHRIS
> This is being wasted on these assholes!

> DIANA
> Huh?

> CHRIS
> Nobody's watching! All they're doing is cheering the gore! They're missing what's going on! This is goddamned art! He finished all of this before he moved onto murder. Completion of the art, to him, meant completion of the artist. And nobody is paying attention!

Diana stares at him.

> DIANA
> You need a drink.

> CHRIS
> Seriously, where did you find these?

> DIANA
> You asked me that already.

He grabs her arm.

> CHRIS
> Did you steal them? How did you get them?

                    DIANA
          Get your hand off me!

                    CHRIS
          Tell me!

                    DIANA
          Fuck a cop, get a banned movie.
          It's how the world works. Get
          off me!

She shakes him loose and steps away from him. The
crowd cheers and his head whips around towards
the screen.

                    CHRIS
          Fuck! I can't believe I missed
          that! I want copies of this!

                    DIANA
          Yeah, whatever.

She looks around. The CROWD is looking crazed.
Small skirmishes continue to erupt throughout
the room.

Beside her, Dick Allen is staring up at the
screen, punching himself in the thigh.

Except that he isn't punching himself: he's
stabbing his leg with a penknife. Blood has
soaked through his pants.

                    DIANA
          Jesus Christ…

Just then, the screen goes blinding white, then the lights come up. Everyone cheers.

Diana turns her attention to the crowd.

> DIANA
> (shouting)
> That's one! One more to go! Ten minutes until showtime, people! Go grab drinks, some popcorn, then hurry back in.

People start out past her. She smiles, exchanges some handshakes.

She looks over at Chris, who is still staring up at the screen.

> CUT TO:

SCENE FOUR:
AS SEEN FROM GOLGOTHA

Boone couldn't believe what he'd read. *"Fuck a cop, get a banned movie. It's how the world works."* That Kearns would write something so lazy was unfathomable. As he'd proven over the past few weeks, nothing was that easy. If he could have fucked a cop to get the last two Borgia films, he would have done without question. Instead, he'd spent weeks crawling on his belly, exploring every corner of Carcosa's vaults, long after he'd been reassigned to one of the Contact Printers. His work was left to pile up. The first second he could, he'd slip away, from beneath the lazy eyes of his so-called superiors, and invade the vaults to continue his quest.

Every night, he emerged sweaty and filthy, covered with dirt and the celluloid remnants of history. It took a week to locate *Rape of the Archangel*. Though Copper's VHS copy was decent, a quick glance revealed that the can contained both the negative and the work prints of *Archangel*. Of course, that would read so much better than a VHS dub, no matter how good the source had been.

After another week he'd started to give up hope. Despair hit him when he found the can reading *Borgia / The Pioneer*, only to tear open the lid and find it empty, with only a plastic opaque "black bag" inside. He howled, hurling the can into the darkness, his rage chasing it away.

Shel called him every day now, desperation thick in his voice and growing worse with each call. The man Boone thought in charge of his destiny sounding increasingly like a junky reaching the end of his last fix. "Did you find them yet? Jesus—how long do you fucking need?"

And: "I got you in there, you ungrateful son of a bitch. Don't you *dare* let me down!"

And then: "I'm sorry. It's been stressful here lately. Management is on my ass, you know? So, how's progress?"

Thus far, nobody had questioned him on his time spent in the vault. No one at Carcosa seemed to notice him. If they did, they didn't seem to care. As the days ground by, his co-workers shuffled unseeing in and out of the shadows. He worked with Morlocks, he realized. But he had no delusions that he was an Eloi.

On the last Friday of a month he couldn't recall, Boone's patience left him. He'd found the empty *Pioneer* can in a pool of darkness, his foot sending it skittering into the light like a big, flat beetle. Its emptiness mocked him. With a shout of hideous rage, Boone attacked the nearest shelf, sending cans flying into the air, crashing to the concrete. Bolted to the floor, he couldn't topple them, so he had to satisfy himself with manual destruction. Cans and cans spilled film, new and ancient, a ticker-tape parade honoring his failure. Seizing them up, he sailed them like a discus into the yawning shadows to explode against walls and other shelves.

From one can, he ripped a reel from its bag like a mad abortionist and unspooled its contents with violent hands. Attacking film cans one by one, he heard the movies screaming as he ripped them apart. Taking hold of a release print of *Killer's Kiss*, he rendered a reel into confetti, gathering up whole piles of ruined celluloid, stuffing it into his mouth to induce a flixing overload. It didn't come—the high beaten down by horrorstruck adrenaline.

Weeping, he collapsed to the floor, listening to the dying echoes of his rampage. And then Copper's Cinemagog smiled upon him. As if in a movie. As only could happen in a movie. There on the single untouched shelf before him, lined in a neat row, waiting for his discovery, were the rest of the Borgia films. *The Magus* on the left, bracketing *The Pioneer* with *Osculum Infame*. There for his taking all along. Unless put there during his tirade by the deity disgusted by his breakdown. "Here," it seemed to say. "Just take them and fucking go!"

He laughed like Dwight Frye as he gathered up the cans,

peeking inside to check the contents. The empty can had been a fluke, or a distraction. A red herring. *The Pioneer* was right there, in an almost identical rusting can. *The Magus* in his left hand. *Osculum*—so far from destroyed!—in his right. The cans warmed at his touch, begging him, almost sensually, for rescue. Like the *Temple of Doom* Sankara stones, the cans seemed to glow when held together.

Removing his jacket, he wrapped up the films, tying the sleeves to make a little jealous bundle all his own. It was still hours before the end of his shift. Carrying the bundle closer to the entryway, Boone stashed his treasure in a nook between the wall and a badly installed wooden shelf. Much later, after he'd spent his hours obsessing over his findings, making multiple trips to the dingy restroom just so he could sneak inside and confirm their continued existence, he'd retrieve the prints and return to The Squat. The screening was upon them.

SCENE DELETED:
OUT THERE

Free from his manacles, Kearns rubbed some feeling into the raw places on his wrists and ankles. Glowering at the world, he kicked open the door of his prison trailer and stormed across the parking lot. He figured he had maybe five minutes before word got around that he'd been formally ejected from the Studio. They would come and they would drag him away screaming. But here was a window of freedom and damned if he wasn't going to climb in and start a fight.

Five months he'd banged away at that script making every change they asked for. He'd learned his lesson on his previous script and that subsequent production. Five months he'd kept his ego in check, banging the keys every day for the money. To be part of The Big Scene Out There. That's what he'd wanted wasn't it? It's what every screenwriter wants: The Big Scene. Expected another round of "notes" from Higher Ups, from the Suits, from the director, Legacy Lad. His teeth were already grinding as he opened the daily email from Higher Up. No suggestions this time. Just a draft of a script he barely recognized as his own, changed down to the character names, and a pink slip telling him to F.O.

"F.O." Code from the Higher Ups for "Fuck Off."

Bare feet sizzling on the black top, he crossed the road and ducked under the wooden gate arm. The security guard inside more or less waved as he passed.

"'The writer always gets fired', right?" He told himself. "Goldman wrote that in *Adventures of the Screen Trade*. What makes you better?"

The weight of the shackles, like phantom limbs, pulling down on his arms and legs. Chained to that radiator, like a POW or a werewolf on full moon night. Five months in that Spartan trailer. Banging out change, after change, after change. His original pitch had been simple, almost elegant: simple slasher movie, done with a brand new style by hot new director, Legacy Lad. Killer driven mad by "forbidden movie", hunts sorority girls in an abandoned theater, then they hunt back. Could be made for pennies. Would attract the kids and bring in millions. Hell, release it during the summer they'd get their $50 million dollar opening weekend. Ten times their investment.

But someone Higher Up took notice, had a vision. More changes but not from Legacy Lad, just from the Suits. And then, day before yesterday, a new name in the CC: Lee B. Maybe this was only his second picture but he knew what that addition meant. Legacy Lad was out, Lee B. was in. New director. New vision.

New script.

New writer.

Never complained about the change. Or the glitch air conditioner that let in just enough of the heat from Out There to remind him how very closely the place resembled Hell. Someone owed him a goddamned explanation.

Two more guards, actual police, standing outside the hanger doors. The third policeman asked, "Is it about a bicycle?" but Kearns had no time for non-sequiturs.

Jabbed his thumb against his chest. "Writer," he said. Aimed thumb at door. "Lee B.?"

Instead of pepper spraying him until he drowned, the third policeman nodded and opened the door. Before Kearns could step through, he noticed how much was different—despite the phalanx of lights inside, the soundstage was significantly darker, cooler air tumbled over him. The noise that followed the air was far removed from the traffic sounds behind him. A thousand teamsters cursing, equipment banged metal against metal; footsteps across catwalks sounding like an army of robots taking position for battle. Kearns blinked against the shift in light and shadow, then stepped through the door. Either the policeman closed it behind him, or it swung shut on its own, sealing him inside the chaos.

"Chaos on set!" someone called, or maybe he imagined. If real, it was stating the obvious. Bodies moved around him, stepping through the invisible barrier between concrete soundstage and the breathtaking set. Inside the hanger, they'd built an Art Deco movie theater complete with massive red velvet curtains, limitless golden ropes holding them open, revealing a shimmering silver-white movie screen beyond. Rows upon rows of perfectly upholstered blood-red seats bracketed by exquisitely carved armrests and bases. A movie theater by way of a cathedral—even the bit of the ceiling visible above the screen, built out only a few feet over the rest of the set, was domed and flanked by the *masques comedia del arte*: Comedy smiling too broadly, too sadistically, on the left; Tragedy twisted in agony on the right, a bullet hole in its forehead weeping blood.

It was majestic and it was wrong. For five months he'd described the fictional Selznick Theater as a decaying wreck, a junkie corpse of a theater, something salvaged from an apocalypse. Not this—glittering and new and were those walls actually marble inlaid? Were those great doors real mahogany?

Too much to comprehend. The discordance, of worship versus rape, of ideas. Where was *his* theater? This didn't go up overnight—how long had they been ignoring him? Without looking down, he knew that his right wrist was bleeding again, seeping through the raw-rubbed pores. Kearns grabbed the first person he saw with a clipboard, young girl, dark brown hair in pony tail, hipster glasses, fresh out of school. Spinning her around, clasping her shoulders, his red face turning hers white, he hissed, inches from her mouth: "Lee B."

Trembling hand—scared to the point of palsy—raised a walkie to her young lips. "I need Lee. Now."

From some distant other place, a voice crackled through the speaker. "He's bus—"

Ripping the walkie from her hand, Kearns didn't let that officious spook finish its declaration of haughty authority. Squeezing the talk button hard enough to white-knuckle his hand, Kearns vomited his rage over the walking. "This is Kearns. The *writer*. Where is this 'Lee B.'? Show. Him. To. Me."

No reply from the walkie. Just the hollow sound of radio silence.

The size of the building, the scope, the madness of pre-set production—it was all meant to make him feel small. *Just* the writer. Just one of the infinite monkeys providing word doodles for the masters. Rage grew him in leagues. The question came out with the crash of a perfect storm: *"Where is he?"*

The question had not gone out over the walkie; his demand echoed against the walls swallowing the entirety of that expansive set. No one stopped to look at him, acknowledge him in any way (well, the girl PA had obviously wet herself). And yet everything, almost imperceptibly, slowed down. You had to be watching to notice. And *just the writer* had been watching.

Hydraulics whined and a crane bucket lowered. Standing in the bucket, beside a very large, expensive looking camera wearing a giant lens, was a gracefully-aging matinee idol, smiling around a black cigarillo with white tip, staring down at him through a director's loupe. With the subtlest of gestures, the man in the khaki, with the silk ascot and the riding boots, stopped the bucket just off the floor.

Just enough to loom that much taller over Kearns.

The Director regarded him with no little amusement. For a moment, he reminded Kearns of Eli Cross—Peter O'Toole's sinister movie director in Richard Rush's *The Stunt Man*, particularly the way O'Toole traveled in a chair lift on a crane, always overseeing the action. The Director dropped the loupe, let it thump against his solid chest, and said around his cigarillo, "Lee Benway. At your service."

Forced to look up at the man, if only at a slight incline, brought Kearns' rage to steam. Holding the bundle of printouts—blue and gold and green pages—in a tight fist he shoved them forward in Benway's direction. "What is this shit?"

Removing the cigar but not the smile, Benway said, "And

who is asking?"

"Kearns," he said. "I'm the writer," he said. "And before you have my ass thrown out of here, I want to know who changed my words!"

"Thrown out? Not if I have anything to say about it." Benway opened the waist-high door of the bucket and stepped down onto the dark concrete of the sound stage. He remained taller than Kearns, by just enough inches. Smiling his Burt Lancaster smile, wearing his Cary Grant chin, Kirk Douglas' jaw, Robert Mitchum's chest, Benway moved too fast for Kearns' eyes to register—the man clasped either side of the writer's face and kissed him. Hard. On the lips. For longer than even a joke would dictate.

Releasing Kearns' face, Benway threw his head back and roared with laughter. Like Victor Mature. Then he clapped both of the smaller man's shoulders. "Jesus, God, is it good to meet you! They wouldn't let me near you. Can you imagine?"

Kearns had no words. Fortunately Benway had them all.

"I mean, here you are, my Chandler, my Steinbeck, my Brackett, and I can't even talk to you directly. Can you believe those bastards? Those *fucking* bastards! Ha! Suits!" The last word he spat onto the ground. "So you got the new draft, I take it?"

Mouth open, the almost-sentence stumbled out slowly. "I…they…fired today."

"That's what they think!"

Suddenly, Benway's arm was across Kearns' shoulders and he was most definitely being marched forward. The prized Jew shown around the new death camp. (Strike that last bit. It'll never play with politically correct in the cities.) "Listen," the director said, "don't take those bits of confetti personally, okay? Your script was brilliant. Basic, but lovingly-told. I was in tears. Not literally, but it was what attracted me to the project."

"What happened to—?" was as far as he got.

"Legacy Lad? Shipped out. New assignment. Listen, kid, Kearns—I just wanna tell you, this new draft was just to get your attention."

"What?"

"I knew they had you squatting away in the ol' Red Lodge like some unclean thing. But you weren't fighting. Some of those notes from Higher Up were infantile, but you put them in! Now I understand, you had a rough time on your first show, what was it?"

"*Daycare of the Dead*," said Kearns, more than a little dizzy as Benway continually spun him in a new direction as they talked.

"I read that. I did. Honest to whoever you like. The first draft, anyway. That's what got you on the map out here. You think I wouldn't have read it?"

"I… the advice I got was to be outrageous. Write something maddening."

"It. Was. *Gorgeous*. Zombies overplayed? Not the way you wrote them. Zombie toddlers! Terrifying. No wonder there was a bidding war for it. No wonder you got suckered in."

A stab of anger. *Daycare* had been over and done with thirteen months ago, but the wound was still fresh. *The writer always gets fired.*

"But you had to have known—deep down, some part of you? What's the first thing the winning Studio did?"

"Cut its balls off," Kearns said.

Benway stopped and jabbed a forefinger at his chest. "Exactly. They take out the pedophile angle and what did they put in? Tainted juice boxes. Fucking juice boxes! Best they could do. Because they're hollow, man. Nothing inside them but a hamster on a wheel driving them towards where they think the money is. God, I hated to see what they did to your work."

It was true, everything that Benway said. *Daycare* became a watered-down PG-13 jump-scare flick. Nasty as his original was, it pushed taboos. It *said* something. In the final cut, every single zombie toddler was shot off-screen. So that uninvolved parents could just drop off their brats and leave for dinner.

Daycare of the Dead became its own title: the babysitter for America's texting youth. They'd created this generation. The Suits, Out There, chiseled away at the average attention span, over periods of decades, until only the consumer remained. But then the entire project was killed. Disasterous test-screenings. Even watered-down and flavorless, Middle America didn't want to face the responsibility the film implied. "Not *our* fault our kids are disaffected! It's because of video games! Violence on TV! Liberal agenda!"

The finished movie was shelved. Castrated and cuckolded, then hidden away forever.

The result of the production left Kearns scarred, but it had gotten him Out There. Put money in his pocket. Put him on this: *"Feature Presentation."* The story of a movie that made killers, "based on a true story". They reeled him in and made him an unwilling blood donor to keep their Suit-asses tight.

Did you hear the one about the actress who was so stupid she fucked the writer?

Jesus, this set was the biggest thing he'd ever seen. The theater stretched on and on until the darkness of the stage swallowed its tail. People moving in and out and around, carrying spools of cable, tools, light stands, Century stands, Mighty Mole Richardsons, Beefy Babies, mounting Red Heads and 10Ks. Multiple Obies were lashed to the cameras. The littlest lights, designed by Lucien Ballard and named for Merle Oberon, to cast a shine to hide her scars and put starshine sparkle in her eyes.

"What I couldn't figure out was why you weren't fighting at all? Suits said you didn't even seem mad. You've only been Out Here two years and they've already shredded your soul? I don't buy it. I don't buy it and I didn't buy it. So I knew the new rainbow paper would get you going."

Kearns looked at him, "So the new draft was a dodge?"

A guilty shrug from Benway. "Not as such, no. That's my director's polish. Before you say anything, it's my prerogative and it's in my contract. Yours too, if you care to look."

The boil returned, sweat sizzling on his skin. "So what you're telling me is that's it. Nothing of mine remains. Here you are extoling my virtues and you replace it all."

The smile didn't drop. Not a millimeter. "Fer chrissakes, man, will you look at the big picture. Look around you!" With a flash of Fairbanks, Benway mounted the small proscenium stage in a single bound. "You inspired all of this! We wouldn't be here right now if it weren't for your work."

Punctuating his words with a fury of flung paper, pages scattering in every direction like raging birds. "This isn't my work! This is pristine! My theater was a crumbling corpse! Where in any of my drafts does… does *this* exist?"

Gliding through the air, Benway was on the ground and at his side in an instant. He put his hand against Kearns' chest. "Right here," he said. "It's all right here and you know it."

Looking down at the hand then up at the man, Kearns said, slowly: "Bull…*shit!*" He stumbled back, breaking the connection, the touch that bound them on a molecular level. "Bullshit, Frank Capra! My story was sold on the idea of art as corruption! That something like a movie could turn people primal!"

"But that's not the story you *wanted* to tell," Benway said, taking a step forward and regaining ground. "Don't 'bullshit' me, man. When it comes to bullshit, I'm King of the Mountain and excreted it all myself. Twice the size of Kilimanjaro. How many times has that story been done? Ooh, the evil horror movie that makes savages of us all. Makes us rape and pillage and mutilate! *Demons* come to mind? How about Carpenter's *Cigarette Burns*? What about *Anguish*?"

"*Demons* and *Anguish* just take place in theaters. You might as well hit me with *Targets* or *Dead End Drive-In.*"

"And again, there is none so blind as those with vision," the director said, with a sad shake of his head, then turning chin towards ceiling. "Forgive him, Great Cinemagog, he knows not how he sins."

"Oh, Christ, now you're invoking the Dark Gods? That better have been irony!"

"Kearns, kid, my friend." Benway took another step towards him, arms outstretched, perfect width for a hug or a crucifixion. "Will you please forget what I quote-unquote did to your script? It's all going to be okay."

"How?"

"Two words: Associate Producer."

Kearns stared at him. "That's the title you give the sandwich guy when you don't want to tip him."

"*State and Main!*" Benway said. He was right about the source of the line, but damned if Kearns was going to give him the satisfaction.

"You want pull? You want to do something on this show that's meaningful? You did the hard part: you brought us all together. Rise, Sir Knight, because I've just upgraded your title. You're a rich, white landowner now. And therefore you have the right to vote."

"I'm no Suit."

"Good! I battle enough of those. Besides, it's not like the Higher Ups ever deign to come down to set. All they care about are the dailies and those are going to be smashing. My guy? My D.P.? Thanks be to Latham-ascdop, God of Cinematography! My guy—lemme ask you: heard of Greg Tolland, Peter Suschitzky? What about Andrew Lesnie?"

"Yeah."

"Blind men. Scrambling in the dark like moles. My guy spins sunshine into gold. Into Oscars, my friend."

"So who do you got?"

"The Shadow Walker, my good man."

No further explanation. Kearns was seized again in the iron grip of sinister friendship, led back to the edge of the set. All around him, walkies squawked, bull horns bellowed—orders to work faster, harder, 'Time is money,' sez Yapim, God of Producers. (Jesus, the useless shit they taught you in film school.)

The aroma of Christmas found its way to Kearns' nose. Without warning, the shadows had birthed a cloth-covered table, easily thirty feet long, cooked food spanning one end to the other, with chefs in white stationed at intervals, near the turkey, the roast beef, the honey ham. "I don't know what they had on your last show," Benway said. "But this is *our* Craft Services. And this is for everybody. Grips, P.A.s, union, non-union, journalists—the groupies. Eh? Who doesn't like groupies? And on a set like this, they know when to keep their mouths shut… and when to open them again."

Near the close end of the table was a cart on wheels, similarly draped, and on it was a naked girl, maybe 20-years-old, lounging on her stomach. From the nape of her neck to the cleft of her perfect backside, ran four rows of crystal white powder. Benway stood beside her and she handed him something green and cylindrical—Kearns was sure it was a rolled thousand-dollar bill, and through the contorted face of Grover Cleveland, the director inhaled one entire line. Ending at her ass, he gave the girl's left buttock a nibble, eliciting a semi-forced giggle, then turned back to the writer with that great big smile.

Director Benway.

Dir. Benway.

Dear Benway.

"I haven't even told you a metric *fraction* of our plans, my friend. Lemme tell you, you set some wheels in motion. Yes you did. The sex in this thing? All real. Not simulated—but not *porn*, mind you! Penetration, just like they're doing in Europe." From nowhere another cigarillo was produced. Already lit. "But what's that you say? 'Freestyle fucking? How utterly banal.' You're absolutely right. Even the dullest American will see right through that. And we're talking pretty damn *dull*. Not stopping there, man, no way no how no sir."

The blow was obviously kicking in. Or was it the

director's natural adrenaline overtaking the drug? He spun on his heel and cast an order into the yawning darkness. "You will please bring out our extras!"

Blackness disgorged a small platoon of men and women in wheel chairs, tired, hard eyes glazed over from some medicinal inducement. Benway skipped backwards as the grips slid the parade of wheelchairs forward, careful to avoid the slightest air of corruption. Each occupant was shackled to the armrests. Anger flashed again in Kearns—he knew how they felt.

"Everyone says they'd do anything to be in the movies. How about a vacation on Death Row? Every single one of those before you, our background actors, all sentenced to die, painfully or not depending on which side of the fence you're on, or maybe the needle, I should say. Each and every one of them trading their state-mandated death for a shot at stardom."

Kearns felt a heft slap on his back, a fatherly/uncle-ly gesture. He hadn't noticed that Benway had even moved before he felt the man's hand. Instead, he was transfixed by the sight of the recently, temporarily, pardoned. He didn't need Benway to tell him that this was only a brief stay of execution.

"Squibs and CG gore: out the door. Old hat, cliché go-away. For suckers like Malick, whenever he gets around to actually making a picture. Like real fucking. But this is unique. A new twist on 'snuff' if you want to be crass."

"They're the victims." Kearns said, stating the obvious to no one in particular.

"Exactly!" Benway lowered his voice, turned Kearns slightly away from the rolling condemned. "Just between you and me, they're more like walking props. But they'll be infamous. In that end massacre, when the SWAT Team bursts through—"

"SWAT Team?"

"—just sprays the audience with gunfire, you're gonna see death the way God or whoever intended. And you'll see dancing. And we'll both see awards. Guaranteed."

Any thought Kearns had for the script, the new draft,

his original drafts, the Pride Parade of colored paper—it all melted away in that moment. Taking his rage with it. Something in Benway's words made his pupils dilate, and now he could see very far into the blackness beyond the set. He could finally make out the bodies of the crew, dark silhouetted against darker, skittering about like the world's biggest ant farm. The crew—thousands of them. And the walking props: hundreds. Criminals hitting the Big Time. The Big Scene.

Kearns inner monologue: That's all anyone asks for, isn't it? Their fifteen minutes in The Big Scene. And they're not all criminals, are they? Look at them. They're not all resigned. Not all hardened by prison. There are volunteers in there. Waiters and waitresses and cash register maestros finally getting their chance. Their first time as Featured Extras. Last time as well. Bright-eyed, eager, excited to die on the Big Screen. They were entering as unknowns and ingénues. Their corpses would be leaving as stars.

Something else. He could feel the darkness looking back. Lights from above—broken up by deliberate flags of black cloth or the thin aluminum "barn doors" mounted in front of the lamps, or diffused through screens, or scattered into patterns by cut out frames colloquially known as "cookies"—shaped the shadows beyond the set. A higher vantage point would reveal the shape better, but even at ground level he could see that the yawning void before him was not a natural cut-off. Instead, the light creeping around and through the deliberately, carefully placed equipment, gave the blackness tendrils. Creeping out from the densest body of dark, tentacular shadows reached out to him fingerlike. Some trick gave the tendrils lazy movement, each long, probing finger of dark swaying in its own manner. No two grew out or danced in the same way. Surely from above the shadows would appear squidlike. This was the black shape of the dark Cinemagog, Lord of all Gods of Celluloid. As the tendrils swayed, so did they beckon.

Kearns shivered and took a step back from the closest

shadow. As if to draw him back in, the mix of marvelous aromas from the craft services set up wafted towards his nose. The sweet and savory, like beckoning fingers. He looked back: men and women in pristine chef's whites were laying out new trays of salads, hors d'oeuvre. A thick, tempting roast, sliced thick and bloody, set down beside an arrangement of severed fingers laid artisanal on beds of arugula. A small bowl of grey eyeballs, still chilled, lights glittering off of the dead retinas. A chafing dish, lid removed, releasing a billow of steam from the piles of glazed hands, pink flesh falling from the phalanges bones. When sliced, what would ooze from that red velvet cake, topped with what did not quite resemble cherries?

With a proud growl, Benway swept Kearns into his arms again and literally swung him around. "It is so good to have you on the team, Kearns. Having you reborn, right here in front of me, leaving behind the ashes of a screenwriter!" Again, the word was spit like the taste was foul. To the world inside the soundstage, Benway shouted, "Director on set!"

Announcement met with echoes of the same. Coming from both the light and the dark.

To Kearns, he gave a little wink and widened his smile. "Producer on set!"

And the echoes came louder, with more urgency, footsteps hurried faster across catwalks and concrete. More lights bloomed. The darkness backed away. Everything inside, whatever Kearns could see or even visualize, bathed in gold.

There must have been a gesture. One of the grips unlocked the shackles from a large, bald man, wearing street clothes and a mask of fatigue encircled by a network of plain black tattoos. Four tear drops of ink dripped from his left eye, frozen in time on his cheek.

They led the man to the edge of the set, and he was met there by a wall, moved into position on casters by the men or women on the other side, out of view. The scenery slid into place and suddenly the condemned man was no longer in what he knew to be reality. This was The Movies.

Benway cried out, "Hot set!" And the talent reacted to the proclamation with a smile.

"What do you say?" the director asked the writer, pressing a German Luger into his right hand. "Wanna shoot some B-roll?"

Kearns stared down at the black weapon in his hand. Heavy. Metal. Glistening in the golden light. Its grip curving perfectly around the arc of his thumb, seeming to sigh and relax into a perfect fit. "As associate producer," Kearns said finally, "I say: Yes I do."

He received another hug in return. "I love you, man! Like a fucking brother." To the condemned man, Benway said, "You hear that? This man right here is about to make you famous. A star, my man. A big star."

Beefed up with pride, the man stood straighter before the new backdrop. Benway called over the First A.D., another girl with another pony tail and another pair of hipster glasses. He nodded and she called out: "Roll sound!"

From the darkness came the answer, "Speed!" It was followed immediately by "Camera rolling!"

"No need for a slate on this one, kids," said Benway, winking at Kearns over his shoulder. "This is just a camera test."

The condemned man's smile fell just a little, reflecting a glimmer of disappointment, as Kearns raised the pistol.

SCENE FIVE:
COPPER'S SANCTUM

Like Copper, Orson's elevator didn't go to the top floor. It was one of the reasons the older editor liked working in the tower attic. The means to get there was treacherous. Only the determined would bother making the journey up the cramped, narrow passage of protesting wooden stairs to the labyrinth of rooms left unfinished since the 1930s. Who knew what was in the air he breathed as he worked, dust trickling down from the ceiling in a cascade of motes glittering in the bluish screen light cutting through the darkness. Sometimes it felt as if at any moment he and his entire editing bay would crash through the surrendering floorboards and send him plummeting to oblivion. Would he even notice long enough to stop cutting? Could he make one final edit before he was crushed to pulp beneath the ancient machine?

Copper worked in digital now, but there was a time when he only sculpted in film. Those days were long gone, but his first project, *Spires*, shot so long ago on 16mm, was still a work in progress. Hence the ancient flatbed Moviola he'd rescued from basement storage, he and Rusty alone schlepping it into the sole service elevator, and then breaking it down and transporting the impossibly heavy parts one at a time up that perilous passageway.

For the last year he molded *Spires* workprint. Trimming away, adding back in, finding a place for even two-frame trims excised from somewhere else. Nothing would be wasted. Everything would be reconfigured. By now, the workprint was little more than a stiff reel of tape splices and repairs, but the movie... the movie was finally speaking to him. Telling him how to finish it. Whispering to him at night, even while it lay dormant while he, and the Moviola, collapsed from exhaustion.

Spires, he knew, was a spell. He was studying the incantation, learning from the spell itself, how to properly recite it and bring it to power. *Spires* was his offering to his Dark God of the Movies, the powerful Cinemagog, who oversaw all film, having crushed the Greek muses beneath his hooves less than a hundred years before, Terpsichore and Calliope trampled to nothingness in his wake.

Copper never had visitors. In the weeks following Boone's return and the fervor surrounding the impending Borgia screening, Copper had retreated even further to his roost, rarely emerging except for supplies, food mainly, cravings that snuck up on him without warning. Only Rusty Pennick, his acolyte and apprentice, was allowed safe and unfettered passage to and from the Sanctum. Before Boone and Borgia, Copper made conscious effort to join the festivities in the Common Room, at least once a week if he remembered, or when Rusty could coax him out of the darkness. Recently, he'd had no desire to join in on Borgiamania. He felt no revulsion, no disillusion that his fellow artists were so obsessed with the work of a murderer and—by all accounts—utter hack. Just disinterest. Fabulous disinterest that spurred him to concentrate harder on *Spires* and unlock his own mysteries of the universe. As soon as the spell was complete.

So Boone's knock on the landing was almost a shock. *Almost* an intrusion. But Tom Boone had been a close friend during their time in the educational trenches and should, of course, be welcomed. But the truth was Copper resented the intrusion. Fortunately, the thin monitor light had sapped away the energy to display resentment, or any other emotion. Though startled by the knock, he forced himself to stop mid-edit, swivel in his chair, and greet his visitor with as much enthusiasm as he could fake. Which was, as it turned out, none at all.

Boone waved first, or rather held up a hand, palm out, almost inviting the old editor to sniff it and determine he was friendly. "Hey," he said weakly. In his other hand, he held the black plastic light-blocking bag that held the last two Borgia films. "I need your help."

In his mind, Copper heard a glimmer of his old self exclaim, "Of course, buddy! Anything you need!" But what emerged from his mouth was a dull, "With what?"

Boone held up the black bag. Copper looked from the bag then back to Boone. Suddenly, Boone was uncomfortable, ashamed at having disturbed his old friend at all. Maybe Alyce had been right. He should have given the films to Rusty and left Copper alone. But that didn't seem right. Copper was an Addict; he should be in on the adventure. "I basically stole these from Carcosa," he said, gaining a little courage through the recount of his heist. "I can't take them back to telecine. I need you to transfer them for me."

Waiting for Copper to respond was like watching a fairy tale king wake slowly from enchanted slumber. King Théoden still bewitched by Sauruman. Then the fog seemed to lift from his eyes and his brain finally acknowledged that Boone was there. "All I have is an elbow," he said, referring to a device like a periscope, mirrored inside, so that a projector at one end could shine its bounty into the lens of a camera at the other. It was a poor telecine process, but it was the best they had at their disposal. And Copper had the only one in the building.

Without any movement from the editor, it was impossible for Boone to judge what his old friend was thinking. Copper sat motionless, looking exhausted and worn, life leeched away from too many weeks spent in flickering darkness. Finally, there came an almost imperceptible shrug. "When do you need them?"

"Soon as you can," Boone answered, setting the bag down gently on the floor. Then, even more hesitantly, toeing them closer to Copper. The silence that filled the space between them started to clog his lungs. "The, uh, the others I should be getting back from the lab at the end of the week," he added, extraneously and unhelpfully. But the words carved away some of the silence.

"I'm not watching these with you," Copper said, his voice rattling out of the dry cage of his chest. "But I'll put them together for you. I know how they go." He glanced down at the bag, his eyes fixed like they were miles away but still in view. "Bring the tapes when you get them back."

Copper's words hung in the air. "Put them together for you"—what did he mean by that? The films were already assembled. He just needed them transferred. "Ok, thanks. I appreciate it."

"You know who I've been thinking about?"

The question startled Boone. It may have even startled Copper, who did look confused as to where the query originated. Boone shook his head, watched as Copper swiveled in his chair, back to the screen and the labor at hand. "Ambrose Bierce," he said. "And Richard Stanley."

Richard Stanley. Director of *Hardware* and *Dust Devil*. A notoriously strange artist, considered to be a mystic by some, due to the time spent wandering South Africa. The few films he'd made had a common theme of a wandering stranger, on a journey with no destination, separate from "real" time. "Ambrose Bierce" meant little to Boone. He mustn't have been a filmmaker. But "Stanley" was something Boone could work with.

"Cool," he said, trying to engage with the editor. "Did you see the doc Severin put out on Stanley? *Lost Soul*? About when Val Kilmer fucked him over on *Island of Doctor Moreau*—"

"A film is a spell," Copper said, sucking the conversation from the air and crumpling it into a meaningless ball. "You need to find the right order—the order it needs to be in for it to work. Hollywood thinks that 'spell' means 'formula'. Which is why they rarely get it right Out There. Formulas aren't the same as incantations. Formulas lack in art." Slowly, he swiveled in his chair again, fixed his watery blue eyes on Boone. "Ya know?"

Boone didn't. Nor did he want to know. Part of him wanted to seize his old friend's hand, drag him out of the chair, down the stairs, and back into the land of light and the living. Except that the lower floors were no better illuminated. The living were no better animated. Plus, Copper was working. Boone respected that.

So he gave a nod as a response and turned to leave.

"Friday," said Copper's voice behind him. "I'll send the files down with Rusty."

Really, that was all Boone hoped for. He descended the stairs and left Copper to his film, his edit, and the work that lay before him.

                                        CUT TO:

INT. LOBBY

Diana rubs her eyes. She looks past the crowd as they file back into the theater.

Near the mouth of the empty corridor stands The Flickering Man.

He smiles at her and turns to walk into another theater.

                    DIANA
          Hey!

Chasing after him, she pushes through the crowd.

EMPTY THEATER

Like before, the Flickering Man has vanished.

                    DIANA
          Fuck!

She looks at her watch and speaks into the walkie-talkie.

                    DIANA
          Norm,   things   set   for   movie
          two?

There's no response.

                    DIANA
          Norm? Shit!

She rushes back up stairs.

                                        CUT TO:

LOBBY

Sarah pushes away from Dave.

                    SARAH
          I'm not going back in there!

                    DAVE
          Sarah.

                    SARAH
          No, Dave. If we're trapped,
          fine. But I'm not watching
          another sick, horrible movie!

She stomps down the corridor. Dave doesn't
attempt to go after her. He returns to the
theater.

                                        CUT TO:

THEATER

The crowd is restless, the mood distinctly

antagonistic. Dave is shoved aside almost immediately by Keith, pushing through people, roughly. He barks at them to move out of his way.

Chris stands where he was at the rear, chewing on his thumbnail.

He is flanked on both sides by groping couples - the first Punk Boy and Girl on one side, Pike and Krusty on the other.

PROJECTION ROOM

Diana bursts through the door.

> DIANA
> Norm, when I call you, fucking
> answer!

The room is empty.

> DIANA
> Norm!

No answer.

> DIANA
> Fuck!

She stomps over to the projector, trying to teach herself how to run it by reading the diagrams.She speaks into the walkie-talkie.

> DIANA
> Keith, did you see Norm down

there at all?

                    KEITH'S VOICE
          I can't keep track of all of
          your people, Diana.

                    DIANA
          Is that a no?

                    KEITH'S VOICE
          That's a no.

                    DIANA
          Fine. I'm starting.

                    KEITH'S VOICE
          Whatever.

THE PROJECTOR

Everything seems to be laced up. She stabs a
large red button on the lacing column.

The machinery starts up with a whine. The lights
in the theater begin to dim automatically.

She pokes her head through the window to check
the focus. The crowd is cheering, but not
enthusiastically - the sound is too primal.

She hears the door SLAM behind her.

                    DIANA
          Norm, you mother fucker!

She turns around.

Norm stands behind her. He's gouged his eyes out. Blood streams down his face. His hands are smeared.

                    NORM
         I'm not watching this anymore.

Diana is too stunned to scream. Norm lifts up a sharpened slice of metal and drags it across his throat.

Blood spurts across her face.

With a strangled cry, she pushes past him as he drops to the floor.

HALLWAY

Diana flings herself out of the room. She's scrambling from the room nearly on all fours.

She gets around the corner and presses her back against the wall, having an anxiety attack. She presses her hands against her eyes.

Her breathing slows, as she forces herself to calm down.

                    DIANA
         Motherfucker played you. It
         was make-up and you know it!
         You just got punked, Diana.
         Fucker played you and you let
         him!

With a frustrated scream, she opens her eyes.

The Flickering Man is smiling down at her.

                    DIANA
          You! Who the hell are you?

He turns and walks down the stairs.

                    DIANA
          Hey! Don't walk away from me!

She hurries after him, but he's moving fast.

He makes it into the theater before she can get
to him.

THEATER

And of course, as she opens the door, he's
nowhere to be found.

The images on the screen are, if possible, more
gruesome than before.

The crowd is still cheering each onscreen
mutilation, but it sounds like they're hypnotized.

Diana whirls on Chris.

                    DIANA
          Who came in before I did?

                    CHRIS
          I was watching the movie.

                    DIANA
          I saw a man come in here and
          he was flickering.

                    CHRIS

> What do you mean he was
> flickering?

                    DIANA
> I don't know how else to
> describe it. Norm pretended
> to kill himself, and then
> there was this man standing
> there and he was…

She stops and thinks about what she's saying.

                    DIANA
                    (to herself)
> Jesus Christ, Norm killed
> himself.

                    CHRIS
                    (barely listening)
> Just now?

                    DIANA
> Yes, Jesus! Why aren't you
> listening to me? I have to
> find that man!

She storms out. We FOLLOW HER to:

LOBBY

Diana slams the door behind her.

Critic Harry Murdoch lunges at her. She gasps.

Blood pours from his mouth.

He's clutching at a hole in his chest.

                    HARRY
          Stop the movies, Diana!

                    DIANA
          Christ, why are you assholes
          doing this to me?

                    HARRY
          It's the movies! It's true!
          They're going mad!

                    DIANA
          Get off me. And tell your little
          effects artists I'm going to
          kick their asses!

There's a snarl behind her. Dick Allen leaps
onto Harry's back, stabbing at his neck and
shoulders.

Diana screams and stumbles backwards.

                    HARRY
            Help me! Diana! Turn off the
            projector!

Diana picks up the walkie-talkie.

                    DIANA
            Keith! Get out in the lobby,
            now! Keith!

Harry's screams turn wet as Dick severs his
artery.

Keith bursts through the door. He sees Dick

murdering Harry.

Dick looks up and snarls at him.

Keith is all reaction. He pulls a pistol from a hidden holster and shoots Dick in the head.

Diana can't believe what she just saw.

Keith pauses for a moment. Harry looks up at him, gurgling.

Keith shoots Harry too.

Diana gapes at him. Keith shrugs.

KEITH

Couldn't let him suffer.

Like a zombie, he returns to the theater.

Diana moves like a sleepwalker. She gets to her feet and returns to the theater.

THEATER

She surveys the crowd, seeing them for the first time.

There is madness surrounding her.

The crowd is in a frenzy. There are pockets of violence all around her. Fights have broken out. Couples and groups are having rough sex in the corners.

A GIRL is chewing through her wrists and smearing her face with blood.

Diana rushes out and slams the door behind her.

STAIRWAY

Diana is running up the steps towards the projection room.

                    DIANA
          Take the loss, Diana. Screw
          the gimmick. If this gets out,
          you're ruined! Gotta stop the
          show!

She flings open the projection room door. The Flickering Man is standing in front of her, between her and the projector.

                    DIANA
          Get out of my way!

She throws a punch at him.

Her fist passes through him. She stares at him, astonished.

                    DIANA
          You're Luther Borgia.

The Flickering Man smiles and nods.

                    DIANA
          It isn't bullshit. Those
          movies are bringing you back.

Another smile. Another nod.

                    DIANA
          Fuck   your   resurrection.

          You're not ruining my career.

She goes to move through him, but something stops her. She gasps.

Looking down, she sees a knife in her belly.

Chris Balun steps through Borgia, pushing the knife further into her stomach.

                    CHRIS
          The film has to end.

Diana gasps, blood spilling from her mouth.

                    CHRIS
          Completion of the art means
          the completion of the artist.
          The film has to end, Diana.

He pushes the knife up to the hilt. Diana coughs blood. He helps her slide to the floor.

                    CHRIS
          You've done a wonderful thing,
          Diana.

He brushes the hair from her face and holds her as she dies.

As the light leaves her eyes, he stands, nods at Borgia, and moves to the projection window, stepping over Norm's body as he does so.

                              FADE TO BLACK.

CHAPTER FIVE

"In commercial films, the occult is a subject for horror, but in my films, it's more friendly. That's not to say I don't know the difference between a demon and an angel, because I do."

—Kenneth Anger

SCENE ONE:
LUKE AND SETH GO SCREEN HOPPING

Seth spent two days and nights in Cris' bedroom, popping pain pills to help him sleep through her shoots. Filming S&M was noisy, but the Vicodins made that better. Gradually, his strength returned and he managed to move down to an empty room down the hall, courtesy of the as-yet unmet Alyce Reynolds, the Squat's benefactor. The room was squalid, thick with dust undisturbed for an immeasurable amount of time. With him he'd brought only his clothes, now clean of blood thanks to Cris, and the film cans. And also two sets of her many pairs of handcuffs—one to secure the cans together, the second to secure it to a pipe in the back of the bedroom closet. He had a little money on him, for food and new clothes, but leaving the Squat was not yet an option.

Several times he'd snuck a glance out of a covered window and saw shadowy men on the streets below, hanging out beneath the yellow-green glow of the sodium lamp outside of The Arc, hats low over their eyes, gunsels out of central casting. They didn't seem to be watching Orson Hall, but neither did they seem like they weren't. Best to stay inside. He'd give some cash to Bev, Cris' production assistant, send her out for supplies that ease the burden of his seclusion.

As to be expected, cell service was spotty at best. Too much electronic interference spilling from the rest of the rooms. Electromagnetic waves from countless televisions, playing all day and all night. It was no surprise that he couldn't get a signal, couldn't alert his contacts at f.p.s., the underground

"Film Preservation Society," that would take the film cans and rescue them from destruction.

A television had been included with the room, as well as a DVD player, but without anything to play, antenna reception bringing little success beyond faint, local stations, there was nothing with which to pass the time. He'd have to borrow entertainment from Cris, including frames to flix upon, until he could figure out his next move.

The maddening nothingness filling the waking hours, he found himself staring at the ceiling, remembering the past life when he'd lived in the building, sharing a suite with Luke Widdowes and Gantry Garrett, gliding through their classes and the extracurricular films and dreaming about the day when they'd escape the hallowed halls of education and get Out There, revolutionize the movie business.

They didn't.

After graduation, Gantry knocked up his girlfriend, moved in with her and her parents, then settled into the white trash, blue-collar life he'd dreamed of escaping. That was over a decade ago and they hadn't spoken since.

Luke had gone his own way, as he'd always done.

Seth and Luke had virtually grown up together, different

school districts the only things separating them from each other and their shared interests. Together, they were a single unit of brilliance and pretention and fuck anyone who couldn't see that. Outside of their very limited circle were only the mouth-breathers, the banjo players, the uncultured heathens who flocked to the blockbusters and the new releases, feeding the mediocre beast and the tepid output from Out There. Death to the *Daddy Day Cares* and *Shreks* of the world. Spielberg and Lucas should be impaled, *Cannibal Holocaust*-style, for what they did to their classics and the childhoods of all who loved *Star Wars* and *E.T.*

"Kubrick?" Luke exclaimed, arguing with Gantry one afternoon. "Kubrick isn't worthy to lick the leader of *New York, New York!*"

"Just because you didn't get *Eyes Wide Shut*—" Gantry protested, returning volley.

"I got it just fine. Once I got it, I didn't want it!"

That's how Addicts spoke to each other. They could only communicate through references, equating life experiences to famous scenes.

"I walked through Delia Park this morning and the light hit the trees like the opening shot of *Miller's Crossing.*"

Representational language, based on a shortened lifespan of shared second-hand experience. The movies they watched became the lives they lived. The only purpose of living was to collect those movies. Gather them, devour them, store them away for future reference. The only way they could interpret their own world.

Whole days could be lost in the pursuit of this collection—taking bus after bus to visit the most remote home video rental places, or flea markets for second-hand VHS, especially the rare horrors that came in the "Big Boxes", slathered with lurid, bloodsoaked coverart. Flixing hadn't yet been discovered, so the participation in watching the movie was only a one-way conversation. Yet it was the most important one.

Seth remembered:

Emerging from the porno theater where they'd spent the night, the morning sun hit them hard, their pupils slammed shut. Both Luke and Seth scrambled for their sunglasses, frantically searching blindly through coat pockets, the brightness backing them up into the sliver of shadow given off by The Garden Theater's marquee. Sufficiently shielded from the glare of the Great Hot Destroyer, only then were they able to resume their plan.

The pair had been on a screen-hopping jag since Thursday evening, classes blown-off in favor of this latest semi-quarterly cinematic endurance test. It was something they did, as hard-core film addicts, traveling the city and the four borough-states visiting one movie-plex after another, until the day was eaten away. This time around their goal was the so-far unattempted three-day personal film festival.

Having begun with a dusk-'til-dawn video screening of Alexandro Jodorowsky—*Fando y Lis, El Topo, Holy Mountain, Santa Sangre*, and a very rare print of *Tusk*—the decision had been made over rejuvenating cups of coffee early Friday morning.

The Jodorowsky fest landing on a Thursday had been a fluke and by the time credits rolled on *Tusk*, only two other people remained, the rest of the audience succumbing to fatigue and an upcoming work/school day. Filling in the hours between last call and morning rush hour had always been a problem during marathons—returning to the apartment for DVDs was considered cheating the unwritten rules. Once Friday's screening of *The Rocky Horror Picture Show* at the Arc had let out, the only theater left open at 2:30 am had been The Garden Triple-X. After two, the theater's repertoire consisted of a repeat of the previous evening's program which usually meant a mixture of whatever had been on-hand. Now that the world's pornography was moving to the Internet, fewer and fewer patrons were willing to pay-for-"play" in the celluloid XXX-world. But since The Garden was mob-owned, the theater fronted for whatever other illegal activities were to be had after midnight, so management demanded the continuation of the 24-hour cycle established in the '70s.

Despite the ratty condition of the seats—asbestos-laced stuffing erupting from torn cushions, wooden armrests missing or pocked with cigarette burns, plus the tangible aroma of bleach and pine Lysol—if you could ignore the overall seediness of the theater, The Garden wasn't a bad place to spend the night and it certainly wasn't their first time there for refuge. For one thing, after midnight the counter-guy never checked IDs, so Luke's lamentable under-21 status was never an issue. For another, the dealers and pros knew who had come for the movies and who was there for the other reasons. Luke and Seth were the only ones anymore who came in for the movies.

Friday night's program had been a lucky land: back-to-back screenings of *The Opening of Misty Beethoven*, Rinse Dream's *Café Flesh*, and the weird German edit of *Throat Sprockets*. Both of them had seen the movies before, so resisting the urge to sleep through them would be less of a challenge than if the films in rotation were something newer. Even so, it was best to sleep in shifts, with the other keeping an eye out for transient pick-pockets or molesters who would risk a beating to cop a feel on a slumbering stranger. Rats, too, were a problem at The Garden, the largest of them the size of dachshunds, trundling up from the subways in search of nourishment, be it dropped popcorn or dangling fingers.

At 8am the counter-guy, also rodent-like, who by this point was also the projectionist, flipped on the house-lights to sweep out the strung-outs, homeless, and students. When roused, Seth and Luke made it a point to protest less than the bums to ensure they'd be allowed back. Since they had no interest in the downstairs games or behind-the-exit-curtain tug-and-moan sessions, the pair were considered low risk and good business. They bid the ratman counter-guy a good morning as they stumbled into the wall of sunlight beyond the tinted doors.

Over coffee and a high-protein breakfast at Shain's Diner, they loomed over both the newspaper and the subway schedules and planned their assault. To avoid wasting any time, they'd have to take two trains out to the West End to the Belotti 24, one of the big chains but the only one that started its first-run premieres at 10am during the dying summer. First up would be either *Witching and Bitching* or *Hawks of the Seas 2*, depending on which side of 10:30 the trains arrived.

Ordering half the cold-cut menu for supplies, Luke and Seth packed and repacked their provisions. The Blue Eagle store next door provided the sugar-rush staples in movie theater-sized boxes at a discount so there'd be no need to waste time or money at the concessions stands. Water bottles were legal and permitted, so no skullduggery was required save for filling them with caffeinated liquids at free-refill gas stations. Again, prices for theater wares were astronomical and to be avoided on principal. Between the two of them they had two summer passes to the Belotti chains, a free ticket each for the Roman East, and about sixty-two dollars and change. Technically, the Belotti passes were good for one movie only per visit, but the pair were determined on multiple screenings. Most of those tricks required nothing more than stealth and timing. This wasn't their first marathon. Like Mallory and Franklin from *The Guns of Navarone*, they were prepared for their mission.

Traveling away from Bethlehem that early in the morning meant that they had the outbound trains largely to themselves. Both legs of the trip were shared with only a few old yentas and their shopping bags, the occasional sleeping wino and the sparse commuters returning from their third-shift occupations. To pass the time, Luke and Seth played an Addict game:

> Luke: "*The Loved One.*"
> Seth: "*The Gruesome Twosome.*"
> Luke: "*Three O'clock High.*"
> Seth: "*I Quattro dell'apocalisse. Four of the Apocalypse.*"

Luke: *"Five Deadly Venoms."*

Seth: *"The Sixth Sense."*

Luke: "Too easy."

Seth: *"Six Pack.* And you don't get *The Magnificent Seven* or *The Seven Samurai."*

Luke: "Fine, *Return of the Secaucus 7."*

Seth: *"The Private Life of Henry the VIII."*

Luke: "Nice. *The Ninth Gate."*

Seth: *"The 10th Victim."*

Luke: "No, it's *'The Seventh Victim'."*

Seth: "That's the short story. Or the Val Lewton film."

Luke: "No, the one with Mastroianni is—no, sorry, you're right."

Seth: *"The 10th Victim."*

Luke: *"The Eleventh Hour.* 1922," he added.

The game continued until the bus reached its destination. Once they paid for their initial entrance and got inside, they really went to work. First they stashed their backpacks inside the drop ceilings of the men's restroom. In the bags were quick-change outfits for later, to throw off the first shift ushers, usually the most diligent of the day, older and full of coffee courage and conviction. The men's room visit also served as a diversionary tactic, to confuse the ticket takers as to which theater was really their destination. Next came the casual stroll to the first cavernous cubicle and film of the day. They never went anywhere together, one moving to sit next to the other only after the final trailer played and the houselights dropped to darkness.

Once film #1 was complete, they staggered their exit, avoiding eye contact with the cleanup crew who swept away popcorn debris and readied the house for the next showing. Cleanup ushers rarely looked up from their dustpans. It was a mechanical job, performed by mechanical people for a menial wage. They weren't the sentries.

Film #2 was sometimes tricky. Often the second screening

would occur before a shift-change—hence the need for a return to the men's room and disguise retrieval. Off came the black trenchcoats that were the *couture* of their generation. On went something colorful to distract the moderately eagle-eyed from their faces. Another staggered entry into whatever was playing next. On occasion, early afternoon meant a wait for the next screening, which sometimes meant a hideaway inside a toilet stall. Fortunately, they packed books to pass the time. In between screenings, you never spoke to your conspirator.

Film #3 was always the easiest. The older ushers ended their shifts and yielded their stations to younger employees who came equipped with dead eyes and zero interest in the world around them. Nobody asked to see ticket stubs at this stage of the game.

But Film #4 was when the management finally began to catch on. That's when it became necessary to mad dash from the safety of men's room to theater, barrel-rolling and dodging tracer bullets from the better-armed assistant managers. Sometimes the more determined—those up for promotion or reeling from recent discipline—would pursue them into the darkened theater, but even if they were the only patrons, they always managed to evade capture. Some unspoken rule between management and screen-thieves. Once inside the house, you were home free once the movie started.

A fifth screening at any multiplex was considered ill-advised, even for the most experienced theater-jumpers. To pull off a fifth screening usually meant slogging through the air ducts and commando rappelling down to the seats. It was usually best to pack it in after Film #4 and find another movie house to haunt.

During peak seasons, summer and fall, Bethlehem in general and the Welles in particular overflowed with theatrical venues, the multiplexes a buffet for the flicker freaks. Even if they could, there was no need for flixing back then. The adrenaline surge was enough. And that infinite hush between the final trailer and the start of the movie. That singular moment of indescribable, anticipatory bliss. In those days, that was the high they pursued. That moment made junkies of them all. That moment made the first Addicts.

The Digital Revolution did little to change that rush, at least as far as Seth was concerned. He mourned the loss of the home video industry, even when the last Blockbuster shut its doors, as miserable and commercially cynical as that chain was, the shelves still held the potential for wonder. Scrolling through online collections was never as satisfying as an afternoon wasted wandering the stacks of even the chintziest VHS rental store. "Normal" people went antiquing for the same reason. The opportunity to find the Holy Grail nestled between knock-off Hummels and faux-chintz bric-a-brac. Every video store held the potential of discovery: an uncut copy of *The Devils* amidst the sea of *Home Alone II*.

That was all years ago. Born too late, Seth had missed the era of the suit-and-tie crowd, dolled up to see the latest matinee. Even the age of smoking in theaters, where the haze from the crowd's cigars and cigarettes, duplicated the projected image midway through the house, suspending images momentarily before they reached the big, welcoming silvered screen. (An early memory: a pre-show snipe, two lighters discussing how inappropriate it was to "Flick your Bic" in the darkened theater.)

Gone were the opening curtains. Gone were the ushers in smart bellboy uniforms, unlatching a velvet rope as you entered. Gone were the "bank nights", the giveaway crockery, the double-bills, the five cartoons and the newsreels. Gone were the printed tickets hand-torn by glove-clad hands. Replaced by cable and Hulu and the digital download. He'd been born too late for the pageantry. Now even the semblance of "event" was ground to dust beneath the drone of progress. "Time," the announcer announced, "marches on!"

Born too late, Seth had missed the era of The Show.

But he hadn't missed out on the magic. Not entirely.

His personal culture still counted those experiences among his formative years. Now, older, and with metal in his body and a weariness in his bones—from too many complicated screenings, too many fights over copyright, too many liberations of "lost" films from decadent collectors—he rarely, if ever, went theater hopping these days.

Even if he did, there was no fun in doing it alone. Luke Widdowes was long gone, swallowed by the rest of the world outside of Seth's narrow perception. He had no comrades with which to defy authority and commit the "theft" of multiple screenings from a neighborhood googolplex.

One afternoon, bored of his own silence and unable to spectate another of Cris's bondage productions without snickering in spite of himself, he wandered past the wrought-iron railings of the upper floors and ventured lower, to where "The Kids" hung out between, or instead of, going to class. He'd peek in on the common room and spend a moment in the doorway, overcome with sudden sadness. Because he couldn't identify the movie playing on the central TV and that was an appalling notion. Was he so out of touch now?

Not that it mattered. Whatever played on the main TV failed to cast its spell. Of the half-dozen or so Kids lounging about on garbage-night rescued couches, split and bleeding beanbag chairs, not a one watched the movie unspooling before them. Instead, the personal devices, the little hand-held leeches cast in metal and plastic and magic touch-screen technology, held them in thrall. The sound was a din, a cacophony of electronica masquerading as score, drowning out whatever dialogue the unidentifiable actors were spewing. Instead, all eyes were turned downward, towards the screens each held in their laps. Maybe they were all flixing to their own personal groove as well, but the whole visual simply saddened him.

Modern, larval-stage Addicts had no use for the physical media. The world was at their disposal for download onto screens no wider than your palm. The instant gratification generation.

The last thing they'd murdered was that hush between trailer and feature. That hush was replaced by a spinning wheel and a notice of "buffering". The sensuality of that moment—the reverence, somewhere between religion and orgasm—was gone forever. Digital projection took away the subliminal chatter of projector gates and platter systems, even eliminated the comforting flicker of 24-frames-per-second flashing across your eyes, simulating movement. 1s and 0s duplicated real movement and the fantasy world was so much smoother now. Cleaner. The electro-chemical sorcery surgically-excised from the movie-going experience.

Disgust rising, Seth turned away from the sorry scene and nearly ran into a couple passing behind him. Girl and a boy—not as young as "The Kids" in the common room, but still younger than him, therefore "Kids" in his mind. "Sorry," he mumbled.

The girl looked at him with big dark eyes shrouded by long hair, studying his face. She frowned slightly, then nodded. "Oh, you're the guy staying with Leni up on five."

Seth nodded in reply. "Yeah. Well, I was. She found me a vacant room down the hall."

"Oh," the girl said. "Right."

There was an awkward pause, made worse by pain creeping from his side. The meds were wearing off and he could feel the wound weeping against the bandage. He'd have to change the dressing soon and he wasn't exactly in the mood for a chat with strangers who somehow knew his business. Then it hit him. "You're Alyce, right? Ms. Reynolds?"

Her reply was a thin smile that failed to mask her suspicion.

"Well," he said, before realizing he didn't really have anything to say. So he went for bland nicety. "Thanks very much for giving me refuge, as it were. I used room here when I was a student. Jesus, almost twenty years ago…"

Weak charm. It failed to disarm her. Uncomfortable under

her scrutiny, Seth glanced over at the boy—younger man—next to her, eyes fixed with a far-away stare, face criss-crossed with perf tracks. The guy was a flicker freak, fresh off a flix bender judging by the freshness of the wound pattern. From the look in his eye, he was flixing still.

Seth's side was starting to throb, even as he applied pressure—surreptitiously, he hoped—with his right hand. Suddenly, he realized etiquette would require an offering. Wincing as he took his hand away, he tried to cover with a smile as he offered it to Alyce. "Seth," he said. The girl didn't take it, but the boy seized it with a drunkard's grip. "Boone," the boy said.

Recognition. "Oh yeah. You're trying to run down all the Borgia films, right?"

"Not trying," Boone said, eyes refusing to fix on a spot. "Got 'em all. Waiting for the last two to be transferred."

Ice-cold needles shot through Seth's veins. The word 'fuck' sprang to mind.

"Can't wait to see them all," the boy continued. "We're going to screen them in the basement this weekend, all goes as planned. You should come."

Alyce's sharp look went unnoticed by Boone, but not by Seth, who held his tight smile but only barely. "I, uh… seen 'em," he mumbled, and attempted to turn away. The boy caught his arm.

"Bullshit," he said. Then, "Really?"

"Yeah. Back in '08." He tried again to escape, but Boone held fast, probably unaware he now held a hostage.

"No shit? Did you know Chris Balun?"

A fist-sized lump formed in Seth's throat, searing where the ice-water veins weren't freezing. "Yeah," he said. "Yeah, I did. Back when he ran *Movie Outlaw*."

"I used to write for them! First under Chris, then Ed Salinger—"

"Good mag. Miss it. Well, it was nice—"

"Seriously, man, you've got to come. I've never met anyone who'd seen them all the way through. So I guess it's bullshit that they make everyone go crazy."

Screams. Blood. Pain. Fire. Screamingscreamingscreaming.

"Sure," Seth answered. "Just hype because they're rare. Knock offs of Kenneth Anger you want my opinion. Not even worth showing."

"Still," Boone said. "Unseen since '08. It's going to be pretty awesome. Seriously, I'd love if you did a Q&A. Or a quick intro."

"Love to. Can't." Pulling his arm free, he lifted his borrowed *Re-Animator* t-shirt and showed off the now-bloody bandage. "Nursing a wound. Should really get back to bed. Ms. Reynolds, thanks again." To Boone, he said, "Good luck with the screening. Don't be too disappointed."

"In the films?"

"If you don't go berserk." He flashed another tight smile and hurried away, feeling Alyce's gaze on the back of his neck as he beat a retreat.

There are two ways to watch The Divine Heresy, Seth thought. *One after the other, like any other marathon… or the way Borgia intended.* Only three people knew about "the right way", and two of them were dead. He wasn't about to shed any light on the matter. Obviously, neither was Chris. That left only Luther Borgia. And he couldn't tell anyone.

Unless the movies were played "the right way".

Then Luther could have his say about all sorts of things.

SCENE TWO:

CALM

Boone rode a flix high from four frames of *Some Like It Hot*. Carcosa was making new release prints and plenty of rejected sections found their way into the garbage bins along dozens of other prints deemed "unacceptable" by the QC crew. Overflowing barrels of 35mm cast-off celluloid. It was like a buffet or a farmer's market for the flicker freak. When no one was around, Boone stuffed his pockets with frames. A few more weeks and he could be set for life.

Orson Hall had two common rooms: one for The Kids on the ground floor and one on five especially for The Addicts. With the powdery taste of Marilyn Monroe in his mind, Boone stumbled into The Addicts' room and found Kearns half-conscious on the couch, John Woo's *Heroes Shed No Tears* on the flatscreen playing to an audience of none. Or one-half at the most. Perf tracks criss-crossed Kearns' bare chest, mostly scabbed-over, which meant he was about to start yet another bender.

Slumping down next to him, Boone pried a strip of frames from Kearns' open hand, held them to the light. A strip of darkness, no way to tell what the screenwriter was on without a taste. Tearing off the top frame, Boone popped the film into his mouth, then immediately spit it out. "Fuck! Ugh! What the hell is this?"

"*House on the Edge of the Park*," Kearns answered, his voice coming from very far away. "Found it in Copper's attic."

"Tastes like death. What were you doing up there, anyway?"

"Went to look for him. Had a question. Don't ask me what. Don't remember. Wasn't there anyway. Found that in his trim bin."

That felt like a violation, a line crossed. Addicts respected each other's spaces. That attic had been Copper's for longer than any of them had been around. "No Rusty?" he asked.

"Wasn't looking for Rusty," Kearns said. Never once did he look in Boone's direction.

A question rose to Boone's mind, chasing away his admonition. "Hey, why did you make Chris the villain in your Borgia script?"

"Fit the story," Kearns said.

"Yeah, but he was a good guy."

"Real good guy."

"So?"

"So that's what *they* wanted me to do. That was one of their notes. I fought them. Sure." He waved a hand in the air, gesturing at the futility, showing off the manacle scar on his wrist. "But that's what Fucking Lee Benway wanted. So Chris went under the bus."

"Shitty thing to do to him."

"Changed his name in, like, the sixth draft. To 'Chris Lucas'," he smiled at the name. The joke was lost on Boone. Then Kearns shrugged. "Not like the movie ever got made. So fucking what?"

Resting his head back, Boone tried to find the spot on the ceiling that held Kearns' attention. But while Kearns was flixing on darkness and brutality, Boone was still on the heady high of Sugar Kane, Josephine, and Daphne.

"Not like Chris was the hero in real life, anyway."

It took some effort, but Boone turned his head to look at his friend. Or was it now pronounced "friend"? "What do you mean?" He was startled to find Kearns staring back.

"He let those people die. The people in the audience. Locked them in, set the place on fire."

"Fuck you."

"Completely true. In the FBI file and everything."

Still incredulous: "So why didn't he go down for murder?"

Kearns shrugged. "Redacted," he said. "But it happened.

Those movies fucked 'em all up and he did what he had to do. Feds must've understood that."

"Bullshit."

"Whatever. You weren't there."

"Neither were you."

"You got me there, Tom." Kearns let out a sigh. Something rattled inside his chest with it. Boone turned back to the ceiling. They sat there, in silence, for a long time.

                                        CUT TO:

THEATER

We CRANE DOWN from Chris' face as he smiles and watches both the movie and the show in the crowd. The madness is spreading.

Edward, the bass player, and Phoebe are in the back. Edward is hypnotized by the film; Phoebe is laughing at a joke she just told, drunk, and not watching the film. She pulls her flask out of her purse and a joint falls onto the floor. She picks it up.

                    PHOEBE
          Awesome! I forgot I had this!

She holds it up to Edward. He looks at it for a moment, then looks back at the screen.

                    PHOEBE
          Come on. Let's get out of
          here. This crowd's getting
          rough. I hate crowds.

She pulls on his lapels. He resists for a second,

then follows her.

CORRIDOR

She leads him down the hall, unsteady on her feet.

QUICK CUTS: EXIT DOORS

Sarah is pulling on various sets of locked doors, looking for a way out. They're all locked.

She gives a little scream of frustration, then leans against one of them, defeated.

PARTY ROOM

We see a young woman, NICOLE, who we recognize as the girl from the opening, put down her drink and stagger dazed out of the party room. The camera moves past her to:

KURT AND THOM

Who are near the back of the room, looking miserable.

Kurt is glaring into his empty beer bottle. His grumpy face is turning to rage and his face reddens.

Thom smiles at a dazed looking Donna who just stares at him.

It makes him uncomfortable.

He turns to Kurt, opens his mouth to say something.

                    KURT

                You motherfucker!

Without warning, Kurt smashes the bottle against
Thom's face.

He's on top of Thom, stabbing him in the face
and throat with the shattered glass remains.

                        KURT
            I could have been somebody!
            I should be famous right now!
            It's your fault! It's your
            fault.

Thom is flailing beneath Kurt, drowning in his
own blood.

Tony is over in a shot, dragging Kurt away.

DONNA AND SHAUN

look over at Thom as he gurgles. They walk

over to him, like moths to a flame.

Donna reaches down, dabbing her fingers into the
wounds. She rubs the blood across her face.

SUPPLY CLOSET

The door is cracking as it is being pummeled
from the inside. A hole explodes from the center
of it, propelled by an ax head.

Dirk reaches through the hole and opens the
door.

He moves, jerkily, through the door and back
into the hallway, swinging the ax wide as he

does.

MEN'S ROOM

The door swings open. Phoebe pushes a compliant Edward into the restroom. She's laughing drunkenly. She takes a swig from her flask, forces the flask to Edward's lips. He swallows obligingly and she kisses him hard.

> PHOEBE
> You should fly me out to the set the next time you shoot. I'll give you full coverage. You won't be sorry. I'll totally do you right.

Edward stares at her, smiling a strange smile.

She returns it.

Edward punches her hard in the face twice, sending her sprawling through a stall door. He's on her before she can protest, punching her again.

His hands close around her throat, strangling her. She struggles against his grasp.

Before she loses consciousness, she knees him very hard in the groin.

Edward lets go, staggers back. Phoebe is up, gagging and gasping for air.

> PHOEBE
> You son of a bitch!

With a strangled cry, she kicks him in the face. He flips onto his back, spitting teeth.

Phoebe is in a primal rage. She stomps down on his face and skull with her stiletto heels, puncturing his cheeks, his eyes and throat. With another stomp, she leaves the shoe behind in his chest.

She lets out a shriek and staggers back against the sink, crying and hurt.

She inspects her face - swollen and bleeding. This lets loose a new series of tears.

PHOEBE
Why? Jesus Christ!

She sees the shoe imbedded in his chest. She's making near incoherent noises now.

She staggers through the door.

CORRIDOR

She limps towards the theater.

Before she can reach the theater door -

Dirk steps out of the shadows and buries the ax in her back.

Phoebe's scream trails off into a gurgling gasp as she pitches forward through the door.

THEATER

Phoebe lands face-first on the floor. Nobody notices as Dirk walks in after her, and pries the ax from her back.

A SCREAM rips through the theater. This gets people's attention. The CROWD turns.

Nicole is in the back, staring at Phoebe's body, horrified.

DIRK

turns to look at her, circling around to get in front of her.

Soon, he's between her and the angry-looking crowd. Their eyes are glazed, bloody.

Nicole turns and runs screaming from the theater.

The crowd follows.

LOBBY

We see a repeat of the slow-mo run as Nicole flees the angry crowd.

She reaches the door, but, of course, it's chained.

THE CROWD

reaches her and the CAMERA PULLS AWAY as they reach her, weapons raised.

As her scream is drowned out, we see Sarah staring horrified as the crowd brutalizes Nicole.

She backs away, pressing herself against the wall, trying to stay out of sight of the angry crowd.

CUT TO:

COPPER SLIPS BETWEEN
THE FRAMES

With the rest of his crew down in the common room, passing around bowls of celluloid frames and flixing to whatever was on the movie channels, Copper was in the attic bleeding onto his art. Rewinding the 16mm film, cranking with the left hand, keeping tension on the feed reel with his right, the edges of the celluloid, razor sharp where it wasn't jagged from ancient layers of splicing tape, reopened the old wounds in his fingertips. But it didn't matter. He was basically flensing away his fingerprints, but again, it didn't matter. This was his workprint; he'd bled over it for years. Done with it now, he was one with it now.

Practically-speaking, it was a pyrrhic victory. While he'd started the project on film, he'd had to finish on digital video, as "film", the medium, slowly, maddeningly went extinct. It had taken years, but the business had killed it. The electro-chemical process was dead. Long live creation and fabrication in binary code. Where once was Cinema is now Digital. But he still worshipped the old gods. He replaced all the cuts, matched the edge numbers to the corresponding negative, and was preparing to store it all in a cool, dry place.

All filmmakers, in the end, are stored in a cool, dry place. (In a perfect world, they only die at sundown, when the light is clean and yellow. What the Cinematographers call "Golden Hour.")

Last night, away from Mya with barely a call, while his crew stayed down in the common room and passed around bowls of film frames, sucking on them and flixing to whatever was on one of the streaming channels, Copper had finished his movie. It had taken eleven years and three different formats— Super-8mm blown up to 16mm, 16mm transferred to digital— and finally, last night, using Final Cut Pro 7.5, he clicked "Save" and let the backup hard drives do their work. He had reached

Picture Lock. He had finished all the post-sound. The movie, called *Spires* at the start, now *The Eyes' Cathedral*, was finished. But there was still work to be done. The shadows inside his head told him that time was running out.

Conceived as *Spires,* the first cut was ten minutes long and had been his senior thesis film. College-aged Copper had taken all the pain and misery from His Life Thus Far and captured it with a Bolex. He incorporated footage his teenaged-self had shot on an old Eumig Vienette Super-8 camera his Grandfather had bought in Austria. (He still had it, lovingly packed away in one of the corners of the studio. It looked like a *Star Trek* phaser and filming with it felt like he was literally shooting his troubles at point-blank range.) The blow-up to 16mm had cost a small fortune and the lab had forgotten to ink in edge numbers so he'd had to conform the negative shot-by-shot by eye. He made two mistakes, resulting in a flash frame in the third minute, and a repeated shot in the sixth, rendering the next two shots out of sync.

Because of those two mistakes, there had been eleven walk-outs during the Senior Screening. Prior to *Spires,* Senior Screenings for years and years held by the academy as the graduation had never had a single walk-out. Not one. Eleven was an impressive number. He was told that one of the older women, after rushing for the door, had gotten physically ill in the ladies room. Unlikely, but he liked to think it happened and after a while the story became legend. When Mark Bowman dramatized the scene in his little opening to the limited VHS release of *Spires,* the story became truth. Images he'd created out of his own pain became shared pain with eleven viewers. Eleven viewers understood him. What it was like when your brain grows teeth and gnaws at the inside of your skull.

Eleven became his magic number. *Spires* had been the first *real* movie in his filmography. Expanding it into *Cathedral* made it number eleven. In between, there had been violence. There had been bleakness. There had been a void into which he poured all of his pain. His movies became infamous for their violence but mostly for their despair. "There is no happiness or hope in a Copper Film," wrote Seth Salem for *Movie Outlaw*, reviewing number six, *Black Rainbow*. "They also don't *end*. Once his movie has had its way and is done with you, the credits roll and it kicks you bloody into the gutter. You aren't a viewer; you're its whore."

That quote followed him everywhere for the rest of his career.

It was the sound that his brain shadows made.

*****

"Oh, Christ!" Boone said as the videotape ended. "Why did you make me watch that?"

Copper smiled serenely. They'd just finished with a Hungarian cannibal film, which included real documentary footage of an infamous criminal extolling the virtue of a human-based diet. The movie, *Kibaszott Cannibals Kibaszott hullák,* was never released in the United States. In fact, by the time Copper had found a pirate copy, it had already been banned in six countries.

"Because it's real, man," Copper explained.

"You said it was a mockumentary."

"Well, it is and it isn't. See, the director, Zoltán Yildiz, had been inspired by the case of Bernd Brandes, who requested his friend to eat him. Now that guy, Armin Meiwes, was a German who's now serving life in prison." Copper stabbed the rewind button on the remote. The VCR whirred, time-code spinning backwards. He stopped it without looking and stabbed Play then Pause. The image froze exactly where he'd wanted it to: on the image of the film's central unnamed cannibal criminal, looking quite normal. Even serene. "*That* guy has no name. He was found in Hungary with no identification, only the clothes on his back. And what he's talking about is having been raised by a dude who was not his father, who killed people and fed them to him over like thirty years."

"I got that," Boone said. "That stuff was at least subtitled. What about the movie that's actually around it? Was that documentary?

Was it snuff?"

"It was re-creation. Yildiz loved both stories so much that he combined them and added the doc footage later. That stuff you see at the end—"

"Yeah, just tell me those were special effects, okay? Don't try to sell me some Buttgereit shit that it was a real morgue corpse."

"Who knows?" Copper's red-and-grey beard couldn't conceal his smile. "Yildiz said in an interview that they were eating cold pork roast."

"Okay, I ask again: *Why* do you make me watch these things? Why do you make me watch *Cannibal Ferrox* and *Sprski Film* and *In a Glass Cage* or *The Atrocity Circle*? I mean, I love razor-edge horror but seriously, Cop'? Why do you do these things to me?"

It made Copper laugh. "Boone, man, you have to get between the frames and see what's behind them. See what inspired the artist and see what was on his mind. These aren't films-by-committee, dude. They were made for reasons."

"Well, *Sprski Film* was a total con. It wasn't political. 'Newborn porn'? Gimme a fu—"

"That's beside the point. Look, you watched *Kibaszott* and all the others and they got a reaction out of you, didn't they?"

"This one almost got my lunch out of me." Boone was getting defensive. "And I'm no toddler with this stuff."

And laughter roared out of Copper. "I never said you were! But when's the last time you actually felt something after a movie? When it wasn't being forced on you like Spielberg's bouncing emotion ball?"

That got a grudging grunt of agreement. But Boone

wasn't about to say that Copper was right. "Okay, fine. What was behind the frames on that one?"

Another smile, another shrug. "That there's evil in the world. That there's poison inside us all," he said. "And if you can get it all out on film, you've captured it."

*****

The Eye's Cathedral, into which he'd poured his history, three generations of alcoholism and abuse and helplessness and hatred, was complete. While the Kids stayed downstairs flixing, his crew had lost interest in making their own movies, Mya unsatisfied with his infrequent texts, his aversion to her question, "When are you coming home?", Copper remained focused and finished his work. Now he needed to find his own way through the frames. Help from the gods of film would be needed to outrun the shadows, gouging the insides of his skull, telling him to hurt the ones he loved.

When he'd met Mya, he was sure that she would silence the shadows for good. With her kindness. With her laughter. And nothing devious, hateful, deceptive behind it. For the first time in his life, a woman he loved told him, "I love you," and he was able to believe it.

Until recently, when the claws and shrieks of the shadows, all in His voice, started to drown her out.

So he had to finish *Cathedral*, reshape the inaugural *Spires*, and complete his work. It would be more difficult in absence of Mya's warm smile, but for most of his life, he'd worked in the cold anyway.

Rusty asked Boone, "You've seen *Spires*, right? The original cut?"

And Boone replied, "Copper's short? Of course."

"Well you know the scars on the main character's back in the beginning? Those are actually Copper's."

"I just thought it was good make-up."

"No," Rusty said. "Andy's dad used to beat the shit out of him. Almost killed his mom."

"Fuck," Boone said. "So what happened?"

"I don't know. Copper doesn't really talk about it. All I know is, he was around until Copper was fourteen and then he just went away."

"What does that mean?"

"Copper put a stop to it. The old guy in the beginning of the film—"

"During the barbecue scene?"

"Yeah. That's Copper's dad. And it's the only footage he ever took of the old man. Might be the last footage ever taken of him."

"You're overselling it," Boone said. "I get it. Copper's a dark guy."

Rusty didn't respond and eventually Boone's attention was drawn elsewhere. Among the Kids, Rusty was different. He didn't already know everything, had few pre-conceived notions about 'art' or 'Art', was open to everything. Because of Copper.

When Rusty was much younger than the Kid he was now, when he was something his mother wanted him to be, Copper was there for him, gave him a map to follow rather than wandering aimless and angry. Every time Copper spoke to him, the message was, "Shut up, you're *not* worthless."

With Copper's help, Rusty found the means to *create*. He wasn't one of the Kids who sat around flixing, sucking frames of film and drifting in and out of past narratives. Thanks to Copper, Rusty had found the inner peace that came from externalizing the darkness, entombing it on film and tape and hard drive. Because of Copper, Rusty had a man to look up to.

And he was certain—absolutely certain—that Copper was unaware of just how deeply he'd affected this Kid.

*****

"I'll never hurt you," Mya said to Copper in the dark.

"I know," he said.

"But do you believe me?"

And Copper thought about the past relationships he'd held but couldn't hold *onto*. Connections held with women and other people. He'd grown up in a world absent of trust, absent of health, absent, almost, of warmth entirely. When things inevitably went south, with girlfriends, fiancees, brothers… No matter what the circumstances, he always blamed himself. And the shadows. They were his inheritence. The last remaining vestiges of the first man he was supposed to love. The man who's pounded his love's absence into Copper's skull nearly every day since he was born. Still, even now that he was long gone.

Other people had followed in that man's footsteps since Copper's teenaged years. These other people, women, lovers, replaced and redoubled the pain already dished out. Yet Mya…

"But do you believe me?" she repeated.

Much to his surprise, he told the truth: "Yes."

*****

There were nights, however, when the shadows wouldn't stop their tearing, their cursing and plotting. Some nights, they'd fill his head with images of those he loved (without qualification), shredded skin and broken bones. The shadows projected blood onto his hands.

Copper had raised his hand to only one person in his life. Then never again. No matter what the shadows told, of deceit and betrayal and lies.

Echoing louder now, their screams of rage bouncing off the inside of his skull, skirting the claw marks in bone, making a picket-fence noise of blood red, they were getting much harder to ignore.

*****

Before he could export the final movie, in synch, color corrected, with sound, score and credits, Copper had a few things to do. Back in the day, before digital took over completely, with all the new gods that came with the format, you thanked and celebrated the gods of the old format, the Gods who lived in the sprocket holes, the Gods that lived in the camera gate.

Nevermind the crucified god of his father or the dude who flew away on his winged horse. Nobody killed in the names of the Film Gods. These were the gods of creation, not destruction.

Before he'd even considered a return to his persistence of vision religion, he was giving them thanks. Before laying in each shot, he trimmed away the film leading up to the *clack* of the clapper, marking the start, and thus paid tribute to both Kem-Daly and Audisseus, bringing sound and image together in a single frame. Each referral to his shot log was a silent prayer to Vastane the Adversary, assistant to all producers. Any time he begged for a few bucks to buy another reel or pay down his lab bill, Ifirs, the red-eyed god of Executive Producers, looked down on him and smiled.

These were old names, and yet still young. Filmmaking as a medium was still in its infancy, yet it was dying, replaced by new technologies and new deities guiding the minds of men.

The attic, the studio, had only the illumination of the computer screen to beat back the darkness. Sitting down at his desk, he halved the light, and within the external shadows were the Gods of Film and Filmmaking, enraging the shrieking behind his eyes. Shards of cold light knifed the darkness, a pattern formed by room's geometry, his own body, and lit as if by Latham-ascdop himself, the Master of Light and Dark. Enveloping them all, his tendrils and vast wings formed of broken shadow, Cinemagog, god of all film gods, watched him.

Copper felt a stab of guilt, using the New Technology to

honor the old, but they understood. Formats change but art will remain. Film, video, 24 or 29 frames-per-second, it's all a way to capture time. The more you put into a production, the more you can extract from yourself. Leave it behind. That was one of the secrets. It's a reason camera stock is called *negative*.

The computer cursor hovered over the "Export" icon, turning from arrow to pointing finger, as if one of the gods was giving instruction. *The Eye's Cathedral* was his first film and his last. Thinking that way risked the melodramatic but it was still true. He'd put so much of himself into it. Maybe all of himself. He knew what was behind the frames.

Copper clicked the button and the computer did the rest. In an hour, maybe two (or four or six, the computer's processor was being argumentative), Copper's work would be done.

*****

When Copper hadn't come down from his studio for a couple of days, only Rusty and Boone found it unusual. The Kids were unaware of everyone's comings and goings, particularly those of the older Apostles living on the upper floors.

But then Mya called and said that Copper hadn't been home either, had anyone seen him? Rusty mounted the steps. Boone was right behind him.

In the midst of editing, every Apostle lost some days. It's what happened. You go without sleep, without food, and you don't even miss it. You're lost in the rhythm of the edit. When you carved film, the abyss went even deeper. It was your whole body working with the medium, not just the index finger pointing and clicking.

The studio was empty, except for dust mites dancing in a sunbeam streaming from the one smudgy window. Copper's chair was empty. The computer screen was asleep. Rusty nudged the mouse and woke it up. A little window hovered over the program's editing display. "Export Complete."

*****

Days later, still no Copper. After she'd watched, alone through a waterfall of grief, the final cut of *Cathedral,* Mya's terror morphed into an understanding sadness. Before she packed up his things, emptying the studio, she left a note for Rusty on the computer screen and he shared it with Boone: "Watch Closely".

When they did, taking in the familiar footage from *Spires* and marveling at the new footage built around it, the movie was disturbing. As expected. The main actor, long moved away, changed into Copper twenty minutes in. Necessity, naturally. He hadn't wanted to audition a replacement. They understood. They'd worked on the movie too over the years. But there'd been no script, no map they'd ever seen. Just some storyboards and what Copper set up on the day.

They watched it twice together and it was all Copper. A bleak and violent story with no happy ending, no conclusion to speak of. Just a cliff-drop into the darkness as the main character, now Copper, sought to kill the God of his father. The God who was his father. Something that, in the end, changed nothing.

Neither Kid nor Apostle back in their tears. They missed this good man, even though he was there—right there—on the screen in front of them. On the screen, instead of by their sides.

*****

Boone had been halfway out the front door, on the way to a double-feature, when Rusty called him up. Back in the studio, Rusty, his eyes still wet and swollen, ran the footage again in fast-forward, his eyes searching the images. "Here," he said. "You get this ten or eleven times."

"What?" Boone asked, leaning in, weakened by the emptiness of the studio. "Something subliminal? Flash frame?"

Rusty shook his head and paused the movie. With the mouse he advanced the image frame by frame. "There."

On the screen was Copper. Not the main character but Copper as they'd seen him just last week. Looking over his shoulder directly into the lens. Smiling. Copper's character never smiled in the film. The smile seemed to be just for them.

"So it is a flash frame." Boone said. "Ten of them?"

"It's not a flash frame, it's a half-frame roll." Rusty said. "The rest of the movie is in twenty-four f.p.s., but these are little glitches, something you'd get at 29 fps. Video speed."

Boone nodded. Of course he knew, but he wasn't sure he understood. "How did he export it? What format?"

"Doesn't matter. It's either a glitch or he did it intentionally. It's like he's behind the movie."

"Are you telling me—?"

"I'm not telling you anything. But there it is."

*****

Rusty and Mya took *The Eye's Cathedral* on the festival circuit. It always played as a tribute to Copper. Rusty said that each screening was a beacon, in the hope of bringing Copper back home. But Mya knew differently. She knew that Copper was both in the movie and *in* the movie. For all its bleak story, its never-ending ending, for eleven undetectable fractions of a second, Copper lived there, surrounded by all of his pain but frozen away from him. Unable to touch him ever again.

Smiling. Just for her. Just for his friends. Behind the frames.

SCENE THREE:
POST COPPER / COPPER IN POST

Copper had vanished.

They found his studio empty, his masterpiece rendered and saved on his Mac. There was no trace to be found of their old college buddy. Just a week ago, he and Boone and Rusty were sitting in the common room, discussing "extreme" movies and, as Copper liked to say, how it was important to see "between the frames" for the true meaning of a film.

Then, the night of the power surge that sent everyone in Orson into a scrambling panic, unplugging their DVD players and computers from the sparking outlets, Copper vanished into the darkness.

After Copper's disappearance—confirmed by Rusty and Boone, who emerged from the loft with haunted looks that were at the same time oddly serene—the Addicts had raided his studio. To fund his feature, Copper had worked as a projectionist at The Arc. While there, he'd cannibalized the booth, appropriating every trailer and snipe and ad left behind by others before him. Like every projectionist, he skimmed frames from the prints he built and tore down. Like every projectionist, his hands were a road map of scars left behind by the film edges traveling at high rate between his fingers, fingerprints sanded away by the speeding sprocket holes.

When their friend had gone, slipping between the frames of his film in service to his dark gods, Kearns claimed a dozen boxes of snipes. With them, he could flix forever. He could flix his life away. The loud and colorful chaos of *Cool World* could amp up his blood and leave him twisted in the oblivion of his mind, only to be rescued by the high impact gunfire from *The Killer*. Copper had been quite the collector.

What was left unscavenged fell to Rusty's possession. It seemed only fair that whatever dregs and spoils unwanted went to the editor's favorite student, almost a son. Over the course of a day and without help, Rusty moved his belongings from his room on three to Copper's previous dwelling. Again, it seemed right and nobody contested the space.

What nagged at Boone the most was not Copper's transcendence—he and Rusty found the old editor living between the frames of his masterpiece, an ascension courtesy of the man's Dark Gods, they presumed (and did not question)—but the whereabouts of the last two Borgia films. Panic shot through him when Copper went away. What would he tell Shel the Agent? That the last pieces of the puzzle were gone? Possibly snatched away by some overeager Addict who wouldn't know what he had until he slid a length of frames down his throat? The idea was appalling.

For hours, Boone grilled everyone he knew who'd pillaged Copper's space. "Did you see film cans in a black bag?" *No, no* and *no*, they all answered. But Josh wouldn't meet his eye, ducked the question twice. He became convinced that this was the particular Addict he was looking for. Determined to get an answer, he tracked the Addict up and down the hallways until he was able to corner him outside the common room on five. In his building rage, he'd backed Josh against the railing.

"You're the only one left, man," he said to Josh. "You knew I took the films to Copper. Fuck are they?"

"No idea," came the resentful answer.

Not good enough. "I went through hell to get those."

"Why are you asking me?"

Boone dropped his voice down low, transforming it into Thug #2 from every prison film: "I find out you took them, I will rain hell upon you!"

"Fuck you, dude!"

Boone lashed out, grabbed double-handfuls of Josh's t-shirt, yanked him up and then back. Cursing, he advanced until Josh's upper half dangled over the iron railing. "What the fuck—get off me!"

"Won't need the movies to make me kill, you understand?

I'll do it on my own! You fucking *dare* cheat me?"

Suddenly there were arms around him, dragging him back, helping Josh onto the floor even while they struggled to hold him. Kearns and Alyce helped put space between the two men. Josh, red-faced, angry, offended, shouted profanity at the indignity. Boone returned the volley of insults. Their voices echoed through the iron grillwork emptiness above and below.

Half-carried, half-dragged, Boone found himself back in the common room, shoved onto the couch while Josh retreated. He babbled incoherently in his rage as Alyce tried to soothe him. "It's okay," she told him. "They'll turn up." There was no anger in her voice. No umbrage. As if she understood perfectly all of his concerns, all of his panic. Her hands were cool against his flushed, sweaty face. The softness of her voice dampened the angry barking coming from Kearns, who was calling him an asshole, an idiot, someone who'd lost his mind in the face of two lost movies that amounted to nothing. He mocked Boone's obsession. Yet none of it had any impact. Not while Alyce whispered to him, calmed him. Nothing could hurt him further.

After Kearns stomped off, Boone gave himself time to breathe while Alyce rocked him. If the films were gone, what then? *Archangel* he could replace with Copper's VHS, but not *Golgotha*. Not *Osculum*. The screening would be incomplete. Without the set, the screening would be nothing. All of it for nothing. Nothing.

The concept refused to take root in his mind. "Lost?" They'd *been* lost. Forgotten. Forbidden. Until he came along. Until, with Shel's help, they'd at long last been recovered. And then stolen again. It wasn't fair. It wasn't right. He'd take down the building brick-by-brick to find them again. If he had to kill Josh to find them, so be it—

"Hey, Tom?" said a halting voice, one thick with both caution and disgust. He looked up and saw Rusty in the doorway, a black plastic bag in his hand. The younger man—older than "The Kids" but so much younger than the Addicts—came no closer. From the doorway he tossed the bag into Boone's lap. The contents of the bag rattled, muffled sounds of plastic on metal. Boone didn't have to open the bag to know that his panic could be stifled now. Perhaps forever.

"He transferred them to a flash drive," Rusty said. "There are three files, including a master."

That was the last thing Rusty said before he turned away. It was the last thing Rusty would ever say to Boone. Quietly, the younger man advanced up the steps to Copper's loft and closed the door behind him.

The anger leeching from him as he held the bag in his hands, Boone sat back against Alyce, a whole body sigh escaped his chest and his muscles relaxed at once. "Saturday," he whispered.

Silently, Alyce nodded, forced a tight smile for nobody's benefit. "I'll spread the word," she said.

CUT TO:

CORRIDOR

Sarah creeps along the wall, unable to believe what she's just seen.

As she backs away, a shape comes out of the shadows.

A hand closes over her shoulder.

Sarah screams, then stifles it with her hand as she sees Diana, bleeding bad.

DIANA

> Get away from them. Hide, quick!

Sarah helps her into an empty theater.

LOBBY

A GUNSHOT echoes.

Another Security Guard, TONY, is trying to break up the mob.

He's backed by a group of horrified looking PARTY-ROOMERS.

His shirt is still bloody from dragging KURT away.

                    TONY
          What the fuck is going on
          here?

The Crowd turns to stare him down. Tony doesn't like the looks of this.

                    TONY
          Keith? Keith, I need back up.

                    KEITH
          Right here, buddy.

Keith steps around the corner and shoots Tony in the head.

The Party-Roomers scream.

The Crowd turns on them.

There are more of the murderous crowd than there are Party-Roomers. Things get messy quick.

PARTY ROOM

Kurt is on the floor, hands cuffed behind him.

He's mumbling to himself. He gets to his knees and starts banging his head against the wall.

>   KURT
> I wrote "Aurora Borealis"!
> I wrote "Aurora Borealis"!

Soon, the wall beneath his head is splattered with blood.

EMPTY THEATER

Diana doesn't have much longer to go.

>   DIANA
>   They were right. The movies
>   are cursed. Thought it was a
>   scam.

>   SARAH
>   Don't talk. I'll call for
>   help.

>   DIANA
>   There is no help. They're all
>   mad. You have to stop the
>   movie.

>   SARAH
>   Shh. You're hurt really bad.

>   DIANA
>   I know I'm hurt, you stupid
>   bitch! I'm dying! I'm holding
>   my fucking guts in. So listen
>   to me. Get up to the projection

room. Pull the plug on the
projector. If the movie ends
he'll be alive again.

                 SARAH
What? Who will be?

                 DIANA
Jesus, I catered to idiots.
The movies are bringing their
creator back to life. He was
a serial killer!

                 SARAH
You can't be serious.

                 DIANA
Yeah, my dying breath is just
a practical joke on you. Look,
throw me back out there, all
right. Get away from me.

                 SARAH
Okay! Where is the projection
room?

                 DIANA
Upstairs. On the left. Just
pull the plug. Don't let the
movie end. You hear me? Don't…
Don't let the movie … end.

Diana dies. Sarah can't believe it.

                 SARAH
No. No, don't die. Wait! I

               don't   understand   what's
               happening!

She looks up. Borgia, still flickering and grainy,
smiles and applauds.

Sarah stands, ready for an attack.

Borgia bows, indicating that she's free to leave.

She edges past him, he doesn't move towards her.
Slowly, she opens the door and peeks out.

THROUGH THE DOOR: SARAH'S P.O.V.

The Crowd is filing back into the theater.

Sarah recognizes Dave, near the back, moving
with the rest.

SARAH

Panting, throws herself through the door, grabs
Dave, still moving, and drags him into another
empty theater across the hall.

                    SARAH
          David!

ANOTHER EMPTY THEATER

Sarah slams the doors behind them and leans
against them.

                    SARAH
          We have to get out of here. We
          don't have much time. Are you
          okay? David?

David turns to her, the entire right side of his body bloody.

                    SARAH
     Oh, Jesus!

                    DAVE
     Hi, Sarah. You gonna watch
     the end of the movie with me?

                    SARAH
     We have to shut the movie
     down! That woman who put
     the whole thing on, she was
     stabbed, David!

                    DAVE
     Stop the movie? We can't do
     that.

                    SARAH
     We have to! Everyone's crazy
     because of it. Oh, David, are
     you okay?

                    DAVE
     I'm fine, Sarah. But you can't
     stop the movie.

                    SARAH
     We have to!

He holds up a piece of broken glass. She flinches.

                    DAVE
     Once you see it, you can't

unsee it.

He smiles, wide, and begins cutting into his face.

                         DAVE
              You can't unsee it!

Laughing, he turns on her. She screams and throws herself into the hallway.

HALLWAY

Sarah runs from Dave, who stops just inside the door, watching her run.

Smiling, Dave calmly walks across the hall and goes back into the theater.

THEATER

Is an orgy of blood and pain. The crowd has turned to each other.

Pike and Krusty have cornered one of the NURSES, dragging her across the room. They throw her down and leap on her. Krusty holds her down while Pike rapes her.

Ralph and Dan are watching nearby. Wordlessly, they walk over and start to help, each holding one of the nurse's legs.

Other PUNKS are stabbing each other.

Donna and Shaun are biting into each other's arms, slowly cannibalizing each other.

Throats are slit with jagged pieces of metal and

glass.

Dirk is hacking into another NURSE with the ax.

LOBBY

Sarah races across the lobby, holding a hand against her mouth.

The Lobby is littered with bodies and blood. There are a few Party-Roomers still alive, crawling towards her, horribly wounded.

She skirts around them, heading towards the stairs.

Borgia smiles at her and bows again, allowing her to pass and run up the stairs.

UPSTAIRS CORRIDOR

There are two rooms: Projection Room A and B.

She tries the knobs of both. They're locked.

Frantic, she looks around the hallway. She grabs a fire extinguisher from the wall and begins to bang it against the knob of Projection Room A.

BORGIA

rounds the corner, still smiling. He drums his fingers on the wall. The fingers make noise. Surprised, he looks down at his hand. He's still grainy, but he's no longer flickering. This pleases him.

SARAH

doesn't know what's happening with him, but it

renews her attack on the door.

The knob falls to the ground. She hurls herself against the door. It swings open and she falls through it, hitting the floor hard.

It's the wrong room.

                    SARAH
          No!

The projector in this room is dark and silent. She looks back at Borgia who is laughing.

Sarah runs into the room, looking for another access.

There is a second door to the right but it only leads to a breakdown table.

She runs to the projector's windows.

They're too small to fit through.

There's no way to get to the next room from here.

Sarah gives a shriek of frustration. And runs towards the door.

Borgia blocks her way. As he speaks, we can hear projector noise in his voice.

                    BORGIA
          Nice   effort,   miss.   Really.
          But maybe we should just sit
          quietly and wait for the movie
          to finish.

                    SARAH
You! You're the filmmaker!

                    BORGIA
Clever girl.

                    SARAH
The movie is bringing you back
to life.

                    BORGIA
The artist lives through his
art.

                    SARAH
How? How is this happening?

                    BORGIA
Movies are powerful things,
kid. You put your heart
and soul into filming one,
literally bleeding over the
film, and then you show it to
people who can tear it apart
just like that. Diminishing
everything you've done.
Soulless critics who can't
create for themselves, so
they destroy what others have
done. It's a cruel business.

                    SARAH
Bullshit! Bullshit! You're a
murderer.

                    BORGIA

You know, I didn't think I'd
be able to say that with a
straight face. Maybe I should
have done more acting. What
do you think?

                SARAH
All this is your fault.

                BORGIA
Let's face it: anybody can
make a movie. Takes talent to
orchestrate a massacre.

                SARAH
I'll stop it! I'll shut down
the movie!

                BORGIA
Yeah? How?

He reaches out and pushes her. She falls backward.

                BORGIA
Set up. Execution. Climax.
Dénouement.

He kicks her in the side.

Sarah gasps, and crawls away from him.

                BORGIA
My movies were pure horror,
kid. No special effects. Just
life and death on screen.
Nobody wanted to admit it.

> Even when the bodies showed
> up, they still called me a
> fake.

She's crawling away from him.

                    BORGIA
          You have no idea how painful it
          is to have your art ignored.

Another kick, and Sarah rolls down the stairs.

                    BORGIA
          But, after a while, the movies
          became secondary. I found
          real art in the murder. Human
          flesh - that's my medium.

                    SARAH
          Poseur!

                    BORGIA
          Aw, that's not nice.

Borgia comes down the stairs after her.

Sarah rolls painfully and gets to her feet.
She's hurt.

Borgia takes his time, savoring the pursuit.
He's almost dancing.

There's a YOUNG MAN in the hallway, stabbing a
Swiss Army Knife into another BOY.

Sarah rushes past him.

Borgia grabs the man's wrist in mid-thrust, takes the blade from his hand, slides it across the man's throat.

Borgia sighs with pleasure as the man coughs and dies.

                    BORGIA
          Beautiful!

Sarah limps towards the theater.

THEATER

The doors part, Sarah stumbles into the room. Nobody looks at her.

The orgy of pain and mutilation continues. It's like a bloody mosh pit. Those who aren't stabbing and clawing each other are having wild sex on the floor.

Sarah pushes her way through the crowd.

The MOVIE is still spilling its red images across the screen.

Sarah isn't sure what to do, but she makes her way towards the screen.

THE DOORS

swing open again and Borgia enters, elegantly.

Chris is near the back, face and hands bloody. He waves at Borgia, who returns the gesture.

Dirk turns, ax still in hand, sees Borgia. Borgia plunges the knife blade into Dirk's throat and takes the ax from his hands.

Dirk drops. Borgia walks down the aisle towards Sarah.

SARAH

gets to the screen and reaches up into the light.

BORGIA

stumbles.

THE IMAGES

burn her hand.

Sarah screams and pulls back a bleeding arm.

Pike looks up from the bloody nurse at his feet (who is being ridden by Ralph now) and screams at Sarah. He throws a jagged piece of metal at her.

Sarah dodges the object. It slashes the screen.

BORGIA

Screams as a bloody gash opens up across his leg. He drops to the floor. Sarah Looks frantically for a weapon. Borgia gets to his feet and limps towards her, his face a mask of rage.

CHRIS

Appears at her side, a knife in hand, slashing at her. He tries to step towards her and trips over a bloody body at his feet.

Chris falls, dropping the knife. Sarah leaps for it, grabbing it up.

BORGIA

Is coming closer, swinging the ax.

SARAH

Knife in hand, stands up directly into the path of the projection.

Her face, back, hands and arms begin to bubble and bleed. She screams and slashes into the screen.

Each cut blows a black tear into the screen.

Black voids in the picture.

BORGIA

Screams with each cut, as bloody gashes open up he drops to the floor. The Crowd hoists him up, and he dies, held above them.

The ax slips from his hands.

Reverently, the crowd lowers him to the floor.

ON THE RUINED SCREEN

The movie ends. The tail leader comes up and the theater is bathed in hard white light.

SARAH

Bloody, collapses to the floor, hugging her knees in exhaustion.

THE CROWD

Turns to her, enraged.

CHRIS

Takes the knife from her hand. He passes it to
Dave. Sarah holds her hand out to Dave.

                    SARAH
          I stopped him. I stopped him.

Chris shakes his head and Dave stabs her. She
stares at him in shock.

                    SARA
          Why?

                    CHRIS
          Once you see it, you can't
          unsee it.

The Crowd howls and comes for her. Sarah screams.

PIKE

Stands over her with what looks like a pointed
crowbar. He raises it up and grins.

                    PIKE
          It's only a movie!

He slams the axe down and we -

                                   CUT TO BLACK

CREDITS

CHAPTER SIX
SHOW TIME

"There is nothing that says more about its creator than the work itself."

— Akira Kurosawa, Something Like
an Autobiography, p. 89

Kids and Addicts alike grabbed every spare chair, beanbag, sofa cushion, and bedspread they could lay hands upon and dragged them down into the spacious basement of Orson Hall. Spanning beneath the building, the basement was used for laundry facilities and storage, but it had served as a makeshift screening room on more than one occasion. It was the only space big enough to house them all. And nearly everyone was there, fidgeting and impatient, as Boone and Kearns set up the screen.

Up all night, Boone toiled on his laptop to bring all of the digitized films together into one program that would play them in tandem. Once hooked up to the digital projector, there was no more work to be done. He could concentrate solely on what hidden mysteries the films had to offer. Tonight was to honor a dead artist—madman or not—and watch his creation, the first screening in over a decade. Excitement was electric. Burnt ozone hung in the air, spawned from no particular source.

The few folding chairs to be found were set up near the back of the cinderblock and concrete room, while others sprawled out on the floor on blankets and beanbags. In the middle of the row sat Shel the Agent, his arms crossed and face satisfied, but legs bouncing in anticipation, belying his cool demeanor. "You really pulled it off, Tom," he said when he'd arrived. "I knew you'd do it. I knew I could trust you. Rest of the Agency is gonna turn green, I'll tell you what." Shel shook a proud finger in Boone's face, his face a grin of hubris.

"You want to do the intro?" Boone asked him. But the Agent shook his head, grin unwavering.

"It's all yours," said the Agent. "Your show all the way."

Boone didn't move from behind the table holding the laptop and the projector. He simply raised his voice over the murmuring crowd. "Thanks and welcome," he said. "You all know what this is all about. The first screening of all five of the films of Luther Borgia, rumored to drive people insane upon completion. That's why we're all here. To see if we'll lose our minds too. So let's do it!"

There was a smattering of cheers, whoops and applause from the Kids.

Without fanfare, Boone hit the Spacebar and *The Magus* bloomed to life on screen. The first image was startling: two coal-black eyes staring out at the viewer from a sea of darkness, the face obscured by the frame. From the little speakers, the film's tinny narration clawed forth. "In the beginning," the soundtrack wheezed, "was the Word made flesh."

And thus the screening began.

("The Archetype Murderer: The Serial Killer as Artist" by Chris Balun. *Movie Outlaw*, Vol. 3, No. 1. 1999. Continued from page 26.)

Each of the Borgia films runs between 21 and 23 minutes, with *From Golgotha to Gomorra* [sic] coming in the longest at

23:13. While each film stands on its own, it becomes clearer that each is part of a larger story of The Magus's journey. Beginning with his own titular story, wherein the Magician (played by Borgia himself) stages a bloody show for a audience of decaying socialites, the stage performer becomes a sorcerer during the course of the arc of the quintet.

As he progresses through each level of, ostensibly, Hell, The Magus claws his way from the bounds of Earth, both physical and spiritual, until he finally comes face-to-face, we're to presume, with God. In the final minutes of *From Golgotha to Gomorrah* [sic], the Magician reaches into God's mouth, pulls out his tongue in a graphic display of carnage, and eats it, taking on the power of The Creator, and forcing the sun to set forever.

His more lavish set-pieces were meant to be the zenith of blasphemy: the unsimulated fellatio of Christ on the cross in *Golgotha*, for example, or the literal cannibalism of the Son of God in *The Magus* (and embarrassingly repeated in *Rape of the Archangel*). While Borgia attempts to be heretical with these films, the theme of an artist taking on the mantle of God was not a new concept in the '70s any more than it is now. It's the artistic hubris, laughing in the face of God, meant to be blasphemous but merely coming off as clumsy and pretentious. Borgia's passion for filmmaking was not matched by talent, unfortunately, and each of the five films (with the exception, perhaps, of *The Pioneer*, whose vistas of the Redwood Forest, filmed during a vacation years before, are gorgeous and striking) feels amateurish, cheap, and familiar.

Borgia's use of childish sets, cardboard and plywood flats salvaged from local theater productions, do little for the production values. Neither, unfortunately, do the notorious on-screen murders. It's telling that even with real human beings at his disposal, Borgia's filming of the tortures, particularly of Etta Tarquinio in *Rape of the Archangel*, does little to dispel the overall shoddiness of the production. The pain and terror in Tarquinio's crying eyes are, of course, genuine. Her blood is real. Her entrails, when removed from her abdominal cavity, are real. But because the rest of the art design is lacking, it is easy to see how her truly horrifying death was shrugged off as cheap special effect.

It was this sort of critical dismissal that so enraged Luther Borgia. But in the end, his reign of terror and murder comes to nothing. Etta Tarquinio died for nothing. Heather Grenedy died for nothing. As did Amelia and Elizabeth Street and Mildred Ozcnawitzki, at the hands of his vicious grandfather (whose own lack of discernable film talent could at least be excused by the newness of the technology).

Ultimately, there's very little to be said in favor of *The Divine Heresy*, outside of its status as a curio quintet.

One exception is an almost throwaway bit of dialogue during the predominantly silent sophomore film, *The Pioneer*. During the opening sequence, where the Magician (again played by Borgia, as he did in all of the films save *Archangel*) stumbles out of a cave after a hundred years, according to the interstitial card, squinting against the sunlight, trips over a mound of dirt in the crotch of a tree. Digging through the mound, he uncovers a Bolex movie camera, which gives him special powers, particularly the ability to see the gods who preside over artists. Or "Artists" to accurately quote another title card. Through the lens he sees a towering figure in silhouette against the sun, a lens flare blooming between the figure's legs. The voice-over gives name to this god: "Cinemagog, Father of Filmmaking".

It's this strange little nod towards a new mythology that has crept into filmmakers' lexicon, while the source of the name often goes unknown. "Cinemagog" is Borgia's "Rosebud was the sled". Other filmmakers and students have built tongue-in-cheek religions around the concept of Cinemagog, and spawned the creation and naming of dozens of similar "gods", such as Dolirostrum, god of Cinematographers, Kem-Daly, the god of Editors, and most bizarrely, Ifrirs, the god of Executive Producers. These deities are often invoked in the same way as the "Flying Spaghetti Monster" or "The Church of the Sub-Genius." The modern-day muses with the temperament of the Furies.

No doubt Borgia would be chagrined that a toss-away line in his second film would be his lasting heritage, even after his own name was long forgotten by filmmakers and scholars alike. Something meant to be a joke was given greater meaning than any of the rest of his portentous imagery. As the women he murdered now rest in relative peace following his execution, Borgia's own hopes at immortality collapsed and burned around him. Only the name "Cinemagog" was left behind, the concept turned into something more-or-less positive. At least, it puts name to whoever we curse during those long hours of production.

Luther Borgia, his films all but lost, deliberately forgotten, spends eternity in the Hell of Obscurity. A level he'd never dreamed of during the course of his *Divine Heresy*.

*****

When *From Gomorrah to Golgotha* ended, with its lingering gaze fixed on a repeat of the opening shot of a sheer cliff wall, the light switched abruptly to dull video blue and no one in the basement moved. A little less than two hours had passed—the first leg of a marathon for many of the Addicts and Kids. It wasn't a stunned silence that had enveloped them. It was something borne from an entire room of people collectively unimpressed. For all of the build-up these forbidden films had, they'd unspooled into twenty-minute clumps of mediocrity. Finally, beginning from somewhere in the middle of the room, laughter erupted, then grew cacophonous as the absurdity infected the crowd. It wasn't madness that consumed them; it was derision.

While Boone sat in stunned silence, his cheeks burning with surprising shame, the rest of the party was gleeful, ripping on the films as they exchanged lofty reviews of what they'd witness, universally judged to, more or less, "suck balls". The Kids, at first secretly giddy at the prospect of hanging out with the older Addicts, were merciless in their appraisal, arguing as to which of the five films was a bigger piece of shit. "We should have all gone crazy out of fucking boredom!" declared one of the youngsters, though Boone would be hard-pressed to identify which one.

"Ooh, look at me, I'm Luther Borgia," said one girl. "I don't know how to frame a close-up so that the face stays in focus."

"I'm fucking the ground! I'm fucking the trees!" said another.

"Look out, God! Luther's gonna getcha!"

Only the Addicts stayed silent.

Gradually, the party broke up, with no little amount of ironic disappointment that they weren't all steeped in each other's blood. Fifteen minutes later, only the Addicts remained. Along with Shel the Agent, who wore a blank, unreadable mask, his eyes nonreflective in the blue dim of the basement.

Once it was just them, just "the family," Kearns nodded. "Now let's watch them the right way."

Reaching over Boone's shoulder, he flexed his fingers over the laptop, fired up an editing program and fiddled with some settings. All the while, Boone sat motionless while Alyce squeezed his hand.

That was it? he thought. All the anxiety and the searching and the theft? For what? For what?

It *was* shame he felt. He'd bought into the hype, like some online newsgroupie. He'd been hoping for something transcendent, something worthy of all of the fuss and fanfare and forbidden fruits. Instead, he could only sit there and bask in the absurdity he'd just witnessed. He'd made better films in grade school. Borgia was no genius. He was a sub-basement John Waters wannabe. It was good that the motherfucker was dead.

"Okay," Kearns said, mostly to himself. Again, to himself, he nodded, then pressed a button on the laptop. The projector's bulb nova-ed. The extended opening shot of the cliff-face of *From Gomorrah to Golgotha* filled the screen and their retinas.

Then the wide mad eyes of *The Magus* faded up, superimposed over the wall. Over that closed the red-lipped mouth of *Osculum Infame*, then the Spinning Wheel from *The Pioneer,* and finally the burning, flapping swan's wing of *Rape of the Archangel.* Each film's signature pre-title image laid one on top of the other, forming a singular, dense symbol. Luther Borgia summed up in multiple-exposure.

Every Addict had the same thought at the same moment: How is this possible?

Luther Borgia, a heavy-handed symbolist who seemed to intentionally misunderstand both Catholicism and Thelema, whose masterwork, by the standards of modern day the shock value, was lifelessly mundane. Even the outrageous crucifixion fellatio—extolled in the cult film books—seemed lacking. Unsimulated and as vile as anything from *Pink Flamingos,* but minus the sense of humor. Not even the sacrifices, the genuine murders, redeemed the art—which was the most horrible critique of all.

But run together, each film overlaying the last, the quintet of shorts were a cacophony of light and shadow and color and noise. The reverse Stations of the Cross unfolding against the ridges of the cave, pierced by the blowtorch flame in the dead center—the images unified. As if that was the intention all along. As if that were really the grand design.

But how could that be? How could Borgia—a film school dropout, his own killings, like his art, imitations of things that came before—have planned it all out? Especially as so much of *The Pioneer,* nearly all of *The Magus,* seemed so accidental? So uninformed?

Combined, the five films told one dark and secret story.

The Divine Heresy was no adolescent revenge fantasy, told in chapters. It was a primal scream in layers; a Bosch painting treated like a *MAD* fold-in. The quintet was not a sum of its parts; the five films were separations from the whole, layers conceived and shot and formed over a series of well-planned years.

"Like an x-ray of an entire deck of Tarot, seeing every card at the same time." The thought originated with Lys and spread wordlessly through the rest of their minds. With it came the endorphin rush that trapped them all in time.

Described in their own cinephage language: the duration of *The Divine Heresy* was that first breathless moment as the house lights dimmed, the curtains opened, and just—*just*—as the studio card began to appear. That frozen, orgasmic second before real magic began. That glimpse into the unknown and all-possible.

Before education reacted. Before the mind began its silent background critique of theme and *mise-en-scene*. Before all the noise gathered in the frontal lobe.

That one weightless,

airless,

near-lightless moment…

before the movie started.

The Divine Heresy was everything that was or could happen in that infinite blackness of the pre-fade. Where the dream began to unspool. Every thought, plot, speech, person, fight, fuck, chase, dance, possibility…

It all came at them at once. And their eyes reflected it all back again. Light meeting light in the space between screen and audience. That perfect spot where identity stopped.

Finally, Borgia's bookends worked as they should: the eyes closed, the wheel slowed, the flames died, the mouth opened to black and the wall faded to nothing. It was all over before, it seemed, it had barely begun. Video blue smeared through the darkness. The exhibition was over.

Slowly, each of the Addicts turned to look at each other. At first, none of the faces seemed familiar. In the blue, brains recalibrated, retuning to the vibrations of reality and they recognized themselves again: Boone, Lys, Kearns, Josh, and one of the Kids, Maya.

Behind them, Shel the Agent wept tears of blood.

Washed in blue, his face twisted in both ecstasy and agony, Shel nodded and whispered to himself. Finally, his eyes snapped down from the screen, leveled and fixed on his audience-mates. He stood with a calcified slowness, smoothing the front of his suit jacket, straightening his tie…

…before he launched himself toward them all, snarling and sprawling and scattering the metal chairs in a violent wake. His fist found Maya first, connecting with the side of her head and knocking her to the ground. There was no aim in his rage, just blind, abyss-gazed madness.

Their herd attacked, the Addicts retaliated. Jumping evolution, the sheep turned and fell on him like a pack of wolves. The soundtrack of their group mind filled with kettledrums and trumpet blasts, Zulu war cries and *"Warriors…come out to play-yaaay!"*

Kearns stomped down on Shel's head, just as Edward Norton had done to the gangbanger in *American History X.*

Boone's teeth found Shel's hand wrapped around a chairback and he gnawed the man's knuckle like James Caan's "Sonny" in *The Godfather.*

They beat him like Terry Malloy. Like The Man with No Name. Like Walken in *Dogs of War.* They beat him like he was Mel Gibson's Christ.

Shel fought them back. Like Oldboy. Like Lee Marvin. Like Lee J. Cobb in *Thieves' Highway.* He was Santa Ana's Army, Sitting Bull's Indians, Quantrill's Raiders, and *The Towering Inferno.* "I am Godzilla!" he shouted in Treat Williams' voice. "You are *Japan!*"

At last, his fury had them scattered. He had his gun

out before they could regroup. Now he was on the "Top of the World, Ma." Tom Cruise at the end of fucking *Taps*.

Shel the Agent opened his mouth. Flickering light poured out like a projector beam. Abstract images, conjured impossibly from inside him, splashed their faces as he turned, targeting each of the group. Overpowering the danger, the light mesmerized them, even moreso than its inconceivable source. Instead of the gun, they saw only the light blazing from the Agent's open mouth. The Film of his soul, a prologue to their death.

Just like in the Silents, before the rules had really kicked in, the Addicts met their *deus ex machina* as *The Divine Heresy* spilled again across the screen, the projection emanating from the Agent's open mouth. The Director's Cut. The Criterion Collection. All five opening images reopening space-time cinema. The Voice of His Master, overlaid five times, halted Shel the Agent in his tracks, even as his shadow bisected the picture. At the surprise encore, his mouth snapped shut, cutting off his internal light, and darkness filled the void around him. Now, as before, the only illumination came from the dead video blue on the screen.

Their savior God of the Machine stepped out from the darkness behind the blinding eye of the projector, a length of film stock wrapped around his closed fists. That was the garrote he slipped around Shel's neck before the Agent knew what was happening.

Seth—the older guy from upstairs, the one with the bullet wound and secret film cans—tightened the celluloid noose, the edges slicing through throat flesh as well as his own knuckle-skin. Breath caught in Shel's lungs stayed where it was. His mouth hung wide as he stood gaping and gulping for air, bloody eyes bulging from their slick sockets, his internal light sputtering against the dark of his maw.

Someone jostled the laptop and *The Divine Heresy* restarted, blooming across the screen, drowning the blue.

It took a moment for their stunned brains to realize that

the Agent's grasping fingers were not reaching for them. They clutched at the beam of projector light slashing the darkness. Shel the Agent wanted to hold the movie in his hands, cling to the images as he died. To touch Borgia's masterpiece with his own skin. As the first unified fade out began, Shel the Agent went to black with it.

Dust motes danced in twin beams of light: the first from the projector, the second, growing dimmer by the minute, from Shel's own mouth. His soul sputtered to darkness. And Seth let the body hit the floor.

With the impact, the floor shattered into a web of cracks and thunder. Structural violence hurled the Addicts off their feet. The invincible cement armor heaved again, first up and then down, sucking Shel's body into its jagged wound. The Agent's corpse vanished into this new chasm. The pit roared and shuddered in response.

Now the survivors were scrambling, reaching for each other, for Seth's outstretched arms. The whole of the Welles spasmed as the foundation gave way to nothingness, leaving the six of them dangling from the suspended staircase.

A moment of calm. The personification of the lazy screenwriter's cue for the line, "This can't be good."

From deep, deep down inside that blackness beneath them, a light sputtered to life, like a Star being Born. With it came the lost, lonely, distant chatter of a projector. Against the light, far below: thin shadows, long arms, wide wings, dancing in the pit.

Then the carved arches burst into their world, borne by marble Doric columns. A red velvet curtain unfurling between and then receding, revealing the silvered screen behind it. Gold-trimmed seats of matching crimson fabric emerged from the chasm like teeth in a lower jaw. Carpeted aisle ways carved through the rows. Balcony boxes bloomed from the walls.

Their offering to Borgia's god, to Cinemagog, the God of Film Itself, was deemed acceptable. Now this grand theater was their obvious reward. It was no trick of the yellow lights, glowing warm and welcoming from their recesses in the walls. The impossible theater was there. For the cinephages, Cinemagog had vomited up their Heaven.

"Movies are mass hallucinations with popcorn," no one said.

It was many long minutes before the Addicts took their first tentative steps onto the newly formed aisle. Like early primates descending from the trees, the six of them, crouching and ready to once again fight or flee, slowly found their seats. They all half-expected to see shiny gold ticket stubs, freshly ripped, in the palms of their hands. For that reason, no one dared look down.

As they settled, terrified and elated, that infinite moment came upon them again. That feeling of free-fall before the fade-in. With it, this time, came a new feeling:

As the curtains parted further and the lights dimmed and that cosmic wonder engulfed them—

—they felt, on the backs of their necks, something watching *them*.

On the gorgeous, virgin screen, the MGM Lion was just beginning to appear.

Just as *they* were beginning to appear, to whatever eyes stared out behind them.

Ferris Bueller famously broke the fourth wall. *The Purple Rose of Cairo* broke the fifth.

As the lion's roar filled the air around them, they idly wondered which wall they'd just broken through.

Behind them, something unseen was definitely blinking. Adjusting to the changing light.

CHAPTER SEVEN

"This film is about the perverted love affair between homo sapiens and lady violence. In common with its subject, it is necessarily horrifying, paradoxical and absurd. To make such a film means accepting that the subject is loaded with every taboo in the book. You seem to want to emasculate (1) the most savage and (2) the most affectionate scenes in our movie. If Performance does not upset audiences it is nothing. If this fact upsets you, the alternative is to sell it fast and no more bullshit. Your misguided censorship will ultimately diminish said audiences in quality and quantity."

—Telegram from Donald Cammell
and Mick Jagger to Ted Ashley,
president of Warner Bros., 1970.

SCENE ONE:
THE SECRET CINEMA

The theater in the basement remained the secret of the Six. Alyce changed the locks on all of the doors leading down, kept the keys to herself. No one outside of the Addicts was to venture downstairs. Some of the Kids grumbled, then left to do their laundry across the street.

"What are you seeing?" Alyce whispered to Boone in the darkness. For her, *The Princess Bride* unfolded on the giant screen.

"*Blade Runner*," Boone said. And behind his eyes, a flying car banked around a building, its entire side an electronic billboard shilling whatever the advertising Geisha wanted it to.

They sat together in the overstuffed seats, staring up at the same screen and seeing completely different things. It was like that for each of them. The theatre played just for them, turning their thoughts and desires into images flashed back onto their retinas. While they watched, the curtains whispered in a nonexistent breeze while the screen breathed with invisible current. All impossible. But if this was the legacy of *The Divine Heresy*, it certainly beat mass murder.

Thematically, they realized, this flew in the face of established development. They'd witnessed something forbidden, obscene to the gods, they should have been blinded for it. They should have gone appropriately insane, and set upon one another like starving hyena. Instead, they were rewarded, granted The Quickening, blessed with the movie theater that played to only them. Instead of Orpheus losing Persephone, they were humanity greeted by Prometheus, granted the gift of fire. Perhaps somewhere Borgia was having his liver chewed out by Cinemagog's giant vulture, but the Addicts were no worse for the wear.

That night, Alyce saw The Flickering Man for the first time.

She'd left Boone asleep in his apartment, *The Great Escape* playing on TV to his closed eyes, and made her way back to her own room. Though she hated to leave him, loving his arms around her while she relaxed, there was something about her own bed too alluring to ignore. And she felt good; better, in fact, than she could remember ever feeling. Something about surviving the screening, even if the danger was just mass hysteria cooked up in their own imaginations. It made her feel stronger. Like an explorer returning home to regale the media with her adventures.

Rounding the corner, she saw the smiling bearded man standing just outside her door. He wore a neat dark suit, simple and inelegant. Something you'd wear to a trial. His entire body flickered, almost imperceptibly, but just out of phase with her own eyes. It was as if he were a projection, beamed from an invisible source. He raised a hand—bloody, she saw, slick with red wet—and waved at her. It was a greeting, and it sent her stumbling backwards in shock. The flickering man took a step towards her and opened his mouth. From deep inside his incorporeal body, she heard the faint sound of chattering, like a projector gate, rumbling up through his open mouth.

Recognition came easy. She'd spent hours watching his face. It was The Magus himself, Luther Borgia. He stood in front of her door, flickering at 24 frames-per-second. When she screamed, he vanished.

Of course he vanished. There could be no evidence of his existence. She'd have to appear a fool to her peers. Someone naïve. Someone who couldn't handle her forbidden films without ensuing nightmares. Words wouldn't comfort her, nor would Boone's vague murmurings of support, promises of belief. Luther Borgia had appeared to her.

Nobody gave a good goddamn.

SCENE TWO:
KEARNS MEETS A MUGWUMP

Down in the Secret Cinema, Kearns flixed to *Videodrome* and found himself inside the film's vicious pirate TV signal. Barefoot on the metal grate floor, he had Fucking Lee Benway chained to the wet red clay wall, strangling him with his own bare hands. Knuckles white from the effort, Kearns dug his thumbs into the man's throat, squeezing the Adam's apple, collapsing the trachea, feeling cartilage pop beneath his grip, watching the man's face go from red to purple in seconds. Fucking Lee Benway's eyes bulged from their sockets, blood vessels exploding in petechial hemorrhage.

When the director's body went slack, the chains held his body upright. Kearns relaxed his grip, flexed his fingers to relieve the cramping, bent at the waist to give his erection some room to breathe. In just a few minutes, Benway would be alive again and they could start all over.

There were other victims, chained and bound to the wet walls. Boone and Alyce, bleeding and broken, slumped barely conscious, hanging from their wrists, too weak to move. Every way he turned, Kearns found more and more victims awaiting their turn or suffering from their wounds. He stopped recognizing faces. The room, seemingly finite, had no shortage of bodies on which to inflict misery.

Shuddering—from cold, from exertion, from the sheer thrill of the bloodletting—Kearns found a flail in his hands, lumps of lead knotted into the ends, an instrument of Biblical torture. He approached a girl, shackled and blindfolded, vaguely recognizing her as one of the "Kids" from the *Divine Heresy* screening. Myra? Mina? It didn't matter. He planned to use the flail to remove any and all distinguishing features from her skull. Her lips were parted in anticipation—

—He came out of his flixing fantasy with a violent gasp and heaved the sparse contents of his stomach into the aisle.

Hanging limp over the armrest, he watched the frame he'd been suckling curl up in the puddle of stomach acid even as the carpet absorbed the liquid.

More and more often, his flixing regimen ended with violence and sickness. It had been a long time since he'd found any joy in escapism, but the now-frequent brutality was causing him true concern. Particularly with his body's physiological—and sexual—response. Nothing chased away the black emptiness that kept him inert for hours at a time. The photochemical reactions of the film frames on his system only dredged up more horror and more chaos.

There was no outlet, no release.

No escape.

Before the Secret Cinema had risen from the depths of their unintended ritual, he had been able to battle the darkness with frames, with pot, with alcohol and his never-ending movie marathon. Now, sunk down low in the theater chair, gazing at anything the Cinema wanted to show him, there was no pleasure.

He just wanted it all to end.

Before his eyes, up on the screen, he saw himself returned to the *Videodrome* set. Like Max Renn in the film, his own hand had fused with a Walther PPK, flesh and metal melted together into a lump of venal monstrosity. Like Max Renn at the film's end, he put the gun to his temple and pulled the trigger.

He'd expected the movie screen to explode with guts and viscera. That was, after all, what happened to the veined, pulsing television in the movie. Instead, he was painfully reminded that, even with the film emulsion coursing through his body, swirling around in his mind's eye, it was still only a movie. Hallucination. Whatever you wanted to call it. The Secret Cinema could only *show*. It couldn't *do*. It couldn't remove him from himself.

Sooner or later, lacking the strength to tackle his own problem head on, he was going to hurt someone.

In the dark, Kearns wept, and watched his cinematic self turn back to Lee Benway and destroy the man again.

****

"They're leveling The Arc next week," one of the Kids said.

Boone and Kearns had just emerged from the basement, having screened *Visitor Q* and *Forbidden Zone*, respectively. As they entered the common room on one, the news caught them off guard.

"Who is?" Kearns demanded.

The Kid didn't look up from his tablet, staring down into the window of the Internet while a cartoon played in one open window, text scrolling in another. "Some revitalization project," he replied. But this was unhelpful.

"The what?"

"It's been all over the news. They're doing something with The Welles. Redoing it, I guess," the Kid said. "To attract tourists."

"Bullshit," Kearns said, under his breath and to no one in particular. "Bullshit. The Welles is fine the way it is."

"Did you know it wasn't spelled with two 'e's until after World War II. It used to just be called 'the wells' because that's where all the wells were. In Colonial times. If you wanted water, you walked down to 'the wells.' Then all the theaters went up in the '50s."

The Kid droned on but Kearns had stopped listening. Instead, he repeated, "Bullshit. Bullshit!" Until Boone slapped his shoulder and brought him out of it.

"Fuck's with you?" Boone said.

"Didn't you hear? They're murdering The Arc."

"So what? It's practically a slum anyway. Maybe they'll put up something better. With stadium seating and Surround Sound."

"Boone! They're *leveling* The Arc!"

Kearns realized the sentimentality was lost on Boone. What was there to understand? During his entire time shackled Out There his memories of growing up, going to movies at The Arc, were all that kept him together. During the endless rewrites, where he was never fed until the appropriate amount of pages were turned in, he could remember seeing *Return of the Jedi* as a child at The Arc, seeing all of the adventures of *Indiana Jones*, all three *Back to the Future*s. He could look upon those memories and remember why he'd gotten into the business. He could remember why he wanted to write movies. Why Fucking Lee Benway had been his hero, back when he was simply known as "Directed by Lee Benway".

Some squad of politicians had decreed his theater unworthy of preservation. They'd decided that his home, his memories, held nothing of importance to future generations. They were going to flatten it and move on, erect a Starbucks in its place, turn The Welles into another Disney-fied shopping destination.

Impotent with anger, Kearns turned away from his friend and went back to his room alone. There was nothing he could do to stop it. For the past week, he'd been entombed in the basement theater, The Arc not even an afterthought. So who knew how long this demolition had been planned? Time was meaningless now that they had the basement theater to themselves.

Kicking the door shut, Kearns collapsed face-down on his nasty, ancient sofa. It had been rescued from a curb, still damp from morning dew, and schlepped to Orson back during his sophomore days. In the room it remained, a reminder of how everything could be salvaged. But there was no comfort in that. How could he salvage The Arc? Would he if he could?

The sofa smelled like mildew and the ten years' worth of the asses that sat upon it. He could smell spilled beer deep inside the cushions. Other odors he couldn't identify. The fibers were hammered flat, yet still seemed to stick to his face as he turned his head.

Across the room, a bearded man sat cross-legged on his floor, smiling and motionless. The bearded man disrupted the meager light, seeming to flicker in the gloom. Correction: the bearded man *was* flickering. At 24 frames-per-second.

Suddenly, Kearns was exhausted. All energy had drained from his body. In that moment, a decision was made. Meanwhile the flickering man continued to smile, contented.

Sleep was useless to attempt. Barely the strength to sit up, bathe in the omnipresent blue light of the TV, but his mind was flapping on its reel. There'd be no sleep. Sluggish fingers found the remote wedged between the cushions. From deep within him, he summoned the will to push PLAY. *Naked Lunch* flooded the screen, Peter Weller as William Lee as William S. Burroughs in Tangiers, in the market, buying the meat of the giant black centipede. One of Kearns' favorite films, and no, the irony was not lost on him that the namesake of his life's bane had sprung from the text inspiring the film. But Fucking Lee Benway'd never read a book in his life, let alone the cut-up drug-soaked brilliance of William S.

"Consider the lonely, loathsome flicker freak," came the thin voice of his mentor. There was William S., a skin scarecrow, a cigarette of mostly-ash suspended between two willow branch fingers. Swimming eyes in a hollow face turned towards Kearns, the face a mask of gentle affection, but, nonetheless, dripping with disgust. "Content to devour the art and devotions of those who came before him, his foot will never leave a print beneath it. He is all eyes in a world of hands."

On the word, William S. reached towards the foul-smelling, beaked creature beside him. "Lacking liver," is how the author described the mugwump in *Naked Lunch*. William S. began to stroke the creature's erect penis, coaxing forth its "addictive jism". William S., by the rules of his own work, was addicted to mugwump juice and, therefore, a "reptile."

"Worse than a reptile," the corpse-man continued,

plucking the word from Kearns' head, "worse than a junkie two-days past a fix. The flicker-freak wears full-body track marks that tick down the wasted days, like notches on a jailhouse wall."

"Goddamn hell, this old fucked up faggot is right!"

The new voice was gruff and angry and just as familiar. Kearns was being judged and found wanting by his past heroes. While Jack Kerouac and Alan Ginsberg fucked violently in the corner, Hunter S. Thompson strode front and center, poking Kearns' bare perf-ridden chest with the barrel of a .44 Magnum.

"You sit here and eat that garbage, watch *that* garbage, and the outside world erases your memory! Don't get me wrong. I'd be the last person to condemn a satisfying drug binge, but goddamn it all, you idiotic gibbon, you festering pustule, you're not even doing it for the thrills! You're not feeling! You're seeing, you're hearing—sometimes you taste, granted. But do you touch? Are you touched? No and who would? You adolescent! Hiding? From what? Failure? That shit'll find you in a locked bank vault. Failure oozes through the cracks. And so what?"

"And so what?" echoed William S. "The natives of Zimbabwe believed that a photographer could capture their souls with his machine given to him by trickster gods. If this is true, then what damage could be done with a movie camera? Would the soul be shredded and spread across twenty-four frames-per-second?"

Thompson kicked at him, almost losing a shoe. "You keep your goddamn mouth shut, commie bastard!" He jabbed the pistol in the mugwump's direction. "And keep whatever the hell that is away from me or I'll put a bullet through its eye socket!" Turning back to Kearns, Raoul Duke continued his tirade. "Quit watching! Quick sucking on the frames! Clean yourself out with some booze, good weed. Rinse your head with some blotter acid and get back to goddamn work. You wanna shame the priest back to their vestries? Get it down on paper and turn that blood pounding in your ears into a goddamned Viking roar!" And there came that trademark squeal, that anguished pig noise that

Hunter made often, and often for no reason at all.

"You got two choices, way I see it." Thompson paced, removed his green visor, ran a large hand over his bald head. His eyes blazed behind sunglasses, smoldering in the half-dark of the room. "You get back to work, make things, put grandiose lunatics like *that*—" he stabbed the gun accusatory at the Flickering Man's direction—"back in the black bag where they belong. Then you stop being God's perfect sucker." He paused, dragging long on the cigarette holder clenched in his teeth. "Or two: go down with the goddamned ship."

The mad journalist spread his arms wide, then let them fall, as if strings had been snipped. "Or, fuck you, what do I know?" He turned his back and repeated, "What do I know?"

Kearns felt his blood go corpse cold. Beside him, the mugwump had vanished along with Ginsberg and Kerouac, but William S. remained, cigarette still smoldering, but burnt down to the filter, still enough heat to sear the frail skin. The skin of his face had shrunk, pulling back the lids and lips, eyes and teeth bulging, as if the skull were attempting to escape the flesh altogether.

Sometime before Burroughs' most recent death, Thompson was revealed a fraud. It wasn't the great writer at all, but his doppelganger, Johnny Depp at both the zenith and nadir of his career. A lovely duplicate but a duplicate just the same. He hadn't been dispensing Duke's wisdom; he'd been running lines.

"But did it *sound* true?" Hunter S. Depp demanded.

Kearns shrugged, the last of his energy reserves. "Fuck do I know?"

Johnny S. Thompson turned back to him, blowing smoke through his nose. With the barrel of the pistol, he again indicated Luther Borgia, smiling and flickering and hunched in the corner. "His sentiments exactly, motherfucker," he nodded. "His sentiments exactly."

SCENE THREE:
SETH AND THE NEW FLESH

Strangling the madman in the basement had wreaked havoc on Seth's wound. Another one of Cris' borrowed t-shirts was plastered to his side by blood. Pain blossomed like fireworks. But none of it registered. Not when that theater rose from that hellish pit they'd made. Popular vernacular had drained the word "awesome" of all meaning until that moment. When the velvet curtains parted, revealing the massive screen hung between the old fashioned colonnades, Seth finally understood the word "awe." In its entirety.

He'd murdered a complete stranger. Whoever he'd been to Alyce and Boone and their friends meant nothing to Seth. The bloody tears weeping from the man's dead eyes; that was all he needed to know. The man, whoever he had been, was gone for good. *The Divine Heresy*, in all of its intended glory, had opened up the universe and revealed to the victim all of its secrets. Once exposed, the man was infected, and wouldn't stop until he'd opened the eyes of all the others, bathed them in their own blood, and showed them what he'd seen. Seth put an end to all that with a loop of unbreakable film stock.

Ilford Stock. One of the strongest strands of celluloid ever made. Wound onto a core tucked away in the corner of the basement where he'd crouched and waited all through the first showing. Against his better judgment, he'd joined the private screening, just in case. Rather, "Just to see."

"I have better things to do," Cris had told him, even before he asked if she was planning to attend. "Editing. I need to polish a new script."

He snorted at the thought of her using a script. She called him a prude. He called her a misogynist and sent her into a frothing feedback loop. He managed to duck everything she threw at him as he retreated through her door.

But he was relieved beyond words that the screening held

no interest for her. It was one less thing to worry about as he sat there in the back, against the wall, unnoticed by the rest of the audience, and told himself there was nothing to fear. The films by themselves were harmless junk. There'd be less mass hysteria and more fidgeting boredom. By the end of the final film, he finally relaxed, chided himself for an idiot while listening to the dwindling crowd tear Luther Borgia a new critical asshole.

Then the taller guy, the strung-out one who looked like a withered corpse from a Hogarth etching, did something with the laptop by the projector. The *Divine Heresy* blazed onto the screen, its pieces assembled and fused in Director's Cut harmony. Worry returned and Dr. Jekyll'd into pure terror. From the darkness, Seth watched and waited for the first casualty to make itself known.

The past flooded back, slapping over him like a thick fire blanket. He and Chris Balun dodging swinging fists clenching splintered armrests, shattered bottles, whatever the crazed patrons weeping blood could find for weaponry. Barreling towards the Exit, he tripped over a pair of girls who'd spilled into the aisle. Copulating, was his first thought. ("Fucking", was the actual word.) Then he realized that the girl on top was not a natural redhead. That her blonde hair was sopping with the blood of the girl beneath her. The girl whose face she was eating.

Hands tore at him, seizing clumps of hair, his sleeves, pant legs. Kicking, biting, he fought them off through sheer force of will and drunken adrenaline. A jagged hangnail found the corner of his right eye and tore. His vision blurred, burned, watered, and still he fought through.

Through the shrieking and writhing crowd he saw Chris at the Exit door, shouting for him to hurry. On the narrow stage beneath the screen still splattered with Borgia's nightmare, was the artist himself, both in life and as part of the film, existing in two planes of reality. The more blood that was shed, the more "real" the artist became.

Luther Borgia didn't look at him as Seth clawed his way

towards the door. Luther Borgia saw only the adoring crowd, undulating in adoration, ululating praise and hosannas. Luther Borgia's masterpiece had touched so, so many.

Seth didn't know where the gasoline had come from, or when Balun had chained shut the rest of the doors. In no time, they were safe outside the alley watching the first flames lick their way up the walls. Moments later, the screaming inside got so much louder.

There in the basement of the decrepit dormitory, only the tall man, almost as old and out of place as Seth himself, was touched by Borgia's glory. Attacking the others who only fought back without shedding a single bloody tear of their own. Realizing that the man would never stop, not until someone was dead at his hands, Seth found the spooled trailer, made his garrote, and made his choice.

Nothing had prepared him for the Hell that came afterward. What could have warned him about the yawning pit that swallowed first the corpse at his feet and then attempted the rest? In what ancient tome did it decree that a sacrifice to a dark god, risen by a forbidden film, would be rewarded by an impossible movie theater? One that played whatever you wanted, whenever you wanted. The Coliseum for Instant Gratification courtesy of something lurking beyond all rational thought.

> *Exterminate all rational thought.*
> *Long live the New Flesh.*
> *Do what thou wilt shall be the whole of the Law.*
> *Don't dream it, be it.*
> *Buy the ticket, take the ride.*

Unlike the others, he didn't linger. While Boone and his friends, "The Addicts," as Cris called them, stared transfixed at whatever played across their eyes, Seth was able to tear his gaze free from *Singin' in the Rain*. He moved, but no one else did.

At the end of his row sat Alyce, clutching Boone's hand tight enough that her knuckles gleamed white in the darkness. Seth approached her and she did not turn. Moreover, she did not blink. Neither did Boone.

Lowering her face close to hers, Seth looked into her eyes. What was reflected on the surface of her cornea was not *Singin' in the Rain*. It was, in fact, *The Wizard of Oz*, and it held her face trapped in tearful wonder and joy. Seth couldn't see what played for Boone, not with Alyce between them, and he did not wish to break whatever trance held her. He knew, anyway, that Boone was not seeing *The Wizard of Oz*.

What made this screening so different from the last? Why hadn't The Addicts' eyes welled with blood? Why had the older man, his victim, been the only one affected by Borgia's twisted play? Suddenly, he didn't want to know.

Via the ancient, shuddering elevator, Seth returned to his floor, hand pressed to his running wound, blood mixing with the cuts in his palms and the creases of his fingers, where the film garrote bit into him too.

Cris' door was ajar, which had to be intentional. Weakened from adrenaline drain and pending shock, Seth leaned in her doorway. Across the room, two of her blonder models, virtual twins to his eyes, young and smooth and painted to look only slightly older, spotted him and snapped to attention. The girl on the left offered her bare foot to the girl on the right. As the latter sucked on her toes, the first girl belted out "Hooray for Hollywood!"

"Hey, Seth," said Cris, her smile a sadistic beam. "Is this fetish closer to your heart?"

Sadly, her joke was ruined when he collapsed to the floor, blood welling up beneath him. "Hooray for Hollywood" ended with a shrill scream. Though probably not for the first time.

As Cris and the models hurried over to him, hoisting him up and applying pressure to his wound, a bright shadow passed by in the hallway. There was no denying it. It wasn't a vision produced by blood-loss and mounting hysteria. The shadow was flickering. And bearded. And smiling.

SCENE FOUR:
REQUIEM FOR THE ARC THEATER

The City of Bethlehem demolished The Arc on a Saturday. No press had been invited. No fanfare raised. It was as if the town fathers had decided to eradicate some shameful bit of its history. Only the Addicts seemed to mourn.

On the TV in the Common Room on five, a yellow sticky-note read "Play Me." Josh discovered it first and did as he was told.

Blooming to life, the screen filled with the image of what he recognized as the inside of the Arc, down in the first row, just near the curtained exit and off to the right side.

Outside the window, Josh could hear as the construction trucks rolled up to the theater across the street. They were wheeling in a wrecking ball on a crane.

On the screen, louder, yet muffled in that odd way video presented sound, also came the sound of trucks and commotion. This was no video but a live feed. Into the image stepped Kearns.

Running to the door, Josh called for the others. It was still early, but he doubted that Boone or Alyce had spent the night down in the secret theater. They hadn't. Their sleepy, yawning selves emerged from Alyce's room, blinking against the intruding shafts of sunlight knifing through the gloom from the skylights above. "The fuck?" Boone said through a yawn.

"Kearns is about to get himself killed."

Within the few seconds it took for Boone and Alyce to reach the room,

Kearns had already started what they could only assume was his final monologue.

"—learned something over the past few days," the Kearns image said. "There's nothing left here for me. Not once the Arc is gone."

The man's face seemed even more hollow and haunted than ever before. For months he'd appeared to them sleep-deprived, half-starved, slowly dying from his singular diet of flixing. Apparently his patience for slow suicide had worn away. "I'm never going back Out There, even if that was a possibility. Fucking Lee Benway," he muttered under his breath. They would have been disappointed had he not.

"How can I be expected to stay here as a spectator?" he asked them.

Alarmed, Boone glanced at Alyce, but found her face unreadable. If she'd ever shed a tear for Kearns, it wouldn't be now.

"You all saw it too. Those…creatures out in the darkness. The ones who lived down there in that pit. Right? I don't think all that stuff Copper used to say is bullshit any more. There are…*gods*. Of film and filmmaking. We unlocked—" Machinery noise drowned him out for a moment, reducing the image to a silent opening and closing of the mouth. Then he was audible again. "I don't know how else to get there. There's nothing beneath the floor of the secret theater. So I'm going with the Arc. We'll go together."

"Jesus," Josh muttered. "He's just across the street!" He turned towards the window, closed and hidden behind a *Terminator II* poster. Tearing it down, he yelled towards the street. "Hey! Someone's in there!" Wasted effort. Even if he'd bothered opening the window, the construction workers wouldn't have heard. Had Josh made the slightest bit of effort to run downstairs and across the street, to even attempt to save his friend, it would have been too late. Josh knew that in the back of his mind, but doing nothing at all just seemed incalculably wrong. He also knew that this was what Kearns wanted. His "Hey!" would assuage any guilt he'd feel later. It was a pre-emptive, moral strike. Having done next to nothing, his conscience was clean.

Neither Boone nor Alyce even considered a move. Not

to stop or save. They stared at Kearns' image with unreadable faces. A thought that passed between them: This was an answer to a couple of problems. There was that yearning possibility that Kearns was right. Like Copper slipping between the frames of his own film, maybe this was Kearns way of, as he said, "getting behind the screen."

For the first time in months, Kearns smiled.

The wrecking ball exploded through the wall behind him, turning Kearns' video image into a Tetris screen. Moiré patterns broke up the picture, jumping it to blue and then back to scene: Kearns, hurled aside by the force, engulfed by the rolling cloud of dust and debris.

For just an instant, before the camera gave out, there he was again: standing, as if he hadn't been the slightest bit affected by the destruction. Kearns still smiled straight into the camera, gave them a thumbs up. Then the ceiling caved in and the screen went black.

Josh leapt first, stabbing REWIND on the DVR, and Bobby K. reconstituted before them on the monitor. Twice. Going frame-by-frame, like searching for Copper, they watched the catastrophic turn miraculous.

Kearns, standing, wearing his sad and demented expression.

The Wall behind him, destroyed with dust and fury.

Kearns, knocked forward by the impact.

Geometric squares of video color and black and white.

Two frames of "Lost Signal" blue.

Continuation of Kearns, vanishing past the bottom of the frame—

—yet still standing, maintaining his place, his smile, his posture.

Hold.

Hold.

Rolling cloud.

Collapsing ceiling.

Black frames cut to blue.

They argued over one another, processing what they'd seen. Sliding his finger over the remote, Josh rolled the footage back and forth frames at a time. As Kearns falls forward, he leaves an image of himself behind. Not a ghost or a mistranslation of digital data. This was an afterimage of Robert Kearns. It existed for twenty-two frames. Less than a second.

The image was out-of-sync with the camera shutter. As the Nikon captured the final moments at 30 frames-per-second, the twenty-two frame Kearns image *rolled*. The second Kearns was a projected image, running at 24 f.p.s.

Projected from where?

It had been live footage, streamed right to their feed. No time for an effect. Kearns was there, gone, there again, then nothing.

Rushing down the street, they were kept at bay by police stringing yellow tape between plastic saw horses. Men in yellow hard-hats waved at the dust cloud, already dispersing, revealing the rubble which had been, minutes ago, The Arc Theater. The final line in the sand for Bobby Kearns. Many hours later, a bulldozer found his body, crumpled and pulverized by the former Nickelodeon, the former Palace, the Arc Theatre, Jewel of the Welles.

SCENE FIVE:
BOONE AND BORGIA

News got around about Kearns. Within hours, the entirety of Orson was in heavy debate. Moral and ethical questions were raised and contested. Before too long, several factions had emerged, with Kearns' supporters becoming worshippers, and the detractors evolving into zealots. By mid-afternoon, Kearns was a legend on his way to demigod status.

For Boone, the Kearns question went beyond discussion. He'd known the man for over a decade, going on two. He knew the Kearns who'd graduated, happy, optimistic. Then he met the Kearns who'd escaped his bondage Out There. They'd been completely different men. That he checked himself out came as no surprise. Shock, however, was something different.

Boone spent the rest of the day in the Secret Cinema, watching movies that both he and Kearns had enjoyed together. Which turned out to be no easy feat. The two men had vastly different tastes inspired by the entirety of their upbringing and personalities. What they could agree on—*The Third Man, Miller's Crossing,* and *The Maltese Falcon*—played before his mind's eye.

But the Secret Cinema seemed no longer interested in entertainment. Subtly at first, before it even registered to Boone's eye, the Secret Cinema was changing the films. Lines of dialogue he'd never heard before:

"You think this is about ego?" asked Orson Welles as Harry Lime, moments before the film's majestic chase through the sewers of Vienna. "This is about transcendence. This is about becoming greater than you'd ever hoped to be."

It was a clumsy line, out of place with the rest of the film. It stood out. Boone knew the movie backwards and forwards. That line had never been there before. He wondered if the Secret Cinema was showing an alternate version. Something lost to the physical world but stored Elsewhere.

In *Miller's Crossing*, Gabriel Byrne, as gangster Tom Regan, turned directly to the camera and addressed the audience. "Art is about something bigger than its ingredients. Art is a doorway to the rest of the universe."

In *The Maltese Falcon*, Sam Spade's final goodbye to Bridget O'Shaunessey included the phrase, "The black bird is just a door-way, kid. Just another doorway." For a moment, Bogart looked exactly like Rupert Borgia. Following the film's famous final line, referring to the Falcon statuette as "the stuff that dreams are made of", Spade looked directly at the camera— directly at Boone—and in Borgia's voice said, "Just let me in, Boone. And everything will be set right."

The direct address didn't startle him—the absence of surprise was the real shock. Why shouldn't Borgia be speaking to him through the films? It was Shel's machinations that set the search in motion, but it was all Boone's effort that brought the screening to life. It had been his journey, very much a classic hero's journey, he thought. Borgia no doubt respected that. Bringing those films to light had been Boone's greatest accomplishment—his films, his life's work, be damned.

Mary Astor replied to Borgia's Spade, her face imploring, but with Kearns' voice: "We unlocked that secret, Sam. That's why most people go mad. Watching those movies. They weren't ready to see what we saw. But we'd been prepared. Don't you see? We've been preparing our entire lives. What else did we ever do with our time? We watched movies. Discussed them. Read about them. We *ate them*, Sam. To prepare ourselves. Condition our bodies for what lies on the other side of the screen."

At the close of *The Maltese Falcon*, the Secret Cinema screen did not return to blank silver. Instead, it showed The Magus, The Artist, staring smiling, but intently, directly at Boone.

What more did "real" life have to offer? The entirety of his life had been dedicated to movies. Study that went well beyond class-assigned homework. Borgia *understood* movies. They were depictions of life reordered into something logical, coherent. Necessary. His own attempts at adding to film history had been only marginally successful. What he'd always wanted was to merge with the art form. He'd wanted to *become* a movie.

Once he understood that desire, which came into such clear definition as he sat matching Borgia's eyes, everything was thrown into sharp clarity. Life is hard, bright, the edges too sharp and bereft of sprocket holes, the path directionless, decisions unclear. Luther Borgia had found a means around all of that. He'd found a place outside of the physical, where meaning was easily understood.

Boone wanted that. More than anything, he wanted that clarity. He needed that understanding. To the Borgia image he said out loud, "Come on in."

As the Borgia image smiled, satisfied and genuinely joyful, the Secret Cinema screen shattered like glass. The silver cloth disintegrated into a million shards and sprayed across the floor of the stage.

Revealing a dark, starlined infinity. The gateway to meaning. Without hesitation, Boone stepped into the void.

SCENE SIX:
THE FLICKERING MEN IN ALYCE'S LIFE

Alyce rolled over and found her bed empty. She'd fallen asleep with Boone beside her, stroking her hair as he flixed on *American Pop*. They'd been discussing the Secret Cinema. They both could feel it calling them. They'd spent days on end downstairs, snuggled into the overstuffed chairs, watching whatever came to mind.

They'd tried a number of times to sync up and watch the same thing. Though they'd settled on *Jaws*, what played for her eyes was *A Night to Remember*. What played for him, he told her, was *Repulsion*. The theater had a way of knowing what you really wanted.

Since the first screening, they hadn't run into the Kid, Maya, again. Not in the theater, not in any of the Kids' floors. Truth be told, they didn't look particularly hard for her. She wasn't one of The Addicts. Before the Screening, neither of them had known her name. She was simply an Extra, a seat-filler. She was likely off somewhere, occupying space in the background for someone else's story.

Though Boone spent the day downstairs mourning for Kearns, Alyce felt surprisingly invigorated by the screenwriter's intentional demise. Something about watching Kearns finally seize hold of his destiny and let go of his past, though tragic, was inspiring. While Boone engaged with the Secret Cinema, instead of joining him, she'd thrown herself into her screenplay. Miraculously, all of her blocks had vanished. She typed with a ferocity she hadn't known in years.

When Boone finally emerged from the basement, he'd been withdrawn, distracted. There was something off about his eyes—his pupils were too wide, perhaps, or the brown iris had gone greener. It didn't immediately occur to her that Luther Borgia had had hazel eyes.

Hearing the door open in the next room, Alyce struggled

from the clinging sheets and climbed out of bed. Shrugging into an oversized Elvira t-shirt, she called for Boone in a half-whisper. No idea what time it was. None of the DVD players displayed clocks any more.

The door was wide open. All was dark in the iron-wrought hallway. "Boone?" she called again, louder, not caring who she woke up. Down the catwalk and around the corner, a dim light shined.

Flickered.

She steeled herself. No half-ghost after-image of a dead murderer was going to stop her from finding Boone. Had Borgia taken him? Coaxed him out of bed without her knowing? Could he hurt them? He was little more than a shadow made of light. What could he do beyond…influence?

Bare feet on bare floor, soles slapping against the cracked linoleum and the old wood revealed beneath. She wasn't afraid.

She wasn't afraid. "Boone!"

Around the corner, she found Boone. Flickering at 24-frames-per-second.

His ghostly image was tinged with a slight blue, flickering, rolling, but silent and smiling serenely. The sight stopped her in her tracks, she muffled a scream with a tight fist held to her open mouth. Legs suddenly weak, she sat down hard. Boone remained smiling, standing over her, offering her no assistance. He took a step forward.

Then she saw the source of the projection. Again, it was Boone. Further down the hallway, behind the flickering image of himself, naked, eyes closed, sleepwalking—the light poured from his open mouth.

Just as it had done to Shel the Agent, *The Divine Heresy* had turned Boone into a walking magic lantern, producing a hologram of himself, an image at peace with its state of existence. The projected Boone held its hand out to her.

Instinctively, she scuttled away, tearing her heels and her thighs on jagged thorns of linoleum. The Boone Image took another step and backed her against the wall. His ghostly hand reached out to caress her face. She felt nothing, not even a change in temperature as the image flattened against her cheek. The image was without depth. It was safe.

Leaping forward, she barreled through the projection and ran to Boone, the real Boone, standing upright and open-mouthed just a few feet away. She called his name, seized his shoulders, shook him awake. His eyes snapped open. His mouth snapped shut. The Image Boone vanished.

Disoriented, Boone looked around, confused as to his location, as to why his lover was sobbing into his bare chest. He looked past her. At the flickering man down the hall, waving at them with a friendly, beckoning gesture.

CUTAWAYS

From his place at the railing two floors up, Seth watched the entire display. Unable to sleep, hot and restless, he'd moved into the hallway, wishing he smoked just to pass the time. Only a few minutes had gone by when he saw Boone emerge from around the corner on five. Or, at least, the brighter image of him preceding his physical body. It was like witnessing a sleepwalker's astral projection.

Soon, Alyce followed, and behind her was Borgia himself, lurking in the surrounding darkness. Seth watched as both flickering images bracketed her along the catwalk.

It wasn't until all parties had departed that Seth exhaled the breath he didn't realize he was holding.

*****

The Arc wasn't the only thing that crumbled. Destruction of the theater seemed to affect the ghastly evolution the Squat was experiencing. The horrors were ramping up.

With still no contact from *f.p.s.*, Seth wandered the halls, restless, looking in on The Kids' common room, as the Addicts' room on five sat vacant. What need did they have of a common room when the Secret Cinema gave them everything they wanted? Not that there were many Addicts left. The guy in the attic—the guy whose movie he'd seen, Copper?—had vanished. The screenwriter who'd worked with Lee Benway apparently went down with the Arc. Hadn't he heard someone mention that another someone had drowned in their apartment, on a floor above his? Or was that just a fiction inspired by one of their endlessly-playing movies?

Since half of the building had been present for the first round of *The Divine Heresy*, he'd kept an eye out for tell-tale signs of Borgia poisoning. Could the films affect the casual mind, even without the "proper" presentation? He didn't know.

So he watched for bloody tears or sudden bursts of violence. His regular paranoia had him crouched and waiting regardless. At least now he felt primed for something more specific.

More Kids were popping up with perf-track scars on their faces. As they passed by him in the hall, looking so young to his eyes, he took note of which tracks were older and healing and which were still freshly crusted over. Apparently, the all-night marathons had grown in popularity, but was that Borgia's influence or simply an effect of mid-terms? Did these Kids even go to class any more?

It was the ones with different scars that really worried him. He'd counted three Kids—two boys and one girl—who had slashed the corners of their mouths into wider grins. He imagined them achieving their Black Dahlia-cum-Joker smiles with the blades of a guillotine splicer.

Others had recently turned their foreheads into flesh-billboards for arcane symbols he didn't quite recognize. Even when he'd been in school, there was a persistent danger for some film students to fall in with a darker edge of cinema worship. The more vulnerable found themselves aligned with the mysterious Gods of Film, and would sometimes carve the strange symbols of Cinemagog and his ilk into their flesh. This was nothing new. He knew guys in the industry who still bore remnants of those juvenile marks.

Impossible to tell what was potentially Borgia nonsense and what was regular student nonsense. What angst was real and what was manufactured? Or was it all manufactured?

There'd been multiple reported sightings of the Flickering Man, Luther Borgia himself. Even Cris had seen him, standing off to the side during takes, watching her models doing a scene, exuding a voyeuristic nastiness that was usually reserved for the other side of the computer screen. She was used to having viewers, but not being viewed. "But," she told Seth later, "neither of the girls seemed to notice him at all."

"That makes sense," he said. "They weren't at the

screening."

She reminded him: "Neither. The fuck. Was I."

One evening he took Cris with him down to the Kids common room—"I don't want to feel like the creepy uncle skeezing on the girls," he added, "or guys." They sat near the wall on the floor, their backs to the little kitchenette island buried beneath empty chip bags, old beer bottles, the accumulated refuse of twenty children away from home for the first time with no one to tell them to clean up.

The Kids had on *Bottle Rocket*. They laughed, smoked, drank. They flixed. In the corners, unconcerned and uninhibited, they fucked. This was a tribe, he recognized, a clan of modern cave dwellers enthralled by their flashing shadows. Their whole civilization was this room.

Wandering down the hall to one of the communal bathrooms, Seth startled a girl sitting in an open stall on the floor. On the john behind her sat Luther Borgia, who stroked her hair as she slowly cut stripes into her forearm with a utility razor blade. She looked up at Seth as he entered, but apart from brief surprise, she barely registered that he was there. The horror was awkward. Literally, he had no immediate course of action. Should he stop her? And risk Borgia losing an armed acolyte? Or would they both ignore him. Borgia certainly hadn't acknowledged his presence.

Satisfied with the work done on her arm, the girl took the blade to her face. Between thumb and forefinger, she squeezed her earlobe and stretched it away from her skull. The razor slid through the soft flesh neatly, and with a wet whisper Seth would take to his grave.

It was only then he noticed the bloody hand prints that dotted the walls, the mirrors, the sinks, even the ceiling in spots. Then he noticed the twin streams of blood trickling from under the door of the stall next to the girl's. The girl noticed it too. Her face broke into a broad, toothy smile, delighted and bright. Laughing, she banged her fist on the facility wall. From the closed stall came a bubbling sound, a gurgling—a laugh through a throat gargling blood. Blood on the walls, down the side of the girl's face, down the collar of the t-shirt she wore as a nightgown. Along the seams of the tile, racing towards his shoes.

"This is going to get worse," he told Cris, who'd watched, while he was gone, a girl chew through her own lip, oblivious to the pain and damage and coppery taste. "I don't know what to do."

"You've seen this before?"

He nodded. "And what did you do last time?" she asked.

"I burned the place to the ground. And everyone in it."

They returned to her room, neither of them saying a word during the elevator ride. Once they were behind her locked door, Cris looked at him. "Got a Plan B?"

He did, but he couldn't articulate it. Not yet. The idea was still turning around in his mind. He thought of Goddard's Edict: "A photograph is truth. Cinema is truth at 24-frames-per-second."

He thought of the white man's superstition that primitive cultures believe that a photograph stole a person's soul. What did that mean for a film strip? Was the soul shredded and spread across thousands of frames? The query led him to Borgia, the man who'd spread his soul across the hundreds of thousands of frames that made up his five little masterpieces. He thought of the "spell" that released those soul fragments, those atomic particles of spirit, and allowed the man to walk, flickering, through the halls of the Squat and infect the minds of a brand new audience. The viewers, the viewed. Electricity conducted via eye-contact.

Filming captured the spirit. Replaying the captured images released the spirit. What would happen if those reassembled fragments were filmed again? Could the Devil be exiled the same way twice?

All these thoughts battled and swirled in Seth's mind, a

literal brainstorm tossing about inside his skull. But to Cris, he didn't say a word.

SCENE DELETED:
THE LOVERS GRIM

Jewell and Jed knew that the older people, the ones who'd gone Out There and come back broken and shattered, retreating into cocoons of the familiar, referred to their class as "The Kids." The insult was just something to endure, because there was some truth to it. They were younger, they were still learning. Maybe they hadn't seen every goddamn movie made since the invention of the hand-crank camera. Maybe they didn't give a shit. Fuck Méliès and the fucking Lumières. Fuck D.W. Griffith and Welles and John Fucking Racist-Ass Ford. Let's talk about the new artists, the ones still alive, still working. The guys making the art right now. What did it matter where film came from? Where it was going—*that* was what they needed to know.

"Film." Even the medium was wrong. "Film" is dead! Long live Digital! As far as they were concerned, Jewell and Jed and the others in their class, "film" was good for only one thing. You couldn't flix on a digital file.

Using just the tip of her tongue, Jewell teased the single razor thin frame of film out of the palm of her hand. It hung suspended between the two of them, their lips so close to touching, before she drew it back and gently gripped the edges between her teeth, revealed by her smile. The frame was one of five they'd been saving, from a new release print of George A. Romero's magnum opus, *Dawn of the Dead*. It had been safely stored with the other four, gently tucked away inside a first-edition hardback of Danny Peary's *Cult Movies*.

Jed's mouth closed over hers and the frame disappeared, held between his tongue and hers. Swaying their tongues back and forth, to and fro, into his mouth then hers, already they could feel the film's effects seeping into their blood stream.

Emulsion dissolving away with their shared saliva, the power of the movie, its contents and all that went into creating it, electrifying their nervous systems. Jewell riding him, straddling his lap tantric-style, as they shared the frame.

Behind them, the flatscreen TV mounted over the head of the bed played their favorite greatest hits. Other couples—norms, muggles, mundanes, straights, vanillas—had "their" songs to make love to. For Jed and Jewell, it was a carefully-selected compilation of their favorite death scenes. A mirror at the foot of the bed, another over the bed, allowed them perfect visual from all angles: themselves and the screen. Flixing and fucking and happy anniversary.

As she impaled herself upon him, as he held her face gently in the cup of his hand, she whispered in his ear, "Let's see if we can tackle this *petit morte*, supersize it to *le grande*." He shuddered and the tremor passed into her. And the opening volley, Krug and company murdering Mari Collingwood, roared to life: Wes Craven's classic sleaze-and-destroy, *The Last House on the Left*. Jed was inside Jewell, just as David Hess as Krug reached into Sandra Peabody as Mari's abdomen, making external what was internal, pulling hand over hand.

Thrusting in time to the irregular pulse of the scene, Jewell raked her long nails along Jed's back and sides. Little troughs, furrows, instantly filled with blood, while he nibbled her throat. Holding the tiniest bit of flesh between his teeth, he bit down and she gasped, and hot blood dripped into his mouth, over his tongue and over the frame.

Last House ended abruptly and another treasure, *Blood Feast* from the Godfather of Gore, Herschell Gordon Lewis, blossomed crimson. Now the bed was a stone altar to the Egyptian God of the Dead. He was Rantes, she was the nubile Suzette Fremont as played by Connie Mason, and her heart was beating and spurting in his hands. Blood streamed between her breasts, over both pierced nipples, momentarily obscuring her ankh tattoo in the hollow of her collarbone. Flixing harder now, it was as if H.G. himself stood beside them and beamed in approval.

Separating from him, she spun onto her stomach and clawed at the dirt beneath her, clawing up mud and pine needles as she fought to crawl away, like the perfect little victim. He'd grown a burlap hood to hide his face, just like Jason in *Friday the 13th Part 3* in "Super 3-Dm," though the print was clean and in two dimensions only. His machete sailed down, slicing through air and her neck. Tearing at her thong with his free hand as her legs still kicked. Even with the blade millimeters away from severing her spine, she continued to fight him. His entire palm came down hard on her left buttock, instantly leaving a raised handprint behind, and if her windpipe was still connected she would have cried out in happy terror.

Another hard cut to a brand new scene and now he was beneath her (she would not always be the prey, not always be the Final Girl, nor would he constantly play predator) and the chainsaw in her hands screamed and spewed gasoline smoke. Viscous red sprayed over her face, her bare breasts, blotting out all traces of white along her curves. (Her curves—he loved the shape of her. She was built like a woman, not the modern day depiction of starving teenaged androgyne.) His scream of horror and agony also filled with blood. Jewell raised the running tool of destruction over her head and let out a triumphant howl, the running blade still shaking off his life's liquid. He saw now the stitched seams between her breasts and shoulder blades, criss-crossing over her face. Jewell wearing a patchwork girl-suit. Leather Jewell.

A favorite now, the very literal climax of *Nekromantik II*. Her back arched as he spasmed beneath her as she roughly sawed off his head. More blood spewed, continued to spew, would continue to spew and the night was still young.

Passing the dissolving frame back and forth between them, the hooks and chains shot out of the darkness, tearing into them both. He placed a gold coin on her exposed heart, she castrated him with the barber's scissors while he remained inside her. They wallowed in wet red.

Deep breaths from both as the montage started, all of the best and most twisted from the David Cronenberg collection. Their hips slammed together, flesh pressing flesh, the very atoms of their bodies fusing and unfusing as the rhythm increased to a primal atonal beat. Her hand slid into a slit in his stomach. His touch withdrew tumors from deep inside her brain. His touch so intense she swore he was on both sides of her at once. Something slithered out of her mouth—the frame curled into a flesh tube?— wriggling and slithering until it found an opening into him. Eyes rolled showing white then boiling in the sockets. Fetal creatures beating at them with tiny fists, their body temperatures growing hot and white hot as an appendage grew from her armpit and impaled his hand as he struggled to impale her further. Veins bulging, swelling, straining against the confines of their skin, showing them the future of fireballs and vivisection and now the car crashes, the shrieking metal and sparking chrome tumbling end over end in the air and over black asphalt, safety glass shattering into billions of pebbles shredding their bodies and finally gas tanks exploded and so, at that moment... at that moment… at that wonderful moment…

… so did their heads.

Tissue, brain matter, white bone, shredded organs, bits and pieces and glops of red slid down the walls and dripped from the mirror ceiling. Jed and Jewell blended together in the charnel carnal afterglow.

From the sanguine sheets, they regrew whole, their bodies reassembling, him separating from her though they were still joined, fused, like emulsion to celluloid. The frame of film was dissolved, consumed, like the actions of the zombie that had been captured via the magic of photo-electric chemistry.

Easing herself up, just a little, she slid away from him and collapsed and all the blood was draining away while they panted and laughed and the final scene played behind them. Jed held Jewell just as James Spader held Kara Unger at the end of *Crash*. Jewell's body was contorted in sweat-slick bliss, just as Unger's was twisted post car (intentional) accident. And they heard themselves delivering Spader's final line, like a whispered prayer of hope and happiness. Laying exhausted and smiling and loving each other, bodies intact. They laughed, then said, softly, with Spader, "Maybe next time, my love." Blood now a slick of perspiration, their skin glistening in the flickering light.

"Maybe next time."

SCENE SEVEN:
JOSH SHOULD HYDRATE

After a week, Josh realized he didn't need the Secret Cinema any longer. His television started to behave like the magic basement screen: anything he wanted to watch was there before him. Magical still: it was interactive.

It started with *The Ring*. Not the Japanese original, but the American remake, which he preferred. In fact, most of his favorite movies were the ones the other Addicts despised, a fact that brought him greater joy. He loved seeing the looks on others' faces when he declared his love for *Die Hard II*, proclaimed *The Phantom Menace* to be the best of the *Star Wars* series. His room was plastered with posters for *Jaws IV, License to Kill, Supergirl.* He'd made them sit through *Ishtar* just to watch them suffer.

During the first victim's view of *The Ring*'s haunted video, where the tortured ghost, Sadako, crawling from her stone well and out of the TV screen, the scene didn't stop where he'd expected. Over the dozen or so times he'd watched it, Sadako had never emerged from *his* television set. Because that would have been ridiculous. Even moreso if she'd crawled across the room, face hidden within her long, trailing black hair, slithered up his lap, and put her head between his legs.

Which is what happened.

He'd just assumed it was an erotic vision brought about by flixing on *Showgirls*. But when he put his hand on the back of her head, he could feel her hair and scalp beneath his palm. He felt her ragged nails dig into his naked thighs. Her ghost mouth was moist, a chill damp around his penis, her tongue colder still. But that didn't stop his orgasm.

With a violent shudder in the darkness, he shouted out loud as he spasmed. Then Sadako was gone and the movie played on. Once again, he was alone in the room. Quickly, he changed movies, his fumbling hands knocking over stacks of DVDs as he hurried to find the right one. Soon it was Kara Zor-

El, cousin to Kal-El, daughter of Krypton, played by Helen Slater, who emerged from his TV set. Contrary to the film, she behaved just like Sadako, slithering from the glass and crawling across the floor on hands and knees. This time he felt the whisper of her blond hair against his legs, heard the rustle of her costume, a fabric his fingertips couldn't identify. When she was done with her initial tease, she turned from him, still on her hands and knees, and flipped her tiny skirt over her waist, beckoning to him with big blue eyes. There in the darkness.

Over the course of two or three days—time was unclear—he'd experienced Pon-Far with Lt. Saavak. Had a tryst with both Kaylee and Inarra aboard the Companion's perfumed shuttle in *Serenity*. Found himself buried beneath all three of the—*modern*—Charlie's Angels, with Lucy Liu's Alex straddling him first. Later, it was he who brought the Silk Spectre to climax, forcing her body against the controls of the Owlship, spitting a tongue of flame across the sky while Leonard Cohen sang "Hallelulia," while he held the end of the chain that led to Slave Leia, lounging against a bed of cushions. In sheer decadence, he bedded every woman in *Sin City*—every gun-wielding Valkyrie submitting to him. To follow up, he allowed all of Frank Miller's bastardized *Spirit* women to take their turn with him.

He couldn't remember the last time he ate or drank anything. Nor could he remember flixing since his TV became his sex portal to Movieland. Nor did he mind being watched, constantly, by the flickering man in the corner. Not even when he transformed Terry Farrell into a Female Cenobite, used her hooks and chains against her.

At once used up and exhausted, Josh sank to the floor and watched *Weird Science*, desperately hoping that Kelly LeBrock wouldn't come calling midway through. He considered switching to something without erotic danger and almost settled on *The Thing* before he realized that all of the characters in that film were men, and none of them had seen a woman in some time. He had no desire to be cornholed by R.J. MacReady. Or worse, by Wilford Brimley.

As he fired up *Sucker Punch*, he became aware that his TV was watching him back. At some point during his sex vacation, the TV had gained eyelids, complete with long lashes, which blinked periodically as he stared into its pupil. Sometimes moisture would gather at the corners; large tears would drop onto his already-ruined carpet. Midway through *Josie and the Pussycats*—his body was ready to go again, with Jenna Malone or Tara Reid—the movie faded away, replaced by an image of himself in his room.

The TV blinked around the mirror scene, but the vision didn't change back. Irritation grew. He was eager for a romp with cute girls in cat ears. The remote did nothing. The TV blinked at him in defiance.

Dropping the remote the floor, he stood up fast, fought a dizzy spell brought on by extreme dehydration, and reached for the television's manual switches. On the screen, the Video Josh did the same. Only the Video Josh reached out from the confines of the glass and seized hold of the Real Josh's hand.

Alarmed, he pulled back, but the Video Josh's grip was stronger than his own. It pulled him forward. As his hand passed through the glass surface, he fought back, bracing his feet against the entertainment center as he pulled, struggling to free his captured limb. The Video Josh held on with both hands and yanked harder.

There was no sensation as he slipped through the blinking portal. Not even a change of air temperature. Just the feeling of falling. Falling. Falling.

Until he was firmly on the ground. No impact. No sudden halt in decent. First he felt the falling. Next he was safe on his feet. Somewhere off in the distance, a boat horn sounded, scattering complaining seagulls. Then the smell of low tide hit his nostrils, the rancid stench sent him reeling as he covered his mouth and nose with his sleeve. A white sleeve stained yellow, stinking of beer and sweat. Awareness of his surroundings slammed him hard.

He stood on a cobblestone walkway along the bank of a filthy river, fourth or fifth in line behind a row of vagrants and sailors stretching before and behind him. An old fashioned car—something out of *The Untouchables* or the 1955 parts of *Back to the Future*—sat parked on the road beside them. Water lapped over the breakers; trash and debris washed onto the stones. At the head of the line, where a greying man stared down, waiting his turn, was a filthy mattress dumped on the ground. On the mattress was a sailor, naked from the waist down, finishing up with the moaning woman beneath him.

This wasn't one of his movies. This was one of Copper's. Who was the woman? Her filthy blonde hair sweat-matted against her face, her make-up smeared, mascara running. He recognized the face from *Single White Female* and suddenly realized what movie he was in. Definitely one of Copper's favorites. *Last Exit to Brooklyn.*

For no reason, he remembered the character's name: Tralala. Played by Jennifer Jason Leigh. And he was at the end of the film. Where a broken, rejected Tralala, drunk and at rock bottom, pulls a train with the boys on the docks. The gang bang will kill her.

No. Not my movie!

He wanted to run. Get out of line and run as fast as he could. But to where? Where was his portal on this side of the glass?

The sailor finished up and climbed off of Tralala, leaving a bruised and bleeding woman on the mattress. The next man stepped forward, dropping his pants as she weakly beckoned him to hurry. The line advanced. Josh felt rough hands shove him forward. To keep the line moving.

Even then, his body wouldn't obey. He couldn't leave the line. He couldn't bark at the man who'd shoved him. Long, long minutes went by. Tears rolled down his face as he helplessly dropped his own trousers and stumbled forward, laying on top of her, breathing in the coppery smell of blood, urine, and alcohol sweat. Tralala seized a handful of his hair and it hurt, but her grip weakened once he was inside of her.

Wordlessly, he begged. He thought of the flickering man and pleaded with him to stop this.

Because this wasn't *his movie*.

Only a few minutes had passed before he realized that Tralala no longer held his hair. Her eyes remained open, fixed on the sky above her. He was still inside her as her body grew cold.

It still wasn't over.

He thought of the Eyelid TV.

Please. Please! For the love of God —

Then there were rough hands on the back of his neck. He felt male flesh pressing against his thighs. Whoever was in line behind him was determined to have his turn. Josh couldn't withdraw from the dead and cold Tralala. He couldn't fight off the man mounting him now.

Please! Please! Please!

Blink!

CHAPTER EIGHT

"I don't like the idea of "understanding" a film. I don't believe that rational understanding is an essential element in the reception of any work of art. Either a film has something to say to you or it hasn't. If you are moved by it, you don't need it explained to you. If not, no explanation can make you moved by it."

— Federico Fellini

"Cinema is the ultimate pervert art. It doesn't give you what you desire—it tells you how to desire."

— Slavoj i ek ("The Pervert's Guide to Cinema," 2006)

"For a moment the feeling crept over me that my work, my vision, is going to destroy me, and for a fleeting moment I let myself take a long, hard look at myself, something I would not otherwise do--out of instinct, on principle, out of self-preservation--look at myself with objective curiosity to see whether my vision has not destroyed me already. I found it comforting to note that I was still breathing."

— Werner Herzog, "Conquest of the Useless: Reflections from the Making of Fitzcarraldo."

SCENE ONE:
SETH AND OOMPAH

"You're doing the right thing," Seth told himself. "It's the classic third-act sacrifice." He'd taken the last booth in Shain's Diner, his back to the wall so he could watch the door and avoid re-enacting the end of every Wild Bill Hickok movie. He stirred another packet of sugar into his bitter blue-black coffee. Above him, the fluorescents flickered like a projector. Beneath the table were the dusty soup cans, resting safely between his feet. Straddling the cans gave him the feeling of safety, but it did nothing to assuage his sick guilt. His stomach clenched at the sound of the little bell chiming above the door, announcing his contact's dramatic arrival.

He didn't know what to expect. That morning, he'd taken a roll of gaffer's tape and marked an 'X' into his window. That was the universal sign in spy movies for "I'm ready to talk." Usually, it was to signal a contact. He had no contacts. Only the men in dark suits that stood across the street from his window. Would they know what he needed in return?

That afternoon, he watched a folded slip of paper slide under his door. Of course, there was no one to be found on the other side.

The paper was an old flier, advertising last Halloween's showing of *The Rocky Horror Picture Show* on the Griffith campus. Written on the other side was "Shain's Diner. 4pm. We'll bring what you need. You bring what's ours."

Stepping outside of the Squat for the first time in weeks, Seth was immediately slammed with anxiety. Cris had divined his primary concern: "It's a trap," she said, and not in a jokey, Admiral Akbar way. "As soon as you step outside with those cans, they'll gun you down. Nobody here is going to take the time to even hose you off the sidewalk."

"If I don't go," he said, "there won't be anyone left to complain."

Outside the front door was a world that was bigger than he remembered, a yawning stretch of buildings and teeming with humanity, any one of them could mean him harm. He paused in the doorway, a can in each hand, and waited for the terminating bullet. It didn't come. Only self-consciousness at standing in one place for so long. People passed him by on the street, not a one of them giving him a second glance. Adjusting his grip on the uncomfortably narrow steel handles, he turned West and walked toward Shain's.

Diner light illuminated the Agent's face beneath the brim of his black fedora: the big reveal, subverting audience anticipation. The contact in the black duster and the shining black boots, tall as Lee Marvin in *The Killers* and dressed as smartly, was not Terry from *f.p.s.*, or any of the James Bonds, or even Bobby Kearns defying death to return in the final reel. Instead, it was an agent from the MPAA—"Oompah"—carrying a metal briefcase, approaching Seth's booth. True to formula, Seth recognized this agent and was surprised by his lack of surprise because it was a twist he'd seen coming. The Agent was Luke Widdowes.

It wouldn't have been anyone else. Story dictated that he turn the McGuffin over to the Evil Society, make his Deal with the Devil, a trade for the Secret Weapon, in order to Save the Day. For the Agent to be an Unknown, an extra, would be a dramatic betrayal. Thematic necessity: it had to be his former best friend, his one-time companion turned sworn enemy.

As he slid into the booth across from Seth, Luke removed his fedora, revealed his Yul Brynner-smooth scalp, his familiar Raymond Massey forehead, and wide Richard Widmark-as-Tommy Udo grin filled with Burt Lancaster's teeth. "Snappy opening remark," Luke said in greeting. And Seth had to smile. Despite the growing nausea at both his personal betrayal and the dramatic irony, it was classic and perfect contrivance. "Witty retort," he said.

Luke gave his coffee order to the waitress, Roz. Because

she worked at Shain's—which had always been as far from the typical "INT. DINER" setting you could get while still reading as a restaurant—Roz didn't look like she came from Central Casting, wasn't a miscast Michelle Pfeiffer in *Frankie and Johnny*. She fit in reality and it unnerved both men in a way neither could explain.

"So," Seth began, sipping his coffee for dramatic effect, "did you know it was me when you took that shot from the alley?"

Luke smiled, shrugged appropriately. "If I'd wanted to kill you…" He intentionally trailed off.

"Yeah, yeah," Seth said, and laughed in spite of himself.

Roz delivered the Agent's coffee, providing him with the business he'd need for the rest of the scene, wherein the two old friends would catch up, trade their pleasantries and veiled threats, then conclude their business, leaving the situation open-ended for a possible sequel, depending on how it played with the crowds. There was no sense in fighting it.

"Should I bother asking what lured you to the Dark Side?" Seth asked.

Luke did his duty and played his part. Staying true to character, Luke only answered after dragging his tongue-stud across his teeth, making that picket fence noise that was his trademark all those years ago. "You'd think I followed the money but really, it was just the path of least resistance."

"Still making 'introductions'?"

"It's what I do."

Seth nodded. With a scraping of metal across linoleum, they made their exchange. Two soup cans and their accompanying reels for the square metal briefcase. Seth asked the appropriate question. "Is it loaded?"

"Yep. And the barrel is attached," Luke replied.

Seth stole a quick glance at the metal briefcase at his feet. It was thicker than normal, more a padded carrying case for the tool inside. He knew what it was without being told. It should work perfectly for what he needed it for. At the very least, it would give him and Cris a fighting chance to stop whatever Borgia from turning the Squat into whatever abyss he planned to make his home. It was the Secret Weapon.

"Just for fun," Seth continued. "I threw in a 25mm prime and a 10mm wide. In case you ever actually want to use it as a camera."

"Battery or wind?"

"Hand-wound. But you shouldn't have to crank too often. I tried it out last night. It runs nice.

Worth the trade. I made sure of it. Capture the footage. Put it all back in the can where it belongs." Luke tapped one of the soup cans with his foot. "I trust that when we lace this up, it's not going to be a driver's ed. scare film or something? You didn't switch it out with *Blood on the Asphalt* or *Our Friend the Atom*?"

"Even if I'd had the time," Seth said. "It's all there. I didn't give you a ringer filled with my whites."

Luke smiled at *The Big Lebowski* reference. "Nice."

"What're they gonna do with it?"

"Not my department," Luke said. "But if I had to guess, it'll go to restoration, get a big premiere and then, probably, Blu-Ray. Or maybe they'll put the old TCM version on there as an extra."

"Or maybe they'll stick it in one of those *Raiders*-type warehouses and lock it away again?"

His old friend gave him a vague combination of nod and shrug. "Maybe. Hiding it again isn't really in anyone's best interest." He shifted his posture to an odd angle. Seth realized that Luke had to be running his hand over the metal casings. As if to confirm for the audience, a little metallic noise came from under the table, which could only be explained by the Agent playing with the steel plate that acted as a latch. Like Rene` Belloq appreciating the Ark hidden inside its wooden crate. It seemed as if Luke was seconds away from spray-painting the cans with the MPAA's logo equivalent of a swastika, to alert the world of its new ownership. The mask of smugness slipped away for just a second. "Did you…did you check it out?"

"I didn't want to risk lacing it up. I unspooled a little of each reel, though. The tinting doesn't seem to have faded much. It's…pretty amazing."

Luke nodded, solemnly, reverently. Then the friend vanished again into its opportunistic shell. "So the Borgia films, huh?"

"Yeah," Seth said.

"How bad?"

"Bad. Bad enough for the trade. Obviously."

"Yeah, well…Positions reversed, I'd have given the print to Terry."

"The entirety of The Welles is *In the Mouth of Madness*, man. We read aloud from the 'Necronomicon Ex Mortis'."

"'The Book of the Dead of the Dead'," Luke said, picking up on Seth's *Army of Darkness* cue. "Remember to say the words. *Klatuu Barada Nikto*. Every little solitary syllable."

"Yeah, yeah." Seth reached for his coffee. A thought stopped his hand. He looked up.

"No," Luke said. "I'm not coming with you. And I'm not just saying that so I can show up again at the last minute. These are going into my trunk and I'm driving back to Manhattan."

Luke laughed when Seth didn't reply. "I'm serious. I'm not playing Han Solo or the Brad Dexter part from *Magnificent Seven*. I'm not going to turn around and help save the day, dude. You know why?"

"Because this isn't a movie."

"Because I really don't give a shit. And not just because this is your problem or my job, or that I'm getting any kind of bonus for delivering this. Which I totally am, by the way."

"You know what you sound like?"

"Of course I do. But I'm not the secretly altruistic Anti-Hero. Seth, I'm not a trope. And I'm not hip to the idea of dying while performing some heroic last-minute gambit. I'm really, honestly, getting in my car and driving away. If I do over 70 all the way there, I'll be back home in my apartment in five hours. I'll probably grab a beer, check my email, go to bed, and in the morning, deliver this long-lost print to my bosses. And all the way home, I'll hope that you get through this bullshit alive and maybe we can grab a drink in a couple of weeks or something. Once you get the hell out of this shit-hole once and for all. What I'm not going to do is pretend I'm a character in the movie of your life."

"You do understand what's going on? Those movies really *did* alter our reality."

"I believe you. But I'm going to keep my reality the way it is."

Seth looked at him. "Your reality? Where you dress like a '40s gangster and shoot at film critics."

"My reality where I work for a legitimate corporation and occasionally go up against thieves of intellectual property."

"You just tipped your hand." Seth made a gun out of his thumb and forefinger. "The MPAA doesn't publically consider itself to be a corporation."

"Seth, grow up, man. Seriously."

There should have been a closing line. A gesture. A dramatic finishing of his coffee, or a final, standing drag on a cigarette, ala *Goodfellas*. But like Luke, the Agent, the former best friend and now antagonist, rudely and coldly pointed out, this wasn't a beat in a screenplay. He placed his hat on his head and extended his open hand across the table. "Don't get yourself killed. Come visit me next month. I put one of my cards in the case."

Seth didn't respond. He stared into his nearly empty cup as Luke gathered up the soup cans, dropped a five dollar bill on the table, stood up to leave. "Good to see you again. Sorry I shot you." He gestured with the can in his giant right hand. "It's really cool that you found these. I can't wait to check it out."

"It won't live up to all the hype, of course."

"It's *London After Midnight*," he said. "Even if it's boring as hell, it's still gonna be really cool."

Watching Luke leave, a couple of scenarios ran through Seth's mind, all of them ending with his old friend arriving back at his New York apartment and reverently opening the first of the cans. Light from inside will beam out, illuminating Luke's face like the Ark's holy light. Or, more appropriately, the deathly blaze of the *Kiss Me Deadly* isotope.

Either way, resulting in the Agent's flesh-melting and fiery end.

SCENE TWO:
AND THEN THERE WERE TWO

Rusty left that morning. With multiple backpacks stuffed with equipment, spools, tapes, sundry, Rusty struggled his burden down the narrow attic staircase and into the elevator. He ran into Alyce on the way out.

"I've got Copper in here," he told her, hoisting up the plastic handle holding the old iMac box together. "And I've got all of my stuff too. Tell Boone he can have whatever is left."

"Why don't you tell him yourself?" she asked.

He shrugged. "Who would I tell? Ghost Boone or his comatose body?" She didn't know the precise details, but she could guess. Boone hadn't been himself for a while. Rusty shrugged and attempted a smile. "You know," his voice cracked and he tried to hide it behind a cough. "You guys should make a movie. Just pool all your resources and do something together."

The words seemed so far away. Rusty was speaking at a distance she couldn't discern. He nodded again, emphatically. "Seriously. Do something. Do *anything*."

"We will," she said, lying brightly. "I promise."

A third nod, with downcast eyes. "Don't you think it's weird?" he said to the floor. "Twelve floors of filmmakers. Nobody's even taking selfies." One last attempt at a smile, then he turned away from her.

Looking at Rusty, she wanted to hug him goodbye. He'd been The Addicts' little brother. Their mascot. More than Copper's acolyte. Or surrogate son.

But she didn't.

She couldn't even watch him trundle his stuff through the door for the last time.

Returning to her room, Boone was asleep on the bed, propped sitting up against the headboard, eyes closed, mouth slack. And from his mouth came the Projection, the Other Boone, who stood smiling and waiting for her, flickering at 24 frames-per-second.

The deep sob, violent and wracking, caught her completely by surprise. Violently, she turned from the Other Boone and hurried out her door again. Leaning over the railing, gasping for air, she looked down. Down to the first floor, the wide-open atrium where the elevators met the stairs. There were Kids all up and down the stairways, passing in the halls. So many of them walking, eyes shut, mouths open, preceded by their own projections, their own Other Selves. They were a Flickering Army now, the epidemic had spread.

Wiping tears away with the heel of her hand, she turned abruptly. And passed right through The Other Boone, nearly knocking down the sleepwalking Real Boone in the process. Somehow, she was between them, real and projection, and yet could see them both clearly. Whatever light source gave the Other Boone his life and depth was strong enough to pass through her solid body. Even when she waved her hand in the cone-shaped beam of light, she was unable to interrupt the image. The light was denser than solid. The image was more real than reality.

SCENE THREE:
THE CLIMAX

"If someone asks you if you're a god," Seth said to himself, "you say 'yes'."

Across the street from the Squat, Seth stared up at the towering building, slightly disappointed that it was not engulfed in a swirling, twisted vortex of cosmos and clouds, its roof topped with a temple for Zuul. At the very least, he'd been expecting a sparkling rift in the time-space continuum. Still, beneath the slate-gray sky, the crumbling structure seemed to shimmer.

Stepping closer, the shimmer came into sharper focus. Seth realized he was looking at the idea of a building. Instead of cracked stone, the Squat was now made up of hundreds of thousands of millions of moving pictures, each one the size of a 35mm frame of film. Every movie ever made, playing out simultaneously on an infinite loop, the rectangular images edged together like magic windows. His brain worked to identify as many as it could—*How the West Was Won, Serpico, Fantasia, Battle Beyond the Stars, Sunrise, Cabinet of Caligari, Weekend at Bernie's, Greed, Heroes Shed No Tears, Forbidden Zone, Café Flesh, Kramer Vs. Kramer, Rebel Without a Cause, Jigoku, Red River, Cutthroats Nine, Come and See*—so many images, so much movement, at the same overwhelming time. Solid, but not. A photomontage of perpetual motion. The Squat: now an infinite celluloid citadel, a shrine to Cinemagog, the God of All Film, the Endless Watcher. Seth stepped back. It was easier to process the building as a shimmer.

Kneeling on the sidewalk, he opened the briefcase and began to assemble the camera. He felt the god's unblinking gaze upon him.

While The Squat pulsed and morphed, like Linklatter's animated interpretation of Philip K. Dick's camo-suits in *A Scanner Darkly*, Seth concentrated on the Bolex. He mounted all three lenses into the carousel then unscrewed their aluminum caps. Now three eyes—one red, one green, one blue—stared back at him, blinking themselves awake. So this was his weapon against the dark and deadly gods of cinema. Of course it was.

There was something else in the case: a tightly wound tube of 35mm, courtesy of Luke. Without a core, the film was funnel shaped, tapering from the inside out. He shoved it into his pocket. Maybe his friend wasn't coming to help him, wouldn't be filling the role of secondary hero, but Luke played his part just the same. Seth guessed at the contents of the film and, if he was right, this would be more important than even the blinking three-eyed Bolex camera. Standing, he cranked the camera spring to a full wind and approached the main door.

Hell had descended. Instead of the rotting foyer and the shattered tile, Seth stood on the edge of a grand ballroom. Men in military uniforms spun women in flowing dresses, turning them into blossoms beneath the crystal candle-lit chandelier. Unnatural colors assaulted his eyes. Reality was absent entirely. Vertigo threatened to swallow him as a part of his consciousness swooped and arched above the dancers. He was in Abel Gance's *Napoleon*, a revolutionary film. The auteur liberated the locked-down cameras of the silent era by mounting them on wheeled platforms. In the case of the ballroom scene, on a swinging trapeze. The sequence was hand-tinted, like so many silents of the time, hence the hard color scheme, vivid but fading from age.

Before he could raise the camera, the spinning dancers parted in the center. Seth half-expected to see Rupert Borgia reincarnated and welcoming. Instead, the crowd revealed Shel, the Agent, his eyes bright with madness. They hadn't killed him. They'd transformed him. By forcing him between the frames, they'd made Shel the Agent one with Cinemagog. As the man smiled at Seth, his face began to peel in strips, the skin sloughing away to reveal the celluloid beneath. The filmstrip tendrils whipped and waved violently, like trims fighting a rough air current.

Seth's vision lurched, then trisected, the scene filling his eyes in three panels: his P.O.V. staring down the transformed Shel; the swinging high-angle master shot; and finally himself in a full-body shot, frozen in place, the Bolex useless in his hand. Gance had pioneered the use of multi-plane split screen, a process dubbed "Polyvision", a forerunner of CinemaScope, though it was not employed during the *Napoleon* ballroom scene. Still, his brain struggled to comprehend the simultaneity, the three perspectives overwhelmed his senses, threatened to collapse his nervous system.

Then Shel, with his undulating, featureless face, took a step towards him. That was all the motivation Seth needed. Bolting forward, he didn't bother with the Bolex, he just made for the ornate doors on the other side of the room. Buffeted by swirling dancers, taking a wide berth around the shivering Shel, Seth hurled himself at the exit. Behind him, laughter filled the air—a canned sound, unnatural and post-dubbed, but the wickedness was genuine.

Outside the ballroom, things were much worse. One end of the crumbling hallway had turned sleek white and chrome; the other end, to his right, was flat, barren sun-scorched land without walls. Armies advanced from both sides: Imperial Stormtroopers from the left, Zulu warriors on the right. Princess Leia's Blockade Runner merging with Isandlwana. Soon, Lord Vader would meet King Cetshwayo. Seth kept moving, leaping towards the collapsing plastic door folding and vanishing into desert space, leaving behind the laser blasts and ululating warriors.

Emerging in a new environment, dim and smelling of mildew, and again familiar. This time, the familiarity was genuine and not manufactured by the cinematic flashing shadows made flesh. Water dripped onto his face. Rain was falling through holes in the ceiling. Somehow, he'd reached the unfinished top of the building without climbing. The walkways were iron gratings, lined with filigreed guardrails. As much The Squat as *Blade Runner*'s Bradbury Building set. Who would he run into first? Alyce? Boone? Or Roy Baty?

Soundtrack wrapped around him, though he couldn't quite identify it—was it Bernard Hermann's *Psycho* score or Richard Band's sound-alike opening for *Re-Animator*? Regardless, a massive sting of crashing cymbals sounded as the wall beside his head exploded, punched in by a gigantic black gorilla fist. Willis O'Brien's *King Kong*, moving with antique certainty, feeling for him. Nose filled with the pungent stench of wet animal fur, Seth crabwalked from the grasping paw. He wasn't going down like Fay Wray. Or Jessica Lange. Or even the seemingly boneless Naomi Watts in the Jackson remake. Kong would have to find another mate.

As the paw grasped, the walkway began to twist and crumble. Succumbing to gravity, Seth slid backwards towards a railing that he knew would give way. It was an action movie necessity. The iron fulfilled its duty with a wrenching scream. Torn from its mooring, the railing fell into space and Seth went with it. With a death grip on the Bolex, his free hand found a jagged length of metal rail. His shoulder screamed hot as it took his weight. Suspended above the yawning abyss that replaced the floors below, Seth found the terror too-familiar, reminded again of *Blade Runner* but also James Stewart in *Vertigo*. The distance beneath his feet telescoped to infinity. Another quake from the destructive paw and safety slipped from his grasp. Seth plummeted into darkness at an incredible speed, arms flailing like the final movements of a Disney villain.

Cold water cut his scream short. The yawning nothingness turned into ocean. Breaking the surface, he gasped for air and prayed that the special Bolex was watertight. Then he saw the dorsal fin pierce the waves, speeding towards him, spurred on by urgent tuba and cello harmonics. Of course, it was "Bruce", the misfiring mechanical shark from *Jaws*, only now functioning at peak capacity. Its torpedo-shaped head surfaced, a roar escaping the maw that was mostly teeth. He could smell the beast's previous meal on its breath, the scraps of bloody flesh caught between its razorteeth.

In blind panic now, reason abandoned him. Seth couldn't tell himself that "none of this is real," or even "You don't know what you're dealing with," or even "You just don't get it, do you?" None of the Wretched Clichés came fast enough. There was only the instinct for flight, or in this case *swim*. Away from Bruce the Shark as fast as he could with one arm. Without looking back, he knew the Great White was just inches behind him, toying with him before the teeth sawed him in two, just like it did to Captain Quint.

He hit the submerged door hard, finding it with his face. With the shark's gaping mouth of razors filling his vision, Seth was sucked him backwards as the door gave way, riding a wave of escaped water that washed him into another room. Sputtering, gagging, Seth scrambled onto a sodden stuffed chair. Shaking from cold and terror, he watched the killing machine thrash and snap against the too-narrow doorway. Then the soggy wood splintered and tore apart and Bruce the Shark released itself into the room. It gave off another irrational roar and sped towards him, half out of the water already.

Now or never time. The classic split-second last resort. Seth, the hero of the scene, raised the Bolex and he squeezed the chrome trigger. Inside, the sprocket wheels whirred with life, the gate chattered against all the light the blinking eye-lens could take in. He closed his own eyes tight. He did not want to see those teeth when this gambit failed.

But there was no agonized rending of flesh and bone. Bruce the Shark was gone, captured by the Bolex, the image frozen in seconds measured 24 frames at a time. Already the water was draining away, spilling through gaps in the doors and floor and windows. He felt his clothes already start to dry. So it worked. The Ultimate Secret Weapon saved the day. Of course it did. Thematic design. Even these dark gods had to play by the

Syd Field rules of narrative.

As he gulped the air, he recognized the room as Cris's. The woman the rest of the Addicts knew as "Leni," the fetish-film director, was pressed up against the far corner of the room, straddling the floral couch that had been featured in so many of her clips. Her black hair plastered to her porcelain face, water dripping from her chin, Cris gave him a look of death. "Jesus-fucking-Christ,

Seth!" she screamed. "The *fuck* is going on?"

Standard quips came to mind, snappy sarcastic retorts that would play well in a trailer. Instead, with urgency: "Where are your girls?"

"Gone," Cris said, climbing down from the couch to stand in ankle-deep water. "Some ran, some just vanished."

"Vanished?"

"Wanda, she… she melted away. Bubbled like burnt film."

"Of course she did."

"She *melted*, Seth! The fuck is that all about? Is this because of your little film festival? Your forbidden Borgia movies opened some kind of portal?"

He nodded, wiping stinging seawater from his eyes. "Of course they did."

"And you knew it would happen!"

At that he shook his head. "Last time, half the audience went nuts and killed the other half. There were no sharks or gorilla paws."

"The *last time*? You weren't bullshitting about that screening?"

"Why would I? I helped Chris Balun burn a hundred people to death."

"So what's with—?"

"I don't know!"

Beneath their feet, the floor transformed. It became a swinging rope bridge, suspended in the air above yet another yawning abyss. "We should go," he said.

Cris, grasping the rope railing, already moving towards the door. "Don't you mean, 'Let's get the hell out of here'?"

"Just hold on tight," said Seth. "The second you open the door, this thing is going to collapse."

"How do you know?"

"Rope bridges *always* collapse."

For this, he got an eye-roll. Cris opened the door. On the other side, crowded into the narrow hallway, were Shel the Agent and his back up, the snarling Nazi nightmare monsters from *American Werewolf in London*. The Agent smiled and once again his face split into writhing tendrils of celluloid. The snarling creatures in their dark uniforms bared their bloody teeth and raised their Uzis. Cris was only halfway through her shocked exclamation of profanity before Seth leapt forward, grabbed her around the waist with one arm while wrapping his other around the rope railing. Just as the structure burst from its moorings and sent them sailing backwards into space.

Nothing halted their descent. Like a pendulum, the rope bridge swung to the zenith of its arc before descending again. Momentum and friction worked against the movement and they slowed slightly as the bridge climbed again. Already rotted with age and weather, with a puff of dust and the sound of fiber violence, the ropes snapped, the bridge collapsed, dropping the pair into free fall.

For about six feet. They landed hard on a stone floor, wind knocked from their lungs. As they gasped, their company came into view: dozens of brown-skinned men in white tunics and turbans, staring down at them.

Cris groaned. "What now?"

"Thuggees," said Seth.

"*Temple of Doom?*"

"*Gunga Din.*"

They'd interrupted a ritual of some kind. Dozens of religious killers, stranglers in the name and honor of the Hindu

Goddess of Death, Kali, circled them and stared down with menace. Neither of them moved, or spoke, or dared to breathe. Seth scanned the crowd, recognizing a few from his multiple viewings of one of his favorite movies. But the faces belonged to uncredited extras, their names lost to history. Cary Grant was nowhere in sight.

The absence of the classic leading man—his boundless charm, dimpled chin, *Gunga Din* representing Grant in the best shape of his career—struck Seth like a slap but in a way he couldn't explain. While pursued by Bruce the Shark, he didn't take the time to puzzle over the whereabouts of Roy Scheider's Sherriff Brody. Why was the non-presence of Sgt. Archibald Cutter so significant?

Because the head of the cult, the pinch-faced man credited as "Guru," played by Eduardo Ciannelli, was pushing his way towards them through the crowd. Grant's Cutter should be there. To stroll in and calmly rescue them with the announcement, "Right. You're all under arrest." If they were in *Gunga Din* at the moment Seth recognized, Cutter should be there. What was the point of splicing into this particular movie otherwise?

Though he couldn't see beyond the hovering sea of stern faces, he understood that the entirety of Orson Hall had been swallowed by the Addicts' dark side. Somewhere within the building Kids were being eaten alive by Umberto Lenzi cannibals; hoards of zombies—fast, slow, rage-filled, and instinctually-driven—chewed flesh from bone. Somewhere, the dwarf killer in the red plastic rain slicker from *Don't Look Now* had cloned itself a dozen times over, transformed into *Phantasm*'s killer Jawas and fury children from Cronenberg's *Brood*. Terror ran through every floor because Dr. Morbius' Id Monster was loose. *The Shining*'s elevator dinged and released a cascade of blood. The obsessive darkness of a thousand film students ran free in the building, nightmares squirming and writhing, piles of maggots forming and reforming as the worst and blackest dangers. "They're in the fucking room! Game over, man! Game over!" As they tumbled into piles of razor wire.

Without Sgt. Cutter in that cavern, Seth and Cris were alone and drowning in but a fraction of what movies had to offer. Cinema was a perfect amalgam of light and shadow, of sound and silence. But just then, the world was devoid of joy. Like *Fantasia's* Chernybog, like *Lord of the Rings'* Balrog, the infinite dark that was Cinemagog's wings blotted out light and hope.

As Ciannelli's Thuggee Guru drew closer, Seth reached out and squeezed Cris' hand as he raised the Bolex to his eye. One of the cultists behind him slipped a Rum l scarf garrote over his head, cut off his air. Seth attempted to gasp but his throat was closed. Thematic reversal of his murder of Shel. Dropping Cris's hand, Seth clawed at the cloth crushing his larynx. With a growl, Cris punched and fought against the assassins. Dark spots danced in front of Seth's eyes and his vision began to smear.

"Right! You're all under arrest!"

The familiar voice, right down to the mild Cockney intonation, stopped Ciannelli in his tracks and all but halted the assassination. Seth's determined murderer didn't loosen his grasp, but the garrote stopped tightening.

The crowd split, giving way to the smug Sgt. Archibald Cutter, strolling with hands clasped behind his back, his whole demeanor exuding authority. 35-year-old Cary Grant, born Archie Alexander Leach, appeared out of nothing and right on cue. Their savior. The impossibly handsome leading man gave them a wink. Then the Thuggee group swallowed him whole.

Air returned. Refilling his lungs was Seth's sole point of concentration as Cris dragged him towards the double glass doors at the rear of the temple. They weren't abandoning Cutter—he'd be captured, tortured, but would soon be rescued by Victor McLaglan, Douglas Fairbanks, Jr., and Sam Jaffe. Archie had bought them time and they couldn't waste it.

Ankle-deep snow filled the hallway beyond the temple and an icy wind of straight pins raked at their skin. What would come for them next? Wampas? *The White Buffalo*? Clint Eastwood from *The Eiger Sanction*?

Cris leaned hard against the door, bracing for a wave of Thuggees that didn't come. "What the hell just happened? Did Cary Grant just save us?"

"Yes."

"How is that possible?"

"Because that's what happens in *Gunga Din*."

"I feel like I should argue with you…"

Light snow swirled around them, dancing in the Arctic half-light, the cold turning their breath to clouds. Aside from the whistle of wind, the snowy world inside that hallway was quiet. Far in the distance, Seth made out a horse leading two men behind it. The men were tethered together by a length of rope so they wouldn't get separated in the worsening weather. Seth knew that the man in the rear suffered from snow blindness. He also knew their names: Peachy Carnehan and Daniel "Danny" Dravot. They were traveling to Kafiristan to establish themselves as gods. Seth and Cris had escaped one Kipling adaptation and stumbled into another. This time, it was *The Man Who Would Be King*, starring Michael Caine and Sean Connery. The two likable anti-heroes were just beginning their journey.

Over the wind, he heard Cris ask him, "Do you see another door anywhere?" But Seth didn't answer. He watched Peachy and Danny make their torturous progress through the deep snow while his brain chewed over the situation. All other floors of Orson Hall were probably under siege by the Humongous and his desert raiders; by Clarence Boddicker and his drug-dealing scumbags; by the Crazies and those loyal to the Duke of New York. Upstairs were Leatherface and his cannibal family; downstairs were Freddy Kruger, Michael Meyers, and Krug & Co. But where was Max Rockatansky? Where was Robocop? Where were Snake Plisskin, Ellen Ripley, Captain

Marvel, Jack Burton, Jackie Chan, and Shane? Or any of the Rooster Cogburns or—for Christ's sake—the platoon of James Bonds?

Far off in the distance, he heard Cris' voice, "Seth? What do we do now? Seth?"

In the deep shadows of Cinemagog and the rest of the elder deiwos—Ifirs and Dolirostrum and Vastane the Adversary and so many more—the Squat was over-run by a century of cinematic conflict. But where were the protagonists? Where was the pre-requisite Happy Ending?

The answer came to him a millisecond after his brain asked the question. Reaching into his jacket pocket, his hand found Luke's tight spool of 35mm. The Other Secret Weapon.

"Here," he said, handing Cris the Bolex. When the lens-eyes blinked at her she jumped, but only slightly. With ragged fingernails, he clawed at the paper tape holding the film coil. Freed, the plastic unraveled into concentric circles, threatening to leap from his hand. He managed to tear four frames from the end with his teeth and let the film melt inside his mouth, felt the movie surge through his system. The scene's soundtrack filled his head, the bright music wishing him, and everyone:

"Good morning / Good mor-ning. /
It's great to stay up late! /
Good morning / Good morning to you…"

Gene Kelly, Debbie Reynolds, and Donald O'Connor appeared before him, arms linked and smiles wide. Not exactly his first choices for a commando squad but they had the necessary weapon: hope.

With his teeth, he tore away another few frames and forced them into Cris' hand as he took back the camera. "Are you out of your fucking mind? I'm not flixing now!"

"Just do it!" His words came from the desperation to make her understand, but it was free from anger and frustration. "Good Morning" overwhelmed his pessimistic terror. Shocked at his outburst, Cris shoved the film frames into her mouth.

Then it was as if "Good Morning" boosted itself into stereo. He knew it played in her head as well.

"*Singin' in the Rain*?" she said. "That's your answer?"

"It's always the answer!"

Moving in perfect, seemingly effortless unison, the dancing trio from the M-G-Musical produced a door from thin air. Opening it, they waved the flixing pair through. Taking Cris' hand once again, Seth followed the *Singin'* stars' lead, pausing just for a moment to look back at Peachy and Danny, continuing their painful progress across the frozen tundra beyond. Even in their arduous struggle, the Men Who Would Be Kings seemed to have a new spring in their step. "Good Morning" fought the infected reality around them.

On the other side of the door was that blasted, skull-littered hellscape from *The Terminator*'s war-torn future. As the metallic skeletal robots murdered human soldiers in their path, Seth could already sense that the tide was turning. Lee Marvin and his *Big Red One* platoon appeared on a ridge, their M-16s reducing the T-800s to scrap. Following them were John Cassavettes and the rest of *The Dirty Dozen*—including Trini Alverado's Jiminez, resurrected, as if he'd never even mentioned a raise to the producers—and behind them came Brad Pitt's *Inglorious Basterds*, and *The Warriors*, *The Losers*, *The Black Six*, the *Time Bandits*, and every one who'd ever been a member of *The Magnificent Seven*, George Kennedy included, while Spinal Tap performed "Hell Hole" one hill over. Closing in ranks were Sarah Conner and Ellen Ripley, Princess Leia and Queen Amidala; Anita Mui and Maggie Cheung and Michelle Yeoh, *The Heroic Trio*; motorcycles roared, driven by Tura Satana, Jeannie Epper, Pam Grier, and Zoe Bell, all followed by a battalion of Final Girls headed up by Laurie Strode and Nancy Thompson. Doc Holliday and the Earp Brothers were joined by Harry Tuttle and the rest of *Brazil*'s air conditioning repairmen resistance. Joe-Don Baker and The Rock, both *Walking Tall*, brandishing their clubs; *Billy Jack* advanced with the *Hard Boiled* Tequila, double-fisting blazing .45s; a muffled gunshot from deep in the distance signaled that *Quigley* had returned from *Down Under*.

Dodging bullets and explosions, as if they had memorized a map of the perils, Seth and Cris dashed through the chaos and destruction. Way off in the distance, *Sinbad*'s Cyclops battled an Imperial AT-AT, stop-motion vs. Go-Motion, in epic Harryhausen / Tippet style. And "Good Morning" played on.

"Why didn't the screening affect you?" Cris asked him that morning.

"Maybe because I'd seen them before."

"But the others—"

He shrugged helplessly. "I don't know. Maybe because I was working at the time. Shooting days and writing nights. Maybe I'm Superman."

Maybe I didn't buy into Borgia's bullshit and he knew that.

Maybe I'm just not that important.

There was no answer. It was throwaway sloppy. A gaping, unforgivable plot hole. Rank amateur plotting.

But it was true. Seth found himself in the role of The Chosen One—that most hackneyed of shortcuts to character. He could wield the Secret Weapon. He could save the day.

In the middle of the battlefield stood a door, with frosted glass shot-through with spiderweb cracks, splintered wood, peeling veneer, a brass knob polished smooth by time and infinite turning hands. It was escape. It was freedom.

Dodging Sherman tanks and Imperial speeder bikes, Seth shoved Cris ahead of him, filming as he ran. The Bolex's infinite wind and unblinking eyes captured the maddened world around them. A razor-wielding David Hess—this time as the rapist, Alex, from *The House on the Edge of the Park* — bubbled away and vanished beneath the Bolex's gaze. So did the Nazi nightmares from *American Werewolf in London*. So did the fucking Balrog hurrying towards them, flaming whip lashing at the roiling ground at their feet. The Bolex took it in, reduced its monstrosity, made it go away.

Bombs exploded around them. With each impact came a Wilhelm Scream accompanying flying bodies, destroyed by shrapnel and flame. The door was still yards away and hordes of enemies were bearing down.

From high atop a hill stood Rupert Borgia, no longer flickering, no longer smiling but laughing. Miles and miles away, surrounded by the churning sea of space surrounded by the shadowy smoke figures of Cinemagog and the Deiwos, Rupert Borgia roared with laughter, his satisfaction rising above the din of war and carnage. So far away, and yet Seth could see him quite clearly, his mind's eye zooming from ground to heavens with just a blink. If only the Bolex had a zoom, he could wipe that look off the Man Who Laughs.

An eruption sent them tumbling. A thought occurred, a gamble. They helped each other to their feet, the door still an infinity away. Without speaking, he stopped her. They stood their ground. She shouted at him, but he never heard her voice. The world exploded.

Impact shot them through the air. No jagged debris, only mild heat and swift wind. In movies, explosions were friendly. They blew the heroes to safety. As long as he held the Bolex in his hand and "Good Morning" in his head, they would remain the heroes of this story.

Too strong, the force of the blast had them overshoot the door. They went tumbling past, kicking up dirt and bones as they rolled. "Up! Up!" he shouted, but his words were lost. Seizing Cris' hand, he yanked her to her feet and half-dragged her back towards the door.

He heard her voice pierce the howling wind. "Other side!" Pointing at the door. Wanting him to circle around. Another gamble: he didn't think it made a difference.

As a Peter Jackson Oliphant stomped into their path, threatening to jellify anything in the path of feet the size of office buildings, Seth's hand found the doorknob and he gave it a vicious yank.

Considering it had no hinges, the door swung open almost too easily. And beyond its threshold was dark and quiet reality. Abaddon Street, yawning for a mile in both directions, revealed by the open door. Its lone streetlight switched from Green to Yellow to Red.

Rupert Borgia roared in fury. Having grown to an impossible size, the Artist held a Kid in each hand. Enraged, he hurled one to the ground. The Kid fell for miles before he wet cratered into the ground. The other Kid, Borgia brought to his mouth, chewing off the boy's head, a perfect parody of Lucifer devouring Judas, as per Dante's Inferno. The Artist offered the spurting body to Seth, his face an expression of "See? Do you see what I can do?"

But there was the threshold of freedom before them. Inches from their face was an escape from this Ragnarök. Then the universe switched to slow motion. All movement slowed, 48 frames-per-second, then 72 fps, then 96, 130, Bullet Time. Swinging Cris on the end of his arm, he watched his old friend slide through the opening. Her feet landed squarely on the sidewalk beyond the door.

Braced against the doorway, she pulled for him to follow.

With the world in glacial speed, Seth's eyes left freedom and fell upon a catwalk. A metal grating, it stood apart from the impossible network of staircases that surrounded it, jutting off to one side like an afterthought. The staircases were arranged in M.C. Escher's famous nightmare of physics, as seen in *Jim Henson's Labyrinth*. It teemed with crawling, hissing monstrosities that he was sure were once the rest of The Kids, scuttling and slithering up walls, across ceilings, spider-walking down staircases that sprouted from dead ends and sealed doors.

On the catwalk stood Alyce and Boone. Between them was Boone's projection. Alyce was screaming but her words couldn't reach Seth's ears. He could tell from her body language that she was begging. Boone's projection advanced upon her, without an ounce of love in its flickering, out-of-phase eyes.

The distraction was all it took. A tremor shot through the ground and sent Seth sprawling backwards, his hand leaving the safety of Cris's grasp. Her face turned to a mask of disbelief—she shouted, quite appropriately, a good long "No!" as the door between them closed. Once he hit the ground, the door to freedom shattered. Debris littered the space where it stood and the hellscape extended beyond. The path to freedom was gone.

Borgia, the Auteur God, laughed in triumph. The sound boomed through the chaotic basin. Scrambling to his feet, he raised the Bolex to his eye, even as Borgia's massive hand shoveled him up.

It was the Kong paw all over again, only this didn't feel like flesh. Borgia's hand seemed to be made entirely of static electricity, blue energy crackling harmlessly around him even as the grip tightened. The crotch of the giant thumb pinned his elbow to his side, crooking his arm to a painful angle, preventing his finger from reaching the Bolex's trigger. He held on tight to the camera, but it was just a useless appendage.

The fist raised him up. Up. The God, all the while, laughing at the sport.

Did it recognize him? Seth wondered. From that first screening years and years ago? Was this the Triumphant Revenge?

SCENE FOUR:
THE OTHERS

Up and down the staircases, around hallways, upside down along ceilings, clear across walls, The Other Boone chased Alyce with murder in its eyes. Running and tumbling, falling up over the impossible geography, Alyce found herself rolling sideways along what she felt was the cobblestone floor, but was really a canted wall. Gravity held her to surfaces at random. The Other Boone, and the Boone behind it, the source of the projection, had no trouble navigating the madness space.

"Stop!" The begging should have sickened her but she was terrified. Her whole world annihilated in an eyeblink, physics lost to some whim of insanity. There was no explanation her mind could dredge up that made any sense of her current existence. To Alyce, the swirling insanity was dwarfed by the image of Boone, the man she loved, approaching her in seething hatred, his physical body dragged along behind it. "Please! Boone—whatever this is! Fight it!"

If he heard her, he gave no indication. Halfway up the wall, Alyce scrambled away from The Other Boone's reaching hand. When his fingers finally met her face, she felt only soft static, heard only a gentle crackle of new sheets fresh from the dryer. The Other Boone passed right through her.

Astonished, The Other Boone grabbed for her hair, but its two dimensions flatted across her scalp. The Other Boone took a step back as it realized its impotence. The Other Boone screamed—the sound of a projector collapsing under its own weight.

Pushing herself away from the wall, Alyce sprawled at The Other Boone's feet, her sharp knees and elbows finding every sharp stone beneath her. Looking up, she saw the Other Boone grief-stricken, agonized at the thought of failing its new master. She felt no fear then, no resentment. Not even hatred for Borgia, or his films, or this horror he visited upon them all. (That they'd asked for. That they'd *hoped* for.)

She saw only the image of her lover twisted in pain. All she'd ever wanted to do—*ever*—was to provide Boone comfort. Love. (*Obsession.*) Alyce let herself go limp.

Her body bucked. Once. Twice. Then violently, arching her torso forward, bending her back off the floor. Light pulsed its way up through her chest, bulging her throat slightly—and impossibly—as it forced its way out of her mouth. With a chatter, conical light spilled from Alyce's mouth, and before The Other Boone now stood The Other Alyce.

Bookended by their meat bodies, the Projected Lovers stood before each other. The Other Alyce reached out and caressed The Other Boone's cheek. There was an imperceptible hum as image flesh met image flesh. Anguish melting away, The Other Boone stared down at The Other Alyce, and a tender smile broke across its face. The Other Alyce coughed a happy sob as each recognized the other.

They'd transcended.

Was this what it was like on the other side of the frames?

The Other Boone wrapped its arms around The Other Alyce. The pair held each other wile the rest of the world crumbled around them. While their flesh bodies ceased breathing and went slack against the stones. The Other Lovers held each other until their light began to flicker. They held each other as the light faded away entirely.

SCENE FIVE:

CINEMAGOG

The Borgia God was speaking, but Seth was damned if he understood a word. *The problem with thousand-foot men-projections*, he thought, *was that they only spoke 'wind machine'.* Hot rushing air scoured him as he struggled against the giant's fist, but he couldn't work out what it said.

Seth could guess. Some orgasmic monologue about the triumph of its plans, the mastery of its scheme. How it was ruler of the entire universe now. That there was nothing anyone could do to stop it. Its Art was unleashed. It would devour the world. Especially its critics. And blah blah blah fucking blah.

The problem with bad guys, Seth thought, is that they never go to the movies.

They don't know about the Final Act Twists. About the classic Hail Mary pass. Every hero gets one last go, when all seems at the most hopeless and lost, to Save The Day.

(*Unless this is some nihilistic indie horror…*)

(*Unless this is some Russian war allegory…*)

Fuck it, he thought. *My movie is directed by Capra.*

And Capra, he thought, as his elbow finally worked free, *is all about The Happy Ending.*

Seth raised the Bolex, extending his arm to its length, and squeezed the trigger.

The Borgia God made the same face all villains make at the end. From Jaffar to Hans Gruber to the Stay-Puft Marshmallow Man: that look of horrified, hilarious surprise.

The special effects were disappointing. Borgia didn't melt or crack and explode. There was no unearthly howl as the Bolex captured its flickering frames—and all the frames in between—and ceased it to be. At once, Borgia was there—towering, massive, winning—then he wasn't.

The next moment, Seth was falling.

The descent was swift. Gravity tore the Bolex from his

grasp and he watched the eye-lenses close serenely. The motor, he imagined, had wound down.

As Borgia vanished, it was his universe that collapsed. The dark gods of Cinemagog and his ilk retreated into the shadows and the angry booming clouds. The warscape far beneath his feet heaved once and then disintegrated. He found himself falling through layers of sand.

The universe was a powder of silver emulsion.

Tumbling end over end now through the vast dark expanse, he was astonished to find that his fear had evaporated. Replaced by an exhilaration to see What Came Next.

There should be one last glimpse of the fantastic. One last burst of mystery and promise.

As if on cue, this new universe responded with a dazzling display of color whizzing past him, accentuating his rapid descent into the unknown. This was his trip through *The Black Hole*. He was in Willy Wonka's terrifying tunnel. Falling at warp factor seven, past the jump to light speed, color bending around him as friction became a matter of opinion. Nothing would slow his descent now.

He was a comet. He was Icarus about to be reborn.

Far out there in the cosmos, Cinemagog watched his descent. With bright eyes, the color of a newly-hung silver screen.

Deep inside his body, he felt warmth begin to spread. Light was pouring from his fingertips. He could see it trailing from his mouth like a plasma tail. The credits were about to roll. He could almost see The Other Side. He looked down at his body and saw it glow.

"My god," he said, in Keir Dullea's voice. "I'm full of stars."

DELETED SCENES

WHAT HAPPENED TO THE GUY
BEFORE ME?

The ancient machine was screaming.

Shuddering, roaring with mechanical rage, grinding, snarling noises bouncing off the grey cinderblock walls. The din of metal upon concrete poured into the dark hallway as the Oxberry optical printer seemed to be bouncing scraping towards the open door. The take-up motor stalled, the upper reel stopped. Film began to unspool onto the floor.

Unable to offer any help whatsoever, Nick watched as Jim cursed, diving for the toggle switch that would put the machine into "brake". Instantly, the aged mechanical creature ceased its tantrum, but sharp-smelling liquid still hissed through the hoses and the Oxberry continued to hum a malevolent warning.

"Fu—" Jim caught himself. "Sorry," he said, without turning around, peering at the take-up motor, searching for the problem. "Swear too much."

"Doesn't bother me," Nick said, trying to sound as nonchalant as possible, even though his nerves still jangled from the unexpected eruption.

"Machine's sixty-some years old," Jim said, still not turning around. He'd produced a screwdriver and pried at something behind the upper metal reel. "I used to joke that there was a Japanese soldier inside that didn't know the war was over." Cursed again under his breath; something snapped under his screwdriver blade. Satisfied, he began to push against the rim of the reel, taking up the slackened spilled celluloid strip.

"I didn't even know they still printed movies like this any more," Nick said. "I thought it was all digital these days."

"Well, yes and no," Jim said, and began peering around at other parts of the decrepit machine, examining its feed reel, drive belts. *It's like watching a mechanic fix one of those huge cars from the '70s,* Nick thought, *like a Buick Skylark, or something. Shit, this thing looks like it was built out of an Army surplus tank.* The machine seemed to glower, faceless, from its position in the corner of the room. It was huge—the length of one of those aforethought cars—comprised of two metal cabinets supporting a projector on one end and a camera on the other, connected in between by a bellows and a little glass gate into and out of which pale yellow liquid flowed, constantly recycling through old rubber hoses.

"Most prints for theaters are made on a contact printer," Jim continued.

"Which means the original negative is pressed against a strip of virgin stock to make a new print. Contact printer does this at a high speed."

Nodding—for his own benefit, as Jim was still not looking at him—Nick remembered seeing one of those types of printers on the trip down the near pitch-black hall just outside the room. Nearly every room at this end of the Carcosa FilmLab was mineshaft black, save for dim orange lights set into the high ceilings at the mouth of the hall, "safe lights" that wouldn't accidentally expose and ruin unprocessed film stock. It was just a glance, but he saw one of the wardrobe-sized metal cabinets spin two strips of film through even larger, glass-enclosed phone-booth-looking enclosures on either end. There hadn't been a single living person in that room when they passed. The machines just ran themselves.

"This bitch," Jim said, tapping the Oxberry with his screwdriver and finally turning back to Nick, "is usually used to blow up sixteen millimeter prints to thirty-five mil' negs, or vice versa. Or you can combine two images if you're making a matte—you know what a matte is, right? They don't really use them much any more."

"Yeah," Nick replied. "Like the old Harryhausen movies. Mattes blocked out one side of the frame and left that part unexposed so that Harryhausen could animate the dragon on the other side, or whatever."

Jim nodded, "Yeah, more or less."

"All done on computers now," Nick said. And Jim grimaced again.

"Numbers," the older man said. "Mouse clicks. Programs. No art to anything any more."

Over Jim's shoulder, Nick saw something white flash momentarily in the doorway. Nothing but black beyond, though, when he looked. Just his eyes, he thought, seeking more light. Since the raw film was housed inside a magazine set on top of the camera, the optical printing room wasn't as dark as the contact printing area. Flickering fluorescent tubes high above cast a weak, sick wash over everything. Not bright—just enough light to see but not nearly enough to comfort. The older man's face had taken a slight green hue from the fluorescents and Nick was sure he didn't look much better.

"Anyway," Jim continued, "We're making new negs here right now. It's a big job. Need a couple hundred new sixteens from the thirty-five inter-positives. I'll explain that later. It's called a 'blow down'—that's what we call it here, anyway. Shorthand. And that's pretty much all we're doing. And that's why we need three shifts. The Oxberry's going to go twenty-four hours a day."

"Weekends too or no?" Nick asked, dreading the answer.

"Originally weekends too, but the clients didn't want to pay that much overtime, so it's just five days a week now."

Nick breathed a sigh of relief. It was a short sigh. He was still going to lose his evenings. 9pm to 5am in a dark, foul-smelling concrete cave for the foreseeable future. *Welcome to a career in film,* he thought. Again. "What's the movie?" he asked.

Instead of answering, Jim reached over and flipped a silver lever. "Take a look," he said, indicating a viewfinder set next to the bellows of the camera. Peering in, Nick saw an orange-washed medium-shot image of a crucified man, his face twisted in agony, jaw clenched, teeth bared—a headband of thorns cutting into his brow. Blood streamed down his face. "Christ," Nick said, and felt immediately stupid again.

"Exactly," Jim said, unable to contain his pleasure at the joke. "Client's a evangelical group, taking this movie all over the world. We're making subtitles for it in nearly every human language."

"Mass indoctrination through cinema," Nick mumbled and drew the lever shut.

"That's about it," said Jim. "They're sending missionaries out with projectors and generators. In some places, they'll be using sheep as screens."

"Seriously?"

"I dunno," Jim said. "I'd like to think that was a joke." He shrugged. "Anyway, that's the big job."

Nick found the science and mechanics fascinating. It was a far cry from the editing software he was used to. He felt a little like an archaeologist, exploring an ancient civilization and its tribal rituals.

"Are you religious?" Jim asked. Surprised at the question, Nick wasn't sure how to respond.

"Uh, not particularly. Isn't it illegal to ask that?"

"Only if you didn't already have the job," Jim said. "Relax. None of us are particularly religious either. Just want to make sure the jokes don't piss you off."

"Oh," Nick said. "Hell no. Joke away, I don't care."

"Good," Jim said, grinning. "With this place, you'll definitely need a sense of humor."

While Jim showed him the finer points of coaxing the

machine into operation, Nick jotted notes into an old composition book, sketching out the film paths that the celluloid strip traveled, over and under plastic rollers, marking down which switches did what. He knew his way around a dark room, could change a camera magazine inside a black bag if necessary. That he already understood the electro-chemical process of film had helped him land the job. Again, if only from a technical standpoint, he was now in the film industry. Albeit a quarter-mile underground, in a building that had begun life as a slaughterhouse and currently seemed home to decades of bad karma.

"Tonight," Jim told him, "you're just going to watch this run. I have everything set up, focused and whatnot. You just have to watch and make sure nothing jams, especially on the projector side. Film could seize up in the wetgate and perc' will spill everywhere."

Perc. Perchlorethelyne. A specially-designed fluid that flowed through the glass projector gate, meant to fill in scratches and imperfections. It smelled caustic and gurgle-hissed like a consumptive's lungs as it flowed through the ancient rubber tubes connecting the gate to a reserve jug on the floor beside the machine. "There's an eye-wash station in the corner if you get splashed. Don't touch your face if you get any on your hands."

Nick asked, "Should I wear a mask or gloves?"

"Should you? Yeah. Almost definitely. Good luck finding a mask around here with a new filter. Other than the big thick rubber ones the guys in chem-mix wear, the only gloves around are cotton. That's to keep your fingerprints off the film, not for protection. If you feel better with them, there's a box in the dark room. Perc' soaks right through though, obviously." Jim flashed Nick a quick grin. "Don't worry. If OSHA pays a visit, you'll get a mask, gloves, rubber apron, whatever makes the place look good. Otherwise, try not to inhale too deeply."

Jim wasn't kidding. Carcosa was one of the last film processing plants left in the country, used more for its storage vaults and its 2K film-to-digital scanners than anything else.

Josef 'King' Ghast, owner and president of Carcosa, considered such safety concerns to be frivolous expenses. With the chemicals and the utter lack of sunlight, it was advised that Nick make a habit of taking a daily multivitamin. Above them, fluorescent tubes buzzed and cast their sickly green light through the room, leeching the shadows from anything solid.

"It's not a fun job and it's kind of an awful place to work," Jim said to him, without humor. "Pay's okay, benefits are decent. But basically you're stuck in the ass-end of a concrete submarine for eight hours breathing toxic fumes and fighting with The Bitch here. That's the glamour of show business."

Nick's enthusiasm bubbled and burned away like film against a hot bulb. Anxiety took its place immediately. "Great," he mumbled.

"It's not so bad," Jim said. "You can play music or watch movies on your laptop. Just keep one eye on The Bitch and make sure it isn't spilling film or perc' or running out of sync." The older man indicated a display where the twin red LED readouts counting both projector and camera frames in perfect harmony. "You'll know if it slips. The display will beep at you."

"What do I do if that happens?"

At the rear of the machine was a small panel, meant to be screwed down but merely taped in place. Jim removed the plate and revealed a small bank of tiny yellow lights. Two pairs flashed together like car hazards. Jim showed him how to adjust a screw head and bring the lights in and out of synchronicity. "If this happens tonight, though, just stop the machine and split. Don't even bother clocking out. Leave me a note and I'll rethread everything."

Nick's first instinct was to argue, to insist he could handle changing the mags. But it being his first night solo, he felt more than happy to take the man's advice and just high-tail it should anything go wrong.

"There's a notebook up on the shelves over there," Jim said as he pulled on his coat and gave the machine a last once-over. "All the optical guys here have added to it—tricks, shortcuts, settings. Keep it handy. Good luck and good night."

Once Jim departed, Nick was alone. With the shuddering, clanking, hissing machine which he could tell already did not like him. The decades had taken their toll on the Oxberry, made it mean and angry, given it a malevolent pseudo-sentience. At least, that's how it seemed as he stared at it, watching the film unspool from the reel on the left, while the twin readouts counted out the matched frames on the right. It was the animation that gave it the perception of life and Nick's mind anthropomorphized it even further. Eyeless, the machine studied him back. If The Bitch were an animal, its teeth would be bared, claws out, quills extended, all the ways nature says "Don't Touch."

There was no cell service this deep under ground and apparently the King didn't believe in Wi-Fi. Any music Nick played from his phone was drowned out by the snarling Oxberry. Just another six hours to go before the shift ended.

Out of desperation, he grabbed both the machine's operating manual and the short-cut notebook left behind by previous operators. He felt suddenly determined that The Bitch would not defeat him. This resolve surprised him.

Twenty minutes into the operation manual and Nick felt his will to live slipping away. The machine complained and chugged along, the noise enveloping him, vibrating his body, making his blood fizz. It still wasn't enough to keep him from dozing off and drooling onto one of the murky diagrams. Combatting the boredom was near impossible. He paced the room, measuring one wall to the next, heel-toe style.

There were three other optical printers in the room, none of them Oxberrys and none of them apparently in any kind of working condition. Two were shrouded by dusty drop cloths. The third, a JK directly across from the Oxberry, stared out at the room, the projector end stripped down, probably cannibalized for spare parts for the active, hungry, angry primary creature hissing and draining in the corner. The lens at the end of the JK's camera stared at him like an unblinking eye.

Feeling suddenly claustrophobic, Nick stepped into the tomb-dark hallway, peered into the blackness swallowing everything beyond the pale light from the optical room. Like a mirage, a dim orange safety light indicated the very end of the hallway, which led into the main cleaning and staging area. Beyond that was a break room with coffee and snack vending machines. Caffeine was desperately needed, but he'd have to cross the length of black totality of the hallway to get there. For some reason that seemed daunting. The concrete walls muffled the Oxberry's groans, but still sent ominous noise oozing up the walls and across the ceiling. A trick of the lack of light: he swore he saw a pale colorless thing slither into one of the contact printing rooms, like an eyeless snake born in the dark. A chill entered the soles of his feet and climbed his spine. With a shiver, he abandoned thoughts of coffee and returned to the Oxberry room.

Tomorrow he'd remember to bring books and his laptop. Or maybe a baseball and glove, sit against the wall and while away his time like Steve McQueen in *The Great Escape*.

He should practice cleaning film gates with a Q-Tip and acetone, lightly brushing the glass until he'd eliminated all streaks, smears and dust. But the boredom had sapped his motivation. The practice gate sat untouched on the table next to the bottle of acetone. Instead, he returned to the technicians' notebook.

It was a thick five-subject, spiral-bound job straight out of any high school, bent, broken and creased. The first two dozen pages were filled with figures, f-stops, alignment marks, sketches of the film paths similar to the ones he'd made himself. Pump pressure notes, electronic schematics. A full page listing parts removed from the JK to keep the Oxberry running.

One scrawl caught his eye: "Projector column will move back if struck at base with a rubber mallet (tool drawer)."

Another: "Mag C sprocket wheel replaced, runs smoother

but still jams. Try white grease on bearing *only.*"

With a soul-heavy sigh, he flipped a page, stared at another page filled with faded ink scribblings in changing handwriting. He felt like a monk preparing to illuminate a new manuscript, but kept illiterate to prevent exposure to heresy. It was like gazing at some forbidden Lovecraftian text whose obscene figures drove the reader to madness.

A sentence at the top of the page, inside the 1" margin, the following words: "*Oxberry will respond better to a gentle touch.*" Below that:

"I SAW THE EYE AGAIN."

Before he could ponder the words, the Oxberry let out a grinding shriek and the LED displays began flashing, beeping. Film spilled onto the floor, the take-up reel having again ceased turning. Nick leapt to his feet, his body moving before his brain knew what was happening. Arms spread in alarm, feet shoulder-length apart, Nick stared at the panel of switches and dials. Out of his open mouth spilled a clueless, "Uhhhh," before his hand shot out and found the brake switch before his eyes had processed the information. The Oxberry stopped cold, ceased moaning. Only the sucking sound of the perc' pump remained.

Out loud, to no one but himself, Nick cursed softly. Then louder. He flipped open the viewfinder and peered at the last frozen frame. Christ's twisted, tortured face stared back at him, scalp bleeding from thorn wounds. The perfect image to cap the night. The Christian Messiah sharing his defeat. Spinning the take-up reel by hand, getting the film off the floor and shutting down the pump, Nick relived his awful high school days of athletic failure all over again.

He killed the pump. Absent the hiss and spit, silence filled the room like foam insulation, intensifying his self-loathing. "First day," he said out loud to himself. "Mistakes happen," he thought. "Jerk-off," he finished.

Flipping to the last page of the tech notebook, he scrawled a quick apology to Jim, shut down the antique Apple IIe that drove the Oxberry's shutter-timing motor, and locked the door behind him.

Darkness swallowed the silence. Keeping his eye on the distant pale safety light, he walked briskly down the hallway, trailing a hand along the rough cinderblock wall to ground himself in physical reality. His fingertips felt wet, slimy. Certain that he'd heard the chattering of rodent claws on the floor behind him. When he finally found light again, he allowed himself to breathe.

Chill, blindness, the oily feel of chemicals that soaked through his skin. So much for his first night.

*****

"I saw the eye again." Nick couldn't get the words out of his head. Unsure of what to think, he felt sympathy for the author nonetheless. The crushing atmosphere of Carcosa FilmLab after midnight could get to anyone. Still, what eye? The unblinking lens of the JK? The pale orange safety light of freedom at the end of the fallopian hallway? Maybe Mr. Ghast had a surveillance camera secreted in the room. From what little he knew of the King, this wasn't beyond the realm of suspicion.

Arriving early, Nick ran the gauntlet into the lab. First was the long pathway lined with hurricane fence and topped with razor wire, between two security cameras staring down like sphinxes, condemning all passersby. Then the elderly guard inside his little Photohut booth checked his bag for whatever he was looking for but didn't find. This allowed him passage through the metal detector that remained silent despite the numerous chrome snaps, buckles, and zippers defining his biker jacket. He had a suspicion that the gateway was meant more for intimidation than practical criminal catching. As he reached the door, he remembered that most of the employees in the packaging department were work-release criminals. Then he realized that Ghast saw all his workers equally: as terrorists, threats to his livelihood. On his way towards the lab, he walked by several of these co-workers, their eyes cast-down at their feet, hugging the walls as they passed him.

Anxiety pressed down on him as he approached the black tunnel leading towards the Optical Printing Room. Residual shame from the previous night's failure, fear of the coming recrimination from Jim—or even worse, charitable understanding—seemed to pale compared to whatever swam and slithered in that yawning dark before him. With a deep breath, he crossed the threshold, leaving the dim orange safety light to shrink at his back. The darkness around him had a texture. The grumbling of the autonomous contact printers, the stench of the perc atmosphere, even the obvious drop in temperature as he descended further into the literal bowels of the building, all combined into invisible crushing pressure.

Reaching the cold greenish light of the Optical Room dispelled the pressure but not the sick feeling in his stomach. Inside, the Oxberry grumbled away at a new print. Jim leaned against the bare table, tinkering with an old 35mm gate. He smiled as Nick entered. "Hey," the man said, pointing his screwdriver at Nick. "Good job last night."

The words stopped Nick in midstride. Confusion died unspoken in his mouth, however, as he did not respond with "Huh? What do you mean? I fucked up completely last night." Instead, he returned a tight smile and shrugged out of his jacket.

"So no problems at all? The Bitch didn't harass you?"

Smile frozen, Nick simply shook his head. Bewildered, he wasn't about to incriminate himself. Maybe another worker had finished the job after he'd left.

"The print came out of processing and I checked it out. It turned out ok. Good job," Jim said. "I totally destroyed my first job. Lens spots, air bubbles—you name it. I had to remake that fucking print four times."

Head bobbing like a dashboard dog, Nick managed, "What movie?"

"*Vera Cruz*," he said. "Burt Lancaster. I had to make up three sections and it took forever." Abandoning the gate, Jim stood up, rolled his neck on his shoulders. "How are you feeling about tonight?"

"Uh," Nick said, picking at peeling paint on the edge of the darkroom door, "okay, I guess. Place is a real creepshow at night."

He received an enthusiastic nod and wide grin from the older technician. "It's the ghosts of all the cows that died here in the '30s. Well, that and the general evil."

A shot at King Ghast. Apparently, no single employee had a positive thing to say about the Lab's owner. So far, he'd heard the man described as 'cheat', 'liar', 'sadist' and 'cocksucker'. By all accounts, the King was a corpulent monster, constantly under lawsuit for missed deadlines, employee health care fraud, general emotional abuse. Most recently was a legal battle with Columbia Pictures, which felt that he was holding their prints hostage in his endless vault, extorting exorbitant storage fees. The Lab was a reflection of its President: crumbling, corrupt, dark and damaged.

Reaching over, Jim set the machine into brake. "Hey, I still have a few minutes, I wanted to show you something."

Following the man out of the room and into the dark, they passed through a set of double doors that opened onto an immense and filthy storage room, filled to overflowing with rusted hulks of ancient equipment. "Anyone else working here this late?" Nick asked.

"Just a skeleton crew," Jim replied. "Only other printer is Ronald. You'll run into him sooner or later. He likes to hide in our darkroom and sleep. You'll love him. He is literally a moron. I'm not saying that to be mean. I think he has an IQ in the low 60s. He's told me a number of times that his favorite thing to do to start the day is to eat cold cereal and watch porn."

They stopped at a door at the very back of the room. The unlocked knob turned easily. Inside, stacked flat on wooden pallets, beneath a bare light bulb dangling from a long cord, were hundreds of film cans, many oxidized with rust, labels faded and peeling away. The smell of vinegar hit Nick like a slap. "Guess what these are," Jim said.

Shaking his head, Nick hazarded a guess. "Bad stock?"

"Nitrate prints," Jim replied. "They stopped using this kind of stock after World War II. That smell is the celluloid breaking down into something similar to nitro-glycerin. Notice the complete lack of ventilation in this room."

Nick looked. The ventilation was surely lacking.

"Know what this shit can do? Burn under water."

"Oh," Nick said. "Nice."

"Yessir. If that bulb blows, everything in this room is going to explode, send a fireball shooting down our hallway and collapse the building like a Coke can. No one'll get out alive." Jim let the door slam. Nick jumped. "We work for idiots, man. This is just an insurance nightmare waiting to happen."

*****

The older tech left before Nick could ask about the journal entry and the eye. In truth, he'd deliberately hesitated asking. Still perplexed by the news of the previous night's "good job", Nick spent the first hour of his shift trying to explain it to himself. Maybe that Ronald guy finished things up, on his way to his dark room nap. More likely, Jim came in, saw the Oxberry sitting silently, the film still threaded, ignored the 'Sorry' note and finished things up himself. A ruse to bolster his new apprentice's self-esteem.

Maybe the Oxberry finished the job itself. Waited until Nick took his coward's walk down the hallway then grew limbs, unpacked its magazine, wrapped the exposed film in a black plastic bag and metal can and sent it sliding down the chute into the processing room.

"Why stop there?" he asked himself out loud. "Maybe it

processed the film too. Maybe this is the machine that runs all other machines. When nobody's watching."

Disgusted with himself, he flipped the toggle switch that brought the Ox back to life. He let it run for a few seconds, then flipped the lever for the viewfinder. This automatically braked the machine again, for the purpose of checking the gate for bubbles or any kind of shift out of registration. The image inside was clean, clear inside the liquid perc hiding any imperfections. The twisted face of crucified Christ once again stared out at him through the reticle.

Dropping the switch unpaused the machine. Jim must have made some adjustments. The Oxberry's growl was distinctly different today, more of a purr than a warning growl, but still nowhere near friendly.

Movement from the hallway caught his eye. Something sickly and pale vanished into the gloom. A rat's tail maybe? One with the width of a garden hose. Nick shook his head. The perc fumes were getting to him. But he wasn't about to leave the room and traverse that hallway until he absolutely had to.

"I SAW THE EYE AGAIN."

Again. Even though that was the first instance of any mention of any eye. Just a scrawl in the margin of the stained paper. Nick flipped through the pages. A quick scan revealed more settings, calculations of frame rate verses exposure and bulb temperature. "Super-16mm gate corroded. Sent to repair, 5/7."

"You know, the guy before you loved that Bitch."

The unexpected voice sent a jolt through Nick's nervous system. He jumped in his seat and saw the man in overalls and thick black-rimmed glasses lounging in the doorway, idly scratching his crotch. "I mean, like, I'm sure he fucked it at night."

No possible response came to Nick's mind. But the man didn't seem interested. With an awkward haste, the overalls man tore his hand away from his itch and held it out for Nick to take, lurching forward with an almost drunken gate. His eyes were dark and wide and very dull behind those aquarium-thick glasses. "I'm Ron."

Nick gave his name as he stared at the man's extended hand. In addition to whatever his fingernails had dragged away, the hand was coated with black grit and grease. It was a hand teeming with nastiness. Nick smiled in apology and declined to shake. "I have perc and shit all over me."

The hand hung in the air for another few seconds before Ron dropped it to his side. Beneath the overalls he wore a long-sleeved thermal undershirt. It too was filthy, stained almost black beneath the arms. "I never seen anyone touch a machine like that guy use'ta," Ron continued. "Creepy fucker."

Nick cocked his head. "You're not talking about Jim?"

"Fuck no!" The exclamation was louder than expected. "Guy who used to work this shift. George Prokopec."

"Oh, okay."

"Couldn't hack it. Just stopped coming to work one day. 'S why they hired you."

There was an empty chair across from Nick, but Ron didn't sit down. He continued to loom over him, staring just past him with his dazed shark eyes. At rest, his wet mouth hung open. "Know what I think? I think he was a pervert for machines, but couldn't handle the project. I think he was a fucking atheist. The Jesus movie offended him too much. 'S what I think." Ron stopped talking. Before Nick could respond with even a grunt, the man added, "Fucking atheists. They fuck anything, you know? 'Cause they don't got God in their lives."

Suddenly, the pitch-black hallway had an appeal. Unable to think past the man's horrifying statement, Nick caught a quick glimpse of his future: held hostage in a concrete death trap with a retarded Jesus freak. All he could think to say was, "Okay."

"Yeah," Ron said. "Hey, guess what I'm working on."

"I... can't," Nick said.

"New print of *Schindler's List* for the museum. You ever

see it?"

"The movie or the museum?"

"It's a good movie, I guess," Ron continued, still staring at some point above and to Nick's right. "I didn't dig the scene where they put all the naked women into the showers, though."

"Oh, yeah. That was pretty terrible."

"Seriously. They was way too skinny. I don't like looking at naked chicks that're that skinny. Otherwise, it was pretty good, I guess."

Nick couldn't help himself. "Yeah, I guess it's hard to make starvation and genocide sexy."

"Yeah," Ron said, and continued to stare out at his personal focal point, mouth hanging open, a spit bubble forming on his lower lip.

All Nick could do was nod. The man showed no intention of leaving. "George Prokopec, huh?"

"Yeah," said Ron. "He sure loved that Oxberry. Like a pervert, you know what I mean."

Nick continued nodding. "No." Closing the notebook, he stood and gestured towards the darkroom. "Hey, I don't mean to be rude—Jim wants me to practice loading the mags in the darkroom. I still got a lot to learn."

"Sure."

No movement.

"Nice meeting you," Nick said.

"Uh huh."

With Ron watching, Nick crossed to the darkroom and closed himself inside. Pressing his ear to the door, he listened for any change in the Oxberry's noise, but mostly for the sound of receding footsteps. Ten minutes later, he opened the door a crack. His room was empty, save for the shuddering machine.

With a sigh of relief, Nick stepped out and into a blinding white light. The JK's bulb burned bright behind its lens. It took him a minute to find the machine's off switch. He didn't even question it. Obviously, he'd have to get used to this Ron guy doing all sorts of bizarre things. Returning to his chair and his notebook, Nick tried to remember the difference between autism and Asperger's and wondered which better applied to his newly-discovered coworker.

*****

By the end of his shift, Nick had cleaned and recleaned the practice gate a dozen times and his fingers were dried white by the acetone. The Oxberry hummed along without incident, giving him time to actually practice changing film magazines in the dark. He discovered a jam in one of the 800-foot 16mm mags and surprised himself by clearing it without causing further damage. He'd even managed two trips down the black hallway for coffee and restroom breaks. It still gave him the feeling that he was traveling the length of some great fish's throat, bracing against the creature's inevitable swallowing of him whole. The walls still felt damp and slick beneath his guiding fingertips.

The last five-hundred feet of the project seemed to take forever. Hypnotized, he watched the red LED numbers accumulate while the lights flashed in unison. Out of sheer boredom, he reached for the viewfinder lever and braked the machine to check for bubbles or hairs or whatever. Just a new distracting image to fill his vision for a second. He put his eye to the viewfinder. An eye inside the viewfinder stared back.

His whole body spasmed in surprise and he leaped backwards away from the machine. Idling, the Oxberry hummed and waited for him to put it back to work. Tentatively, he took a step towards the machine, moving slowly to avoid attracting its attention. Its motor growled softly while the pump gurgled its tubercular breaths.

Inside the viewfinder, the eye, bright blue with gold flecks, filled the frame. Nick laughed at himself, disgusted at his surprise. "'I saw the eye again,'" he said to himself, to the Oxberry. The explanation was obvious: it was the Christ actor's eye in extreme close-up, a still image, a single frame. It was sheer chance that he'd stopped the machine on that frame. The same extraordinary chance that had obviously happened to George Prokopec (if indeed he'd been the one to scribble that note). The viewfinder eye seemed to hold his gaze.

Until it blinked.

"Mother-fuck!" Nick screamed, scrambling backwards, colliding with the table and sending notebooks and tools scattering across the floor. "Perc fumes," he said, trying to catch his breath. "I'm fucking hallucinating."

I SAW THE EYE AGAIN.

No force of will allowed him to look again into the viewfinder. Stretching out his arm, he stayed as far from the machine as he could and flipped the brake lever down. The machine resumed its disinterested growl and resumed its job. Numbers continued to accumulate. Film continued to pass through the hissing gate. When the job finished, he didn't risk checking it again. Black tail leader slid past the bulb, announcing the film's end. He killed the pump, then the bulb, then the power. As quickly as he could, he unthreaded the camera magazine, hoisted it from its mount.

Turning towards the dark room a bright light hit him again. The JK was on. The noise he made was not a word, just an exclamation of angry shock. On his way to the dark room he reached behind the crippled machine and yanked the thick plug from the wall. The bulb went dark.

He'd had enough for one night. To hell with the whale-throat hallway and to hell with the pale-white things lurking within. Dropping the film can down the proper processing chute he hurried the hell out of Carcosa just as the sunrise ignited the horizon.

*****

On night number three, he exchanged pleasantries with

Jim, managed to hide from Ron, and then found both the second notebook and the three small cans of film. Each was 100 feet of 16mm on a black metal spool, sealed tight inside a discolored metal can. The notebook was a battered composition book with the common black and white speckled cover. Both had been shoved into a plastic black bag and shoved beneath the rewind table in the darkroom. The dust coating the bag implied that it had been in that place forever.

Flipping through the pages he recognized the handwriting. Same as the obscure notes in the margins of the technical notebook. Only the words were closer together, written in a breathless hurry, eager to get the story down. Something in his chest hitched as he scanned the pages. The word "Oxberry" stood out on every page. This was a diary. George Prokopec's or someone else's? And did it matter?

Forcing himself to take his time, he laced up the projector, started the pump, cleared the gate of the rush of bubbles with an adjustment of the vacuum tube. He double-checked the settings on the camera, used canned air to blow dust from the innards. Taking a deep breath, he lurched towards the viewfinder and checked the focus. With his eye pressed against the eye-piece, he felt something cold and metal caress his cheek.

Again, he leapt back. His hand went to his cheek and came away dry, but the skin buzzed where it had been touched. No part of the Oxberry could have touched his face at that angle. The brake lever was to the right of his chin. There were no other protrusions. But he didn't imagine the touch.

Warily, he got the machine running and growling and backed away from the beast. He took his seat without looking away. After a moment, he dragged the chair to the other end of the table, creating a barrier between himself and the machine. It hummed and hissed away, indifferent to his presence, pretending like nothing had happened.

Jaw set in defiance, Nick flipped open the notebook with more force than he'd intended. With another glance at The Bitch, he started to read.

—get her running properly and she warms to your touch. She'll respond to a caress even quicker than the screwdriver if the sync starts to slip. I tried to talk to Jim about it but it was obvious he didn't know what I was talking about. Maybe she doesn't like him? Her eye is wide in the viewfinder, watching me watch her.

What the hell?

Nick flipped a page. The Oxberry gave a grunt but continued to snarl without causing problems.

—almost ashamed to say that I've discovered how soft she can be. Her ventilation holes in the cabinet are moist as mouths when she's happy. The dial panel takes on a texture, like underbelly skin. I expected an oily taste when I put my mouth to the camera door. Instead, it was sweet.

Ron was right. George Prokopec was a pervert.

—She sucks greedily when I enter her. And she gets jealous. I slipped my finger inside the cabinet and she swallowed my wedding ring. I'll have to think of some explanation—that it slipped off inside the machinery, which is true enough.

I've put in a dozen work-orders to fix the ventilation in the room. The perc fumes make it hard to think, especially with the main door closed and blocked. It's best to push the table against it to ensure privacy. Ronald Milner comes and goes as he pleases and I don't want to share her. Christ knows what he'd try to do with her. I couldn't bear the thought of his filthy hands on her magazine or reels. It's bad enough that he's jerking off in the darkroom when I'm on break.

I think he watches us. I can't figure out how. But I feel eyes on the back of my neck—not just the rats in the lab, or King's surveillance cameras he thinks we don't know about.

Not that she cares. She wants what she wants and she wants me.

Last night, while I was inside her, a tube snaked out of her cabinet. Then she entered me. Perc—I think—like an enema flush—it wasn't cold, like it should have been. Warmed by her body—

After reading that last section, the words stopped being

words. Nick's mind simply stopped comprehending what he read. The familiar alphabet he'd used all his life momentarily transformed into alien symbols. Was this what the boredom and fumes did to you so late at night? Isolated at the edge of the throat of darkness, George Prokopec succumbed to some mental disease. God knows what that perchlorethyline did to your system. And if George was giving himself perc colonics…*Christ.*

Cursing himself out, Nick forced himself to stand and confront the growling machine. Keeping it running, he dragged his fingers along the front of the cabinet. Despite the working motors vibrating the casing, the metal was cold. It didn't yield to his touch. The ventilation holes, the diameter of a silver dollar, were cool and dry, aerating the beast's innards, just as they were designed to do. Form followed function.

George Prokopec was delusional. Obviously. Inarguably.

Leaving his middle finger hooked inside one of the vent holes, he peered into the viewfinder and watched the movie play. Another scene of Golgotha. Instead of Christ flanked by two thieves, crosses and victims stretched on behind him, for miles. Bodies rotting behind the movie Messiah, carrion birds picking at their flesh. Grotesquerie of religion, to be shown in the furthest corners of the world. "This, African bushman, is what our God sacrificed for you. This is the horror of a life without our God."

Suddenly, he felt wet on his hand, and moist softness sucking at his fingers. Jerking his hand away from the casing, he caught the cabinet orifice straining to reclaim him, puckering and pulsing before it returned to its original state of rigid metal. Wiping his violated digit on the leg of his jeans he pointed at it accusingly.

"No!" he scolded. "Unacceptable. I am not George!"

With a screech, the Oxberry gears started to grind. The take-up wheel froze and film spilled onto the floor. The magazine, shaped like Mickey Mouse's ears, bucked against the mount, leaking light and tearing sprocket holes. Offended, the machine raged at him.

"No!" he said again, then lurched for the break toggle. The Oxberry made a furious, metal-shredding noise and shuddered to a halt. Unwilling to touch it again, Nick used the screwdriver to snap open the camera lid. Film had bunched up inside, bulging against the rollers and sprocket wheels, looped and creased and ruined. For a moment, the wheels had a sheen of exposed bone. The ruptured gate seemed swollen and bruised. Using the screwdriver, he plucked at the buckled film and it unfurled like spilled intestines. All of the work was rendered useless, shredded and exposed to the light.

With only the pump hissing, the Oxberry at rest seemed to seethe at his rejection. Even parked, it vibrated with hatred. All Nick could do was glower at the alien beast before him.

"Fuck it," he said, then slammed the door and pushed the table up against it. There was no lock, so a barrier would have to suffice, using George's method of keeping Ron at bay.

Plugging the JK back into the wall, he couldn't help but feel like the Oxberry was watching him with vicious suspicion. He angled the JK towards a blank space of white-washed concrete wall, tore open the fiberglass cabinet and ripped the lid from the first aged metal can. It took several minutes to figure out the lacing pattern of the JK's projector, but soon he had the first 100′ spool loaded and ready for viewing. The switches for both the room's over head fluorescents and its own set of orange safety lights hung on the wall by the door, within reach of the Oxberry. It took him another minute to muster the courage to cross past it and kill the overheads. With just the muted orange wash of illumination, the machine seemed even more malevolent, hissing and gurgling in the dim. He gave it a wide berth as he crossed back to the JK.

One hundred feet of 16mm runs approximately two-and-a-half minutes. The first reel depicted a man, his back to whatever camera source captured the image—the same height and angle as the JK's perspective, so at some point this machine *had* had a camera attached. The silent footage showed the man—balding and slightly hunched, wearing grey coveralls—running his hands over the Oxberry like a child touching velour for the first time. Lowering himself down to his knees, he pressed his face against the machine's cabinet. From the JK's angle, Nick could just make out the man's tongue darting in and out of one of the ventilation holes.

Coughing against the building fumes, Nick tore the finished film from the JK projector and laced up the second spool. Multiple takes this time: the Oxberry alone, dragging itself towards the door with the lurching, lumbering movement a half-ton machine would naturally, unnaturally, have.

A flash frame popped the man—George?—into frame. The Oxberry had returned to its original position and he was pressed against it, his arms spread wide, caressing and massaging the dial panel, which seemed soft and pliant beneath his touch. Frantically, George struggled out of his coveralls, dropping the outfit to his ankles. He was completely naked beneath and he pressed himself harder against the cabinet. Nick was never more grateful for a lack of soundtrack. Only the JK's chattering shutter and the Oxberry's malevolent hiss accompanied the horrible imagery. George's naked buttocks spasmed as the film mercifully bleached and ended.

The third film can remained. Nick didn't even want to touch it. Nausea rose in his gut and his face was flushed. He couldn't blame the fumes.

I HAVE SEEN THE EYE AGAIN.

She responds to a gentle touch.

"Fucking pervert, that George."

While Christ's story unfolded from one end of the machine to the other, George Prokopec and the Oxberry carried on with blasphemous carnality. Impossible. Just…impossible.

Retching once, a dry heave, Nick laced up the final film.

The Oxberry's cabinet face lay open, the door resting on the floor, while George, completely naked and entwined in film spilling from the stalled take-up reel, sucked at the Oxberry's pulsing innards. Even from the JK's distant perspective, Nick could see the veins ribbing across the motors and gears. The drive belts sinewy. Everything within glistening with wet. He couldn't tell if George was struggling against the celluloid tendrils wrapped around his body, or if he was embracing this bondage. As he wriggled closer to the machine, forcing his body deeper inside.

Nick slammed his hand against the JK's power switch and killed the image that would play behind his eyelids for the rest of his life. Across the room, The Bitch vibrated and hummed with a barely-contained fury. And maybe arrogance. They sat, staring at each other, for almost an hour.

Leaving the final film on the JK, Nick crossed the room, turned on the fluorescents. He walked over to the perc pump and shut it down. The hiss and gargle died away. But he knew that the machine was still on, still watching. He could rip the cord from the wall and its life would continue. Leaning back against the closed door, he considered his options. Something scratched and clawed at the other side, perhaps trying to escape the monster throat. He ignored it.

Finally, he reached a decision. Taking the screwdriver from his back pocket, he crouched down behind the machine and pried open the ill-fitting access panel. The other end of the screwdriver held a flashlight. He shined the beam inside.

The Oxberry's innards glistened in the pencil-thin beam. Purple veins latticed across the copper motor. Gears with white gleaming teeth fit together, driving belts of rippled muscle. Forcing himself closer, Nick peered deeper into the literal bowels of the machine.

And found George.

The man had shrunk, withered to the size of a newborn, it's head twice the size of his wizened body. Tubes and wires snaked in and out and around his lumpy, translucent flesh. His large eyes were open, looking at him, but without seeming to see him. They were round and blue with flecks of gold. Instinctively, it blinked against the light and began to suckle a pliable glass tube. Its mouth was toothless, the lips puckered and grey.

Nick clicked off the flashlight, returning the Oxberry's innards to its natural darkness. He replaced the panel the best he could—no part of it would line up correctly with the edges.

He pulled the table away from the doors, opened them wide and let the perc fumes clear. Whatever had scratched at the outside left deep furrows in the paint but did not enter the room.

Something inside his skull clicked, an almost audible sound, and the horror slightly delayed crashed over him like a wave of emotion. Unable to breathe, he gasped at the air outside the room, inhaling the darkness beyond the doors. He crossed the threshold into the building's throat. Keeping his eyes on the final orange light, he walked forward, focusing all his energy on small, deliberate steps.

First something moist and hairy dashed past his leg. He ignored it. One foot in front of the other. Exact center of the hall, equidistant from the contact printing rooms and the line of processing chute-holes. If he stayed along that very path, nothing could reach out from those even-darker areas and grab him.

He paused at the second weak pool of orange light given off by the overheads. The light dissolved around his feet, swallowed by the dark at the floor, a negative zone mist. Sweat merging with unashamed tears, he forced himself to take a deep breath.

Midway through, he heard the terrifying scraping scream of metal on concrete. Without turning around, he tried to order his feet to move forward, resume his exit. The screech barreled down the tunnel again, blowing foul, turgid air against the back of his neck. This screech was accompanied by the sound of something big and mechanical splintering wood.

Unable to move, he focused on prayer—trying desperately to recall his old catechism routines. Then he realized that the Oxberry was laced with Christ. None of the Trinity would rescue him. A miracle: his right foot shot forward and took a step, dragging his body behind him.

A metallic roar, a hiss of tubes, the chunking whirr of an obscene motor—the sounds vibrated his skin through the back of his shirt. He could feel the machine's… breath on his neck. If he took one more step, the machine would nuzzle him. Seduce him. Entwine him and become another spare part, squashed and deranged like ol' George the Pervert. Locked away inside.

So he remained in place. While the hissing, clunking, scraping, breathing, surrounded him, frozen as he was in the space between two pale lights. He stood and waited. He waited for the sounds to die down, for the giant fist of fear to stop shaking his body. He waited to see if his knees would weaken, collapse him to the filth on the concrete floor, allowing the Oxberry to slide right over him. Crush him in its embrace.

Hours and hours later, those sounds did die away. Terror did not topple him. The horrible Bitch machine simply dragged its way back to its nice safe room, metal feet tearing gouges in the cement.

At the end of the hall, the last safety light, the one that indicated rescue just around the corner—food and coffee and sanctuary—flickered once and blinked out. Before him was nothing but yawning, solid black. The nothing prevented him from escaping.

Another century later, Nick returned to the Oxberry Printing Room. He returned the three incriminating spools to their cans, and placed them, along with the battered notebook, back into the plastic black bag. Using his foot, he kicked the bag far beneath the darkroom's rewind bench. For good measure, he stacked boxes of filters in front of the gap.

Returning to the Oxberry, he unlaced the print and allowed it to rewind. He cleaned the gate, used canned air to blow dust from the inside of the camera, carefully, almost tenderly. He emptied the mag, dumped the ruined film. In the darkroom, he reloaded it with fresh stock.

Adjusting the pump pressure, checking the focus, he restarted the job. He needed the job. And now he understood what the job entailed.

As the Oxberry hummed and hissed and growled, Nick studied the creature before him.

A few minutes later, he remembered the airless closet in the back of the building. Nitrate film burned under water. He thought about a single spark that could cause an inferno and cleanse the world of Carcosa.

THE MARIE
BROWNING CODE

How many times had he flixed watching *To Have and Have Not?* Twenty-five? Thirty? Riding the narrative, feeling the spray of the seawater, answering correctly when asked, "Was you ever bit by a dead bee?" But he'd never tried splicing in. Splice in, find Marie Browning (Lauren Bacall) before Harry Morgan (Humphrey Bogart) nicknamed her "Slim", and take her to bed.

Joel unspooled just a few inches of the film from the feed reel, carefully lined up the sprocket holes against the splicer's pins and guillotined away a single frame. Holding the little wafer of plastic between thumb and forefinger, he let it catch the light. There she was: 19-year-old Lauren Bacall in her first role, leaning against the hotel room doorframe, lighting her cigarette from a match, her chin down, looking up and to the right at the off-camera Humphrey Bogart. Giving him "that look". That famous, smoldering "look", daring him to come to her. Joel angled the frame, trying in vain to be the recipient of "that look". Tilting, angling, until the picture vanished into a razor-thin two-dimensional line. Her look was always for Bogie, outside the frame.

Joel's breath caught as he finished the 180-degree flip. The glossy base-side down, now the matte, almost-dull emulsion reversed-image, Bacall looking left now, but still not looking at him. All he wanted to do was slide into that frame, pluck that cigarette from her full lips and kiss her long and hard and forever.

But film was a passive medium, was it not? Silent participation from the viewer. Even flixing could bring her no closer. Not even the illusion of 3D.

With a silent prayer he mouthed the name of the God of All Film Gods, "Cinemagog", and placed the frame on his tongue, his communion, and closed his mouth around it. Tonight would be different. If Jack/ie could do it…

Joel would find his way between the frames, swim against the tide of the narrative and find Marie Browning before she could meet Harry Morgan. She would lead him to her room, across the hall from Harry's, and he would make love to her.

Flixing was easy. Any film freak could do it. Hipsters called users "frame junkies". One single image of celluloid—35mm worked best, especially if you could get your hands on an original camera negative, which was a high few film students could afford and Joel didn't know anyone who'd managed it, but everyone bragged that they had. Everyone had connections to the Carcosa FilmLab. Sure they did. Most he could manage was the same as everyone else: strike a deal with a projectionist in one of the local theaters. They all trimmed from reels during breakdown, before sending the prints back to the studios. All projectionists dealt in frames.

Pure luck brought Joel the trailer. It was a reissue for art houses, probably during the '80s revival of classic films for festivals. He'd found it on ebay, near-pristine and crystal-clear image. Run once, maybe twice? No scratches on the emulsion and very little damage to the base side. Had to sell some blood to scrape up the $150 asking price, but the seller sweetened the deal with a side, a reissue trailer for the 1962 *Cape Fear*. Couldn't pass it up. He'd hate himself forever.

Puberty hit Joel hard but Marie Browning was there to pick him up. It was a secret he'd never shared—who lusted after a babe from 1944? And it wasn't Bacall per se. Maybe *The Big Sleep* got to him now and then. It was always 19-year-old Betty Joan Perske playing Marie Browning in the Howard Hawks' masterpiece, an adaptation of his friend Ernest Hemingway's—the director's words—"worst book. A pile of junk." Of course it'd been a hit—Hawks jettisoned two-thirds of the novel and hired Hemingway rival William Faulkner to rework Jules Furthman's script into a basic rehash of *Casablanca*. Hawks moved the setting from '30s Florida to '40s Port de France,

Martinique, right after the fall of Vichy. Gone was Hemingway's ideal of a Marxist paradise in Cuba, back were the Nazis, their Sympathizers, the Free French and The Good Fight. *To Have and Have Not* was *Casablanca* with lower stakes. The crowds ate it up.

Newcomer Bacall was "discovered" by Hawks' wife, Nancy "Slim" Keith, on the cover of *Vogue Magazine*. She tested and won the role of Marie Browning and threw the elder Bogart for a near-literal loop. He didn't know what was going on, but he ended his third marriage, to abusive alcoholic Mayo Methot, to be with Bacall. Hawks recognized their smoldering chemistry immediately and ordered rewrites. Faulkner reworked the script at the zero hour to make it more of a romantic thriller.

"You do know how to whistle, don't you, Steve? Just put your lips together…and blow."

From that moment on, it was Bogie and Bacall, for each other and for Hollywood's rabid followers, until the old man died in '57. Just like she'd gotten Bogie, and just as Marie had landed Harry, "Slim" had floored a 13-year-old Joel.

Sitting in his apartment in the old Orson Hall, ten years later, Joel attempted his first splice-in. As the frame of film, the delicate emulsion of the image of Marie lighting her cigarette ("You can't see it on screen, but my hands were shaking the entire time," Bacall admitted in her biography), melted onto his tongue, and the movie hit his veins, he stabbed "Play" on the DVD remote and rode into *To Have and Have Not*.

First up was the "WB"—The Warner Brothers' Shield— dissolving into a map of the Caribbean Sea. Titles: "Martinique in the summer of 1940, shortly after the fall of France." Director of Photography: Sid Hickox. Gowns by Milo Anderson. Dissolve from map to the Port de France set, the dock peopled primarily with West Indies natives, and the first motion: native kid in a straw hat, dark button-down shirt, belted white trousers, running and disappearing screen left. Behind him, girl in straw bonnet. Globe lights set on either side of the side door of the Marquis Hotel door. Already in motion Harry Morgan crossed the narrow plaza to the dock office to buy his temporary exit from port. To take the soft, unpleasant Mr. Johnson (Walter Sande) fishing.

After a hundred thousand viewings, Joel knew every inch of the set, every motion, every cross by the extras. He could time them out like musical beats. Only this time, Joel wasn't watching. He was part of things. He'd spliced in. Now he viewed the action from a new angle and realized that he was the American sailor in the dark jacket, dressed like well-to-do Mr. Howell, leaning on a railing just behind the black fisherman with the half-dozen fish hooked together on a line. The fish smell slapped him first but then mingled with the encompassing aromas of the seawater, salt mixed with human sweat, the powdery perfume worn by the woman crossing behind him. The woman with floral dress and white blouse, balancing a covered basket on her head. Finally, he understood that the basket was filled with freshly baked bread for breakfast at the Café.

Taking a quick glance at his hands, Joel saw they were his own, beaded with sweat and sea spray. Behind him: stacks of barrels, boxes, tarped bales. A hurricane lamp hanging on flagpole. From where he stood, he saw only five of the nine slatted shutters in rows of three across the hotel's second floor, the four-pane glass enclosed gas lamp hung eight feet from the ground over painted wooden signs, "VENTE en GROSS CIGARETTES". "ENGRAIS POUR CANNES." Across from him: a black man in cabbie cap, hauling a rope out of water. Next to the man, a kid fishing from behind the dock railing.

From the unfamiliar angle, it took cinematic Joel a moment to find Harry in the sparse crowd. Another woman balancing a filled sack on her head, steadying with both hands, rounded the corner revealed Harry, passing the man with the sack-laded wheel barrow, reaching the booth for the Marine Nationale Police Navigation. He gives his nationality as "Eskimo" and pays five Francs for the port exit. Joel expected Harry's cap to be a shade of navy blue but it was black. There was no color in this world. Just the duotonal universe here in Port de France.

Harry sighed and said to the officious warden, "We're going fishing, same as we've done every day for the last two weeks. We'll be back tonight. And I don't think we'll go more than thirty miles from shore."

"One more thing," Joel said to himself, in perfect time with the officer. "You will go nowhere near the vicinity of territorial waters, St. Vichy or Dominique."

New orders.

Then Morgan crossed right in front of him, winding through the docks predominated by black native workers, some in straw hats, some fishing, most carrying bundles. He was heading towards his single-perch fishing boat, "Queen Conch, Key West, Fla." First, he'd take an empty bottle of beer from Eddie, his first mate passed out atop a coil of rope on the dock, and then dump a bucket of seawater onto the old rummy's face. All of this in the first minute of the film.

According to screen time, Joel had about ten minutes until Marie "Slim" Browning first appeared, standing in the doorway of Morgan's hotel room, asking for a match. How long would that be in "real time", he wondered? According to the script dialogue, given by Hotel manager "Frenchie" Gerard, Slim comes in on an "this afternoon on a plane from the south." From either Rio or Trinidad, if her passport is to be believed. Certainly, the corpulent Captain Renard (played by *Casablanca*'s Marcel Dalio) will question it, but not until later. Harry, Eddie and Johnson will be out fishing until "tonight". How long would that be? By the position of the sun and by common sense, Joel could tell it was early, breakfast time, but what time was that in mid-Wartime France? It could be 7 AM or it could be 9 AM. His sailor wasn't wearing a watch.

Knowing the scene had already changed—he felt the shudder as the master shot cut to the other side of the dock, to focus on Johnson's introduction, Joel decided to act. Quickly, he crossed the small plaza and headed for the door of the Marquis

Hotel, where Harry had emerged. He kept his head down—did the sailor extra ever move? Was he hidden in the background somewhere? Joel tried to adjust screen logic to narrative logic and now what was "real" time logic. He was in the world of *To Have and Have Not*. He'd gotten between the frames and spliced himself in. But what would happen when the scene changed and the narrative stayed with the crew of the Queen Conch, out on the water in front of its rear-projection ocean backdrop and stock footage of marlin fishing?

Joel's hand closed around the doorknob as he got his answer. The world around him faded to mist and his feet vanished beneath him. Cold water drowned his vision. Then the sky leapt above him. Something was tugging at his mouth. He knew what happened. There'd been a dissolve. He was in the next scene. And he was the marlin. Johnson was about to lose an expensive rod and reel. Joel would swim off with it. And Eddie would say, "Mr. Johnson, you're just unlucky."

Instantly, the movie rejected him like a mismatched organ. Thrown back into his world, his dark apartment and the grubby couch, *To Have and Have Not* on his expensive flat screen and him choking and coughing up seawater. Forget screen time versus narrative time, he'd missed meeting Slim by over a mile of film.

*****

By day, she was "Jack," but she'd always been Jack/ie. The slash belonged to her too.

Jack/ie paid her rent working at a drag review at The Pegasus, a gay club downtown. She did four shows weekly, got a salary plus tips, and was in love with Robert Mitchum. She'd seen all of his films. For a year, she never watched anything that Mitchum wasn't in, like some strange artisanal fast from modern movies. During her shows, she sang "The Ballad of Thunder Road" and danced in front of a "greatest hits of

Mitchum" she'd edited together in her VIDEO II class. All the other queens worshipped Bette Davis and Joan Crawford and Judy and Barbara. And they all loved Rock Hudson. But for Jack/ie, it was Bob Mitchum all the way.

During her first year at Griffith Film Academy, she kept her career a secret, but after a drunken tryst with Darryl Wannamaker after an open-bar screening of *The Wizard of Oz*, everyone knew. Darryl denied spending the night in her room. Only it was *his* room, Jack's room, at the time. Darryl followed *Jack* to his bed. Older by about two years and already working on his Senior Thesis film, Darryl had just broken up with another student, May-Cheung, who'd shattered his woeful ideas of Asian women and their submission. Thus, he'd needed comforting. Jack had needed company. The next morning, Darryl awoke to a hangover and no small amount of horror. During his haste to dress and leave the room, he spilled open the top drawer of Jack's dresser, revealing all the Jack/ie wigs and make-up.

That no one rushed to burn Jack/ie at the stake only added to Darryl's humiliation. After that day, it didn't matter what she did or who she was. Everyone else considered Jack/ie a film student, period, no different from the rest of them. Besides, Divine was part of everyone's pantheon. Plus, what group is more open-minded at twenty-years of age than film students ready to splash down in the next artistic New Wave?

Like Joel, like so many others at Griffith, after graduation Jack/ie retained her apartment in what was ostensibly the dorm building, but had come under new management. Bought by a former Griffith student who'd paid her dues to the studio system, the old Orson Building had a no-eviction policy. Student or not, if you could pay some sort of rent, you could stay. By this time, Jack/ie had officially evicted "Jack." The pseudonym was no longer necessary. Her other costumes fit better. She retained the slash. "The slash is silent," she'd say.

A party game they'd all played: "If you could sleep with a character from any film who would it be?" All variations were welcome. If pressed, half the straight guys would admit to having a thing for Bruce Campbell's "Ash" character in *Army of Darkness*. Veronica Sawyer (Winona Ryder) from *Heathers* was also a popular choice.

Out loud, Jack/ie said, "Jason Statham's character in *Crank*. 'Jed Jellomold,' or whatever his name was."

"Chev Chelios," someone would invariably correct.

If pressed harder, depending on whether or not she was still in costume, she would cop to "Jeff Bailey", Mitchum's character in *Out of the Past*. None of the new kids ever got the reference, though. The younger they were, the less likely students were to have seen anything made before their birth-year. It was galling, especially to the frame addicts, the flixing flicker freaks. After a while, she'd just stick to "Jason Bourne" and down whatever free booze was supplied.

Only Joel knew Jack/ie's dark secret. "Max Cady." The psychopathic rapist Mitchum played in *Cape Fear*. A reprehensible character. A complete and utter brutal mind. But to Jack/ie, there was a blistering magnetism about him. She was attracted to the same animal musk that simultaneously drew and repelled Peggy and Nancy Bowden (Polly Bergen and Lori Martin respectively) in the film's censor-buried subtext. To tell the truth, she was just as repulsed by Cady, but that's what made it a proper dark secret. Judgment didn't scare her—screw them all. Every straight boy had his "bad girl" ideal—Matty Walker (Kathleen Turner) from *Body Heat*, Catharine Trammell (Sharon Stone) from *Basic Instinct*. An orgy with all the psycho girls from *Sucker Punch*, that had been tossed out and roundly cheered. All the kids wanted the Scarlet Witch from *The Avengers* to manhandle and tame. All of them wanted to defile Arwen from *Lord of the Rings*. Everybody's sexual fantasies came with baggage and matching carry-ons. That was just Psychology 101.

Cady. Barrel-chested, muscles-rippling, veins throbbing as he attacks Peggy on the boat, forcing her back, back through all of the rooms. Animalistic. A demon. A sheer force of nature.

"Who am I to judge?" Joel said one night, after wine was drunk and secrets shared. "So you have a hard-on for Mitchum."

"First of all," Jack/ie said. "I have a 'girl boner' for Mitchum. First part two, don't gender me. Don't define me. First part fucking three: I am more woman than you'll ever have and more man than you'll ever be."

Joel choked on his drink, spraying the couch cushion between them with booze and spit. "That's awesome. You should get that printed on business cards. You just make that up?"

"Tenth grade," said Jack/ie. "When my step-father saw me wearing my mother's prom dress. We had a rocky relationship after that."

"I'll bet. What was 'second of all?' "

"Second of all," she said, inserting a deep and soulful sigh, drawing out the melodrama, "while I would love to have the real Mr. Bob Mitchum behind me, don't ask me why because I couldn't tell you, Max Cady does something to me deep inside that a team of therapists couldn't explain. And no, my daddy didn't molest me and no, my step-father never laid a hand on me."

"I didn't ask."

"No, you didn't. Most people would have, though."

"How many people have you told?"

"Just you, Joel, honey."

"Why am I so special? Because of my thing for Marie Browning?"

"At least you still have a shot at Bacall. She looks good for, what? Ninety?"

"She died in 2014."

"She did?"

Joel nodded. "And Mitchum looked good up until the day he died."

Jack/ie nodded. "But on the day he died, he was no Max Cady."

"Tell me you've flixed to *Cape Fear*?"

"Of course I have. Same as you've done with *The Big Heat*—I know all about your little fetish for Gloria Graham."

"I'm not denying anything." Joel poured himself another shot of the cheap vodka. At that point in the evening, the bottle was nearly empty and it had stopped burning on the way down. "What I'm saying is maybe you should try, like, *His Kind of Woman*. It was shot ten years before *Cape Fear*, Jeff Milner is a nicer guy but still tough and solid, and Mitchum was at his physical peak."

"Now, look, of course I've flixed to *His Kind of Woman*. Hell, from some angles even Jane Russell turns me on. Vincent Price is sexy as hell in there too. But—"

"No Max Cady?"

"No Max Cady." Jack/ie finished the bottle.

"He's a violent misogynist," Joel said. "He beats up at least two women in the movie and who knows what he gets up to off-screen? What do you think Cady would do to you? What about that story he tells Sam Bowden about his ex-wife?"

"Hey," Jack/ie said. "You proud of every wet dream you ever had?"

"I'm just saying—"

"Kira. *The Dark Crystal*," Jack/ie said. "That's all *I'm* saying."

"Hey, I was a *little* kid—"

"You had a crush on a puppet."

And Joel dropped the subject.

She didn't say anything when his trailer for *To Have and Have Not* showed up in the mail. Even when she saw that hockey puck-sized spool of film on his shelf, with the typed sticker reading *"Cape Fear,"* she still didn't say anything.

But one night she was going to do her set and someone was going to give her a tab of 'x'. Or maybe some fucking queen would make her feel two-feet tall. Or maybe she'd just come home drunk and lonely and feel just pathetic enough that'd she'd beg Joel for just a couple of frames of that trailer. And she'd finally meet Max Cady.

*****

Fortunately for Joel, the *To Have and Have Not* trailer reproduced several seconds of that opening master shot, because it took him more than a dozen tries just to swim through the narrative and fight his way into the lounge at the Hotel Marquis. Every cut, from two-shot to close-up and back, during the establishing conversation with Harry and Johnson and Eddie on the far side of the dock, yanked and tore at Joel, wearing the American sailor as his fiction suit. Learning to move fast, as soon as Harry reached the dock office, Joel sprinted, as casually as he could so as to not re-enter the background, towards the Hotel door. More importantly: to its iron handle. It was his first anchor. Gripping it with both hands, he waited, feeling the tug and the shudder as the narrative struggled to remain with Harry's story. Joel had to ride it out, wait for that dissolve and hang on with mind and body. At his back, he felt that dissolve wash over the master shot, the dock and all its inhabitants, who were going about their lives instead of just filling the background with action. Outside of Harry's story, life continued in *To Have and Have Not*.

The drag of the dissolve was an odd sensation. Even with his back to the Queen Conch he felt the time ripple, getting the boat and its crew from master to the fishing sequence, the marlin stock footage. The ripple was a pool tide of time running through his body, making his eyes swim, his teeth feel smeary. Reality on the dock during the dissolve was liquid, dispersed across a surface by a damp cloth. It was a straight, 24-frame dissolve, the dock superimposed over the stock shot of the boat on the ocean. In film time, it lasted one second. In "real" time, it seemed interminable.

Grunting with the effort to stay in Port du France, Joel felt the dissolve jangle through him like an existential earthquake. Once his body stopped shuddering, he took a tentative step out of the bright Martinque sun and into the dimmer recesses of the lounge. Each time, the first person he encountered was Frenchie Gerard, a flesh and blood man now, no longer "played" by Marcel Dalio. "Some water for the monsieur," he'd call across the room, while Joel made his way to an unoccupied table.

The bartender, a dark-skinned native playing one of several characters referred to as "Emil" (an uncredited Emmett Smith), brought a clear glass. Joel ordered coffee—"*Café, si vous plait.*"—and then asked him when the next plane was due. "In one hour," he was told in accented English.

And thus he'd wait. The hour was too early for alcohol and thus the lounge was virtually deserted. Not even Cricket, the piano player (Hoagy Carmichael in his film debut), nor the rest of the band shared the space. No longer a set designed by Charles Novi, decorated with period artifacts by Casey Roberts, the lounge of the Hotel Marquis was a living thing of dark wood and heavy warm air, smelling of pine cleaner, coffee and rum. Wooden fan blades in the ceiling turning lazily did little to dispel even the early-morning heat. From where he sat, Joel could see the front desk and the caged-in luggage and goods holding pen behind it. A young native woman in a clean white blouse made notes in a ledger while other employees, all in crisp uniforms, moved about performing their duties. His coffee arrived, hot and sweet, and he drank it while waiting for Marie Browning to arrive.

For years, he'd worked out various plans: offer to help her with her bags, "accidentally" bump into her by her room. Once inside the film he realized any plan was unnecessary. Marie would be slightly fatigued from the trip, landing in Port du France as the farthest point her money would take her. She'd be broke, but already on the make. All he'd have to do was sit there, look like he had money and give off the impression that he wasn't a guy who'd miss it, or put up a fuss once it was gone.

A white mini-bus disgorged a handful of passengers, who then formed a line at the Marquis' front desk. Dressed sharply, Frenchie appeared to greet his new guests. Joel nursed his coffee, watched as some were told that rooms were not yet ready, but that they could leave their bags in the cage and move freely about the island, to shop or lunch.

Trying not to look like he was watching, Joel finished the last drops of his coffee, his nerves buzzing and not from the caffeine. He saw her. Just as she turned away from the desk, one of the few without a ready room. Plain, straight gray skirt and the same checked blouse she'd wear later, during her screen introduction. Chin down, eyes cast up, Marie Browning scanned the room. She found him almost immediately. Quickly, he looked down and pretended to fuss with a cufflink. Before long, that dark, smoky voice was in his ear, "Anybody got a match?"

It was just him at the table, so "anybody" meant him. And he'd already searched the uniform's pockets for a box or a book, making sure he wouldn't have to leave to procure one. The pale gray book was already in his hand, before the question was asked. Looking up, he tore a match and struck it against the cover, lighting her cigarette for her, the flame glittering in her gray eyes. "Mind if I sit down? My room's not ready yet."

Any prepared words of welcome caught in his throat. Smiling at her, he waved his hand at the empty chair across from him. As she smoothed her skirt and sat, placing her worn clutch-purse in front of her, Joel caught a waitress's eye. "*Café, si vious plait?*" he asked, holding up a thumb and forefinger, "*Deux.*"

Turning back, he caught Marie's interested gaze. "Thanks," she said. "You speak native pretty well."

He gave her a smile he'd rehearsed for years: easy-going, charming, full of white teeth and what he hoped was generosity. "Actually, that's all I know."

"Just enough to get by?" she suggested, more than asked. He nodded. "Were you a Boy Scout before you were a sailor?"

"Life of misadventure," he said. It sounded like a cool

line, something you'd give Dan Duryea to fill up the air. It didn't mean anything. But it gave her a cue.

"I'd bet you know all the highlights of Martinique." He nodded. "Good. This isn't the only one."

"It is from where I'm sitting."

It was a corny line, but it got him That Look in return. "Slow down, Sailor," she said. "I just landed. As the old saw goes, my arms are still tired."

Their coffee arrived and he made a show out of paying for it. The sailor he wore was loaded. It got her attention; she watched him return the wallet to the jacket's inside pocket, all the while never letting on that she was watching. For all he knew, she just took her time stirring her coffee.

It was work to stay casual when his heart was pounding. The moment was as he'd always imagined it. Now there she was across from him, pale, beautiful, that sharp jawline angled at thirty-degrees. Marie. "What brings you to Port du France?" he asked.

"Just another stop on my way from one place to another. How about you?"

"The marlin," he said quickly.

"Yeah? You have a boat docked around here?" A boat that could take her to somewhere else?

"No. I rent one from its captain," he took a sip. The coffee had the exact same flavor as his previous cup. Not even the slightest deviation. "The Queen Conch, piloted by guy named Morgan. Out of Florida." He added.

Nodding, she kept her eyes down. "Nice work if you can get it."

"Well, what's money?"

"Nothing until you need it."

"Gets you from one place to another," he said, gauging her reaction. Nothing. She was playing this hand close. Later, while playing Morgan, she'd slip, let his judgment get to her. "One look and you made up your mind just what you wanted to think about me," she'd tell him. That was the narrative, though. She was meant to fall for Harry. This was behind-the-frames, off-camera play. To her, Joel was just another mark. He decided to push it. "Of course, I'm not telling you anything you don't already know."

Exhaling a stream of smoke, just past his face, her eyes flashed a little. "Yeah? How's that?"

"Well, beautiful girl like you. I'm sure you've learned how to navigate life pretty well."

"You might want to get to your point, Sailor," she said. "Coffee's getting cold."

It was a challenge, but not a friendly one. Marie Browning was no prostitute. All she was doing was justifying to herself why lifting his wallet, as she would do soon, was nothing to feel guilty about. Before he could return her volley, Frenchie appeared behind her. "Madmoiselle, your room is ready."

"Can I give you a hand with your luggage?" he asked. Clumsily, quickly.

"No, thanks," she said. "Place seems classy. I'm sure they have people for that." With a practiced flick of her wrist, Marie nudged her cloth napkin to the floor. He was meant to retrieve it, as she bent with him, and during the fumble, she'd reach into his open jacket, take the billfold from his pocket. Joel didn't move fast enough. Marie let the napkin remain where it was. "See you around, Sailor."

Patter dried up, Joel didn't respond. A beat too late, he stood as she did, watched as she followed Frenchie up the short staircase to the second floor.

He'd missed his chance. Following screen logic, Marie would freshen up in her room and emerge sometime later to "buy a new hat" from some local boutique that didn't exist on screen. Then she'd meet up with Johnson and, later, Harry Morgan. Mind racing, Joel thought of some excuse to follow them, some reason to knock on her door at the top of the stairs.

A shudder took hold of him then, a full attack on his

nervous system, and he was flung out of the film.

*****

Back in his room, the taste of coffee in his mouth, Joel gasped at the sudden drop of temperature, the harsh return to his own narrative. In sharp contrast to the morning in Martinique, his apartment existed in a dark autumn night. Someone was pounding on his door. His hesitation, the lapse in concentration, coupled with the urgent knock, was all it took to knock him out of *To Have and Have Not*.

Jack/ie was at his door, looked exhausted and pissed off and more than a little drunk. She had her blonde '60s-era wig in her hand. Obviously it didn't go with her smeared and rain-streaked make-up. Joel had never seen her look such a mess. Before he could greet her, she held out her hand—two of the fingernails missing their ceramic tips. "I want Cady," she said.

"Were you in a fight? You okay?"

A hand wave dismissed his concern. "Just cough up the trailer, Joel, honey," Jackie/ie said. "Momma's had a bad night and wants to make it worse."

He hesitated. Again, it was just enough to give another force leeway. Pushing him aside, Jack/ie took long strides from the doorway to the shelf by the TV. It didn't take her long to find the *Cape Fear* trailer stacked among the others there. "I didn't know you had a scope reel of *Braveheart*," she said, possibly more to herself than to him.

"Uh, yeah," Joel said, still a little disoriented. "Listen, are you sure this is a good idea?"

Jack/ie spun on her heel. "You get your Miss Marie to suck you off for loose change yet?"

"What? No! She isn't like that at all."

"Don't judge me, then, and I won't disparage your dream girl." She held up the little puck of film wrapped around a yellow plastic core, to show him she was taking claim of it. To warn him not to stop her.

"Fine," Joel said. "Give your rapist my best."

Jack/ie took long strides past him. In those heels she could have broken both her ankles but it didn't matter. She was making a point. "You're acting like Cady can come out of the film and get us both. You can't affect the movie and the movie can't affect you."

Remembering the sea water he coughed up by the gallons, each time the narrative had flung him into the ocean, Joel wanted to argue. At the very least, he wanted to tell her to be careful. But his nerves were buzzing from the recent first contact with Marie and all he wanted to do was get back into *To Have and Have Not*. So he let Jack/ie have her exit line. She took the trailer and let the door close a little too hard behind her. And the second he was alone again, Joel restarted the DVD and swallowed a frame. Within seconds, he'd be back in Martinique.

*****

Without bothering to put the trailer on a reel, Jack/ie let the film unspool from the core in her hand. Languidly, the celluloid coiled around the empty whiskey bottle on the coffee table. The table had been a garbage night score, found sitting naked on a curb in Yage, waiting for morning when she snagged it. She'd sanded, stripped and restored the wood in less than a week and now it was one of her prized possessions. Tonight, however, it wore rings of condensation—she couldn't be bothered with coasters tonight, not even with the special new Bettie Page ones she'd found in that antique store across from The Pegasus.

It didn't take too much unspooling to find a close-up of Mitchum as Max Cady, sitting in the smoky bar, wearing his white Panama hat, eyeing up Barrie Chase as Diane Taylor like she was something coated in gravy and he hadn't eaten in a long time. Of course—at the risk of being gauche—Cady *hadn't*.

Just got out of the joint for an eight-year stretch on "indecent assault," put there by Sam Bowden's/Gregory Peck's eyewitness testimony.

Of course, they couldn't say "rape," not even in 1962. Notoriously, the censors gave *Cape Fear* a near-impossible time.

It'd been a rotten night, filled with malignant bitches and rude little rent boys who didn't know their place in Pegasus' pecking order. A night of turned ankles, missed cues, a puddle of beer spilled across the stage that she hadn't seen until it was too late. She wanted to be wanted. She wanted to be Max Cady's first meal in eight long years.

When all was said and attempted, Joel's goal of meeting Marie was simpler than Jack/ie meeting Cady. *To Have and Have Not* had a tight structure, a narrative time of only two days, action largely confined to the Hotel Marquis. He knew when Marie was due on screen, to fulfill her destiny with Harry. All Joel had to do was find the other moments, exploit the time off screen.

Cape Fear's time-frame sprawled over weeks, and Cady constantly prowled behind the scenes, stalking the Bowden family from afar, but with all legality. His plans changed constantly, but his goal was to tear Sam Bowden down to nothing. The way he saw things, Bowden's testimony was a crime against manhood. To Cady's mind, he was only having a little fun with a stuck-up little tramp who had put herself above him, forgotten her place. Then Bowden elevated himself above all and looked down at him with judgment, knowing that, as a man, he'd have done the same thing as Cady if fortunes had reversed. Women, you see? They *want it*. So he was going to level ol' Sam Bowden, ruin his wife, even his pretty little bud of a daughter. Destroy the honorable Sam Bowden, esquire, and salt the Earth of his mangled society.

To even *meet* Cady during a splice-in would be a crap-shoot of the finest order. Jack/ie could swallow the right frame and try to flix during the matching scene, but there were no guarantees. Unlike filmmaking, flixing was an inexact art. Total immersion plus astral projection, not to mention some rare alchemy of the electro-chemical process of merging soul with emulsion.

Even drunk, she knew how to put on her make-up, fix up her hair, get into gorgeous mode. Jack/ie slipped into Jackie, then took the well-loved DVD of *Cape Fear* from her own shelf. She let it play as she carefully scissored a frame of that beautiful Mitchum close-up and placed it on her tongue.

*****

Anybody got a match?
Anybody got a match?
Anybody—

Three more shots at his "chance" meeting, then a half-dozen more and Joel was still no closer to cracking the Marie Browning code. Maybe it was hopeless after all. The narrative really was like destiny and refused to be altered. Still, he argued, the audience learns nothing of Marie's time in Martinque before that iconic moment when she met Harry Morgan in the doorway of his room. She buys a new hat, showing the repulsive Renard the receipt. Before that, she makes some time with Mr. Johnson, lifts his wallet, but then Harry intervenes, to "see the look on Johnson's face" when she returns it, still full of the money owed to him. It's never implied that she's a pro—she infers it from Harry's initial treatment of her, his ability to make her feel "cheap" after she picks up a Vichy sailor in the Club du Zombie just to get a fresh bottle of booze for them both. Even if the Hays Code prevented explicit mention of the profession, there was no reason to believe that Marie Browning was a working girl. Just a pretty grifter making her way across the world.

Every time Joel waited for Marie to lift his wallet while fighting the urge to take her in his arms and kiss her. By

Hollywood logic, such an action would either get him slapped or kissed back. Likely both. Then a fade to black, '40s code for sex. Everyone knew what happened during that absence of light and motion. Dissolve to a candle burning, pan to fireworks in the sky—all iconography, shorthand to protect the children. It was all code.

Marie Browning was a code of her own. Joel might know her future like the back of his hand, but swimming against the narrative tide, he felt defeat in the presence of her present.

"As grateful as I am for the company, Sailor," she said as Frenchie appeared behind her once again, "I'm afraid I have to get going. Girl's got to sleep sometime."

It hit him then: her insurance policy. The "thirty-odd dollars" she offers to Harry to turn down Frenchie's job of smuggling in Gaulist refugees, Paul and Hellene de Bursac (Walter Szurovy (Molnar) and Dolores Moran). Harry will scoff at her. "I thought you were broke. You're good. You're awful good." Then he spits her own words back at her, "'I'd walk home if it wasn't for all that water.'"

She won't react. Her eyes will simply narrow and harden. "Who was the girl, Steve?"

"Who was *what* girl?"

"The one who left you with such a high opinion of women? She must have been quite a gal." She'll offer the money to him again, holding it out for him to take. "You think I lied to you about this, don't you? Well, it just happens there's thirty-odd dollars here, not enough for boat fare or any other kind of fare. Just enough to be able to say no if I feel like it. And you can have it if you want it."

But Harry Morgan won't take anything from anybody. Though in that moment, he'll learn something about Marie Browning, the girl he calls "Slim".

As she stood, Joel grabbed her hand. "Wait just a second."

"Look, Sailor, I've had a long morning. I'm not up for being pawed at."

Before Frenchie could intervene on Marie's behalf, Joel reached into his jacket and pulled out the billfold. Then he let go of her wrist. "Sorry. I've had an interesting morning myself." With both hands, he removed the Sailor's money without counting it. Once it was out, it didn't seem like much at all. "Look, sister, you seem like a smart lady and one who can handle herself. And you don't seem like one to take charity."

"You've got me all summed up in the space of a cup of coffee, have you?"

He forced the money into her hand. "Take it from a guy who knows how hard this world can kick you when you're down. Give yourself a little luxury," he said. "Go buy a new hat."

She gave him a funny look, then. It was outside of her repertoire of smoldering mystery and plain-faced candor. Her grey eyes studied him up and down, looking for his angle. Finally, she dropped the money onto the table. "Sorry, but I don't take candy from strangers."

"No," he said. "I guess you're the type who wouldn't take anything from anybody." When he reached for the folded bills, it was her cool hand under his that stopped him.

"Don't figure me so quickly," she said. "A girl likes a little intrigue from time to time." He didn't say anything. She took the money and gave him a small salute. "Thanks," she said. "I think I deserve a new hat."

Again, she turned away and followed Frenchie up the stairs. It was final: he couldn't affect the narrative.

Then she stopped, halfway up the stairs, and looked back at him over her shoulder. "Say, Sailor? Unless you have something better to do, why don't you stick around for a while? Give me a chance to freshen up. I think I'd like to buy you a 'thank you' tie."

Joel smiled up at her. It wasn't the false grin wrapped around the bravado he'd found in the Sailor's suit. It was genuine. Marie Browning said, "Thank you."

Before he could respond, she'd resumed her ascent. Then a pounding noise ripped him out of his splice.

*****

Outside his door, Jack/ie was a crumpled, bloodied mess on the floor. Turning her swollen face up, she strained her cracked and bruised lips into a smile. "Morning, hon'. Give us a hand?"

Joel cursed under his breath and half-dragged Jack/ie to her feet, then half-dragged her some more to the couch. "I knew this would happen," he said during the trip, panting under Jack/ie's weight. She was solid and a half-foot taller. To her credit, she never lost her wig. Slumped on the couch, she looked like a beaten *Laugh-In* era Goldie Hawn. "You did it, didn't you? You spliced in looking for Cady and you found him."

"Did I ever," she said, the words croaking from her ruined throat. The skin of her neck was purple and swollen, with raised bruises in the shape of tightened fingers. "And he was even more beautiful up close, Joel."

Running to the bathroom, he soaked a towel in cold water then held it to her face. "Careful, hon. I think I'm missing a tooth."

Thinking of the seawater he'd puked onto his own floor, he went ahead and asked the question anyway. "How is this even possible? I thought the narrative couldn't affect you."

"Well, I've been wrong before," she said.

"This is awful. We should get you to a hospital."

"And pay with what? My former good looks? Trust me, I've been worse off."

That was a lie. They both knew it. "Fuck, Max Cady—are you insane, Jack? Why not Darth Vader?"

"Actually," she said, "Cady was quite sweet."

"Yeah, I can tell."

Jack/ie put a hand on his arm, looked up at him with

sincerity in her one open green eye. "I'm telling you true, hon'. I met him in a bar, followed him after he first confronts Sam outside of the courthouse. The scene where he takes Bowden's keys from the ignition?"

Joel nodded. He was familiar with *Cape Fear*, after all.

"I didn't have to leap into little ol' Diane, either. I spliced in and I was just another co-ed in a tight sweater. Looked at my reflection in a store window and wouldn't you know, I looked just like me."

Nodding, Joel thought about his assumption of the Sailor, the extra whose face you never see. A background player in film and in the film's life.

"I sidled up to Cady and asked him to buy me a drink, just like that. And it tasted like a real drink and he smelled like I thought he'd smell. Like a man pumped full of himself, all hot after putting a scare into the high and mighty Sam Bowden. I just let him be that man."

Voice gurgling then, she coughed a bloody glob into the towel. Her dignity was shot and she didn't care. Joel was her friend and he didn't care. "I think he fractured your jaw."

"See, I knew what Cady was all about going in," Jack/ie said, rasping. "You don't put a man like that down. Don't put on airs or rag on him for being what he is. I knew what he needed, psychologically-speaking."

"You're psychoanalyzing a Jungian archetype." Joel turned the towel around to a spot that was colder and unbloodied. "Cady is a representation all the primal urges that Sam has repressed in himself."

"I *know* the film's philosophy, Joel, just as well as you. And I'm telling you, he didn't set out to hurt me. He took me back to his place, this one-room flop above a bowling alley. You never see it on screen, but it looks like a place he'd have. It was spare, just the essentials. Not even a fan above the bed. And it was hot in there. My make-up should've been running, we were both sweating up a storm. All he wanted then was a fresh girl to be a man with and I was more than willing to be that girl. His hands were rough, but he was tender."

"Tender, yeah. You might have a detached retina."

"The mistake was mine, Joel."

"Bullshit. Don't start slut-shaming yourself. You're not gonna pull blame-the-victim with me. The guy was written to be an animal."

"It was a miscalculation on my part. I'm being honest." A loud cough rattled out of her chest, followed by the wheeze of a collapsed lung. "See, I thought I could go in there and just be the woman Max needed. Problem wasn't him. Problem was me."

"You're delirious."

"I went in *whole*. It was all me up there in that room with Max Cady."

And the "duh" bulb went off in Joel's head, before Jack/ie finished elaborating.

"Everything was just fine until he slid his hand between my legs. Then I swear he followed me out of the film and tried to finish the job next door."

Blood caked the majority of Jack/ie's face, in the hollows of her ears and nostrils. It was evidence of Cady's rage at being duped, deceived. This violence was beyond what he had visited to Diane Taylor in the film's second act. And the words he doubtlessly used as he rained that violence on Jack/ie would never have gotten past the film's censors. But back behind the frames and off-screen, just like "real" life, anything goes. "He split his knuckles on me," she said. "But that didn't stop him." Another wracking cough. Then, "Didn't even occur to me that I wouldn't be woman enough."

"Stop it," Joel said.

"I still got what I'd wanted. Just didn't enjoy it like I thought I would."

"Okay, enough." Shivering, he reached for the phone but Jack/ie stopped him. How would they explain the injuries? The cops would get involved. They'd both get asked questions neither could answer. Plus the humiliation. Jack/ie'd be the one on trial, not the ghost from 1962.

Even that would have worked in Cady's favor. Central to his plot against the Bowden's was the violation of Sam's wife and daughter, and the ordeal they'd go through in a trial. They'd bring charges [of rape] against Cady, who'd in turn deny it. Peggy would defy Cady late into the movie, she'd testify despite the shame. But what about young Nancy? She'd suffer her own trial in newspapers, in gossip. Forced to relive [the rape] over and over with each retelling. Sam was a lawyer; he knew how nasty lawyers could be. They weren't all fine, upstanding men like Gregory Peck.

So what chance would a someone like Jack/ie have in the face of it? In the "real" world? The truth was that he'd been violated by a shadow dead for decades. But the "reality" would be that some queer got what was coming to him. Even if Jack/ie was willing, Joel felt sick being a part of that.

Jack/ie was in no shape to return to her room, so Joel helped her get into his bed. Painkillers were found—the building still served some as a dormitory after all—sleep was induced. As the sun began to peek in through the grimy window, pink turning to orange in the sky, Joel left his friend and returned to the living room. To the couch. To the TV. *To Have and Have Not.*

Letting the DVD menu play its thirty seconds of score in an endless loop, Joel stared at the image of Marie Browning, wrapped in Harry Morgan's arms. Obviously, the narrative could affect you, but could you affect the narrative? The editing, the storyline, it was all etched in celluloid and that might as well be stone. Regardless of what happened off-screen, Marie and Harry's lives were lived in that span of time between titles, between fade in and fade out. After "The End", their adventures were never recorded. Nothing he could do would alter the onscreen action.

There was nothing he could do to help Jack/ie. He could splice into *Cape Fear* all he wanted, maybe join the gang

Sam hires to beat up Cady under the pier, before he turns the tables on them. Maybe Joel could be the one swinging the bicycle chain. But then Cady would just overpower him. Even if he picked the exact right time, spliced in and slid into Police Chief Mark Dutton, played by Martin Balsam, and took the cop's service revolver and unloaded it right into Cady's face, even if that were possible, nothing would change. The narrative would freeze, reject him. At the very worst, there would come a dissolve and Cady's revenge would resume, as it always had and always would. Artifice captured in time. No matter what he did, *Cape Fear* would always end with a gun gripped in Sam's hand, never fired, while Cady writhed in the mud, waiting for the police to arrest him. Even if he were to flip into Sam, into the very moment when Peck's lawyer character suffers his doubt, unsure even himself if he has it in him to sink to Cady's level and murder his aggressor, nothing Joel could do would nudge Sam into pulling the trigger. Because that wasn't what happened.

In Scorcese's 1992 remake, nature herself took revenge on DeNiro's Max Cady, sucking him under the Cape Fear River. But that justice was manufactured in the remake. In the original, Max Cady lived. Always lived. Would always live.

What he'd done to Jack/ie happened behind the frames. It had no impact on the movie's storyline. Jack/ie had been just another sin on Cady's roster of rage. It had made no difference.

Beside the couch was a nearly-empty bottle of vodka. It had been sitting there for some time. Joel snatched it up, unscrewed the cap and drained it in one burning swallow. It was time for the Sailor to finally have his date with Marie Browning.

He spliced in at the perfect time. Why hadn't he thought of it before? The path to Marie Browning would not be found at the beginning. Not with her whole life with Harry ahead of her. Joel slipped in well past all of that, and found her sitting alone at a table, with a sympathetic Cricket at the piano behind her. He nearly bumped into Morgan as he exited the Hotel, having bought and delivered to Slim a ticket for the next plane out of

Martinique. Joel arrived just in time to hear her sad final line, "Well, it was nice while it lasted."

Gripping the staircase's iron railing, Joel fought the next dissolve. He wouldn't be dragged back to the Queen Conch while Harry and stowaway Eddie picked up the De Bursacs and had their confrontation with the German patrol boat. Through will alone he fought the narrative tide and stayed right where he was, watching Marie finish her drink and finger the plane ticket in front of her. Morgan had left her feeling cheap again, with his noble thoughts of rescuing her. The man she'd been falling for had just walked out of her life, most likely to be killed on the open water. At no point in *To Have and Have Not* would Slim be more vulnerable. Joel the Sailor meant to take full advantage.

This time in, he wasn't wearing the Sailor's duds. Instead, he wore the crisp linen suit of one of the Gaulists, the Free French conspirators. But it was still him inside that new suit. Like Jack/ie, he had "come in whole".

Unsure of his footing, if the film would rip him from his moorings if his hand left the railing, he remained on the stairs and watched Marie gather up what few belongings she had with her. Finally, she picked up the ticket. For his part, Cricket opened his mouth to say—something, anything, but no sound accompanied his awkward empathy for her. But she heard him, in her own way. Without looking at him, she nodded, as if to say, "That's that," and headed for the stairs.

It was obvious she didn't see him there on the stairs until she was almost on top of him. Her head was down, eyes searching the floor for answers. Risking everything, Joel reached out and touched her arm. "Oh, hello Sailor.

How'd you like the show?"

"Are you all right?"

Turning her head to meet his gaze, he saw the storm clouds behind her eyes. Anger and regret. "Not sure I understand the question." Slowly, she moved past him. Two stairs up she hesitated and turned back. "Say," she said. "I never did show you that hat I bought."

There might have been a cut just then. He couldn't remember how they'd gotten to her room so quickly. Yet there they were, the door closed behind them. Her little travel valise lay open on the luggage table next to the bed, across from the striped couch, the little nothing paintings hung on the wall, found somewhere deep in the WB props department. From nowhere she'd produced a bottle of rum and two glasses and they drank the booze straight.

"I don't want to talk, understand?" Her back was to him. Her voice was hard. "I'm not going to be much company and I don't want to be. I don't want to *be* anything right now."

"Marie—"

"And before you get any clever notions in that skull of yours," she began to undo the buttons of her blouse. "This has nothing to do with you."

He was all too aware that *this* is what happened in '40s movies when they faded to black. Since it was all off-camera, all off-narrative, the all-seeing eye of the Hayes Code was blind here. They were behind closed doors.

As she removed her clothes, Marie Browning didn't want help. Certainly not his. Joel stood behind her, awkwardly discarded his linen jacket and laid it on the hideous couch. Doffing his hat, it landed on top of the jacket heap. He watched as each discard revealed new secret layers of '40s lingerie, made of buckles and snaps and panels. Black underthings—that surprised him, but he wasn't sure why. In a single, mercurial movement, Marie lied down across the bed, the very definition of naked. Turning her gray eyes towards him, her look was all demand.

"Well?" Her eyes had no spark, none of the glimmer or mischief he'd first fallen in love with at 13-years-old. "Come get what you came for."

In her entire career, Lauren Bacall had never posed nude, and he was suddenly aware that Marie Browning's body was a construct of his own mind. As he took in her glory, the image shimmered and wouldn't solidify. Marie had an almost zaftig, Bettie Page quality to her, which belied the slim hips Bacall possessed in 1944. None of that mattered any more. Marie Browning lie before him, finally all his.

Taking her hair in handfuls he inhaled the lilac of her shampoo, the vanilla oil at the nape of her neck and behind her ears. He ran his hands over the entirety of her skin, a cascade of satin. Her eyes avoided his. Would he have ignored her tears were she to cry? This was a coupling of spite, of revenge and desperation. The woman beneath him needed something physical to hang onto, now that she was being sent back out into the world again by the one guy who she thought might have everything up to now worth it. Joel was perfectly happy to be the instrument of her revenge. Maybe he should care, but it was too late to "do the right thing", which by now was a construct of artificial Hollywood morality.

Marie wanted to feel cheap. She wanted to earn Harry's casual dismissal. Joel the Sailor would do just the job and he knew she knew it. But while he felt her nails dig into his back, felt her full lips pressed against his, he knew she was feeling nothing in return. And was likely grateful for it.

But why should *he* feel cheap? Why should he feel used? This was what he wanted—had dreamed about for a decade. His younger, less-mature self had been so confident that, with the right patter and the right conditions, he could make Marie Browning fall in love with him, feel for him what she'd later feel for Harry Morgan. Pushing that all aside, Joel decided to live in the moment. Discarding the whys and reasons for, he took what he wanted. Bodies pressed together, their sweat combining and pooling in that sweltering room. Welcoming that final, time-stopping shudder, they both held their breath as it passed. Afterwards, they shared a cigarette.

There was no conversation as they dressed. Their backs to each other, they suited up back into their uniforms. He turned to smile, to say something to her, but she never turned to him. As he retrieved his hat, she held out her hand. "Here," she said. "Give this to Cricket for me."

The plane ticket. Joel understood. While Harry and Eddie were off rescuing the De Bursacs, Marie remained behind. She took a job as a singer for Cricket's band and never made that plane.

In the original screenplay, Marie's story had meant to be complete, so that Harry and Mme. Helene De Bursac could have their own affair, while her husband recovered from his gunshot wound, to further echo *Casablanca*. But Bacall had wooed them all so completely. Dolores Moran's part got whittled away at Hawks request. The studio heads loved Betty's chemistry with Bogie, demanded more. To Hawks' utter dismay, the married Bogie and the very young Bacall began an off-set romance. To nurse his wounds, Hawks turned his attention towards Moran, out of spite, out of his own wounded pride. The legendary romance put an end to "The Battling Bogarts" and Mayo Methot—who'd threatened to shoot her husband on more than one occasion—divorced in '45 would be dead of liver failure in '51. The Hollywood love story of Bogie and Bacall would last until his death in 1957.

Like so many other movies, *To Have and Have Not*'s ending promised "happily ever after," with Harry, Slim and Eddie fleeing Martinique as war criminals, headed for parts unknown. The plane ticket had been their story's turning point.

Standing in the hallway, her door closed to his back, Joel wondered if he'd played a part in her decision to stay. Or had he been simply the method through which the decision was made? Did he alter the narrative in some small way? As the source of money for her new hat—the line that got her slapped with her own passport by Renard's Lt. Coyo (played by TV legend Sheldon Leonard)? Did he give her the resolve to pursue her own "happy ever after"? If this were a time travel story, of course he'd have always been behind the scenes, long before he made the decision to splice in and alter the sea of time. But *To Have and Have Not* was not a story of time. It was a warmed-over melodrama with no real stakes and no real danger, made a hit by audiences thanks to the chemistry of the central characters. Bogie and Bacall, Steve and Slim, that's why the movie had endured.

And he was a schmuck to think he had anything to do with that.

This time, nothing yanked him out of the movie. Placing his hat on his head, Joel simply exited the frame.

Back in his room, in his own clothes, bathed in the glow of the TV, the DVD having returned to its menu screen, his body hummed. But he felt cheated, and reminded himself of the old saw, "be careful what you wish for." Ten years of anticipation and fantasy, the endless screenings where he flixed to her beauty, the weeks of concentration, fighting the film to remain by her side. All of that over in the space of a deleted scene.

Hitting the bathroom, he washed his face, vaguely startled to see it returned to color. The apartment was dark and his eyes were used to a black and white world. He checked in on Jack/ie, still passed out in the bed where he'd left her. Breathing still labored, otherwise motionless.

Feeling suddenly aimless, he returned to the living room, tried to decide if he was tired enough to sleep, when something hard and heavy slammed into the back of his skull.

The blow pitched him forward and he stumbled like a newborn fawn, knees and elbows flailing. Plowing face-first into the battered recliner, he remained there with ringing ears until the assailant grabbed him roughly and spun him around. His first thought was that it was Max Cady, who'd somehow forced his way out of *Cape Fear* to finish the job he'd begun on Jack/ie. The idea petrified him. Cady would beat them both to death. He was capable of it. *Willing.*

Instead, the face he saw before his eyes, absent of all color, still living in monochrome, was Harry Morgan, holding a pistol on him in a shaking hand. "Ain't that silly?" Morgan says in the film, looking at his trembling hand after shooting Renard's silent henchman (Aldo Nadi) through a desk.

"You!" Morgan said, roaring at him. This wasn't Bogie's standard tough guy routine. This was anger and rage and it belonged to Harry Morgan. "I couldn't be sure. Thought I was going crazy. Then I realized, whenever I closed my eyes—your face. Everywhere I looked: your face in different costumes. I could swear once you were Emil. Then another day you were in Frenchie's outfit, disappearing around a corner. How'd you do it? Answer me?"

Joel had no response. Morgan dragged him to his feet by the front of his shirt, then hit him hard in the mouth, knocking him back into the chair. Liquid copper stained his tongue.

"I don't know what you did, but I know it was you!"

"Mister, I don't know you—"

"Quiet!" Morgan barked the word. The boat captain was uneasy on his feet. Drunk? Possibly. But his wide-eyed mania hinted at something else. "I must be losing my mind. This must be what it's like for Eddie, day in and day out. A haze you can't walk out of." The rambling stopped and Morgan turned laser-focused to him once again. "What did you do to her, you rat?"

Maybe Morgan was still bound by the rules of the Hayes Code, couldn't call him anything worse. Couldn't go for the words that were so casually used in modern movies. Or maybe "rat" was the worst thing he could think of. Morgan took a step forward and Joel's entire body retreated back against the chair cushions. Both hands flung palm-out in a plea to stop, to come no closer.

"Couldn't quite put my finger on it. Took me a long time to figure out. She was different somehow. I knew she wouldn't use that ticket. I didn't want her to. I didn't want any of it. Then after it happened, I started remembering two different versions of the story. I held her body in my arms and I knew something wasn't right. Things got tough, yeah, that's life. Especially after Eddie passed. The light was gone out of her and now I'm covered in her blood and I *know* that wasn't supposed to happen. Something changed. It was like we were living two different lives together. And once she was gone, it finally hit me—you. I'd never seen you before. Then it was like I couldn't get away from you. You had the only face in Martinique."

Morgan took another step toward him, his whole body shaking with some cosmic horror he couldn't comprehend. Neither of them could. "You *changed* her. I want to know what you did, you lousy piece of trash! What happened after I left her that ticket? Cricket couldn't say, but he mentioned you. Always lurking about. Watching her. Must have really galled you to see her leave with me, huh? Well? You'd better have something to say quick or so help me…"

But he couldn't speak. What would he say?

"I *remember* us having a happy life. I remember us growing old together. Even as I held her, tried to stop the blood, knowing it was too late—I *remembered* that it was supposed to be different. Not 'hope.' Understand? You changed something. You changed her. I want to know what you did and I want to know why and I want to know *right now*!"

Nothing. Joel's mouth could form no words.

"Get up!" Morgan ordered him with the barrel of the pistol. "Get out of that chair or so help me I'll drag you out of it!"

Joel started to rise, but not fast enough for Morgan's liking. True to his word, he seized a clump of Joel's hair and yanked him to his feet. He felt the pistol digging into his ribs between the two of them, standing almost nose-to-nose. There was booze on Harry's breath, sure, but it had little to do with his mood.

In a heartbeat, Morgan was grinning. It was an ugly smile, all teeth and without humor. Then that bitter Bogart laugh that hit like a slap. "Answers," he said. "I came all the way here looking for answers. To hear it out of your own mouth. That you violated her or…*ha.* Cast some sort of spell. But what difference does it make now?" Morgan glanced around the room and when his eyes came back, they were dead balls of steel. "I like the colors," he said.

Sound exploded between them and a puff of grey smoke wafted towards the ceiling. It was a familiar sound. You could turn on Turner Classic Movies and hear that sound a dozen times a day. It was the Warner Brothers' foley library gunshot track. Just a high, full-throated bang that meant the movie was over soon, because the bad guy just got it in the gut.

Staggering backward with a chest full of molten lava, Joel knew there'd be no blood, no bullet hole. Not from a 1944 Hollywood .38. Just the searing pain in his side tunneling towards his chest, dropping him back into the chair once again.

If this had been a movie, seconds before Morgan pulled the trigger, someone would have burst through the door. Maybe Max Cady, having escaped his own endlessly repeating prison. The men would have squared off—Cady with his barrel chest and hound-dog eyes; Morgan with his bared teeth and righteous anger.

Or Jack/ie would have thrown her own Hail Mary pass, summoning the strength to leave Joel's bed at the first sound of Morgan's wrath, dragged herself to the hallway, flung herself at the assailant or at the very least hurled some dense object at his hand, knocking the gun away. Maybe there would have been a struggle and maybe Joel would have gotten it anyway.

But this was life, as implausible and impossible as life always is. Slumping to the floor, his organs shutting down, pierced by the invisible stock-sound bullet, Joel looked up at Harry Morgan, whose face seemed to flush, very briefly, a deep angry rose. While he pondered how he could have possibly changed the narrative, or if indeed he had, Joel watched as Harry Morgan watched him die. Fade to black.

And then fade back up. A gray moment. Joel still convulsed on the floor, his insides shattering to glass. Morgan was seated on the coffee table, looming over him, his fingers playing with something very small. A frame of film. Morgan held the frame up to the light of the television, and Joel could only guess what was on it. Likely, it was a shot of Marie, of his "Slim," the last remaining frame of her standing in the doorway, chin down, eyes up, giving "That Look" to an off-screen Harry. Always to an off-screen Harry.

Morgan saw that Joel still lived. He held the frame on his palm and demanded, "What's this?"

Joel's lungs held no breath. The blood in his throat would have made speaking impossible. Vaguely, he wondered what would happen if Harry put that frame on his tongue, if he even knew what flixing was. What would happen to a man from a film if he flixed to the film of his life? What would the feedback loop be like?

A final contortion took Joel out of his world. Fade to black and credits.

THE WORTHLESS LIFE AND POINTLESS DEATH OF ANGELA ST. SATAN

"Are 'snuff films' for real? Well, they are and they aren't. Depends on what you think of as a 'snuff film'." Balun took a drag of his cigarette and paused, looking thoughtful. If anyone had any insight into the topic, it was our local underground expert, the Librarian of the Damned Movies. "If you're talking war crime footage, then yeah, of course they are. Taliban executions, beheading via very slow sawing—you can download these any time you want. Bud Dwyer's suicide, that's news footage. Caught by accident but the cameraman didn't turn away. The Findlays' *Slaughter* recut into *Snuff* by whatshisname—guy who punched Roberta in the face when she threatened to sue him or whatever—Allan Shackleton. Obviously that stuff's fake. So are all those quote-unquote underground indies: *Last House on Dead End Street*, *Murder-Set-Pieces*, the *August Undergrounds*— even though the gore is top-notch, the actors got up and went home at the end of the day. So, yeah, for the most part, 'snuff' is urban legend—sucker bait for whack-jobs like Charlie Sheen who thought the *Guinea Pig* movies were real and actually called the cops. But then the internet and camera phones come about and all of a sudden you get these real-life killers recording their shit, putting it on YouTube—*1 Lunatic 1 Icepick*, Luke Magnotta [sic], or those two Russian kids he inspired to make *3 Killers 1 Hammer*... obviously, that's snuff. That's the real deal. There are rumors still that the Manson family filmed some of their kills, and of course, the footage in the Borgia movies have been verified—movies that got the filmmakers convicted like Magnotta and the other two... Yeah.

"But if you're talking lights and sets and boom mics and *Videodrome*, then no. Snuff movies are never a big production. Guys who make real snuff films, over in Serbia and all those countries that used to be in the Soviet Union, those are run-and-gun. Roll film, kill actor, get the fuck out of there. First one I ever saw was just this girl sitting in a room watching television when her biker boyfriend walks in and just shoots her in the head and leaves. He held the camera and the gun. Definitely not big budget..." —"The Last Screening of *The Divine Heresy*," Interview with Chris Balun by Seth Salem, *Exploitation Nation* Vol. 2, #3, March 2004.

*****

My first thought when I heard Angela St. Satan might be dead: "Good."

She was a terrible actress and a worse person who "starred" in a long string of soft-core horror movies. She'd convinced herself that because middle-aged guys jerked off to her she had the talent to make it Out There. On screen she had this vacant, doe-eyed stare and round mouth and enough baby fat that she got away with her "barely legal" schtick until she was almost thirty. It was the camera that added "sweet and innocent". In real life she was arrogant, snotty, had a foul mouth and looked down on everyone she met, especially other women. If she was dead, five other so-called actresses have already taken her place. Making the same stupid movies over and over again, with one hack after another.

Actually, that wasn't true. For all his for-hire hackwork—*Punishment of Sandy, Lilly Strangled at Midnight, Chloroformed Every Night*, and the rest of his one-day fetish-paloozas for pay-per-click sites—Jimmy Brimstone was not only talented but actually tried to get a message across. He was part of a tradition of angry punk filmmakers, albeit a lot of years too late. Critics (myself included) wrote that his movies fit in alongside those of Richard Kern and Nick Zedd—nihilistic, anti-social, sex-and-violence for their own sake because the world wouldn't know the difference. Jimmy B. wasn't preaching anti-humanity, he was celebrating it. And when he wasn't making spank-and-strangle fetish pics with his naked girlfriends, he was actually concentrating on his message, bleak as it was. As far as I was concerned, when it came to the independent underground the message itself doesn't often matter, so long as it's there. Possession of a worldview will allow your body of work to raise that much further to the top. Cream of the crap.

In his "serious" movies, when he focused on his message, that the world was a hollow cinder of rage and despair, Angela St. Satan actually did show signs of life. When Jimmy Brimstone made movies that came from his soiled, charred little heart, he directed her to be the conduit of his message. *Satan General Hospital*, in particular, was a hard movie to take, but really well-shot and directed. Title was total shock value and so was a lot of the footage, but it actually had a viewpoint, male terror and misunderstanding of the female orgasm and concepts like *vagina dentata*. Maybe one of two or three movies where Angela gave a half-decent performance. He introduced real pain into her safe-and-sheltered little existence. Showed her what a miserable cesspool the world was. It may have been bleak, but it was, to him at least, true. Before then, Angela St. Satan had never known that many true things.

Originally, she was little Jenny Something-or-other. Harris, I think. Her daddy was a banker. Her mommy worked for a cosmetics company. She'd never wanted for anything. She'd never gone to bed hungry. She'd never watched her little brother commit suicide by way of a heroin needle, the way Jimmy Brimstone had. A-student with bows in her hair. Jimmy's darkness called to her, and she ran three blocks away to his little pain-and-pleasure den. She was sixteen at the time. He was twenty and much, much older.

A few years later Jimmy sold her to Sappho Studios and she became their hot new thing. Sappho was a better-than-average studio, probably up there with Seduction Cinema or Surrender, used to getting models-turned-hookers off the streets for their lesbianic fantasies. Their movies had decent enough production value and they made buckets of money because they were, more or less, "soft core." No penetration—hell, no men usually. Just female skin on female skin, stretchmarks, tattoos, track marks and all. But "soft core" meant they made it to late-night cable and video chains would stock their titles, so they churned them out as fast as they could shoot them. By the time Angela arrived on their door, even as used up as she already was, to them she looked like a shiny new penny.

Seemed like she did a movie per week with them. The plots rarely changed: college-girl discovers the eroticism of other college-girls, or vampire college girl, or ghost college girl. Sorority of sinful schoolgirls in little plaid skirts, bored housewives, sexy mummies. That kind of stuff. Use your imagination because no one in charge did. Would have saved money if they spent one day shooting the girls in different hats, then edit those shots into the endless sex scenes and pretend towards variety.

Angela was their new star and they put her forward to shine. In front of the lens, she had an innocence about her. A couple of reviewers compared her to Bettie Page, but she didn't have the pin-up queen's charisma. There were half-a-million fan-run websites out there, all eager to land interviews with her, cement her as a new goddess of sexy b-movies. That's just what happened.

Microcinema starlets are sad little creatures. Studios have no idea that they exist—a form of insect they'd never even bothered to fry with their giant magnifying glass. But to their fans, often a collection of sad and pitiful little fanboys, the "Scream Queens", walked on water in all their naked glory, movie after movie after badly-lit, barely audible little movie.

And the Queens, quite often, utterly and completely despised their subjects.

This was all public record. Angela wasn't smart enough to invent a persona to go with her really stupid stage name. It's easy to get dirt on people who don't care who they run their mouths to. I'd interviewed her years back, when she was fresh on the scene. I got snippets of the truth, some I could use, some I was smart enough to keep out. I got paid by the word and I got assignments because I knew how to make anyone sound important. People talked to me, either figuring I knew what was "off the record" and when or just not caring. I had dirt on everyone in this almost-meaningless sub-industry, and I knew all sorts of things about Angela.

I just didn't care. Because I also knew that, at some point, she would either get bored of the game and leave, or get herself a doting husband, most likely rich and ten years older. Not to sound like a Spillane knock-off, but what she got, obviously, was in too deep.

For me, it all started with a string of frantic emails from a middle-aged fanboy who went by the screen name "Les Moore." I knew him from the convention and film fest circuits. Little guy, greasy hair, big gut, thick glasses like aquarium walls. Like George Romero's, which is probably why he chose them. Les had a permanent hard-on for most of Sappho's stable and had it particularly bad for Angela. She thought he had money, so she was nice to him, or at least cruel in ways he didn't notice. He'd blow wad after wad on her pictures and movies, then go home and do the same only literally.

Ten emails from him in one day. All with the subject "Can't find Angela St. Satan". I ignored them all. Delete, delete, delete. That night, the son of a bitch called my cell phone. Don't even ask me why I answered it. Even his voice sounded greasy as he asked for me by name.

"Les, you know it's me."

"Angela's missing."

"Yeah. Read that somewhere."

"We were supposed to shoot. I got an email from her a couple of days ago, said she'd call me about plane tickets."

"Okay," I said. I didn't care.

"No one's heard from her," he said

"Okay," I repeated. Still didn't care. Remained uncaring.

"I called Rosie,"—her roommate last I'd heard—"I called Jimmy Brimstone—no one's heard from her."

"Les, what do you want from me?"

"I think something happened to her."

I should have just hung up. "And?"

"Call around, find out if anyone's talked to her lately!"

"Why?"

"What do you mean, 'why'?"

"I literally could not care less. Why should I call around?"

"Look, I said I think something's happened to her— Eddie Ball! Call Eddie Ball. She just shot with him last week."

"Who the hell is Eddie Ball?"

"He did *Monster Box*. Owns 'Live Death Pictures.'"

"Oh, please—Are you flixing?" Rhetorical.

"I'll email you his info."

All I wanted, with every bit of my soul, was this conversation to be over. "You got his number, you call him."

"I can't. He won't answer me. He'll talk to you. Everyone

knows you."

"Alright, I'll call Eddie Ball. Then you'll leave me alone?"

"You just…" On the other end of the phone, however many miles away, Les Moore actually started to cry. "You gotta find her, man. Please"

"You gotta find a new fixation. Angela will do anyone that—"

He cut me off with a hard whisper, "You don't know her."

"True enough," I said. I hung up. My chair squeaked as I sat back. I had a pile of reviews to write, half-dozen essays to edit, nothing I felt like doing. Add calling Eddie Ball to the very top of that list. I didn't even know who the hell Eddie Ball was, and that irked me. Either he was too new, or I was getting out of touch with the industry again. With new back-yard filmmakers cropping up every day, it was hard to keep track of everyone. I did a quick search of the Internet Movie Database, aka IMDB. Eddie Ball had a couple of features under his belt, four for Sappho, the rest under his own company. His "Actor" section was ridiculous. He'd listed himself as a stunt man in a dozen Studio pictures, and there were three movies, including *Jaws IV*, that were released before he was born. Desperate. Pathetic. One title was listed as "In Production" and Angela St. Satan was the only name associated with it: *Beautiful Underworld*.

I didn't care if Angela St. Satan was alive, dead, missing or dancing on the head of a pin. I didn't give a rat's ass about Les Moore, his piece of mind, or his middle-aged hard-on for a girl half his age already washed up in an industry that worshipped the obscure.

My computer "ding'd" as a new message arrived. Les. Beneath the "(no subject)" slug, Eddie Ball's number floated alone in a sea of white. Gritting my teeth, I reached for the phone, stopped.

Rummaging through my desk drawer, I found the little yellowed envelope I was looking for and slid the contents into my hand. A dozen, maybe two dozen frames of film, 35mm, from my days as a projectionist in the Arc art house theater. I held each one up to the light of my computer, searching. Finally I found one depicting a tired Robert Mitchum in faded color, the tail-end of one of the middle reels from *Fairwell, My Lovely*. 1975. Directed by Dick Richards. Adapted from the Philip Marlowe novel by Raymond Chandler. For trivia's sake, one of Sylvester Stallone's earliest acting gigs as a thug. If I was going to play detective—sorry, *investigative journalist*—I might as well feel like one. I gave myself communion, laying the frame of celluloid on my tongue and let the emulsion dissolve in my mouth. It tasted smoky, like weariness and regret. *Fairwell, My Lovely* was in my veins now. I was flixing and it felt damned good.

Now I was ready for the phone, stabbing out the numbers with my thumb. To get it over with. Why didn't I just…*not* do that? Delete Les' last email, block his phone number and e-dress and just go to bed?

Across the city, Eddie Ball's phone rang three times. Finally, a gravelly, too-many-cigarettes voice: "Love-Death Productions." (Not *Live Death* like Les said. Moron.)

"Eddie Ball, please?" I said.

"Speaking."

I gave him my name, told him I wrote for *Movie Outlaw*. Sometimes one or the other carried weight.

The tone shifted from bored to the phony/sincere-plus-very-hungry known as "interested professional". "Oh, yeah, sure. How you doing?"

"I'm great, Eddie," I said and pulled a name off his IMDB screen. "Cayley Knoxville gave me your number."

"Oh, great. How's she doing? Haven't talked to her in a while."

I had only a vague idea who she was. Another starlet like Angela. "She's doing great. She's out in L.A. now." If that was true, I didn't know it.

"Right. She told me she was going Out There."

"Hey, listen, I heard you were doing a movie with Angela St. Satan."

A cold front blasted through the phone. Finally: "Yeah? Heard about that, huh?"

There it was: the compulsive professional edge. He didn't want to tip his hand, but he didn't want to lose any potential press. Bitch could be blue in a dumpster, but he'd kill her again for the coverage. I knew how to work with guys like this. No matter what he wanted to keep secret—and they always do saying, "I can't really talk about it," implying some big deal in the works that would eventually fall through or didn't exist in the first place. Everyone was ravenous for attention. Everyone wanted to go Out There and get the fame, the money. You could count on one hand the guys and gals who were into filmmaking for the art of it. Like Angela St. Satan—she'd jump on an ice floe like Lillian Gish in a heartbeat, even if she didn't know who Gish had been or what film she'd really done that for.

I asked Eddie Ball the right questions and 'uh huh'ed at the right times. Towards the end of the conversation I'd learned how he'd screwed over at least three of his partners but somehow it was always their fault. That woman's house he trashed after she let him and his Visigoth crew run rampant? She signed a location release—that many people she had to expect a mess. (Holes punched in her walls—bit of a mess?) Then I got to hear that he'd been molested by an older cousin when he was ten. How his mom wound up first in the hospital then in prison when two coke balloons burst in her stomach on her way back from Cor. People love to tell me things.

I suppose I should tell you how I got from here to there, the other phone calls with Eddie that turned into personal meetings in various bars in and around downtown Bethlehem. The introductions he made to other friends of his. The DVDs of his movies he gave me to review. Playing along every time he mentioned getting on the cover of the Halloween issue. I guess I should tell you that I never bother clearing any of this with Bob, my editor, because there was no point in pitching something that wasn't going to happen.

What I should do is explain why I kept up with it. Why I talked to this clown who really did believe he was a serious filmmaker. I really should come clean and tell you why I kept looking for a girl I didn't like or care about, who was probably strung out in some sugar daddy's living room and would be a danger to filmmaking all too soon.

But you don't want to hear about that. Be honest. All you want to hear about is the snuff film party.

As it turned out, Eddie was so eager to impress me he started calling in favors. I shook hands with bartenders and bouncers, guitar players to filmmakers who'd actually gotten stuff made *and* seen, just this side of the B-List, with their monster movies on cable. In one night I'd met three bankers and a financial planner, all of whom were "interested" in working with Eddie "some day", but none of which liked hanging around the twitchy guy with his hipster goatee and shaved head and lazy eye. All of whom opened up and spilled all sorts of shit to me because I had a job that sounded important. Eddie never introduced me as a guy who wrote movie reviews and interviewed flavors-of-the-week. I was always "The Journalist."

Then you couldn't shut them up.

Everything was "off the record", but everyone wanted to be heard. As long as I kept my face neutral, with just a hint of boredom in my eyes because I'd obviously seen it all, every one of them kept talking. They all had war stories they needed to share. Long story short, through Eddie I met Gary, one of his past "financiers" who for fun kept the promise of future finds dangling in front of Eddie's nose. After a few drinks suddenly Gary was eager to impress me too. Everyone wants to be the big man. Now I'm hearing about some of *his* friends.

"I should not be telling you this," he feigned. "These guys could actually kill me, you know?" he dramatized. "But you're cool. I can vouch for you and it'd be no problem." He bragged. And that's how I landed an invitation to a party at Justin Paris' place.

*****

"Next week you're gonna meet Angela's producer," Gary said, (melo)dramatically. But for a sugar daddy, Justin Paris didn't look like much. His house either. The way Gary had described this party I'd expected a long driveway and an iron gate, say a password into a little intercom to gain entrance. I expected 1920s opulence. I pictured the house having gables. Maybe a couple of flying buttress-es. I was prepared for tuxedoes and butlers and brandy snifters. Cuban cigars. Rug made out of sabre-tooth tigers.

Instead, Gary took me to a decent-sized condo inside a gated community. Justin Paris sure wasn't anything fancy. Not the balding, harrumphing old money I'd pictured in my head. He was just a guy, about Gary's height—which is to say taller than me—sporting a $60 dollar haircut designed to look like he'd given it to himself, and a spray of stubble meant to convey, "Fuck it, I made a million dollars today, I don't have to shave." He wore a Red Wings hockey jersey over strategically-ripped blue jeans and black sneakers. Instead of a cigar, he was holding a joint between his thumb and forefinger. I was barely in the door when he offered me a hit. I didn't want to be rude…

Again, Gary looked like he'd just come from work, but had his tie loosened to a "hey, bro" casual. At Justin's invitation I was shown the living room and met my first and only true love: 96" flat screen television. True to his jersey, there was a hockey game on, and three other just-slightly middle-aged guys, with their trainer guts and the occasional sideways baseball cap and bling, were cheering on whoever was winning.

I'd been instructed to call my host Justin. "Justin, I know we've just met, but I want to fuck your TV. Is that rude?"

He laughed in response, slapped my shoulder, held out

the joint. "Everyone wants to fuck my TV," he said, shaking his head. "And they say size doesn't matter."

"Oh, it matters," I said, sucking in the smoothest weed to ever visit my lungs. "I would gladly live in the box it came in."

More introductions were made; each time Gary stressed my title, "The Journalist." All the guys combined probably possessed a third of the world's wealth, grinned, shook my hand, gave their names with a wink and a "Shh." I made note of the names more out of habit than anything else. I wasn't here to bust up a secret cabal of aging frat boys. I was here to watch what I strongly suspected to be Angela St. Satan's final performance. Maybe I was paranoid, but that's what this all seemed to be leading to.

If there was anything sinister about these money monkeys, it didn't register on me. Only Gary seemed nervous, fully aware he was completely out of his pay grade. Not that any of them treated him like he was lower on the ladder. Honestly, I didn't know how far up or down he or any of them were. Except for some questions about *Movie Outlaw* and the most recent movies they'd seen, there was no talk of any real substance. When matters of work did come up, they used business-speak. They knew what they did for a living and they weren't there to fill me in on pointless exposition. They acted like I wouldn't give a shit anyway and they were right. I didn't have a movie to pitch to them, or any land to develop, no stock tips, so they knew I wasn't out for their wallets. Everyone understood: we were all there to watch the movies.

As the sun went down and the drinks were made, they all crashed on the huge room-length couch while I sank into one of the fluffiest chairs my ass had ever met. Honestly, it was like sitting in a big charcoal hug.

"I assume Gary filled you in on the nature of tonight's entertainment," Justin said. The third joint was finished and he was fishing around for something underneath the raft-sized wood coffee table.

"He said you guys watch a lot of 'director's cuts'."

That got a charge out of all of them. The two on the far end toasted and clinked together their giant German beer steins. I had no idea what they were drinking out of them. Something from a cut crystal bottle that I declined.

"Yeah," Justin said and then fixed his eyes on me, still smiling, still friendly. "Not 'grey market' either. Pitch black market. No bootlegs. You have to literally know the filmmakers in order to see this stuff. It's really special."

I nodded. "Awesome."

The guy to Justin's right, I think his name was Peter, asked, "What's the sickest shit you've ever seen?"

"Ah, hell," I said, feigning world-weariness. "I don't know. You mean like *Serbian Film* or like GG Allen videos?"

Next to Pete was a guy named Mike. The guy next to him was also named Mike. The one who spoke had spiked blonde hair. "No, like, what's the next step above slaughterhouse video?"

"Passolini's *Salo*?" I offered. They laughed and they all said, "Worse."

"*Sweet Movie*?"

"Worse. Worse!"

"Okay, fucking… *Men Behind the Sun. Human Centipede II, Imprint—The Angel's Melancholy*."

Every suggestion elicited a "Worse!" Except for the last one. Three-hour German depravity film. Nobody'd seen that. One of the Mike's asked to borrow a copy.

I decided to let out some of my best cynicism. "All right, whatever. What are we talking about? Viet Cong war movies or what? Because if you say 'snuff'—"

"Okay, it's snuff," Paris said. Just as I knew he'd say. Just as he knew I knew he'd say. Pete and Gary and the Mikes laughed and toasted again. I kept my "seen it all" look but to tell the truth my heart was racing.

Snuff movies are the final taboo because of what they

are. Because they're usually so badly done, they should be boring and a chore to watch, except your brain knows what it's seeing. All of your polite societal breeding is screaming that you should not watch. It's just *wrong*. An endurance test of shock movies—I sat through an hour-long Japanese shit-eating contest once, and it had live dispensaries, if you get my meaning—is one thing. But you're not supposed to watch real human murder for entertainment. If you did, you were either living in the sixth century or you were a sociopath. I've met sociopaths; none of these guys gave off the telltale attributes. Sociopaths don't usually run in packs. No matter how much I'd seen in my weary life up until now, including the few *actual* snuff films I'd already seen—i.e. *1 Lunatic 1 Icepick,* the Russian "Dnepropetrovsk maniacs" killing Sergei Yatzenko with hammer and screwdriver, and of course the footage from the Borgia films (the former because they were all over the internet and the news (I avoided Magnotta's kitten-killing vids because there, that's my fucking limit)—my brain was still going to scream "Wrong, Wrong, Wrong!"

Whatever was on tap tonight would likely be grainy, shaky, hand-held, under- or over-lit monstrosities, but in them, some person was going to die before my very eyes. Whether it'll be clearly captured, bloodier or less-bloody than expected, there would be a dead person at the end of those movies, and that was the sole purpose of production. The very end of a person's life preserved for posterity. If this wasn't some runaround from Gary, I knew in my gut that Angela was going to be one of those victims.

I just shrugged, gestured to the TV and then back to myself. "Do it," I said, using all of my cynical macho bravado, receiving cheers and glass-clinks back.

From under the wooden table Justin withdrew two things: the first was a long universal remote like something used to land a spacecraft; the other was a plain glass bowl filled with frames of 35mm film. So these guys were into flixing too.

Of course they were. The drug of choice for the hardcore film lover: you sucked the emulsion off the film and the magic of the movie flows into you. Sort of like taking an acid trip during *The Purple Rose of Cairo.* You became one with both the movie you were watching and the movie you were consuming. Mixed media sensations.

I wasn't above it and I had no stones to throw. In fact, as I might have mentioned, I love flixing.

But here I had no idea what movies were chopped up to fill that big bowl to the brim. From where I sat I could detect different film stocks, mostly 35mm: a lot of theatrical prints, bunch of orange inter-positives and negatives (the transitional stocks used to make prints without damaging the camera negative), purple black & white, and clear color negatives which usually gave the biggest rush. I was already high on weed, vodka shots, and adrenaline. There was no way I was going to devour unknown cinema during a snuff film screening.

Justin passed the bowl and everyone dipped in blind. When it came around to me, it was obvious that this wasn't one of the optional parts of the evening. I held Justin's gaze, his eyes now just a little less friendly, his smile just a little sharper, then I selected a frame and held it between two fingers. He continued to watch me. Moving my hand up to my mouth, I palmed the frame. With Justin still watching me, I did what I always did, and what most people do when they flix: I closed my eyes and shuddered, just a little, as the first taste of the emulsion should have hit me.

Opening my eyes, I gave Justin a wide, goofy grin, then shuddered again, finishing with a guttural *whoop!*

"What'd you get?" Justin asked. I knew it was an important question. I gave an important answer.

"Nothing I've ever had before." I said and gave a thumbs up. An important answer. The right answer. Justin aimed the remote at the TV that was just slightly smaller than an airplane runway and pressed the exact correct button hiding amongst the infinite number of others. The TV bloomed that special blue that induces erections in all Film Addicts. In the top left corner, a little sun spun its rays around. The file was loading. How long would I have to wait before he finally shows me Angela's last movie?

The first file to play was Magnotta's *1 Lunatic 1 Icepick* and I shot Justin a little glare. "Really?" I asked. "Is *Traces of Death* next?"

He had the courtesy to look chagrined. "All right, all right."

"And seriously I am not watching animal murder. You have any squish videos and I'm out." That came out pissier than I meant it to be but it made my point and my challenge. To Justin, I'd just said, "none of this weak shit, rich boy. Show me what you have that's so fucking special." I could read it on his face; his smile was a little stiffer, showing a few more millimeters of sparkling white teeth than he had been. He was keeping it all friendly, but I noticed the other four guys were almost frozen.

Justin pointed the remote at me. "My bad. I forgot this was on the drive. I got the real thing coming right up."

'The Real Thing.' Because a repeat of a horrible murder is just so boring.

Suddenly unfrozen, the other guys resumed their whooping. Their voices were a little thick, though, as the frames they sucked on started to take effect. Who knows what artificial reality flooded their minds. What would guys like this—with too much money and entitlement and the comfort of zero consequence—get off on during an evening of anti-social murder evidence? *Bambi* or *Winnie-the-Pooh*, just for the irony, that extra "that's so wrong" thrill? Would *On Golden Pond* make them feel even more badass? Nonchalantly, I pushed the frame I'd chosen deeper between the chair cushions.

The first one was quick and simple: A man in a smiling Nixon mask, as seen in *Point Break*, looked at the camera then backed out of the frame. Another man, naked, shaggy blonde hair, tied to a chair, head rolling back on his shoulders, obviously out of it. Drugged? No idea. Probably. Nixon's arm came up into frame and the .38 revolver popped off right into the blonde guy's face, blowing a small hole in his left cheek bone, the right side of his face exploded to hamburger meat. Chair and man flew sideways out of frame and the camera operator adjusted quickly, tilting down on a Dutch angle, so everyone could see the river of blood flowing out of the empty crater that used to be a man's face. As quickly as it began, it was over, the image freezing for just a moment on the ruined skull.

It didn't matter who he'd been before the camera started, where he came from, what he could have been but for whatever circumstance sat him in that chair. Wasted potential dissolved in the lumpy mist on the wall and the red lake on the floor.

The next one up was a suicide—teenaged boy, giggling drunkenly with his off-screen co-conspirator. "Okay," he said. "Wait. Okay—" Then he stuck the barrel of a 12-gague shotgun into his mouth. The blast turned the screen white as the camera iris scrambled to find the right exposure again, the focus going in and out. The levels peaked and crunched as the camera mic leapt up and down the decibel scale. Off screen, the buddy who'd pressed "Record" shouted "Jesus! Fuck! Fuck! Shit!" over and over again, in that order, like a chant. The only part left of the star's head was his lower jaw, lower lip sagged down by the shotgun barrel balanced neatly on his chin. Everything above and behind was sopping wet red. Without the familiar top half of a human face, the row of remaining teeth drew your eye, then stopped looking like anything specific. Just meat and teeth. A large glop of cranium and hair stuck to the wall disengaged with a sucking noise, then a hard splat. The sound a baseball would make, dropped into a puddle on concrete. The resolution wasn't great, but on that 96" screen, you could see some upper teeth imbedded in the plaster backdrop.

Next was an assault. Two men with ski-masks and tire-irons wailing on a third man already on the ground. Filmed with a camera phone, the soundtrack was nothing but screams, solid thumps, cracks and wind noise. Good picture on that phone and the guy got in close. You saw fingers snap backwards as he tried to ward off a blow, bones bursting through skin for an instant before another blow caved the side of his head in. Quite literally, his skull collapsed inward, ear and eyeball sucked into the wet crater. After barely a minute, the man stopped making noise, but the assault kept going. Then a voice: *"Yeah! Yeah! You see what happens, motherfucker! We're coming for you too, bitch! You're getting' this too! We got your dough and your blow, cock-smoker!"* Then black.

I glanced at my companions. Except for Justin they were all nestled back against the couch, flixing away to the carnage. And this was carnage. Just sheer brutality. Evidence of the damage one human can deliver unto another. Gary had his eyes closed. I think he was sleeping. One of the Mike's cheered the assailants on, miming their violence blow for blow. I didn't look, but could easily imagine he had a raging hard-on.

Justin was bent forward, elbows on knees, drawn in by the primal reality. Probably used to the images, likely a greatest hits compilation, his favorites. The total erasure of a young man who never saw it coming, whose life ended in a simple moment of terrible noise. Then this victim who'd been hunted down, surrounded, then pulped. His life had led up to entertainment and warning. It was a message for someone, a message he'd received over and over again in the space of a couple of minutes. Dead. Gone. Preserved forever in digital video.

Clip number four snapped to life. Shot on 16mm film, judging from the color and the grain, this one even had a title: for half a second the words "The Brave" flashed on the screen before being replaced by a title card: *One Little Indian.* Another young guy, dusky skin of some non-white ethnicity, dragged in by two shaved gorillas wearing bondage masks, mouths unzippered. No set up, just execution, only scripted this time. And by now I wished I had swallowed the frame, or even had another drink in my hand. Because this one was almost an hour long. This was what everyone thought of hearing the word "Snuff Film". Scripted, planned, staged. Then horror.

First a beating, then they stripped him naked and, like Movie Number One, strapped him to a straight-backed chair. With a hammer and chisel, one banged out his teeth while the other, using pliers, tore out the kid's toe-nails. There was no screaming yet, just guttural shouts and seizure-shakes from pain. No worries, the screams came quick enough.

Peter and one of the Mikes were giggling. Drunken high-pitched chuckles that neither seemed able to control. Peter kicked his feet and winced a little, still smiling at the taboo, as the kid's left ear was removed with a kitchen knife. His nose went next. His torso was a slick sheen of red, without a single other color shining through. Different shades of blood—dermal, venal, arterial, red on darker red coated with red-almost-black. The masked gorilla on the right, his own barrel chest stained crimson, used a little butane torch to heat a soup spoon. A fucking soup spoon. Which he used to scoop out the kid's eye. The kid wasn't even kicking at this point, making only wheezing sounds, likely in shock and only partially-unconscious from the sheer…the utter…

…Fuck.

I stayed stone-faced the whole way through. Don't ask me how. Goddamned Christ this wasn't *Cannibal Holocaust* or *Irreversible* or mother-fucking *Blood-Sucking Freaks*. It wasn't fake bullshit like *Hostel* or *Captive* or *Saw*'s one-through-ninety-seven. There were at least five men in that room, counting the poor bastard in the chair. Four other guys had been paid to make this for fucking *entertainment*. (I looked at every face of every man on that couch. Gary had passed out, so for him that meant there was a god of some kind. The others were transfixed. Justin looked like he was in the middle of either an important lecture or some sort of religious experience.) A boom shadow passed over the victim's body more than once, a person had been employed to make sure the microphone picked up everything. Every hiss and shriek and squish.

Here's the last thing about snuff films: they're not like car-wrecks, you very much *want* to look away. But you don't. If you've invested this much time—three seconds, two minutes or this goddamned screaming *hour*—you keep your eye on the screen.

Maybe you can blame current society. With the horrors of every day life and endless war happening somewhere on the planet, doom and gloom and Armageddon every night before the weather and the news about the pop star who went on another drunken tirade—on some level all of that shit really does numb your nerves, steel your already-girded loins. 'Extreme' with three 'x's and no 'e'—that's what it took to feel *something* in this horrible world.

But that wasn't the whole of it. You keep watching because you can hear the tribal drums beating in you veins. Your entire cellular being remembers when we were barely-upright, teeth and hair and claws and rocks, splitting skulls and eating the hearts of our enemies. Climbing stacks of corpses to get to the top of the food chain. We no longer cull our own herds of the sick and the weak. Civilization told us that it was wrong. Millions of years of evolution took us from tree-trunk clubs to cell phones. Out of the caves and into the condos. But it didn't remove the fascination we have with watching lives end.

You stretch your neck to see around the wrecked cars and the ambulance, hoping to see even a body under a sheet. You stop and stare and gather round and hold up the traffic behind you because right in front of you is evidence of mortality. If you can see it all, or at least the very end, then maybe you'll never die. Or, at least, you can say you looked it in the eye.

Murder, the worst thing—the last thing—one can do to another, is rarely seen by the naked eye. It's all special effects and camera angles and perfect editing. Or it's clinical, cold, a plot device to fill the spaces between commercials. It's what keeps the "myth" of snuff films alive. It's why men like Justin spend money on these terrible, subterranean nightmares of human nature. It's beyond porn.

You have to look.

You *want* to look.

My acting skills kept my eyebrows up, allowed me to yawn like nothing was any big deal. Inside, my psyche was ripping itself a part. Self-loathing filled the raw spaces because fuck me no matter how bad it was, I never looked away. I wanted to watch. Just like Justin.

When "The Brave", the title character in the little drama, slumped to his side the gorillas stepped back and looked at what they'd accomplished. Took it all in. The camera held the shot and then, so abruptly that I jumped, it went to white-on-black titles: THE END.

Well no fucking shit.

The room suddenly bathed in blue. Justin had thumbed the button with the little white square that meant, "Stop".

"Anyone need a break?" he asked. One of the Mikes stretched. Pete elbowed Gary who snored once before opening his eyes. Justin laughed but it wasn't a mean laugh. His head swiveled in my direction.

"What do you think, man?" he said to me. "Worth your time?"

I opened my mouth but nothing came out at first. I had to actually clear my throat in order to say, "Pretty fucked up." From where I have no idea, but I summoned the will to smile. Now, really, I didn't want to see Angela St. Satan's final performance. But I wasn't going to tell him that.

"Okay, no more delays," he said and bounced the remote off the arm of my chair. "I have about six more hours of this kind of stuff on this drive, but you wanna see Angela St. Satan, right?" I shrugged. Justin shook his head. "No, c'mon now. I know you've been asking around about her. Seriously, who would willingly talk to that stupid punk friend of Gary's? Man, I don't envy you. He's a total wad." He turned to Gary and bounced the remote off his thigh. Gary's leg kicked a little. Reflex. "Right?"

Gary's eye's snapped open. He just laughed and nodded, without knowing what he was laughing or nodding at. Like there was a button on Justin's remote that controlled responses too.

The Mother of All TV screens bloomed with words and Justin started scrolling through the menu of files. "What the hell did we call it? Gary, did we really use that moron's title?"

"*Beautiful Underworld*? No. I think you just called it *Angela*."

"Damn, that's boring too. I'm definitely renaming it." Justin turned to me. "Okay, a little set-up. You know I was one of the executive producers on that cable show she did, right? *Nightmare Girls*?"

I didn't. I nodded.

"I met her at the wrap party and soon as she found out I was one of the money guys—what's the line from *The Big Sleep*? 'She tried to sit on my lap when I was still standing'."

That was for me. To remind me he was a movie fan. That his mouth was where his money was.

"After she'd drank and smoked and snorted every damn thing in the room, we wound up in one of the bedrooms and she's on top and all she can talk about was how much she wanted to work with me. No moaning, 'oh yes' or even 'done yet?' Like we were in a pitch meeting and the sex was the Power Point presentation."

Justin turned back to the screen, still scrolling through dozens, maybe a hundred titles. They couldn't be all murder films, right? Somewhere in all that death had to be a couple of Bugs Bunny cartoons? Do they even have a name for someone so psychically damaged?

Not looking at me, he said, "Now this wasn't exactly planned. I'm sure as hell no actor and I wasn't really interested in doing a porno with her, like she suggested. You know, she was wasted at this point. All she wanted to do was ride me into the Studios. She had as good a shot as anyone else. Let's face it, she was hot and would still be hot for a few more years. Why shouldn't she get a series or something for a little while? Like Megan Fox can act, you know?"

Still scrolling. The Mikes both fished out a second round of frames from the bowl, slipping the celluloid on their tongues like they were taking Holy Communion. Then the eye squeeze and the involuntary shudder and meanwhile I'm pretty sure that Justin is scrolling back and forth on purpose so he can tell his story.

"Man, was she a little cunt, though. She fucking yelled at anyone who wasn't me. Demanding weed and blow and this and that and smoke breaks and pee breaks every five minutes. All this was supposed to be was a screen test! Here it is," he said and highlighted a title: *A ST S*. Not even *Angela*. "Now don't judge it too hard. It wasn't really supposed to be anything."

The scene snapped to life and right away I could hear a little chatter on the sound track. The image was smooth, colors saturated. Angela awkwardly lounging on a couch in bright red lingerie, black stockings and garter belt. She was up on one elbow and between the red of her bra and the blue of her couch, the color was almost overwhelming. "Wait," I said. "Is this film? You shot 16 on this?"

"Yeah. And no one knew what they were doing. Watch, the tripod keeps tilting up because that fucking Eddie Ball didn't have the sense to lock it down. He's supposed to be the pro, right? I just bought the film."

On screen, Angela was looking just off frame to the left. Beneath the whore-colored make-up she wore her innocent schoolgirl face. "I've never had such nice underwear on before. I bet you bought it just so I can take it off, though, right?" Then the innocence left. Instantly, her eyes narrowed and she took on the posture of a hunting cat, rolling onto all fours, flipping her hair back. "That's what you want, isn't it, Ted?"

Justin said quickly, "Ted's the name of the character in the script."

"Okay," I said. "Focus keeps going soft. Gary, do you know what camera Eddie was using?"

Gary said, too quickly, "I wasn't there that day."

"It had Mickey Mouse type ears," Justin said, trying to be helpful. He was watching me watch the movie. "The whatdya call it—the magazine. Two round parts where you put the film in. I don't think Ball knew how to use it. Watch—here!"

On cue—since he'd presumably watched it a thousand times—the film jumped and the image smeared for almost a full second until the gate found its register again.

"Any idea why it did that?"

"Film jumped in the gate," I said. "Either a dirty gate or a loose register pin."

"Oh, okay," Justin said, nodding.

There was literally nothing happening. Angela continued to look left, with a look she thought was seductive. In her movies for Sappho, she was always the girl led astray by the experienced lesbians. She wasn't used to being the aggressor and just seemed lost, begging for some sort of direction. "Do you want me to take this off? If I do, will you touch me?"

"Now, what's that big white glare in the corner? Is that because the light is too bright?"

"Yep," I said, "and he's catching the legs of the stand too." The casual tone of my voice surprised me. Maybe I was wrong about Justin. This didn't seem to be going in a snuff direction. Just stiff and awkward like Angela's usual performances. When she wasn't on her back with a girl's head between her legs, she never seemed to know what she was supposed to be doing.

"Just be gentle with me, okay?" Angela said. "I'm not...I mean—what's the fucking line?"

Then Eddie's voice made an appearance on the chattering sound track. "I'm not used to handsome men."

She frowned. "Really? Okay, okay." She cleared her

throat. "You'll just be gentle, right? I'm not used to handsome men like you." Terrible. Like she had learned it phonetically.

"Did you shoot sync sound?" I asked.

"I don't know what that means."

"Did he have a separate sound machine going when you shot this?"

"Oh yeah. Some kind of little digital thing. I didn't know what it was, I just bought it. The microphone is on a stand just over her head."

I nodded and realized I'd pretty much forgotten about the previous movies. They might as well have been indie horror things; my revulsion had vanished. I was just sitting with a guy I was starting to think was pretty cool, talking about filmmaking.

On screen, Angela undid the front hook of her bra and her breasts popped out like twin Jacks-in-the-box. They were natural B-cups and that added to her pedophiliac appeal. There she was: going-on thirty and still looked prepubescent. A schoolgirl for the rest of her life.

The camera bounced down and then shook to the left. "That was my fault," Justin said. "I kicked the tri-pod trying to get around it and Ball and tripping over all the goddamned wires." He laughed and I laughed with him.

Now Justin was in frame, his back to the camera at an awkward angle, baseball cap backwards on his head. Much taller, too, than Angela, the top of the frame removed most of his head above the hat brim. She rubbed her breasts in little semi-circles, more like an exam than anything erotic. "Kiss me," she said, closing her eyes.

The film chattered and blurred again. It didn't catch as quickly this time.

Almost 36 frames—a second and a half—before the focus centered again. "I said 'kiss me.'" The sound was a little ahead of the image now.

"No," on-screen Justin said.

"I said—wait, *line.*"

Screen Justin's hands came up and encircled her throat, showing just how tiny she was compared to him. His fingers met in the back near the base of her skull—it showed when she tried to twist away but he had a tight grip. Then the film jumped again. On the sound track there was just this faint squeak, the image was only a red and blue smear. Then it went white, then orange—the tripod had been kicked again and was aimed at the light in the right corner of the frame. On the sound track, high-heeled shoes clacked against a wooden floor. It sounded like one skidded away. Then a frustrated male voice, "Wait, fuck, stop. The film's tearing. Can't you hear that?" It wasn't Justin's voice. Or Eddie's.

The screen went suddenly blue video blue as the file ended. In the aqua wash of light, Justin looked at me and shrugged. "That guy will never see another buck from me," he said. "I swear to fucking god!" He was annoyed going-on pissed. "It wasn't that great but it's like he blew the 'cum shot'! Fuck, Gary!"

Justin hadn't raised a hand, but Gary flinched anyway.

As fast as it came, the anger drained away again and Justin's face was back to serene. "Whatever, what are you gonna do, right? It was just practice anyway. I ordered one of those 'Red One' cameras on Wednesday."

I found myself adrift in the conversation. "So what happened?"

"What do you mean?"

"She got strangled in all her early movies. That's the first time it looked real. So maybe you have the makings of a director, don't sell yourself short," I said and felt ridiculous saying it.

"No, dude. We were done. I told you, I hadn't planned it, but she—there was just something about her that made me wanna, you know…?"

I could blame the weed or the booze or just the shock of *One Little Indian*. Really, at that moment, I was just stupid. "So, what happened to her? The word is she's missing."

My host had the strangest expression on his face. Somewhere between amused and something darker. "Are you kidding?"

I looked at the Mikes and at Peter. They were staring back at me like I'd just shit on the carpet. Gary looked down at his feet. The air was suddenly very thick.

After a couple of seconds of staring through me, Justin's face snapped back to life. "Oh, okay, wait. Hold on a minute. Mike, grab the light."

Lamplight bloomed. Justin was sifting through the bowl of film frames, searching with two fingers. "There's not much, but I guess you only need a few frames of it, right? Even with 16 mil'?"

I knew what he was talking about. Of course I did. But if no one else was going to spell it out for the new guy, I wasn't about to make noise either.

"Here," he said, and between two fingers were exactly four frames of 16mm negative film, amber-brown in color, the emulsion black and without spaces to separate the consecutive pictures. "It's okay, I made a work print. This is just some of the blur anyway, but it should still work for you, right? I mean, worked fine for me when I did it."

Justin Paris, fledgling executive producer, purveyor of the finest marijuana I'd ever smoked, and my host for the evening, was holding out for me to take, about an inch and a half of snuff film negative. "Take it, it's a gift. Go on," he nudged my leg with his knee. "Since you palmed that frame earlier, this should be nice and pure for you."

He said that completely without malice. No chide, no challenge, no sinister implication. No sign of the guy who I'd just watched maybe strangle a girl. Maybe. With the film blurred out, smeared for feet across an open shutter due to faulty mechanism or operator, she could be alive. Strung out on someone's couch, like I'd said at the beginning. Blowing some guy for crank or for an introduction to another "producer". The smear didn't mean dead.

But of course it did. That was the whole point of the evening, of all the meetings that led up to the evening. I was one of the guys now, bro code and pinky-swear not to narc on them because I was now kind of an accomplice. With that third unknown voice, who was to say it wasn't me? If Justin the Rich said it was. That was all he'd have to do.

The threat was all in my head, though. This was his offering, something to share. "Dude, this is so cool!" the offering said.

What did I say before? I couldn't look away. Because the caveman in me *wanted* to see. So of course I took the frames. I laid the strip of celluloid emulsion down on the length of my tongue. And the film hit me in a nice warm wave.

When you flix, you're there and you're not there. If you don't have a movie playing on TV, it's just you and the contents of the film in your mouth. It wasn't like you could only taste the pictures you were sucking, but you could taste the whole movie, the plot, characters, arcs, production design, lighting, everything technical and artificial. Your mind was both a participant and a by-stander. And you felt what the movie wanted you to feel. Do a frame of *Old Yeller* and you'd be curled in a ball because even though that big goofy dog died off screen and didn't really die at all and went galumphing back to its handler after the scene was over, you still saw that rifle blast put that pup down. And you sobbed because Tommy Kirk sobbed and because it was fucking sad and unfair and he'd been such a great dog during the movie.

A ST. S seeped through my tongue and into my bloodstream and I saw it again from beginning to end only without the smear. The image was crystal, clean, and I was there, the colors blindingly beautiful and Angela St. Satan, little Jenny Harris who wasn't so "little" any more, staring up at me, off-camera, with those big desperately-hungry eyes asking, "Will *you* make me a star?"

The willfully-dumb and deliberately mean girl-shaped

woman I'd met too many times at conventions and film festivals, charging too much money for her autograph, accustomed to having her ass spit-shined by horny losers of all ages from all across the country. A celebrity in the soft-core world. Get naked, lie back, make little cooing noises and goddamn it, *treat me like a star*!

I watched Justin's hands come up and they were my hands even though I was off-camera. Big hands bigger than mine squeezing her soft throat as she stared up with eyes still not comprehending. *You asshole, this isn't how you do a stunt choke. Loosen your fucking grip, you dumb bastard!* Her press-on nails dug into our wrists, clawed the backs of our hands, as her face went blue and her tongue went purple. Already we'd crushed her windpipe and could see ourselves reflected in those big hazel-colored, stupid-filled eyes. *Don't you know who I am?* The clichéd demand, to be followed by, *You'll never work in this town again*, if only she had the breath.

It took time. Not like in the movies, where she'd hang on for a second and go immediately limp. She kicked to get a purchase, some leverage. At some point, it stopped being a conscious action, just the body's primal fight to breathe. Primal.

Because smell couldn't be captured on film, not yet, probably not ever, we were spared the odor of her bladder and bowels emptying. But not the sight of her big brown eyes finally getting the message as they bulged out of her sockets. Literally, they partially escaped their eyelids and bone housings, blood vessels bursting beneath the so-thin membrane of white as the pupils opened wide, leaving only a sliver of green-brown iris. Still, her legs kicked and her arms flailed, no longer remembering how to grip anything let alone the vice-grip fists that trapped the air in her body, letting nothing in or out.

And while the scene flooded through my nervous system I was also staring at Justin Paris, sitting inches away from me in his enormous sunken living room, bathed in the blue wash of the 96" television screen. When the light finally left Angela's eyes I saw his reflection there, as well as the too-calm face watching me flix, and neither face had any real remorse for what he'd done.

There was surprise. Much later, off camera, there was anger.

I felt that anger, but it wasn't Justin's channeling through me. The anger was all mine. For all the horribly bad movies she'd made, Angela St. Satan wanted to be remembered. Worshipped, of course; a star, of course. But she'd convinced herself somewhere along the line that what she did mattered. All those never-ending scenes of tongue-kissing other women, some damaged some not, ambitious women, smarter women, laying on her back with their heads bobbing near her crotch but never making contact because this was soft-core, nothing "porn" about it. All those little coos and moans and autographs signed and DVDs sold, they all led to her two moments of fame. One in a studio production and one on a cable television show. Prostitutes in both but it was screen time. With actors the housewives recognized. Not indie or microbudget or even low budget but real budget with catered food and it was all leading to her being *somebody*.

Because before she met Billy Brimstone, she barely existed. The pretty girl down the street that other pretty girls pretended to like and that boys just wanted to "get with". That wasn't what she wanted and daddy couldn't buy what she wanted so she was going to find a guy who could. Even if it took her a hundred guys to find him.

To this day, no one has found her body. No one thought to investigate Justin Paris because. Just because. Who was she to him? He gave some money to a cable TV show that she had a minor part in. No one in his circle was going to say anything.

I never said anything.

After a while, Angela St. Satan became another one of those girls who just "left the business". She probably met some rich guy or woman and was living happily somewhere in the neighborhood of luxury.

Obviously, *Beautiful Underworld* was never made. Eddie Ball made three or four lousy movies before people stopped talking to him. Then he went away. Gary, Justin, the Mikes, I never heard from them again and they weren't going to call me. Because after I swallowed those last frames of Angela's last moments, I stood up and left without a word.

Nobody chased me or yelled or protested. There was no big showdown, no big revelation of "staring into the face of evil". If anything, I'd probably hurt those guys' feelings.

I knew what had happened to Angela but I *wanted* to see. Her life was brief, her career was briefer and the worst part was that her last performance was something real. Just before her eyes bulged and her tongue went black, comprehension came to her that this was real. That she had *this last moment.*

Because of a bad filmmaker and bad equipment, that last, probably *only,* true moment was lost forever. Maybe it isn't any great loss, but Angela St. Satan was gone forever.

Immortality isn't for everyone.

*****

I never called Les Moore.

MACISTE — IN COLOR!

"Harry Lime is dead…"

It was the voice, of course, that gave it away. The lumpen, tumorous creature before me, leaning on two canes while still filling the carved onyx throne, spoke with that unmistakable velvet tone, that voice that both enthralled and repelled, deep yet somehow emanating from the sinuses. The voice proved that the flashing images on all five walls—scenes from *The Lady from Shanghai*, *The Magnificent Ambersons*, *Kane* of course—the monster before me really was Orson Welles.

And more than anything, it wanted to die.

*****

Three days ago, I was slumped in my recliner, *The Great Escape* on the big screen providing the only light. I was more than twenty hours into a flixing binge, sucking on 35mm frames from a release print of Truffault's *Day for Night*, part of my score from the salt mine vault in Colombia. The easy anxiety of Truffault's masterpiece giving a sweet undertaste to the war adventure before me. As a side-effect, the flix was translating Steve McQueen—but only McQueen—into French. Jacqueline Bisset swirled in my veins. Prior to that, I'd flixed on *Rebecca*, while zoning to *Semi-Tough*. That's how I liked my flixing binges—the visual a dichotomy to the effects of the frames.

The screen of my phone bloomed more blue light, buzzing a racket on the coffee table beneath my bare feet. As I leaned down to grab it, I saw the perforations on my skin oozing tiny rivulets of blood, the exact size and shape of sprocket holes, crisscrossing across my arms and legs and chest, like little railroad tracks. I'd been flixing too long; the perfs were the proof. Didn't care. Grabbed the phone.

From some far and distant point via his own phone, Eddie said, "You're going to meet Orson Welles on Friday." He was my boss, my editor, possibly the closest thing to a friend I had. One day I hoped to meet him.

"Am I?" I knew better than to say something stupid like, *Isn't he dead?*

"You are," said Eddie, "and the interview is your cover. There's a print in his vault we need you to liberate."

"Which 'we?' "

"The Film Preservation Society."

AKA *'f.p.s.'* Terry's outfit. *"N'est*-ce *pas?"*

"What?"

I shook my head to clear the French. Little dribbles of blood went everywhere. "Sorry. Who am I in this?"

"Let's go with 'Joe Hart.'"

"Okay."

"Sending you details, address, dossier, and how does eighteen grand sound?"

"Like this is going to be a rough gig," I said.

"Cake walk."

"An eighteen-grand cake walk?" I blinked blood out of my eyes. "Who'll have eyes on me?"

"Oompah," he said. The MPAA. I cursed. Still in French, though and French was the wrong language for the profanity I needed.

I thumbed the phone off, returning Eddie to the silent abyss. Absently, as McQueen and company tasted their prison camp contraband vodka, I rubbed a bloody thumbprint smooth across the face of the phone, watching as the ridges and whorls smeared away, what was distinct was now a shapeless and ugly glaze on the glass. Just a film.

*****

"Harry Lime was dead." That's the crux of the first act of *The Third Man*, but the film's twist was already blown in the opening credits: "And Orson Welles as Harry Lime." Selznick undercut his own movie with a vanity card. The pedant in me reminded myself that Carol Reed had directed that film, not Welles. But that sequence in the sewers, with Welles' Lime pursued through hard shadows, it *felt* like Welles, and that was all anyone remembered. The gut feeling. That and Anton Karas' zither music…

The cover story was that Welles had faked his death lo these many years, and was emerging to direct his first post-posthumous film. The giveaway was that it was going to be a remake, of all things, Donald Cammel's *Performance*. Wrong project to sell the resurrection. Whatever was backing the Living Welles had clearly something else in mind.

I was given an address to an old brownstone building, in that crumbling neighborhood that had been nicknamed "The Welles." During the settler years, it was where the town's water wells had been located. Generations later, it became the thriving cultural district, boasting more movie houses per mile than any other city in the country. Thus the cute name change that hung on long after the theaters had migrated North. These days, the neighborhood was a ruins. Civilization had chased out the nickelodeons. Now, The Welles was little more than a dangerous slum mired in history, poison ivy growing between the crumbling bricks of the Acropolis.

The brownstone was appropriately dreary, a moldering and sprawling Gormenghast. I walked carefully. Eddie was right: there were eyes on me from every shadow. I couldn't see the Oompah agents, but I knew they were there. Shadows with eyes and weapons.

I was met at the door by a lovely young woman, dark hair, dark eyes, a demeanor bereft of humor. I gave her my credentials. "He's expecting you," she said.

"And you are?"

She stared at me for a moment, trying to consider just how beneath her contempt I was. "Dorothea Bloom," she said. "I'm Mr. Welles' executive officer."

She stepped aside, allowed me passage into the narrow foyer, all dark wood and depression. A massive staircase wound upwards into the gloom. I couldn't see the terminus, if there even was one.

The smell of undisturbed must hung heavy in the air, like a tomb recently breeched. It was chilly, yet somehow still oppressive. "Mr. Welles will receive you in his common room." She gestured down a long dark hallway.

I didn't like that phrase, "will receive you." She gave it an ominous nature.

Nothing adorned the walls in that narrow passage. No carpet hid the buckling wood floor. I couldn't see the ceiling—the dim light from the ugly brass wall sconces wouldn't reach that high—but I imagined the paint curling like dead fingernails, mimicking the walls. Personally, I preferred the vault in that Colombian salt mine, stacked floor to ceiling with rusty film cans. Malaria be damned. Reaching the end of the hallway, Ms. Bloom opened the dark heavy door. Beyond it was light. Beyond it was sound. Inside it smelled like…nothing.

The room was clean, glistening, with chrome pillars offsetting the cream-colored ceiling and steel gray carpet. It was octagonal, a Roman collosseum in miniature, but only just. High up on every wall was a large flatscreen television, and on every screen played one of Welles' movies. No matter where you looked, there was the man in close up, looming over me from all directions like the many faces of God.

There, in its youthful vision, was Michael O'Hara, his character from *Lady of Shanghai*; on another, his wizened Falstaff from *Chimes of Midnight*; on a third, Harry Lime in *The Third Man*; his *Othello*; his *Kane*.

Yet the room was silent. I couldn't even detect the faint electronic whine from the sets. The silence was a physical presence.

In the center of the room sat a tall throne, its back to me, looking for all the world like onyx, into which had been carved yet another variety of faces, some human, most not, all seemingly twisted in hideous agony, as if emerging from a pool of black oil, all clawing over each other for air.

Then came the voice: from everywhere and nowhere, bludgeoning that utter silence to dust. "Come in, Mr. Hart, we've been expecting you."

Before me was the personification of agony. It took a minute to rectify what I was seeing. The creature in the throne was head-to-toe cancerous, a churning of purple tumors, and one brilliant blue eye gleaming from deep within the mass. Apart from tufts sprouting from random areas, the bloated body was hairless. The twisted, swollen fingers of both ballooned hands clutched twin silver dragon's head canes. Slowly, the creature offered one of these hands, saying, simply, "Mr. Hart, I am Orson Welles."

With eyes closed, I would have followed that voice through every level of Hell. With eyes open, it was all I could do to avoid openly recoiling from that scabrous claw, with lumpen masses slouching beneath the tight skein of broken capillaries. As I shook the hand, I felt my breakfast rise into my throat. I managed to choke out, "It's a pleasure." I added, "Sir."

The creature gestured. Behind me, I found a simple hard-backed chair and took a seat. It was difficult to look at this creature and see any aspect of the smiling, mischievous faces that blossomed from the TV sets. But that eye, that voice: unmistakable.

So entranced I was by my own revulsion, I had failed to notice the two men in dark suits standing sentry at the parlor's entranceway. When they finally registered on my shattered brain, my body jumped in reflex. That's all I was at that moment— misfiring reflex as my mind reeled at the impossible. These men had nondescript faces, identical haircuts, identical suits. They were utilitarian—guards, servants, deterrents, whatever. They weren't part of the mission. They were extras. They were walking props. Welles thought so himself as he idly waved a claw in their direction and said, "You gentlemen may go."

However.

He seemed a bit surprised when they did. As they closed the door behind them, sealing me in with this creature on the phone, Ms. Bloom's voice rang out of the ether around us, "Is everything okay, Mr. Welles?"

On the throne, Welles shuddered.

"Yes, Ms. Bloom," he said. "I like my privacy. During interviews," he added.

Then it was silent again.

"I hope you brought along a voice recorder," Welles said to me. I could hear his skin cracking, his bones complaining, as he made the slightest movements. There was pain in that one bright eye. "I'm told they don't even need tapes any more. Or any kind of media."

I produced a little voice recorder from my pocket and held it up for him to see. "That's right. All digital now."

"We live in a world of impermanence." He gestured, slightly, with one of his canes, indicating the television screens. "I know where the prints are to every one of these films. They exist. They are tangible."

"It's all ones and zeros now," I said.

"Math replaced alchemy." Welles nodded, his neck made a terrible noise, as if his skeleton were screaming. "That's an affront to them."

I turned on the recorder. "And who is *them*?"

Welles fell silent, his eye unfocussed, head cocked. I realized he was listening for something. I didn't hear it either.

I didn't care for the silence. I watched the numbers advance on my recorder as it took in nothing. In this sterile room guarded by an unknown number of threatening men, surrounded by the Rushmore faces of Welles, listening to that foggy voice emerge from the cancerous monster—the surrealism was too much to handle. In the face of so much strange, journalist's ego needed stabilizing. I cleared my throat. "I, uh, finally caught *The Other*

Side of the Wind."

The being across from me nodded. "Did you?"

"It's quite amazing, the work they were able to do from your notes."

"I'm right here," he said, the voice catching on its way out of the ruined mouth. "I was denied participation. My 'notes?' I wouldn't know where to start…"

So much regret dripping from those words. The director's eye lost focus. Reluctant to speak again, my attention returned to the recorder recording nothing as the numbers continued to advance. Time marched on without us. I waited. The Welles-thing was silent.

Suddenly, the eye sprang open, wider than it had been previously. There was panic there. Desperation and longing and… what the hell was I even thinking? Just looking at him was causing me physical pain—I couldn't bear to think what he was suffering.

The mouth opened and closed, gasping in its panic. Finally, he spoke, the words coming out rapid and desperate.

"Mr. Hart, I know why you're really here."

"For the interview?"

The lone eye went from blue to battleship gray as it clouded with anger. "Stop it," he said. "Don't talk to me like I'm…" He trailed off, clawing impotently at the solid onyx armrest. With a deep breath, Welles continued. "Outside of this room, down the hallway you used to enter, hidden beneath the staircase, there are two film cans. I've removed them from the vault and placed them there. For you to take. If you leave."

I didn't like the "if" part of that sentence.

"That's your payment, Mr. Hart, should you accept my contract."

I didn't ask. I just cocked an eyebrow. Welles needed no further enticement. "I want you to kill me, Mr. Hart. End my life. Now. Right this very second."

He waited. I waited. Two pieces in play on the chessboard

and already at a stalemate. Finally, I said, "I didn't come here to murder you, Mr. Welles."

"I'm asking you to. Before they return. It has to be done today and I'd prefer it done quickly."

"How would I even…?"

"I know about you, Mr. Hart. I know who you really are, and I'm familiar with your particular skill-set. I know you'll stop at nothing to…obtain certain films for interested parties."

"We're a film preservation society, Mr. Welles." I spread my hands, the picture of innocence. "That's all."

"That's not all. It's never 'all.' Do not insult my intelligence."

"I didn't mean—"

"Where are your questions, Mr. Hart? Where is your intellectual curiosity? You know very well I died in 1985. Ask. Quickly."

"*Performance*?"

He smiled. His laugh was one of displeasure. "If I were to remake anything, it would be a Maciste film. The Italian strongman. I found pleasure in those later in life. What else?"

"Okay…how?"

"How?"

"How? All of it."

"They rescued me from death. Ms. Bloom and those men you saw just now. And more than a dozen others deep inside this house. They had the power to arrest my departure, by means I still don't comprehend." He gestured again to the television screens. "I suspect it has to do with these images. I think I've been preserved. But while my image will never age, my body and spirit have corrupted. Thanks to whatever they did, I'm Dorian Gray's painting, living and breathing."

"For what purpose?"

"Something terrible." He sighed. It took a long time, and the breath that came out rattled and moaned and wheezed. "I don't fully understand them. Or their motives. They've kept me deteriorating for more than three decades and only now am I starting to get a whiff of their plans."

Again, that blue eye darted around the room, scanning empty corners for lurking menace. I followed his gaze. I saw no hidden speakers, no tell-tale signs of bugging devices. Of course, they could be in the televisions. Or set into the throne. The nefarious are defined by their cleverness.

Creaking, groaning, he leaned forward, inviting me to conspire. "These are religious people following a relatively new set of gods," he said. Subtly, his face changed as I shook my head. "I didn't expect you to understand. They worship film."

I shrugged. "So does half the Internet."

"Not the process of filmmaking. They're not artists, Mr. Hart. They're fanatics of a type. They've kept me alive, Mr. Hart, to harvest me."

He fell silent again, allowing me to process his words. But they were meaningless. "I…" he trailed off. His face contorted in frustration, the bright eye vanishing into the cavern inside the twisted flesh. "I…" he said again. Finally, savagely, he twisted the handle of one cane, withdrawing a short dagger from the length.

With a surprising speed, Welles jabbed the point of the dagger into a mound of purpled flesh on his forearm. Digging into the skin, he twisted and prodded the knife until a mass fell from the wound, dragging with it a thin gruel of almost colorless blood. The flat oily smell of Perchloroethylene, a film-processing chemical, flooded the sterile room. I knew that smell very well and I gagged.

Welles dug into his arm, unwinding the mass shifting inside the tumor. It was film, 35mm, spilling from his wound into his lap. It gleamed wet in the light, as if it had just come from the stop bath, ready for projection. He held up a length between his arthritic claws. "You see now? Miles of this, gestating inside me."

I wanted to reach for the film but the rest of my body

recoiled and I sat back. "What is it?"

"Pieces of my life," he said. "My failures." He held the strip up in front of him. A tear fell from his eye onto the film. He swabbed at the droplet with his thumb, mixing the tear into the smear of effluvia still slicking the celluloid. "This is me in *Heart of Darkness*. You see? I would only be seen in reflections—the river, mirrors. You see?"

I didn't lean forward. I didn't want to look.

"There's a mass on my hip. I pulled about fifty feet of *Don Quixote* from it. A sequence I'd never shot. Quixote battling his giant, before he discovers that it is merely a windmill. A forgotten dream. But there it is."

As he returned the dagger to its sheath, the cane slipped from his grasp and clattered against the floor. The sound was dreadful, the echo bouncing around the room. Tears flowed from that one bright eye. "These people, and their god, something calling itself Cinemagog… they're harvesting my unlived life. They're pulling new films from my dreams."

My voice caught on something sincere. As it emerged from my mouth, it morphed into protective sarcasm. "I guess *The Other Side of the Wind* did pretty well."

"At least that wasn't yanked from my body." Suddenly, he was seized by a fit of coughing. His whole body spasmed. That clear, almost-blood oozed from several open wounds as he convulsed. "I can feel it, Mr. Hart. The film churning in my bowels. For thirty years, they've been allowing my failures to gestate."

I couldn't look at him. Ashamed, my eyes searched anywhere in the room for a point devoid of Welles. Between the pitiful thing on the throne and those enormous fucking sets, my wish was denied.

So my eyes settled on the crusty train tracks crisscrossing my forearms. The flixing abuse I'd inflicted upon myself. Sucking a film's essence from the celluloid, letting the electrochemical nightmares flood my system. *Needing* that high to fully connect to a film… Everyone is addicted to something. Could I blame these zealots for doing to Welles something I did to myself? Or was this worse?

"Mr. Hart…who am I to you?"

"You're Orson Welles, one of the greatest filmmakers who ever lived."

"Was I a man? To you? Ever?"

"I was fifteen when you…passed."

"So all I ever was, to you or to anyone, was just a shadow on a screen."

"A substantial shadow."

"A shadow nonetheless." Another deep, horrible sigh. "Tonight, Mr. Hart, those men, Ms. Bloom, and more than a dozen others are going to stretch me out on an altar and cut the film from my body. First, they're going to remove the skin."

Suddenly, all eight television sets were alight with the imagery Welles was narrating. The zealots were dressed in normal clothes, no suits or ceremonial robes. This wasn't a Kenneth Anger set-up before me. Just normal men and women bearing the corpulent creature between them, hoisting him onto a metal gurney. Their altar.

"They'll remove the skin in strips, the exact width of 35mm film. This alone will take hours. And they'll keep me awake for the process. These strips will have a later purpose, but I will never know that purpose."

I saw the creature on every screen, silently screaming as they dug at him with their knives, flensing the skin from his muscles.

"As they do so, they will carefully harvest the film, lovingly respool it onto cores made from bones," he said with a hollow, humorless chuckle. "Don't ask me why. I can't pretend to know their thinking, or the thinking of these gods of theirs."

I was surrounded by this grotesque display, this Technicolor nightmare of men and women butchering my hero, my idol, wherever he was, buried beneath those tumors.

"They are sacrificing me one bit at a time to their gods. To their Cinemagog, to Ifirs, Dolirostrum, Kem-Daly," his voice cracked and croaked. I'd never once before heard these names. "Their gods of film. Their muses bent and twisted and evil. Inspiration through decay and terror… Sometimes, I can see them in between the frames they cut from my body."

Welles had fallen into a sort of reverie. He was no longer speaking to me, but rather using me as a conduit to something greater. I was hearing his desperate prayer for release. He said I'd been hand-picked for the job, but I could have been anyone. Anyone with the hands to hold the knife.

"If I were the Italian hero, Maciste, I would tear down these walls. I would rip them apart with my bare hands…"

I didn't immediately realize that *my* hands were shaking. My entire body was shaking.

"They're going to *harvest me*, Mr. Hart. And they'll sell my failures to the highest bidders. And I suspect, even once they're done, they'll keep me alive. Or whatever of me is left over."

I couldn't bear it any longer. The gory phantasms vanished, replaced once again by the flickering images of Welles in times gone by.

I reached for the cane on the floor.

Before my fingers made contact with the polished wood, an anxious pounding came from the door behind me. The door I hadn't even noticed. The door I had not entered through. "Mr. Welles! Are you okay?" came the panicked voice of Ms. Bloom, from everywhere and nowhere, out of those invisible speakers.

But the frantic pounding was only coming from the door behind me.

I gave the handle a savage twist and pulled the blade from its housing. The pounding increased—then came the sounds of bodies hurled against thick protective wood.

"Hurry, Mr. Hart. Please."

Why couldn't he be Maciste? Why couldn't he bring

these walls down? Why did I have to do this?

The entire room hit its climax—there was Harry Lime fleeing in the sewers, O'Hara lost in the hall of mirrors, Charles Foster Kane looming, lost, alone in his empty tomb of deep focus…

All around me were all the films by Welles that had given me so much pleasure. By way of thanks, I plunged the dagger deep into that one bright, blue, amazing eye.

*****

As I made my escape, I did not look back. Not at the ruined Welles slumped in his throne. My mind was on the outside world. The pounding increased, frenzied. I made my way through the entry door, feeling my way down the dark hallway. What little light there was seemed to scurry away, fearful of what I'd done.

In the dark by the staircase I felt my way around, loathing every spiderweb, until I found two heavy metal film cans hidden away in the shadows. My goal. My salvation. One can bore a label, nearly impossible to read in the dark. A film previously lost, precious. I wondered from whom *it* had been sliced away.

My escape was not prevented. I'd half-expected a crazed Ms. Bloom to leap at me from the shadows, naked and snarling, with teeth in places there *should not be teeth*, and beautiful as she tore the skin from my face. But no. The pounding turned to wailing, far, far behind me.

Throwing open the front door, I hurled myself and the cans into the street. I ran for two blocks, until I was certain there was no pursuit.

I paused beneath a streetlamp to catch my breath. In my haste, I'd forgotten the mission. There were still eyes on me. Always eyes on me. As I hoisted the cans again, I heard the first bullet whiz past my ear. The second bit into my side.

I stumbled, I fell, but I got back up again. I'd just killed a man for these films. I'd be damned if I'd let the enemy get them.

Harry Lime was dead. For good. Forever. I wasn't about to meet him again.

AFTERWORD

While shopping the individual stories in this book, the criticism I most encountered was, "You need a Master's Degree in Film to understand it." I don't think you do.

You have to have seen some movies, yes. And it would be helpful if you've seen them in a theater. But this book is an attempt to explore our obsession with film. One hundred years plus of history of a strange medium that requires one to recreate reality at a great expense. To recreate reality, you need a cadre of folks armed with knowledge of technology, physics, the scientific properties of light and sound and psychology. And lying. Filmmakers have to be skilled liars. It's what "suspension of disbelief" is all about.

Before the Internet gave us instant history, you had to search for it. Sometimes you had to go to strange locations and deal with stranger individuals—folks who shared the same interests as you yet still managed to make that commonality somehow sinister. The harder you had to search for a movie, the sweeter, you were sure, the reward would be. After completing hundreds of such searches, I can safely say that's not always true. It was always about the search. It was always in service of the Obsession.

You don't see Obsession much in modern day film students. This isn't a screed against the "new generation," it's just a sad fact. With the demise of the video store, film obsession largely died with it. It's hard to explore the Internet for great new titles if you don't know what you're looking for. Therefore, it's easy to dismiss what you've never seen, and even easier to dismiss those who feel that every film, no matter how slight or terrible or badly-made, has merit.

You don't need a Master's Degree for this book. You have to have an emotional connection to cinema. As an art form, as a business—filmmaking is never, ever one thing. It's stage magic. It's technological magic. It's playacting. Theater. It's a light show. All wrapped around, hopefully, an inarguable truth.

When we first started as filmmakers, we were considered part of the "Second Wave"—those who started on film and were early adopters of Digital Video. The first wave consisted of guys like Tim Ritter, Kevin Lindenmuth, Ron Bonk, J.R. Bookwalter, and my dear friend Scooter McCrae.

This Second Wave consisted of people like myself, Amy Lynn Best, and Bill Homan, the Polonia Brothers, Chris Seaver, and our good friend, the late Andy Copp.

As far as I'm concerned, Henrique Couto still carries the torch for the New Wave, as do JM Channell, Chris LaMartina, Zane Crosby, Zane Hershberger, Thomas Edward Seymour, Mark Savage, Charles Zimmerman…

After I did the heavy lifting of writing the damned thing, Ryan Hose, Tom Bugaj, Stephanie Bertoni, Alyssa Heron, Dr. Rhonda Baughman, and especially Amy, all stepped up to make sure the crazy thing was readable.

Specifically, I want to thank folks like John Skipp, Jonathan Maberry, Mark Miller, Heather Drain, and L. Andrew Cooper. Also, on a professional level, thank you to Robert A. Kuiper, Tony Timpone, Mike Gingold, Frank Hennenlotter, Lisa Petrucci, and Stephen R. Bissette.

Also, because their films were so essential to the creation of this book: Clive Barker, David Cronenberg, Stuart Gordon, Brian Yuzna, Dennis Paoli, John Carpenter, and Stephen

Sayadian.

Most of the stories that take place in the Carcosa Film Lab are, more or less, true. Labs weren't fun places to work. At least not mine. And while I offer no gratitude to the thankfully late and no-longer lamented WRS Film and Video Laboratory, I owe a debt to many of the folks I met there, particularly Ray Yeo (the star of our first film, *The Resurrection Game*), Russ Scheller, Paul Martello, Paul McCollough, and Bill Powell.

At Pittsburgh Filmmakers, I'd like to thank John Cantine, Tom Megalis, Brady Lewis, Wen-wa Tsao, Tony Buba, and Bob Rutkowski, for the education. In all shapes and forms.

Also Cathy Kelly, Bruce Lentz, John Bulevich, and especially Terry Thome. You guys provided all the movies.

On the filmmaking front, there are almost too many to mention, but off the top of my head: Jasi Jovingo, Mike and Carolyn Haushalter, Alyssa Herron, Chris Mindel and Bette Cassatt, Jason Lane, Eric Thornett, Bart Mastronardi, Alan Rowe Kelly, Jeff Monahan, Justin Wingenfeld, Bill Hahner, Bill Homan, Lloyd and Pat Kaufman, Don Bumgarner, Jerry Gergely, Gino Crognale, Thomas Berdinski, Ken and Pam Kish and our *Cinema Wasteland* family, Greg Ketter and Dreamhaven Books, Will Kaufman, Holt Boggs, Ward Roberts, Travis Betz, Amber Benson, Gary Kent, Brinke Stevens, Linnea Quigley, Bill Johnson, Bill Moseley, Sid Haig, Ed Neal, Michael Berryman, Rich Dalzotto, Sandy Stuhlfire, and Michelle Linhart from *Horror Realm,* and everyone else who supported Happy Cloud Pictures all through the years.

This book is dedicated to the memory of Herschell Gordon Lewis, David F. Friedman, Doris Wishman, Carmine Capobianco, and Gunnar Hansen. And my dear friend William Richert, who would have hated every inch of this book, but would have told me so with love. I miss all of you guys, terribly.

Personally, I want to thank Bill and Mary Watt, April and Darren and Katie, Dan and Mary Best, Liz and Mike and Haley and Danielle, Kristi Derr, Lee Wildermuth… I'm missing people now…

A final note about this new edition… Many of these stories were written in 2005, particularly the screenplay that inspired *The Cinephages*. *The Marie Browning Code* was first conceived of in 2006. While no one here is a bastion of virtue, and indeed, few deserve to get out alive, the character of Jack/ie needed to be updated or, at the very least, the language revolving around her. While she, like everyone else, chose her path, I didn't want her to be singled out as a victim because of how she was born.

I made some other minor alterations here and there as well, as is my nitpicking perogative. The majority of it stands today as written, a bleak, depraved, horrific look at film addiction.

If you want to know what Cinemagog looks like, pick up a copy of Exploitation Nation #5, design by Ryan Hose (who created this book's madness of a cover) and finished by Phillip R. Rogers. He's pretty terrifying. (Cinemagog, not Phil.)

So the next time you sit down to watch a movie, take a moment to wonder if you're being watched as well.

— Mike Watt, December, 2022.

ABOUT THE AUTHOR

Mike Watt has worked in the film industry in one form or another for more than 20 years. With wife and filmmaker Amy Lynn Best, and their partner Bill Homan, he formed Happy Cloud Pictures to produce the 16mm "zombie-noir", *The Resurrection Game*. Following up the cult favorite, HCP produced more than a dozen feature films, shorts, and documentaries, including their most-recent, *Razor Days*.

At the lamentable WRS Film and Video Production house in Pittsburgh, PA, he served as a film inspector, optical printer, animator, film cleaner, editor, packager, and vault attendant. Despite the lab's best efforts and terrible management, no one during his tenure ever died there.

As a journalist and author, he has written about film for dozens of print and online publications. Though he's not sure what the term means, he is considered a "film scholar" by many in his field.

Hot Splices was a good idea born from a terrible screenplay, written for a movie that no one has ever seen. This is an attempt to exorcise some of that.